I0636921

PERSONAL
Challenges

— THE *Personal* SERIES —

K.C. WELLS

Copyright notice

This is a work of fiction. Names, characters, places, and incidents either are the product of the author's imagination or are used fictitiously, and any resemblance to actual persons, living or dead, business establishments, events, or locales is entirely coincidental.

Personal Challenges
Copyright © 2017 by K.C. Wells
Cover Design by Meredith Russell
Photo by Strangeland Photography

Cover content is being used for illustrative purposes only and any person depicted on the cover is a model.

The trademarked products mentioned in this book are the property of their respective owners, and are recognized as such.

All Rights Reserved. No part of this book may be reproduced or transmitted in any form or by any means, including electronic or mechanical, including photocopying, recording, or by any information storage and retrieval system without the written permission of the Publisher, except where permitted by law.

Will and Blake couldn't be happier. They have a beautiful little boy, Nathan, and Sophie finally has the little brother she's been demanding. But all is not bliss in the Davis household. Coping with reality is going to change all their lives.

Rick and Angelo are sick and tired of trying to get a wedding organized. If it was up to them, they'd be married already, but Angelo's mother has plans and they keep getting bigger. Angelo can see problems on the horizon: big, traditional Italian wedding and gay do not go well together.

Something's got to give.

Colin receives an unexpected call from an ex, with bad news. He feels compelled to help, regardless of the consequences. Ed loves Colin's big heart and supports him in his efforts, but when the truth comes out, he finds it difficult to keep a lid on his emotions.

As the coming months unfold, the friends are going to need each other more than ever.

Personal Challenges contains wedding hassles and shenanigans, secrets, heartache, trials and tribulations, and a whole lot of hot loving. Six men, three couples – a family.

Acknowledgments

A huge thank you to my wonderful team:

Jason, my alpha – who puts up with long Skype calls and frequent Facebook chats!

My betas Helena, Bev, Mardee and Lara – thank you, ladies.

Thanks to Stevie Montoy and Ed Davies for their help and advice.

A HUGE thank you to Trina Lane, who provided so much information for Nathan's story.

Thanks for making sure I got all the details correct, and for checking that what I'd written made sense.

Chapter One

February, 2016

Blake Davis glanced up from the couch as the door to the waiting room opened, and grinned at Ed Fellows and Colin Reynolds. "What time do you call this?" he said quietly, so as not to disturb Sophie who was curled up asleep in his lap, her precious rabbit cuddled up to her. He knew this peaceful state wouldn't last long: she'd been dozing on and off during the six hours since they'd arrived at the hospital. He peered at the clock on the wall. "I phoned you hours ago."

Ed gave him a sheepish grin. "We thought you'd 'ave loads of people 'ere, to be honest." He gazed at the empty room. "Where is everyone?"

Sophie chose that moment to make a cute noise, and Colin looked like he'd melted into a pile of goo. "Aww. She's adorable."

Ed turned to his fiancé and snorted. "When she's sleepin', yeah. When she's awake, that's another matter." He met Blake's gaze and winked. "We don't call 'er Cyclone Sophie for nothin'."

Blake tried to suppress his laughter. Ed had done his fair share of babysitting during the last two years, and he always looked the same by the time Blake and Will arrived home—exhausted. "Rick and Angelo have been and gone, as have Lizzie, Dave and the kids. They would have stayed longer, but Molly was cranky and they think Justin is coming down with something, and didn't want to risk him being in the hospital."

"Where's Will?" Colin asked, sitting at the other end of the couch, his gaze focused on Sophie.

Blake smiled. "In the delivery room with Donna. He asked if he could be present and she said yes." He was glad one of them got to witness their little boy's entry into the world. Will had been buzzing about it for weeks.

Ed stared. "She still in labour? 'Ow many hours is it now?"

Blake ran his fingers through his hair, raking over his scalp. "She'd already been in labour for an hour when I called you two. At least there are no complications this time."

Sophie wriggled in his arms and Blake knew the peace was at an end. She yawned and opened her eyes, blinking. "Papa, is he here yet?" she asked, her voice heavy with sleep.

Blake stroked her long, brown hair. "No, sweetheart, not yet."

She pouted. "You said he would be here when I woke up."

"Daddy is with Donna right now, and it shouldn't be long," he told her, hoping his words were prophetic.

Sophie sighed and turned her head. When she caught sight of Ed and Colin, all trace of fatigue vanished. "Uncle Ed! Uncle Colin!" Impatiently she squirmed off Blake's lap and clambered down from the couch to run toward Ed, her rabbit clutched in one hand.

Ed crouched and caught her in his arms, swinging her up into the air. Sophie giggled and screamed with delight. "'Ow's my favourite girl?"

Blake tut-tutted. "Don't let Molly hear you say that. Or Mandy." Ed's niece Mandy adored her uncle, and whenever Blake and Will attended family gatherings, they'd notice how the five year old clung to him like a limpet.

Ed cuddled Sophie to him. "This 'ere is my favourite little girl." He glanced at the soft toy in her hand. "Are you still playing with that rabbit?"

Blake coughed. "Mr. Bunny, if you don't mind. And he goes everywhere with her. It's a wrench on those days when Will throws him in the washing machine."

Sophie curled an arm around Ed's neck. "Daddy gives him an in-jection, so he can sleep while he gets washed."

Ed bit his lip. "Oh he does, does he?" His gaze met Blake's and he smirked.

Blake shook his head. "You should see him. He has a syringe that we use for injecting brandy into the Christmas cake."

Colin stared. "Really?"

"Yep. He injects Mr. Bunny's paw so he won't feel a thing while he's in the washing machine. You should have seen her the first time we washed it. She sat on the floor in front of the machine the whole time, and when it paused during the rinse cycle and there was Mr. Bunny, nose pressed against the glass door..." He could still recall her anguished lament that Mr. Bunny was drowning. That was the last time they'd let her anywhere near the washing machine during its cycle.

"I'm going to have a baby brother," Sophie announced, beaming.

"Is that right?" Ed said with a wide smile.

"Yes, but Papa says he has to sleep in his own room." She scowled. "I want him to sleep in *my* room."

"My turn for a hug?" Colin asked from the couch, his arms held wide.

Sophie's frown disappeared and she held out her arms to him. Ed passed her over, and she sat on Colin's lap, snuggling up against him, clutching Mr. Bunny.

"I remember when you were a baby," Colin told her. "You didn't sleep well sometimes. Maybe Daddy and Papa want you to get a good night's sleep. Because *I* think Sophie gets a bit cranky when she doesn't get enough sleep." He tickled her, and she giggled. When he stopped, she turned her face up toward his.

"I have a picture of my brother. Do you want to see it?"

Colin frowned. "A picture?"

Sophie stretched out her arm toward Blake and made a grabbing hand gesture. Blake reached into his pocket and pulled out his wallet. He withdrew a folded card. "It's the twenty week scan. She was so excited when we showed it to her, and she kept asking to see it so often, that I just keep it on me." He handed her the card and she opened it with a happy little noise, holding it up to show Colin.

Ed was watching his lover with a fond expression. "Before you ask, we are not 'avin' one, all right?"

Colin jerked his head to stare at Ed. "Excuse me?"

"I see 'ow you are when you're around kids, an' the answer is no. You may be nearly thirty-five, mister, but I'm nearly forty, an' that's too bleedin' old to be startin' a family."

Blake cleared his throat and nodded toward Sophie.

Ed's eyes widened. "Oops. Sorry." The little girl appeared not to have noticed his swearing, staring at the scan.

Colin gazed serenely at Ed. "You have me all wrong. The joy of other people's children is that you get to hand them back." He grinned. "But yes, I love being uncle to Mandy, Ben and Lucy. Your nieces and nephew are wonderful." Colin winked. "I value my life with you much more. I think having children might curtail certain... activities, if you get my drift." He glanced at Blake with a grin. "Or have I got that part wrong?"

Blake snorted. "Don't get me started." On a number of occasions he and Will had been caught mid-coitus when their bedroom door opened and Sophie wandered in, having awoken from a bad dream. True, those incidents had also coincided with the odd occasion when they'd forgotten to switch on the baby monitor, so they had no one to blame but themselves.

Blake adored his daughter, and he couldn't wait to hold their son in his arms, but he was under no illusions: lovemaking was going to be on the back burner for a few months to come.

The door opened and Will entered, green scrubs over his clothes. He walked over to Blake, who rose to meet him. "Is everything okay?" Blake asked quickly.

Will nodded. "Donna is fine, and we have a beautiful seven-pound, ten ounce baby boy." His eyes shone. "And he is *so* beautiful, babe." Will looked tired but radiant.

Blake took his husband in his arms and held him close, their cheeks pressed together. "I love you," he whispered.

Will put his arms around him and leaned into him. "Love you, too." Then he chuckled and drew back, grinning. "By the way, Donna says she hopes that's the last one, and that we don't intend to keep on enlarging the Davis Empire. Her surrogacy days are at an end."

Blake frowned. "Is she really all right?"

Will gave a slow nod. "She's just exhausted. I think this pregnancy was hard on her. She said she *is* nearly forty, after all."

Blake stroked Will's cheek. "You look tired too. Can we see the baby yet?"

"He's in the Maternity unit, along with all the other babies. We can go stare at him through the window." He turned, seeking Sophie. "And there's my little girl." Will bent down and Sophie climbed off Colin's lap and ran to him, throwing her arms around his neck. He scooped her up and held her close, nodding to Ed and Colin with a warm smile.

"I'm not little," she insisted, waggling several fingers in Will's face. "I'm nearly four."

"That's right," Blake agreed. "You're a big girl, aren't you?"

"I've got an idea," Ed announced. "Why don't you all go look at the baby, and when you're done, we'll follow you back to your 'ouse, pack an overnight bag for Sophie, and then she can come stay the night with me an' her uncle Colin."

Will's brow knitted. "Why?"

Ed gave a patient sigh. "Because you're both tired, and you could use a quiet night together. And tomorrow is Valentine's Day, right? Why not spend some of it in peace and quiet? We can bring her back later, or bring her here for visiting time, whatever."

"Won't that spoil your plans for a romantic day?" Blake asked.

Colin snorted and stood up from the couch. "Romance? He's bought a Dine in for Two meal from Marks & Spencer's, and there's a new DVD of the England vs Wales Rugby World Cup match from last year, already waiting on top of the DVD player."

Will grinned. "Oh, be still my beating heart. Sounds like the honeymoon is over, guys."

Ed did an eye roll and Colin laughed. "I do believe a wedding comes before a honeymoon, right? We might manage that, one of these days."

Ed gave him a mock glare. "Shut it, you. It's not like we're in any 'urry, is it?"

Colin leaned across and kissed him on the mouth. "Absolutely." He straightened and faced Will and Blake. "But we really don't mind having Sophie for the night." He gazed at the little girl in Will's arms. "Do you want to come and sleep at our house tonight?"

Sophie's face lit up. "Can Tigger sleep on my bed?"

Ed laughed. "Like that cat would sleep anywhere else when you're around." He peered at Blake. "See? No problem. And it's not like we'd have to go miles out of our way to follow you, is it? You only live a mile down the road from us."

Will kissed Blake on the lips. "Say yes, babe." He leaned in closer and whispered, his breath tickling Blake's ear. "And we can make love all... night... long."

"You're tired," Blake remonstrated.

It was Will's turn to do an eye roll. "Tired, maybe, but I'm not dead, and when was the last time we got the chance to..." He gave Sophie a glance before continuing. "Spend a night being as loud as we want?" he concluded.

Blake's libido roared into life. "You're on," he informed Ed and Colin, before taking Will's hand in his. "Now let's go see our son."

He led his husband, daughter and best friends out of the waiting room, his heart full of joy.

Our son.

"Goodnight, sweetheart." Blake kissed the top of Sophie's head. "Have you got Mr. Bunny?"

"Here he is!" she announced triumphantly, holding aloft the off-white soft rabbit whose fur was already starting to thin in several places. She looped her arms around Blake's neck, still holding onto Mr. Bunny. "G'night, Papa."

Blake breathed her in, the smell of soap, clean cotton and the faintest whiff of chocolate. He narrowed his eyes. "And what were you and Daddy doing in the kitchen just now?"

Sophie's eyes were huge. "How did you know we were eating choc—" She clamped her hand over her mouth, blinking furiously.

"Sophie Elizabeth Davis!" Will put his hands on his hips and gave her a hard stare. "Did you just tell on me?" Before she could react, he kissed her cheek. "It's all right, sweet pea. I'm sure Papa already knows we've found his chocolate stash."

Sophie giggled as Blake let out a loud theatrical gasp.

From the front door, Ed laughed his head off. "Serves Papa right for not hiding it well enough." He held out his hand. "Okay, Princess, time we got you to bed."

Sophie did her customary pout. "Daddy lets me stay up late because I'm nearly four."

Ed guffawed. "Yeah, nice try. That cute bottom lip may work on your daddies but it doesn't work on me an' Uncle Colin."

"You speak for yourself," Colin murmured beside him. "I was all for letting her watch some cartoons before bed."

Ed gave him a warning glare but it was too late. Sophie clapped her hands together and all but bounced across the hall carpet into Colin's arms.

Blake shook his head. "Nice one, *Uncle* Ed." Their daughter gave them a cheery wave as Colin carried her out to the car.

"Sorry, guys." Ed looked crestfallen.

Will grinned. "We'll just refuse to feel sorry for you tomorrow when you tell us how long it took the pair of you to get her into bed." When Ed continued to stare at them, Will laughed. "Oh, come *on*, you've babysat for us before. You can't act all surprised now." He copied Sophie's cheery wave. "Good night, *Uncle* Ed."

Ed turned and walked out of the house, mumbling under his breath about it being the last time he'd attempt to do something nice for *them*.

The door closed, and Blake listened to the sound of the car pulling out of the driveway. He sighed when Will slipped his arms around his waist and rested his chin on Blake's shoulder.

"I suppose we need to make up our minds about names," Will said before kissing Blake's ear.

A shiver ran through him. "Now? Do we have to do it *now*?"

Will chuckled and kissed a trail down Blake's neck. "Well, I did have a few other activities in mind." He rubbed Blake's belly in a leisurely circle. "Dinner, for one thing."

Blake was about to complain when his stomach growled.

"See?" Will kissed his cheek. "Light the fire and I'll bring us in something to eat on the couch. Nothing too heavy. I have plans for you later." He patted Blake's arse and left him to go into the kitchen.

Blake set about his task, his dick growing stiff at the thought of Will's plans. He lit the gas fire, watching the flames grow higher as he set it to the required level. When the thought struck him, he couldn't hold it in.

"Do you ever regret our decision to have kids?"

A moment later Will was at the lounge door, staring at him, his forehead furrowed. "Is that a serious question?"

Blake sat back on his haunches on the rug. "Colin got me thinking, that's all."

"What—not wanting kids because it could ruin their sex life?" Will gave a short laugh. "You make it sound like we never get to fuck."

"Not as much as we did before Sophie arrived."

"And that bothers you?" Will came into the room and sat on the arm of the couch. He folded his arms. "Come on, Blake, out with it."

Blake met his husband's gaze. "Okay then. There are times when I miss *us*—being able to spend a day making love if we wanted to, not caring if we made a lot of noise, no matter what room we chose to fuck in—but as for regretting that little girl being in our lives? Never."

"You want to know what I think?" Will smiled. "I think it makes those occasions that we do get to spend time alone, even more precious. Remember when we bought this house, and Sophie went to stay with Lizzie and Dave for a week while we sorted it out?" His smile widened. "I think we christened every room."

Blake grew warm at the memories. "Not to mention the garden." Then he shivered. "Even if I did freeze my arse off. I mean, who makes love outdoors in *December*, for God's sake?"

Will rolled his eyes. "You were in the hot tub, babe. I hardly think that counts as the great outdoors."

Blake huffed. "There were bits of me that felt the chill, I seem to recall."

Will got off the arm of the couch and strolled over to where Blake knelt. He bent low to kiss Blake on the mouth, the kiss deliberate and sensual. "Then maybe we should make the most of tonight. Because very soon, life will change again for both of us."

"What did you have in mind?" Blake murmured against his lips.

"I was thinking some dinner, a shower together, and then the pair of us on the couch. At least we can start there." Will grinned. "What do you say?"

Blake pointed toward the kitchen. "Get in there and rustle up something to eat. Time's a-wastin.'"

Will laughed as he headed back into the kitchen. "Yes, sir."

"How many hours do you think we have?" Blake called out.

"No idea, and I don't care, as long as we spend as many as possible of them naked," Will called back.

Blake could get behind that plan.

Will strolled into the bedroom just in time to catch Blake staring at his naked reflection in the wardrobe mirror door as he finished drying off from his shower. Will grinned. "Well, I wouldn't throw *that* body out of my bed, that's for sure."

Blake turned his head and narrowed his gaze. "You'd better not. I know people." He dropped his towel onto the carpet.

Will gave a theatrical gasp. "Did you just threaten me?"

Blake gave a slow nod. "So play nice and maybe I won't make a couple of phone calls."

Will chuckled and crossed the room to stand behind his husband. He regarded Blake's reflection, reaching around him to leisurely stroke his chest and belly, deliberately ignoring his cock. "That is one sexy man." He kissed Blake's neck, loving the current that rippled through his husband's body. Will played with Blake's nipples, delighting in the shivers he created. Blake's gaze was riveted onto his reflection.

Will licked a trail up his neck and caught Blake's earlobe in his teeth. He tugged gently on it, while he tweaked the stiffening nubs. "Yeah, you like watching us in the mirror, don't you?" He grabbed hold of Blake's hair and jerked his head back so Blake was staring at them both. "Look at this sexy body." With his other hand he caressed Blake's taut belly. "It's been more than ten years, and yet you're still as lean and hard as you were the night of your thirtieth birthday."

Blake chuckled. "Oh, I don't know about that. Gravity and age will have their way eventually."

Will kissed his neck, knowing all too well how much it turned Blake on. "Yes, but you take care of yourself." Blake put his head back against Will's shoulder, a low moan escaping him as Will pinched his nipples harder now. Will whispered into his ear. "I haven't forgotten how much you love it when I take charge." He ground his hard cock against Blake's arse, his own breathing matching Blake's when Blake pushed back, arms reaching back to stroke Will's sides. "Watch, love. Watch my hands stroking your body. See how your cock rises, how it's already showing precome."

"That surprises you?" Blake gasped, hips slowly rotating as he tried to hold Will steady while he rubbed his arse against Will's hot shaft.

Will slid his hands lower to stroke the tops of Blake's thighs. "Look. See how beautiful you are? See these gorgeous thighs? Know what I'm going to do? I'm going to spread them and fuck you, deep and slow and hard."

A loud groan rolled out of Blake. "Fuck, yeah. Want that."

Will traced over the warm skin to grab Blake's arse, squeezing the firm globes and pulling them apart. "This is mine tonight."

Shudders coursed through Blake. "Yes. God, yes. It's all for you."

Will pressed his erect dick between Blake's arse cheeks and rocked his hips, his shaft sliding through the hot crease while he listened to the noises pouring from Blake's lips that spoke of need, desire and pleasure. He loved that they were both versatile, but he also knew how much Blake loved it when Will took a more dominant role. There was a reason their four poster bed had steel rings fitted to the posts, after all.

He grabbed Blake around the throat and jerked his head back to kiss his neck, this time sucking on the fragrant skin there, knowing he was going to leave a mark. *My mark on him.* Fuck, that turned him on.

"Touch me," Blake whispered.

Will chuckled against his neck. "I *am* touching you."

A low growl rumbled out of him. "You know what I mean, you bastard. Touch my cock."

Will tut-tutted. "My my, such language. I'm glad you don't use that filthy mouth when our daughter is around." He rubbed Blake's belly in strong, slow circles, still avoiding his dick that curved up, solid and delicious-looking.

Blake inclined his head and kissed Will's neck, murmuring between kisses. "Please, Will. Please. Touch me."

Will slid one hand down over that firm torso and grasped Blake's cock around its base while he wrapped his arm over Blake's shoulder to hold him across his chest. "You're hard, Mr. Davis, and it's turning me on. Fuck, I want to be inside you so badly right now."

"Want that," Blake whispered. "Want your dick in my arse."

Will began to pull faster on Blake's shaft. "Look at this beautiful cock." Blake's low cries and moans were music to his ears. He pushed Blake roughly until he was up against the mirror, and then Will used his feet to nudge Blake's legs apart. He got down on his knees, spread that gorgeous arse and pressed his face between the hair-covered cheeks to lick the tight pucker he knew awaited him.

Blake's reaction was almost instantaneous. He pushed back, tilting his arse, his hands flat to the mirror. "Fuck, yeah. More."

Will chuckled and set about his task of driving Blake out of his freaking mind.

It didn't take long. Less than a couple of minutes of tongue-fucking and Blake was begging.

"Please, Will. Now. Please. *Please!*"

Not that Will had any desire to delay the inevitable. He tugged Blake toward the couch at the foot of their bed and sat down. "Come on. Ride me." Ordinarily he wanted Blake's talented mouth on his dick but they were both too close. He ached to shoot his load inside Blake. Will held his cock steady while Blake sought the lube from a nearby drawer, Will vibrating with need.

Blake slicked up Will's dick and then sat astride him, guiding his shaft into position. He sank down onto the hot, bare cock and both of them groaned. No sooner was Will buried inside that tight channel than Blake began to bounce on his cock, his hands holding onto the back of the couch.

"You are so beautiful," Will gasped out as Blake rode him hard and fast, impaling himself over and over again. He shoved up into Blake's heat and fucked him, Blake meeting his thrusts with loud cries and groans as he begged Will to fuck him, to fucking *take* him.

"That's it, babe," Will cried out, thrusting up into him. "Let me hear you."

Blake moaned and placing his hands on Will's chest, he bent down to kiss him, their mouths meeting in a heated collision, both of them feeding each other their sighs and groans of pleasure.

"Fuck, I'm so close," Blake gasped out.

"Not yet," Will flung back at him. "I don't want you coming yet." He wrapped his arms around Blake and pulled him down into a lingering kiss, Blake rocking slowly on his shaft, feeding him sounds of urgent need. Will cupped Blake's chin and locked gazes with him. "On your back, babe."

Blake nodded and eased himself off Will's shaft. He lay down on the couch and pulled his legs up toward his chest, exposing his glistening hole. Will knelt before him, spread him wide and thrust all the way into him, shoving him back against the seat cushions. He snapped his hips and fucked Blake, his body slamming up against Blake's arse, his hand wrapped around Blake's cock, hand and dick keeping pace with each other.

"Oh, yeah, like that," Blake yelled, clutching his knees, almost bent double as Will's thrusts increased in speed and force. Their cries grew loud and harsh, and within minutes Blake's dick erupted over his chest. He shuddered, his body jolted, and the tightening muscles around Will's cock were enough to have him filling Blake's arse with his come. Will leaned in and kissed Blake, his breathing ragged, his heartbeat pounding, his dick still wedged inside his husband.

Blake held Will's face in his hands. "Ten years on, and you still rock my world."

Will kissed him, unwilling to pull out and break their connection. He chuckled. "Ten years on, and my knees are complaining about carpet burn."

Blake cackled. "Do I need to order some knee pads?"

Will snorted. "I'm not that old." Carefully, he pulled his softened cock free of Blake's body. "And if you get come on this couch, you'll be the one cleaning it."

Blake burst into laughter. "Oh, really feeling the love here."

Will kissed him again, this time slow and sweet. "How fast can you get it up again? Because the night isn't over yet."

Blake grinned. "If my incentive is that beautiful arse of yours, then in a lot less time than you might think."

If the twitch Will's dick gave at that was anything to go by, it was going to be a long, long night.

He was really going to owe Ed and Colin, big time.

Chapter Two

"Aww, that's great news! Thanks for letting us know. We would've stayed longer at the hospital, but Angelo was expecting a call." The thought was almost enough to burst Rick's happy bubble, so he shoved it aside. "But I do have one question however. How come *you're* sharing this news and not the proud fathers?"

Ed chuckled. "Let's just say they might 'ave other, er... things on their minds. We've got the Cyclone for the night." In the background Rick caught Sophie's giggles.

Now Rick got it. "Say no more. I hope you've battened down the hatches."

Ed snickered. "Right now she's cuddled up with Colin on the couch an' they're watchin' the Muppet Show."

"Are they showing that on TV again?"

Ed coughed, and in the background Colin snorted. "Go on, Ed," he called out. "Tell Rick which of us two owns all the seasons on DVD."

"An' you can shut up an' all," Ed growled.

Rick bit back his laugh. "The Muppets, eh? Well, I'd never have guessed."

"If I 'ear that you've breathed *one word* of this in the office," Ed began, but he was cut off.

"Uncle Ed, hurry, Kermit is on!"

"Yeah, and you know how much you *love* Kermit," Colin added loudly.

This time Rick couldn't hold it in. He gave a loud snort. "Got a thing for frogs, have we?"

"You just wait until Monday, you little shit. Say hi to Angelo for me." The call disconnected.

Rick wasn't all that concerned. He knew Ed would be fine come Monday. What was a more pressing problem was the conversation taking place in the kitchen.

Angelo was on the phone to Elena, and these days, that was never a good thing.

Rick poked his head around the kitchen door. Angelo had his back to him, but what view Rick had was enough to confirm his fears. Angelo's shoulders were hunched over, his voice a monotone. And by the sound of it, his mother was doing all the talking.

No change there, then.

He withdrew as quietly as possible and went into the lounge to retrieve his own phone. *Might as well call Mum.* It didn't look like his plan of a cosy night on the couch with a bottle of wine and a DVD was going to pan out at this rate. Even when Elena's call was finished, Rick would still have to deal with the aftermath.

Mothers-in-law are not conducive to a good sex life.

Except she wasn't his mother-in-law, not yet, and the possibility that it might get worse once they were married was enough to freeze the marrow in his bones. It wasn't that he didn't care for her—he'd grown to love her during the last nine years—but since she'd taken over their wedding plans, she had become a daily fixture in their lives. *Will she let up when it's finally over and we're married? Will she let go of her baby?* Angelo might not be the youngest of her five children—that was his sister, Maria—but he was the youngest son, and it was plain to Rick that she had a special place in her heart for him.

Rick stretched out on the couch, feet resting on the arm, and called his mum.

"Hey, sweetheart." Rick heard the TV on in the background. "Nice timing."

He chuckled. "How can it be nice timing if you're watching TV?"

The background sounds faded and he heard the soft *snick* of a door closing. "You saved me from this really boring series about the Second World War that your Dad has been raving about for weeks."

Rick couldn't resist. "Aw, it's not much to ask, is it? You sitting with him while he watches, pretending to be interested? Isn't that what marriage is all about?"

She groaned. "God, I thought I'd passed this when *you* moved out. I can still remember those nights when that stupid car show you and your dad loved was on TV. You were both glued to the screen and I had to yell at you at least three or four times to come to the dinner table."

Rick guffawed. "Oh, come on, I was sixteen! What sixteen-year-old boy isn't interested in cars?"

"Okay, maybe. Thank God your tastes changed." His mum chuckled. "It was when you started watching that show all about home makeovers that we really knew you were gay."

"Excuse me? Can we avoid the stereotyping, please?" He laughed.

"So, to what do I owe this honour? It must be all of two weeks since you last called me."

Rick sighed into the phone. "When you and Dad decided to get married, did Grandma and Granddad stick their oars in? Or did you get to plan your wedding the way *you* wanted it?"

There was a pause. "Is Elena still interfering?"

Rick stifled a groan. "It's not really interfering. She wants to help us plan it, that's all."

"Rick, you and Angelo were together for six years before he proposed. You were both happy. I say that because I remember, sweetheart. But ever since you announced two years ago that you were going to start planning this wedding, you've been miserable. And I'm sorry, but I lay the blame for that squarely on Elena's doorstep."

He knew she was right. As soon as Angelo told his parents that they were ready to get married, his mother had taken it upon herself to oversee the entire event. Only thing was, neither he nor Angelo had envisaged the process taking this long.

"She comes up with all these ideas, and the whole thing starts to snowball. But that's not the worrying part. She's been in touch with all the family back in Sicily, telling them about the wedding, and she wants to invite them *all*. Do you have any idea how huge his family is? Not that many will actually come to the wedding. I've met a few of them who were very nice, but for the most part, they're really... traditional."

"Is that a polite way of saying they might not be all that happy about a gay wedding?"

He snorted. "That's putting it mildly. We've tried to tell her all these plans will be an expensive waste of time if no one comes, but it's like she only hears what she wants to hear."

His mum made a soothing noise. "It's not like Vittorio is there anymore to put the brakes on." Angelo's dad had passed away unexpectedly six months ago from a heart attack.

"And that's another thing. I think Angelo is afraid of saying anything to upset her because she's only just lost her husband."

"But cosseting her is only going to create problems for you." She sighed down the phone. "This is why we don't talk about your wedding. *This* is why I stay out of it, why I don't offer to help. I figure you two have enough on your plate dealing with Elena."

The door from the kitchen opened and Angelo walked in, phone in hand. One look at his tired expression was enough to tell Rick his fiancé needed him.

"Look, mum, can I call you back another time?"

"Angelo has come in, hasn't he?"

No flies on Mum. "Yes, that's right." Angelo didn't need to know Rick had been discussing him behind his back.

"Sure. Call me next week. And give my love to Angelo."

"Will do." Rick said goodbye and disconnected. He sat up and gazed at Angelo. "Hey," he said softly. "Need a hug?"

Angelo flopped down onto the couch beside him with a sigh. "Is it that obvious?"

Rick shifted closer until he was pressed up against Angelo, his arm across Angelo's waist and Rick's head on his shoulder. Angelo put his arm around him and pulled him closer still. They sat in silence for a moment, Rick breathing in Angelo's spicy cologne, the one that always stirred his senses.

"Mum sends her love."

"That's nice," Angelo said absently, his fingers stroking Rick's hair.

Rick said nothing for a few minutes, preferring instead to rub Angelo's belly with firm strokes. When it became clear Angelo was not about to share, he tilted his head up and kissed Angelo's stubbled chin. "You need a shave, mister."

Angelo chuckled. "I thought you liked my five o'clock shadow. I thought it made me look... dangerous."

Rick laughed. "I never said dangerous, I just said it made you look like the Mafia." He cupped Angelo's cheek. "You don't have to tell me what she wanted. I can guess."

Angelo's heavy sigh tore at his heart. "If I had the guts, I'd tell her we were going to elope."

Rick widened his eyes. "Oh no, you don't. I have friends and family who would kill us if we did that. My side of the church might end up being less populated than yours, but there are loads of people that I want to share our day with. Don't let's deprive them just because your mum wants to put on a three-ring circus."

Angelo's heady groan rolled out of him. "Don't say that. I don't want that any more than you do." Rick caught the edge of pain to his voice and knew its source, even if Angelo didn't come right out and say it.

He shifted again until he was sitting astride Angelo's lap, holding Angelo's face in his hands. Rick gazed into those coal-dark eyes. "I know you miss him." The last four years or so had seen a thawing in Vittorio, something neither of them had foreseen. Perhaps it had been down to nearly losing his son because of hate that had brought about the beginnings of change in him. Whatever the reason, the two men had gotten along so much better during the last year of Vittorio's life.

"I thought he'd be there at the wedding," Angelo whispered, his voice cracking slightly. "I still can't believe he's gone. I wanted more time with him."

Rick nodded, not breaking eye contact. "I know, babe. And part of me believes he'll be watching you walk down the aisle on that day—whenever it is."

Angelo huffed. "If there *is* an aisle. And at the rate *we're* going, I'll be tootling along it in a mobility scooter."

Rick snorted. "Seriously? If I'd known you were this much of an exaggerator..." He grinned. "*Now* I understand why you told me your dick was eleven inches when we first met."

Angelo gaped. "I *never* said that. You—" He snapped his mouth shut at the sight of Rick laughing. Finally he smiled. "You did that on purpose, didn't you?"

Rick gave him as innocent a look as he could muster. "*Maybe*." He leaned in and kissed Angelo on the mouth, savouring the warmth of his lips. When Angelo relaxed beneath him, Rick broke the kiss and sat upright, still straddling Angelo's lap. "To quote from one of your mum's favourite films: 'Everything will be all right in the end. So if it's not all right, it's not yet the end.'"

"You can see an end to all this?" Angelo asked him incredulously.

"Not yet," Rick admitted. "Maybe it's going to require some drastic action on our part to move things along the way we want, but we *will* get there, I promise you," he whispered, before kissing Angelo again.

Angelo sighed into the kiss, his arms coming around Rick to hold him, hands stroking up and down his back. Rick hummed with happiness. *Here* was his Angelo, his man.

Angelo murmured against his lips, "How long has it been?"

Rick knew instantly to what he referred. "Since we made love? A week." One long, long week.

"I'm sorry." Angelo curved his palm around Rick's cheek. "I've let things get on top of me, haven't I?"

"Well, we can soon change that." Rick smiled. "You could get on top of *me*."

Angelo stilled. "You want me to ride you?"

Rick's heart pounded at the idea. Angelo preferred to top, and Rick had no problem with that. But now and again they liked to switch things up a little, and the result was always pleasurable.

He nodded quickly. "You ride me, I fuck you, it all works for me. Here or the bed?"

Angelo's only response was to lower his hands to Rick's waist, where he slid them under Rick's sweater. The muscles in Rick's belly contracted when gentle fingers traced their way over his skin, edging higher. "You always feel good," Angelo murmured. "Your skin is so soft here."

Rick shivered when fingers teased his nipples. "It's a-all part of my plan, to keep you coming back for more." Another shudder. "Just call me Cleopatra."

Those nimble fingers stilled and Angelo scrunched up his eyebrows. "Huh?"

Rick grinned. "I bathe four times a day in asses' milk when you're not around. How else do you think I manage to keep my skin this soft?"

Angelo laughed quietly and pulled Rick down into a kiss. "Ah, I *had* wondered." He shifted position, lying down on the couch and taking Rick with him. Their kisses were tender, Angelo's arms encircling him, both of them making low noises, hums of satisfaction. When Rick moved to straddle Angelo's thigh and began to rock against it, the tempo changed. Angelo's breathing hitched and he gazed up at Rick, eyes wide. "God, yes," he whispered.

Rick nodded and rocked harder, grinding his stiffening shaft against the firm muscles. He dropped his head to Angelo's neck and kissed him there, moving lower while Angelo gave out low moans, his hips in motion. Rick was in heaven. He couldn't remember the last time they'd made out like this, and he lost himself in their kisses and caresses, in the slow rock-and-roll of their bodies against each other. The kisses deepened and then it seemed like their hands were all over each other as Rick dry-humped Angelo's thigh. He tried to slow things down but once his lips met Angelo's throat, he gave in to the rising tide of urgent passion and sucked on his skin, loving how Angelo's moans intensified. Then it was his turn to moan as Angelo kissed his ear, biting gently and tugging on the delicate shell of flesh until Rick was writhing on top of him, his dick harder now, aching as it met with Angelo's equally solid length.

Their eyes met and both of them drew in long breaths.

"I want this to last," Angelo said fervently, one hand stroking the back of Rick's head, the other on his chest.

"Me too," Rick acknowledged. He slipped his hands underneath the soft wool of Angelo's sweater and sighed with pleasure at the feel of the familiar mat of hair that covered his lover. "Don't ever, *ever* think of shaving this all off, do you hear me?"

Angelo laughed softly. "I should think that would be grounds for divorce."

"Too right." Rick meant it. He loved Angelo's body hair, loved its texture, especially when he rubbed his face against it.

It wasn't enough.

"Need more skin," he ground out, before tugging at the offending garment, pulling it up and freeing Angelo's head. Then he was back in Angelo's arms, fingers kneading the firm, furry pecs and brushing over the taut nubs that stood proud.

"My turn." Angelo grabbed hold of Rick's sweater and pulled it off in one movement. Their bare chests met, launching a whole new flurry of kissing and touching. Rick couldn't get enough of Angelo's kisses. By then it was the turn of Angelo's jeans to cause offense. Rick unbuttoned Angelo's fly and tugged the jeans roughly over his hips, leaving his briefs in place.

Not for long. The sight of the damp cotton clinging to Angelo's very erect cock was too much to bear, and Rick removed them, his nostrils flaring as he caught his lover's scent, rich and raw. Angelo's dick stood up, begging for attention, and Rick gave it willingly. He licked a slow line from Angelo's balls to his slit, loving how Angelo shuddered.

Rick paused in his erotic task and met Angelo's gaze. "Fucking love your cock." He took it deep, sliding his lips down toward the root. When Angelo's grunt of pleasure reverberated through him, Rick smiled around a mouthful of dick and brought his hand into play, working the solid shaft, the skin like hot silk over a granite core. When Angelo reached for Rick's zipper, pulling impatiently on it between groans and sighs, Rick knew his lover wanted—no, needed—Rick inside him.

Angelo sat up, naked, and Rick balanced himself, hand on the back of the couch, while Angelo undressed him. Then Rick found himself pushed into a sitting position while Angelo lay on his belly, mouth poised above Rick's cock that jerked and twitched as though eager for what was coming.

Rick pushed out a long breath as Angelo took him deep. When he caught his breath, he gave a low groan. "That's it. Get it nice and hard and wet."

Angelo moaned around it, the sounds increasing in volume when Rick leaned over to push his fingers between Angelo's furry arse cheeks and rub his thumb over his hole. Angelo pushed up with his hips, plainly wanting more.

Rick chuckled. "You keep your mind on your job, getting my dick rock hard to slide into this tight arse." When Angelo groaned loudly, Rick rubbed down his back toward those firm round globes. "Yeah, you like it when I talk dirty, don't you?" Ten years together meant he knew all of Angelo's hot buttons.

Angelo hummed around his cock and began bobbing his head faster, pausing now and then to suck at the rigid shaft, working it with his fingers and reaching lower to cup and gently squeeze Angelo's balls. Rick forgot about pleasuring Angelo's hole and threw his head back against the seat cushion, eyes closed, thrusting up into that wonderful mouth. When his need was white-hot, he tugged Angelo into a kneeling position and kissed him, tongue going deep.

"Now," Angelo gasped when Rick came up for air. "Fuck me now."

Rick chuckled against his lips. "Lube?"

Angelo smiled. "The bottle in the coffee table drawer had run out, so I replaced it this morning."

Rick got up and moved to kneel behind him on the couch. He curved his body to Angelo's back, his rock hard cock pressed into his crack, and kissed the back of Angelo's neck, knowing it would drive his lover nuts. "Gotta love a man who thinks ahead." He chuckled against the warm skin. "Or should that be thinks with his head? One of them, at any rate."

Angelo lowered his head and groaned. "Will you just hurry the fuck up and *fuck* me?" He stretched out his hand toward the coffee table and retrieved the lube, thrusting it into Rick's hand. "Here. Okay?" He opened it one-handed. "And don't bother with fingers. I want to feel the burn."

Rick laughed and rocked harder, Angelo's body moving with him. He stopped long enough to slick up his bare dick, then he slowly pressed the head against Angelo's hot hole, taking his time to ease the thick shaft into his tight channel. When he was fully seated, his cock buried to the hilt inside Angelo's body, Rick let out a heartfelt sigh. It had been way too long.

Angelo grabbed Rick's hand and pulled it to his lips, kissing his fingertips. "I love you," he whispered.

"Love you too," Rick returned, before beginning to move leisurely, withdrawing nearly all the way out of him and then sliding his dick back in like they had all the time in the world.

"Oh, God, yeah, just like that," Angelo moaned. "Fuck, Rick, that's... "

Rick said nothing but kissed Angelo's shoulders and back, his hips rocking slowly as he made love to him. "This is what we both needed," he whispered. "Slow, sweet lovemaking. Save the hard, fast fucks for another time." God, it was heaven inside him, hot, tight heaven that gripped Rick's shaft and sucked him in, Angelo's body wrapped around him.

Angelo twisted to turn his face toward Rick's and they kissed, Rick's tongue keeping the same unhurried pace as his cock. Angelo sighed into the kiss, before lowering his head to the cushion and tilting his arse higher in offering.

Rick knew what that meant. He covered Angelo's body with his own and kissed his neck while he started to thrust harder, deeper, hips getting into a rhythm as they slammed into Angelo's firm arse. He wrapped his arms around Angelo and held him close while he drove his dick into him, their mouths meeting in kisses that grew more heated.

"Oh, yeah." Angelo shifted onto his side and Rick slid in behind him, spooning around him. He hooked his arm under Angelo's knee and stroked his chest, their lips reconnecting as he continued to thrust into that tight body. When he curled his fingers around Angelo's rigid cock, Angelo responded instantly by pushing through his fist, shaft slick from the steady stream of precome that fell from his slit.

Their eyes met. "Love you so much." The words weren't nearly enough to convey what lay in Rick's heart, but they would have to do.

"Love you," Angelo gasped, rolling onto his back and bringing his legs up to wrap them around Rick's waist. Rick knew the signs: it was their favourite position for orgasm. Angelo cupped the back of Rick's head and kissed him as Rick began to thrust hard, slamming into him, hips pistoning as he drove his dick all the way inside Angelo.

"Don't stop," Angelo begged, his hand jerking his cock faster, his body trembling.

"Not stopping until we both come," Rick panted, picking up speed.

Seconds later Angelo arched his back as come shot over his belly, his mouth wide in a silent cry. Rick lost himself for a moment in the beauty of Angelo overcome by his climax, but then Angelo's internal muscles clamped down on Rick's cock and he too shot his load.

"Love that feeling," Angelo stammered out, "the way your dick throbs when you come inside me. I'll never get enough of that."

Rick fought to get his breath back, his body jolted as wave upon wave of pleasure crashed over him, pulsing through him and leaving him shaking. He lay on top of Angelo, stroking his shoulder and face as he kissed him, unwilling to break their connection. When his heartbeat had returned to somewhere near normal, Rick raised his chin and looked Angelo in the eye.

"And I'll never get enough of making love with you." He kissed Angelo's forehead. Both of them sighed as he eased his softened cock from Angelo's body and rested his head on Angelo's shoulder. They lay like that for several minutes, the ticking of the clock the only sound.

"This wasn't quite what I had in mind for this evening," Rick murmured against Angelo's chest, his fingers tugging gently at the abundant hair there.

Angelo snickered. "Oh? What did you have planned?"

"Us on the couch, drinking wine and watching a DVD."

Angelo chuckled. "Well, we're on the couch, aren't we?"

Rick laughed at that. "Yup. And at least we got to mess around, which is more than Ed and Colin will get to do tonight." Suddenly it dawned on him. "Shit! I forgot to tell you. The baby finally put in an appearance."

Angelo burst into laughter. "And I get to hear about this now?"

"What do you expect? You distracted me. Anyway, everything's wonderful, the baby is healthy, Donna is fine, and Ed and Colin took Sophie for the night so those two could have a night to themselves." He snuggled into Angelo's arms. "See? I knew it was the right thing to leave the hospital when we did. Otherwise one of *us* might have suggested minding her, and then we wouldn't have got to do this."

"*This*," Angelo said, before kissing him on top of his head, "was wonderful. Not sure I feel like watching TV though."

Rick slid his hand between their sticky bodies and wrapped it around Angelo's flaccid cock. "Well, how about we snuggle under the duvet? I'm sure we'll think of *something* to do."

Angelo's shiver told him all he needed to know.

Chapter Three

"Colin, there's a call come through for you. I told him you were on your lunch, but he's fairly insistent."

Colin took one glance at his bowl of mushroom soup and sighed. "Does *he* have a name?" It had been a busy morning. Two of the architects were on his back, demanding to know why their designs weren't in their inboxes *now*. The urge to retort that he wasn't a miracle worker had been *right there...* Even *he* couldn't conjure up CAD models when he'd only had the designs for three hours. Fortunately he was always someone who put his brain into gear before putting his mouth into action. He'd done his best to soothe their entitled feathers, but as soon as the calls had finished, he'd put an e-mail together for the senior partners.

Colin believed in covering his back, especially where prima donnas were concerned.

Marion laughed. "Sorry. I should have said that first. My mind's all over the place this morning."

"Hmm. I wonder why." He smiled to himself. The company's receptionist had arrived at work that morning buzzing with news: her boyfriend had proposed to her the previous day.

Well, he chose the right day for it. Most of Colin's Valentine's Day had been spent playing with a four-year-old, not that he'd minded. Except now he had a better understanding of why Ed referred to Sophie as the Cyclone. She appeared to possess boundless energy and the capacity to turn a tidy room into the aftermath of a nuclear holocaust.

No wonder Ed was always too tired for sex after babysitting Sophie for the night.

Marion giggled, pulling him back into the present. "Anyway, his name is Ray Tranter."

For a moment Colin was confused. *Her fiancé is called Ray Tranter? What a coincidence.* Colin's first serious relationship had been with a guy of that name. Then it sank in, and he was shocked into silence. *Ray? Ray is calling me? What the hell?*

It had to be getting on for thirteen years since they'd last spoken.

"Colin? Are you still there?"

He pulled himself together. "Yeah, sorry about that. Sure, put him through." Colin thought quickly over the last years. There'd been very little in the way of communication between them, apart from the Christmas cards they exchanged every year, and even they'd contained little more than a couple of lines. Colin assumed by the postmarks that Ray was still lecturing in Edinburgh, the job he'd left Manchester for all those years ago.

A few lines every December. Not much to show for three years of being together, but after the way Ray had left, Colin was thankful to receive anything.

I wonder if he's changed much? Thirteen years wasn't that long, but then Colin didn't recognize the man in his own mirror sometimes. Playing rugby had given him a lot more muscle than he'd had as a student.

"Colin?" Ray's voice was deeper, rougher, like he smoked a pack a day, but it was definitely him. That gravelly voice was burned into Colin's memory. *I could listen to him talk for hours back then.*

"Hey, wow. This is a surprise."

Ray chuckled. "Yeah, though I suspect it's more of a shock after all this time."

That was the truth. "How did you find this number?" Colin had told him of the move to London when he'd gotten his present job, about eight years ago, but hadn't gone into details. He wasn't even sure he possessed Ray's phone number: Ray certainly didn't have his.

And it's not like he ever asked me for it. Exchanging cards with his ex after all these years was strange enough.

"It wasn't easy. I've been looking online for nearly six months. It was only finding a photo of your company last month that gave me a break. You'd won some award or other."

"Oh, when we won the RIBA Regional award last year?" Winning an award from the Royal Institute of British Architects had been the company's crowning achievement. "Yes, that was amazing." He paused for a minute. "Is there a particular reason why you wanted to talk to me? I mean, it's been a while." He chuckled. "Unless it was something you couldn't write in a Christmas card."

"I was thinking about you yesterday." Ray's voice softened.

"Oh?" It took a second or two for Colin to realize why. "Oh. Right." Their first date had been Valentine's day, 2000.

"You remember, then."

Colin smiled. "As first dates go, it was pretty memorable." Ray had taken him to the Curry Mile in Rusholme, to a popular Indian restaurant.

Ray snorted. "That's putting it mildly. How many days of lectures did you miss because of food poisoning? I'm still amazed that you went out with me again after that."

"It wouldn't surprise you to know that I've never eaten that dish since."

Ray laughed, but ended abruptly when he started coughing, a deep, hacking cough that went on for several seconds.

"Oh, that doesn't sound good." Colin knew there was a nasty bout of flu making the rounds.

"Yeah, well, I'll get over it."

Something he'd said jarred in Colin's mind. "You said you've been trying to find a number for me for six months? Why didn't you just write to me and ask me for it? You know where I live, after all."

"I wanted to surprise you."

"Well, you certainly did that. Are you still lecturing?"

Ray cleared his throat. "No, I took early retirement."

"Oh, a man of leisure. Nice. What are you finding to do with all that time you now have?"

The pause that followed Colin's words stretched to more than ten seconds. "Ray? You still there?"

"Sorry, I got distracted for a moment. Look, something's just come up, and I'll have to finish this call. Another time?"

"Sure." Colin had an uneasy feeling in his gut and he had no idea why. "Listen, why don't I give you my mobile number?"

"That sounds like a good idea. Maybe—if you don't mind, that is—I could have your e-mail address too?"

Colin blinked. "Sure. No problem." He rattled off the number and address, and then repeated them. "Thanks for calling."

"It was good to hear your voice after all this time." Sincerity rang through Ray's words.

Colin's belly clenched. "Same here. Get rid of that cough."

Ray chuckled. "You haven't changed a bit. Still trying to take care of me." Before Colin could reply, he'd disconnected the call.

Colin placed the phone on his desk and stared at it. *Okay, that was... weird.* He couldn't put his finger on it, but something had felt off. It wasn't until he was on his way to the staff kitchen to heat up his soup that he realized Ray hadn't given him *his* number. *I should have asked him for it.* Then he reflected. *Why would I want to call him?* Their relationship had been over a long time, and he wasn't sure it was such a good thing to rake up the past.

Especially if that call was anything to go by. A couple of minutes talking to Ray and Colin's stomach was churning.

By the time Colin had dried the dishes and put them away, Ed had come to a decision. He couldn't let the evening continue without saying something.

"So, you gonna tell me what's on yer mind?" The second the words had left his lips, he berated himself for their lack of tact. Colin often told him it was an endearing quality, Ed's habit of speaking his thoughts out loud, unfiltered.

What he means is, I'm blunt. It wasn't as if Ed was about to change. He was too long in the tooth for that.

Colin merely arched his eyebrows. "What makes you think there's something on my mind?" He poured himself another glass of wine.

Ed pointed to the bottle and snorted. "One, I know ya, an' two, since when do you have more than two glasses of wine of an evenin'?"

Colin smiled. "I didn't realize I was such a creature of habit." He held up the bottle. "Do you want the last bit?"

Ed grinned. "Thought you'd never ask."

Colin poured out the last of the wine and handed him the glass. Ed followed him into the lounge and joined him on the couch, displacing Tigger, who leaped off and went into the kitchen, presumably in search of more food. *That cat is gettin' to be a little fatty.* His attention was diverted when he observed the slight furrowing of Colin's brow, the tightness around his mouth. "Okay, out with it."

Colin took a sip of wine and sighed. "It's probably nothing."

"Let me be the judge of that." The tension Ed had felt for the last hour or so dissipated at Colin's words. *That's it, love. Tell me.* He didn't push, however. It was enough that Colin was prepared to discuss whatever was occupying his thoughts.

"You remember our first Christmas together, when I received a card from someone called Ray, and you asked me who that was?"

Ed frowned. "Yeah. A uni mate, wasn't he? He always sends you a card."

Colin nodded. "Well, he called me at work today, out of the blue."

When nothing else was forthcoming, Ed put down his wine glass and stared at his lover. "And? Why should that get your knickers in a twist?"

Colin chuckled, exactly the reaction Ed had wanted to provoke. "You have a lovely turn of phrase, do you know that?"

Ed preened, knowing it would make him smile. "Yep. It's part of me charm. Now talk to me."

Colin took another drink and then put down his glass. "What I told you about Ray wasn't strictly true. We did meet at university, yes, but..." His gaze met Ed's. "He was my first."

"An' he still sends you Christmas cards? Friendly bloke." Ed wasn't bothered by that. He knew with all his heart that the love he and Colin shared was solid to the core.

Colin laughed. "That's one way of putting it, I suppose. I'm still surprised that he keeps on sending them, to be honest. But as long as he does, I'll send one in return." He glanced down to where his hands lay clasped in his lap. "The thing is, we weren't your typical boyfriends."

Now *that* got Ed's attention. "Oh? Tell me more." What intrigued him was the fact that Colin couldn't look him in the eye. *Just who is this Ray bloke?*

Colin cleared his throat. "He was... one of the lecturers."

Ed gaped. "You were 'avin' it off with a lecturer? You dirty little git."

Colin jerked his head up. "Excuse me?" His mouth fell open.

Ed snickered. "No, seriously, I'm impressed. 'Ow old were ya? Eighteen, nineteen?" He waggled his eyebrows. "Got a thing for older guys, 'ave ya? Not that *I* can talk, me bein' a cradle snatcher."

Colin gave him an amused glance. "You are only five years older than me, mister."

Ed laughed. "Well, don't stop there. Tell me about you an' Ray. 'Ow did you manage to keep that a secret? 'Cause I don't imagine that's the sort of thing he'd 'ave liked spread around, know what I mean?" He winked.

Colin groaned. "You have *no* idea. It helped that he wasn't one of my lecturers."

Ed shrugged. "Okay. Not so bad then, I suppose. I 'ad visions of your eyes meetin' across a crowded lecture 'all, you passin' notes to each other with your assignments, that sort of thing." It was a side to Colin he hadn't expected.

Colin chuckled. "Nothing quite so romantic. I ran into him in a gay bar near Canal Street. I'd seen him around campus so I knew straight away who he was. We met there a few times before he asked me out."

"'Ow long were you together?"

"Just over three years. When I was in my final year, he was offered a position at the University of Edinburgh. It was too good an opportunity to miss. He left at the end of the summer and that was the last I saw of him."

"Did you part on good terms?" Ed noted Colin's wistful expression. It was obvious Ray had meant a lot to him.

There was a pause before Colin nodded. "What we had was good, but you know what they say. All good things must come to an end. I guess he spoiled me for other men, though. All the guys who came after him just didn't measure up. It wasn't until four years later that I met someone who became part of my life, and you already know about him."

Ed cast his mind back to when they'd first met. "Oh yeah. Matt." The little shit that had tried to get back with Colin. He pushed the thought aside. That was ancient history. "So he called ya? Why?"

Colin sighed and reached for his wine glass. "That's what's puzzling me. I don't know. I get the impression he wanted to say more, but maybe lost his nerve. All I know is he ended the call pretty swiftly. He did want my number and e-mail address though." He gave a shrug. "Maybe he'll be in touch."

Ed shifted closer until his thigh was touching Colin's. "So," he began, his voice softer, "he was your first, eh?"

Colin slowly turned his head. "I know that tone of voice. It gets all deep and seductive when you start thinking with your dick."

Ed gave a theatrical gasp. "I 'ave no idea what you're talkin' about." He grinned. "It just got me thinkin' about our first time, that's all."

Colin laughed. "Believe me, the two experiences were nothing alike." He stroked Ed's thigh. "I had to ply you with alcohol to get you to relax, and your heart was pounding like a frightened rabbit's until I got you to calm down."

Ed snorted. "Calm down? You rimmed me almost to the point of comin'." Colin burst into laughter, and Ed joined in. "I was putty in your 'ands after that." He cocked his head to one side. "So 'ow was *your* first time all that different?"

Colin snickered. "Both Ray and I were horny as hell, impatient to get each other's clothes off. I could hardly wait to get inside him, and when he got close, he made me pull out before he put on a condom and fucked me."

"What—you did each other? The first time?"

Colin arched his eyebrows. "Don't tell me you're not familiar with the concept of a flip-fuck, Mr. Fellows. I've seen your browsing history, remember?" He smirked.

Ed gave him a hard stare. "There is nothin' wrong with watchin' porn." He grinned. "We've 'ad some very nice times after I've been, 'ow shall I put this, 'inspired'?" Just thinking about him and Colin taking turns with each other was making him hard. *Very* hard.

"Not disputing that for an instant," Colin replied quickly. "I'm just pointing out that your surprise is all an act." Casually he reached across to where Ed's erection was making its presence known, and cupped his hand over the bulge. "And this tells me we have better things to do than sit here and talk about my ex."

For a brief moment it occurred to Ed that Colin was avoiding talking about Ray, but the thought didn't stay long, not while Colin was paying such welcome attention to his stiff dick.

"Then let's not waste any more time," Ed ground out. "Get that fine arse of yours into the bedroom."

He had plans for that arse.

"I could kiss you all night," Ed murmured against Colin's lips, his hands cupping the face he loved with every cell, nerve and fibre of his being. Beneath him, Colin sighed and wrapped his legs tighter around Ed's body, pulling him in even closer.

So close, our souls are touching.

The thought shook him. Ed had never been one for such profound contemplation, but being with Colin had changed him. After a string of unsuccessful dates with women, each one more deeply unsatisfying than the last, it had taken one man walking into his life to show him what love was really like. Ed wouldn't change one iota of their life together.

"That's not all you could do all night," Colin said with a chuckle.

Ed stared at him. "And what does that mean?"

Colin reached up to curve his palm around Ed's cheek. "Know what I love about you? Your staying power. I've lost count of how many nights we've made love where you went for hours without coming. It's actually incredible. I don't know how you do it."

"You'd laugh if I told ya."

"Let me guess. You think about your parents having sex." Colin grinned.

Ed laughed. "Ooh, close but no cigar. No, I think about *your* parents havin' sex."

"Ew. That's just... wrong."

Ed raised his eyebrows and rolled off Colin to lie at his side. "Why? I've never met 'em. 'Ave you any idea how much concentration it takes to try an' imagine two people who look like you? It keeps the mind occupied, I can tell ya." He rubbed Colin's belly. "So, you like me stamina, eh?"

Colin covered Ed's hand with his own. "Love it. You know we were talking about Ray earlier? That man couldn't last more than half an hour. In comparison? *You* are a god."

Ed laughed softly. "An' you, flatterer, are after something."

Colin's eyes gleamed. "Damn. You've seen through my dastardly plan." Slowly he rolled onto his belly and leisurely spread his legs wide, tilting his arse higher. His breathing quickened.

Like Ed could turn down the opportunity to tongue-fuck that tight hole.

He knelt up at Colin's side, stroking the firm globes. "Look at you," he whispered. "Lyin' there, waitin' for me."

Colin reached back and pulled his cheeks apart. "You like what you see?"

Ed grinned. "On your 'ands an' knees. I wanna worship this arse."

Colin did as instructed, and Ed leaned over to lick a path down his crack, blowing gently over Colin's hole, watching as it tightened. He smiled to himself. "You love it when I do this."

"God, yes." The pillow muffled Colin's reply, but Ed caught it. He pressed his face between Colin's cheeks and rubbed his bearded chin over the puckered entrance. Colin's soft moan sent the blood rushing to his cock, making it heavy and full.

He pulled the cheeks further apart, stretching Colin's hole, presenting an image so tempting that he couldn't resist. He pushed his tongue inside the loosened ring of muscle, before kissing his hole and licking over it slowly, feeling the tremors that rippled through Colin's body. Ed licked his way down the trench lined with dark blond hair, so dark it was almost brown. He loved the forest of long hair that encircled the hole, the pinkness of the delicate skin when stretched, the way it glistened with his spit. Ed rubbed over it with his thumb, pausing for a moment to push it inside, before withdrawing it and going right back to licking and sucking him there.

"Fuck." Colin's voice was dimmed by the pillow, yet it was still a sound rich in awe.

"Later," Ed said with a chuckle. "I'm 'avin' way too much fun makin' your body dance on me tongue. My cock will get its turn later." He smacked Colin's arse, the sound loud and sharp. "God, I love yer arse. Y'know, you 'ave the arse of a much younger man."

Colin lifted his head from his nest of pillows to stare over his shoulder at Ed. "And just how many younger men's arses have you seen lately?" Before Ed could come back with a witty retort, Colin groaned. "*And* we're back to porn."

Ed smacked him again. "Shut it. I'm enjoyin' meself." He stretched Colin's hole wide again and penetrated it with his tongue, pushing as deep as he could go. When it dripped with saliva, he slowly sank his finger deep into Colin's arse, marvelling at the heat that surrounded it, the softness of the channel that sucked him in, the way Colin rocked back to take more of him inside. Then Ed pulled free and pressed his face into the crease once again, bobbing his head to rub his face over Colin's hole, breathing in the rich, male scent, feeling the warm skin of his arse beneath his fingertips.

Colin groaned and knelt up. "Lie down on your back," he growled.

Ed didn't hesitate. He lay down and Colin squatted over his face, spreading his cheeks to show Ed his prize. Ed tugged him lower and began to tongue-fuck his arse in earnest, Colin writhing above him, low cries and moans pouring from him. Ed dug his fingers into Colin's hips, holding him steady while he probed him again and again with his tongue. When he felt the warm spatter of come on his chest and belly, it made Ed's heart soar. Colin shifted forward and scooping up his load, smeared it over Ed's rigid cock and guided it to his hole.

Ed thrust up into him, filling him to the hilt in one long, hot glide of flesh into heated flesh. The sight of his thick dick sliding in and out of Colin's body sent tingles through him, a burst of electricity down his spine and straight into his balls.

"Sorry, Col," he gasped. "Not gonna be... one of those nights... where I fuck you for hours."

Colin swivelled around, Ed's dick still inside him, and bent over to kiss him, hands stroking Ed's furred chest. "Don't care," he whispered. "Just want to feel you coming inside me."

Ed nodded and proceeded to fuck him, rocking up off the bed to thrust into him while they kissed, feeding each other sighs, grunts and gasps. Colin moaned every time Ed's dick slid over his gland, and the sounds only served to bring his desire and need to boiling point. He wrapped his arms around Colin and held him tight while he pistoned in and out of that hot hole, pumping into him, feeling Colin's channel cling to his shaft.

When he came, he arched up and shot his load deep inside Colin, his dick buried all the way. Colin shuddered above him, each shiver coinciding with every throb of Ed's cock, every pulse of come that filled him. It wasn't long before he came, warmth spattering Ed's belly. Ed clung to him until his heart stopped hammering and Colin lay in his arms, both of them damp with sweat, the air thick with sex and spunk, both of their dicks limp and sticky.

"Way better than porn any day," Ed said, stroking his fingers over Colin's hair.

Colin lifted his chin and smiled. "I'll second that." He kissed Ed lightly on the lips. "And you are just as hot and sexy as you were that first time, do you know that?"

Ed gazed into pale blue eyes. "You can talk. Sexiest fucker I ever met." He kissed him, taking his time, loving how Colin melted into the kiss. "An' I could *still* kiss you all night long."

Colin shifted against him with a grimace. "Maybe *after* we've showered?"

Ed chuckled. "You're on. Cleanliness is next to godliness an' all that. An' after all, I *am* a God. You said so." With a smug smile he dived off the bed, Colin in hot pursuit.

I love my life.

Chapter Four

March 5th

Will opened the front door and beamed when he saw who stood there. "Hey, we were beginning to think you weren't coming." He stepped aside to let Dave, Lizzie and their two children enter the hall. A quick peek at the driveway and the street beyond was enough to tell him parking space was in short supply. *Our new neighbours are going to be severely pissed off.* He did a rapid count up in his head, trying to work out who, if anyone, was left to arrive.

"Yeah, sorry we're late," Dave said earnestly. "Only *someone* couldn't find his puppy, and we couldn't leave the house without it."

Before Will could respond, Justin flung his arms around Will's legs and hugged him so tightly, he nearly toppled over onto the hall rug. "Uncle Will!"

Will bent down and scooped up his godson. "Hey, you get bigger every time I see you! How old are you now? Four?" He grinned and silently counted to three before Justin's eyes widened and his mouth fell open to protest.

"I'm five, Uncle Will! I go to school now with Molly."

"Yeah, and he's a pain." Molly was a very superior seven-year-old, and from all accounts was highly intelligent. She clutched a brightly wrapped parcel. "Is Nathan here?"

Will smiled. "Of course he's here. It's his welcome party." Well, it was partly a 'Come and meet Nathan' and an 'Okay, so we've left it this long to throw a housewarming party' get-together. They'd bought the house just before Christmas, and it had been a mad dash to get everything the way they wanted it in time for Nathan's birth. The housewarming had been forgotten in the rush. "Is that a present for Nathan?"

Molly beamed. "Yes. I chose it myself."

"Well, if you go through this door behind me, you'll find Uncle Blake. Sophie and Nathan are there too."

"Yay!" Molly scooted off through the door.

Justin brandished a scruffy brown soft dachshund under Will's nose. "And see? I found Nounou. He was hiding under the bed the whole time."

Lizzie sighed. "Yes, imagine that." She glanced at her husband with a half-smile. "And Daddy was very good to get down and crawl under there to catch Nounou, wasn't he?"

Will bit his lip. "I hope there weren't too many dust bunnies under there." In his arms, Justin looped his arm around Will's neck and gave Dave an adoring look. Will chuckled. "Because we *all* know who cleans the house when Mummy is at work." Lizzie had only recently returned to full-time work with Trinity, now that both kids were in school and Dave had taken on more of the housework, including doing the shopping and picking up the kids.

Dave scowled. "Enough to have me sneezing within seconds," he muttered. The expression was momentary, however, and he reached out to ruffle Justin's forever unruly curls, before gazing hopefully in the direction of the lounge. "Tell me there's alcohol in there."

Will laughed and glanced at Lizzie. "I see you drew the short straw tonight, Mrs Designated Driver."

"Not exactly." There was less of the Belgian accent that Will recalled from ten years ago when he'd first worked at Trinity Publishing. Something about Lizzie's smile and the sparkle in her eye caught his interest, and he peered closely at her. Lizzie blushed. "I'm not drinking because it's not good for the baby."

Will put down Justin and threw his arms wide for a hug. "Oh, that's marvellous news! Congratulations!" He held her carefully and kissed each cheek. "When are you due?"

"September. I saw the doctor yesterday who confirmed it. I was going to talk with Ed after this weekend." Lizzie smiled. "I guess that's one thing I can cross off my list."

Will relinquished his hold on her, and then shook Dave's hand. "This is all part of a plan, isn't it? You tired of being a house husband already?" He quickly reckoned up in his head how old Lizzie was. Almost the same age as Donna. For a moment, concern for her flared up. "Was this planned?"

Dave shook his head. "To be honest, it was a bit of a surprise. Once we'd gotten over the shock, we started getting excited. And the kids, well, they're ecstatic."

"Before you ask, this will be the last one," Lizzie said quietly. "That was one of the things we discussed with the doctor. She was keen to point out that pregnancies are more risky once you're my age." She locked gazes with Will. "And don't tell me you weren't thinking about that, because I know you too well, Will Davis."

Will smiled. "If you're both happy, that's the main thing. Can't blame me for worrying a little, right?"

Lizzie impulsively kissed him on the cheek. "Sweet man."

"Give me your coats, and then go on in." He helped them out of their coats before ushering them through into the large lounge where most of the guests had already gathered. Once he'd deposited the coats in the cloakroom, he followed Dave, Lizzie and Justin.

Music played quietly, and the air was filled with a blend of piano and voices. The party had the feel of a family gathering, which Will supposed was pretty close to the truth. Most of the guests worked at Trinity publishing, and had been there when Will had joined the company. Donna was there too, along with her two children, sitting on the couch with Blake at one end, holding Nathan in his arms. Sophie, Justin and Molly were standing around him, smiling at the baby. Molly held up a soft toy bear, waving it in front of Nathan's face.

Will had to smile at that. Nathan's room was already full of all manner of soft toys. Sophie had taken it into her head that Nathan would be lonely on his own, so she'd carried all her old toys in there and arranged them around Nathan's cot.

He circulated around the room, refilling glasses and directing guests toward the table that was covered in plates and bowls of party food. Blake caught his gaze and inclined his head toward the empty glass on the small table beside him. Will grinned and hastened to fill it with orange juice. He gazed down at their son, so peaceful, oblivious to the noise and bustle around him.

Blake chuckled. "He's going to be a contrary one, all right. He sleeps through this, but can't seem to spend more than two consecutive hours asleep during the night?"

Will leaned down and kissed Blake on the mouth. "You know it won't always be like this. Remember how Sophie was?"

"Sophie slept more, I'm sure of it," Blake grumbled.

"Let me refill some of the dishes, and then I'll be here to take over for a while." He gestured toward Lizzie, who was on the receiving end of a very enthusiastic hug from Beth. "And you need to talk to Dave and Lizzie."

Blake frowned for a second, and then his eyes widened. "I think I know what they're going to tell me, judging by the look on Beth's face." He shook his head and gazed at Nathan. "Looks like you have another playmate coming your way," he whispered.

"Yeah, and Ed is going to be pissed. It isn't all that long since he got her back to work." Will straightened. "I'll be back." After a glance around the room to make sure nothing was needed urgently, he went into the kitchen and began pulling covered dishes from the fridge.

"So, you two gettin' any sleep?" Ed stood in the doorway, a glass of wine in his hand.

Will snorted. "Yeah, right. If we're not waking up to feed him, he's waking us up with his crying. I don't think either of us has had

a full night's sleep since we brought him home from the hospital."
He sighed. "Thank God the sleepless nights don't last forever. Blake's
right. I seem to remember having more sleep than this when Sophie
was born."

"I guess me askin' if you're gettin' any writin' done would be a
bleedin' waste of time then," Ed said with a chuckle.

Will coughed. "Language, *Uncle* Ed. Little ears pick up
everything, even at this distance, believe me. I will never forget the
day Sophie told her nursery school teacher that she didn't like it
when Daddy and Papa played 'growly bear' in bed. Or how about
the time she told her nursery friend that she'd seen Daddy and Papa
hugging and bouncing."

Ed choked on his wine. "Oops. Did we forget to lock the door?"

Will grimaced. "The door didn't have a lock on it at that point.
You'd better believe it does now. But my God, Ed, the things she
says. I meant it about her hearing everything. Blake mentioned his
package one time, thinking she was out of earshot. Thing was, he
cupped it too. So you can imagine how I felt when Sophie asked me
over breakfast one morning if Papa's package was his stick and two
berries."

Ed gaped. "Oh my Gawd. What did you say?"

Will gave him a sweet smile. "That was the day Sophie learned
that the correct terms were 'penis' and 'testicles.' We thought treating
her like an adult was the way to go. Except it backfired, of course. We
were out walking last summer in the countryside, and a horse trotted
past us. Sophie pointed at it and said in that loud voice all kids seem
to possess when they're embarrassing the hell out of their parents,
'Oh, Daddy, look at that horse's big penis!' I didn't know where to
look."

By now, Ed was laughing so hard, he almost dropped his wine
glass. Will waited until he had control of himself, one eye trained
warily on the glass.

"Don't think I 'aven't noticed 'ow you dodged the question about your writin'," Ed said at last.

Will did an eye roll. "Well, it was a dumb question, given the circumstances. I mean, come *on*, a new baby in the house? When do you imagine I find time to write?"

"Okay, fair point, keep yer 'air on. Can I give you an 'and with anythin'?" Ed grinned. "Or I could get Col to 'elp. He's well trained."

Will arched his eyebrows. "Lucky you. And no, I've got this, thanks. Just going to take these two plates through." Ed got out of his way and Will walked back into the lounge, heading for the food table. He removed the empty plates and took them to the kitchen. When he returned, he found Ed and Colin standing together, their focus on Blake, Sophie and the baby.

Will followed their gaze, staring at his husband, daughter and son, his heart swelling with love. "Look at them, Ed," he said softly. "My family."

"Something I've always meant to ask you," Ed said in a low voice. "I know your 'istory, how your parents threw you out when you were still in your teens, how you lived, how that bloke Richard gave you an 'ome... What made you go down the surrogacy route, rather than adoption? 'Cause I'd 'ave thought you'd want to give some poor kid an 'ome, like Richard did for you. You know, give back a little."

Will turned to face him. To his surprise, hot tears welled up in his eyes, and he quickly wiped them away with his hand. "That's why a huge chunk of my royalties go to places like the one where I lived. *That's* how I give back. But we did discuss it, years ago. It was obvious from the start that we both wanted our children to be just that—ours. Not that Blake was opposed to either option, really. I was the one who pushed for the surrogacy route."

At that moment Blake looked up and their gazes met. *Your turn?* he mouthed.

Will nodded. He patted Ed on the arm and gave Colin a quick smile. "If you'll excuse me?"

Colin returned his smile. "Like I don't know what you're about to do."

Will laughed and walked over to the couch. "I thought you'd never ask."

Blake rose carefully to his feet and eased Nathan into Will's waiting arms. He stood beside Will, both of them gazing at the little baby boy who incredibly was still fast asleep. "Isn't he beautiful?"

Will leaned over and kissed Blake's cheek. "Nearly as beautiful as his Papa. Now go mingle." He sat down gingerly, his arms full of their precious cargo. Donna leaned closer.

"Blake's right, you know. He's a totally gorgeous baby, and if you'd seen *my* two when they were that age, you'd know I don't say that for the sake of it." Gently she stroked the down on top of Nathan's head. "He's absolutely perfect."

Will gazed in adoration at his son. Then he lifted his chin and grinned. "What a pity they have to grow up, right?"

She snorted. "Tell me about it. Mine are just into their teens. You know what advice my mum gave me when my first, Jeremy, arrived? She said, 'all babies should be raised in a barrel, with just a hole for feeding them through. But then they become teenagers? Stop up the hole.'"

Will gasped. "She sounds a right old barrel of laughs, pardon my pun."

Just then Nathan stirred, his eyes fluttering open. Will traced his warm cheek with a finger, his heart melting at the sight.

You are going to have so much love, little man.

It had been far too long since they'd thrown a party, Blake decided. This one had all the hallmarks of being a success. Their guests appeared relaxed and happy, there was no shortage of drinks, alcoholic or otherwise, and between him and Will, they kept the food coming. Once everyone had finished cooing over Nathan, Blake had taken him upstairs to his cot, and the baby monitor was switched on.

Sophie was yawning by nine o'clock. Will had promised she could stay up as long as she remained awake, but Blake knew it wouldn't be long before his little girl would be curling up on the couch. She could be as stubborn as Will, however, and Blake could see she was trying valiantly to keep her eyes open.

He glanced around the room and realized he was missing a couple of guests. Blake slipped from the lounge and went along the hallway to the room which doubled as his office and Will's writing cave. The faint hum of voices from beyond the door that stood ajar told him he'd found Rick and Angelo. He pushed open the door and stuck his head around it.

Angelo was gazing at the prints Dave had done for Blake all those years ago, only now the one of him and Will hung with them, the entire wall given over to the five canvases. Only Angelo was clearly miles away. Rick sat behind him in Will's comfy chair, staring at his laced fingers.

"I thought at the best parties people always ended up in the kitchen," Blake joked, entering the room.

Both men jerked their heads in the direction of the door.

"Sorry, Blake," Rick apologized. "Do you want us out of here?"

"God, no." Blake pushed the door shut behind him and crossed the floor to sit at his desk. "I was going to ask if everything was okay with you two, because you seemed so serious when I looked in."

Angelo sighed and Rick reached for him, pulling him closer. "We just needed a quiet place to talk, that was all."

Blake looked from Rick to Angelo. "What's going on?" He kept his voice low: Nathan's room was above the office.

Angelo snorted. "The wedding, what else?"

Blake folded his arms across his chest. "I've been meaning to call you for a while to talk about this, but lately there never seemed to be enough hours in the day. Have you actually set a date yet?"

Rick let out a low groan. "No." Angelo clasped Rick's hand in his and squeezed it.

Blake stared at them. "What the hell?"

"It's all my fault," Angelo said at last. "I've let this go on for too long."

"Your mother. We're talking about your mother, right?"

Angelo nodded. "We suggest a date, and then she finds a million and one excuses why that date isn't convenient, usually due to one of the Italian families not being able to make it over to the UK for then." Rick said nothing, but his miserable expression, drooping shoulders and distant stare spoke volumes.

"These Italian relatives, are they close relatives?"

Another snort. Angelo scowled. "I've never even met some of them."

Blake cleared his throat. "Okay, I don't mean to offend you, Angelo, but who the fuck is getting married here? It's *your wedding*, guys. You get the final say on who gets invited, all right?" He softened his tone. "I know your mother has been through a rough time, with your father passing, but that doesn't mean the two of you should just roll over and do whatever she wants. This is *your day* we're talking about, a day you want to remember for the rest of your lives. Invite those people *you* want to share it. I know you feel obliged to have the family there, but after listening to a couple of conversations on this subject, it's obvious even to me that your family is *huge*, Angelo. You can't possibly invite them all. And even if you could, you don't organize the date according to which *relatives* can come and which can't." He gave them both a stern glance. "The tail does *not* wag the dog, you got that? I really think it's time you put your collective feet down."

Angelo stared at him open-mouthed, and for a moment Blake was positive he'd overstepped the mark. "I'm sorry, that was rude of me. I sounded like I was your father, didn't I? I didn't mean to come across like I was scolding you."

To his relief, Angelo sagged onto the leather couch that stood under the canvases and put his head in his hands. Rick was at his side in an instant, his arm around Angelo's shoulders. He turned his face up to meet Blake's gaze.

"It's not like you've said anything that we weren't already thinking. And you're right, of course. We do have to do something." He tightened his arm around Angelo. "Eh, babe?"

Blake crouched in front of Angelo. "Trying to appease your family nearly lost you your future husband a few years ago, remember? I don't want this to ruin your day, or your future happiness, because I know you're trying to make everyone happy." He looked into Angelo's dark eyes. "Decide what *you two* want, and then stick to your guns. That doesn't mean you can't make compromises along the way, but make sure she knows this is *your* wedding." He smiled. "And if it were me? I'd start by setting a date and letting her get used to the idea."

Angelo stared at him in silence for several long seconds, before nodding slowly. "You're right," he said simply. He turned to Rick. "Maybe we need to talk about this tomorrow when we go for Sunday lunch with Mum."

Rick nodded, his gaze focused on Angelo. "Whatever you say. I just don't want to see you miserable anymore."

Angelo let out a soft sigh and cupping Rick's cheek, he pulled him into a gentle kiss.

Blake rose and left them to it.

He'd done his good deed for the day—he hoped.

Will found Blake exactly where he'd expected—standing at the foot of Nathan's cot, gazing at their sleeping child. The room was painted in a sunny yellow, with a musical mobile of Winnie the Pooh hanging over the cot, and on a shelf above it, all of Sophie's stuffed animals, staring into it.

Will shivered. "I don't know about you," he whispered to Blake, "but if I woke up to find all those glassy eyes trained on me? I'd have nightmares."

Blake gave a soft chuckle. "That's just you, then. I'm sure Nathan will love them. Think about all the love Sophie lavished on them over the years. There's a lot of love in this small room."

Will liked that. Then he grinned. "Our little girl can be very stubborn, you know. She insisted we didn't need to buy a new mobile for Nathan, not when we already had Winnie from when she was a baby. And although I said he deserved to have a new one, she folded her little arms and stood her ground."

Blake bit his lip. "Hmm. So Sophie is stubborn. I wonder which of us she gets that from." His eyes gleamed.

Will narrowed his gaze. "Oh, I see. *Now* it comes out. I'm stubborn, am I?"

Blake brought his finger to his lips. "Shh. We don't want to wake up Nathan, do we?"

Will arched his eyebrows. "Be careful what you say or I'll change my mind about my plans for this evening." He stared at Nathan, noting his hands balled into tiny fists, his breathing nice and regular. Sophie had come into their lives after a problematic birth, but it had been plain sailing with Nathan. Their perfect little boy.

When he glanced across at Blake, he noted with amusement that his husband was staring at their son in exactly the same manner. *God, what a pair we make.*

He took Blake's hand in his. "I know you could stand there all night, just watching him sleep, but I have something else to occupy you. Plans, remember?"

Blake raised his eyebrows. "Oh?"

Will grinned. "The guests have all gone. Sophie is finally asleep. The party is cleared away. The bed has towels laid out on top of it, and there's a bottle of massage oil standing in warm water."

The happy sigh that fell from Blake's lips as he followed Will from the room was answer enough.

Chapter Five

"No time like the present," Rick whispered as Angelo brought out the tray with the coffee pot, milk jug and sugar bowl and placed them in the middle of the dining table.

Angelo gave him a hard stare. "Do not rush me," he said through gritted teeth. Discussing it the previous night had been one thing—*then* it had seemed a reasonable proposition—but now, in the cold light of an equally cold March Sunday?

Angelo was as nervous as a cat in a room full of rocking horses.

"Thank you, *tesoro*," Mum murmured while he passed around the coffee pot.

"Suck-up," Luca whispered, grinning. Unseen by his mum, Angelo gave him two fingers. Luca just laughed quietly. Beside him, his wife Rachel watched the byplay with a faint smile. After all the years they'd been married, she was more than accustomed to how Angelo's family rolled.

Mum appeared not to have noticed her son's remark. "I'm so glad you and Rick were able to join us for lunch."

"I'm not." Vincente groused. "That meant there was less of Mum's cooking for the rest of us."

Angelo eyed his brother's belly that was already overhanging his belt. Beside him, Rick placed a hand on Angelo's thigh beneath the table, and it didn't take a genius to work out the meaning behind that gesture. *Say nothing.* God, it was tempting though. At forty-eight, his brother had turned into a fat man. No wonder Mum had asked him to play *Babbo Natale* at Christmas. The red Father Christmas costume had fitted him perfectly.

Then it struck him. *Rick really does know me.* It was as if he'd felt Angelo's itch to say something.

Paolo snorted. "You mean more food for *you*, you fat bastard." He caught Angelo's eye and winked. Apparently Paolo had no qualms about speaking his mind.

Mum gasped and gave Paolo an evil glance. "You should not use such language in front of your children."

Paolo's wife Tina gave another explosive snort. "You *are* kidding, right? They're teenagers. Have you heard the language they come out with? I blame the internet and TV." The teenagers in question, two girls and a boy, were no longer at the table but were in the lounge, playing with the PS4 that they'd brought with them. Two of Vincente's three kids were with them, and judging by the laughter, they were having a far better time than the adults.

Mum pursed her lips and said nothing but handed out the coffee cups and side plates.

Maria came in from the kitchen, carrying a large plate on which sat a chocolate cake that made Angelo's mouth water. He tried to ignore Rick who smacked his thigh. Unfortunately, Maria caught it and burst into laughter. "A moment on the lips, a lifetime on the hips, bro, remember? Especially if you want to fit into your wedding suit."

Angelo groaned and Luca cackled. "Way to go, sis. You went and said the W word." He dug Angelo in the ribs with his elbow. "Because it must have been, what, a whole hour since it was last mentioned, right?" The grin he gave Angelo was pure evil.

Mum nodded vigorously. "But we need to discuss this. There is so much to do, so—"

"Mum?" When Angelo was certain he had her attention, he smiled, although his stomach churned and all the hairs in the back of his neck lifted. "Mum, sit down, please. We need to talk."

"Didn't I just say that?" Her expression was one of sheer confusion.

Angelo nodded. "Yes, but there is something Rick and I need to share with you."

Around the table his brothers and sisters-in-law chuckled. Maria did not, however. She met Angelo's gaze and nodded. *Thank God for that.* They had an ally. He should have known Maria would be on their side.

Mum sat and poured herself a cup of coffee. "Well, I'm listening." Her back was stiff, as was her facial expression, and Angelo groaned inwardly to see it.

This is not going to be easy.

Angelo clasped his hands on the white tablecloth, but Rick reached over and took one, lacing their fingers. Angelo gave him a grateful glance before focusing on Mum.

"Rick and I have been talking, and we've come to a decision." He paused to inhale deeply, aware that all eyes were focused on him and that everyone seemed to be holding their breath. Rick simply tightened his grip on Angelo's hand.

Angelo felt like Indiana Jones, about to step off the precipice.

"We're going to set a date in August and we'll take care of the ceremony."

There. He'd gotten the words out.

Mum's jaw dropped and those dark eyes held what could only be described as hurt. She stared at both of them, swallowing a couple of times. Then she coughed. "*You...* are going to organize the wedding?"

Angelo nodded, his heart pounding. "Yes. You don't have to concern yourself with it anymore. Leave all the hassle to me and Rick." He'd figured trying to paint it as though they were doing her a favour might lessen the blow.

Not if her expression was anything to go by. She looked for all the world like Angelo had struck her.

"In August?" She frowned. "But surely there is not enough time. You will never find a church that is still available. Churches get booked up so quickly these days."

"Who says it has to be in a church?" Rick blurted out.

Fuck.

Mum hissed, and Angelo was positive that if she'd had a crucifix nearby, she'd have held it in front of her. "But... it has to be in a church."

"Mum, it can be anywhere," Maria said in a soothing tone. "Nowadays people get married outdoors, on a beach, in a castle, a hotel, you name it."

"And who would perform the ceremony? Some civil servant, when it should be a priest. After all, you are being joined together in the sight of God." She genuflected.

Angelo didn't think this was the right moment to share Rick's beliefs. He had no problem believing in God, but as for some of the assholes who claimed to speak for Him? That was another matter entirely.

"Not a problem." Maria's voice cut through his wool-gathering. Angelo gave her a quizzical glance, and she smiled. "I know someone who would be happy to perform the ceremony."

It took him a minute to realize he knew him too. "Franco?" He and Rick exchanged Christmas cards with the priest, had done since they were first together.

Mum apparently knew his name. "Your friend? The one who is the priest?"

Maria nodded. "Except he's now a prison chaplain. He's still able to conduct weddings, I think. I'm sure he'd be delighted to be a part of this."

That was a great idea. "Maybe we should meet with him to discuss it," he said slowly. Rick nodded in agreement.

Mum bit her lip. "But that still leaves the issue of where you would get married."

"Why don't you leave that to us?" Rick suggested with a warm smile. "One less thing for you to worry about."

Angelo nodded. "And it's not like we're saying we don't want your help." Beside him, Rick nodded too. They'd discussed this part the previous night. "We'd like your input with regards to the reception."

Her eyes lit up. "Truly?"

"Of course. Think about it. The wedding itself will be over fairly quickly. The reception is a much bigger event." At that moment he'd say *anything* to make her smile again. Mum had done little smiling in the last six months, understandably.

It seemed his words had done the trick. Mum nodded, her eyes bright. "This is true. I can help with the seating plans, the choice of menus, the music for the evening... "

"Hey, we can all chip in with ideas for the reception," Luca butted in. "I've had some innovative ideas, things to make your wedding stand out from the crowd." There were murmurs of agreement from around the table, where it became apparent that his siblings were on the same page.

Oh God.

Angelo kept a straight face. "Oh? Such as?"

"How about having *Nonna* as a flower girl?" Paolo suggested with his habitual wicked grin. "She'd love it."

Somehow, Angelo couldn't see his ninety year-old grandmother inching her way up the aisle with her Zimmer frame, strewing rose petals everywhere.

Paolo's suggestion opened the floodgates and everyone started talking at once.

"You could have napkins printed with a word search on them. Give the guests something to do when it gets boring. Of course, knowing you two, we'd have to vet them first. Wouldn't want to shock the Italian rellys, right?"

"Hangover kits! Every seat gets a bag with a hangover kit, containing a bottle of Gatorade, a couple of aspirin, and a coupon for McDonalds."

"How about having a food truck at the venue? That's a great idea!"

"And every guest gets a badge—Team Angelo or Team Rick."

"What about planning something special for your first dance together? You could start out really boring, you know, with a slow number, and then the music changes and you two launch into this choreographed routine that lasts about ten minutes."

"How about fireworks at the end of the night?"

"You need entertainment. I've seen this fantastic act where silk ropes come down from the ceiling, and these dancers are suspended by them."

⁶⟨⁶ᵉ⟩ₓ⟨⁹⟩⁶⟩ ⟩

Rick had to admit, Angelo had lasted longer than he'd anticipated. When Angelo began to bang his head against the table in a slow, steady beat, Rick knew it was time to step in.

"Great suggestions, guys. You've, er, certainly given us something to think about."

Angelo jerked his head up at that, his eyes wide. "Great? Are you fucking *kidding* me?"

That got an instant reaction from Elena, who glared at Angelo.

Not that he noticed. He pointed at Tina. "No. No badges. This is not bloody Twilight, all right?" Then Paolo. "*Nonna*? A flower girl? Seriously?" He levelled a finger at Vincente. "A dance routine? Well, that would be wonderful except for one eeny weeny, teeny tiny problem—I can't dance and Rick has two left feet."

Rick did his best not to react. He wasn't about to tell them that he and Angelo had met in a gay club, and that Angelo on the dance floor was a thing of beauty to behold. *Far be it from me to stop him in full flow.*

Angelo wasn't finished. "Silk rope acrobats? At the reception?" He rolled his eyes. "You'll be suggesting clowns next."

Luca grinned. "Aw, come on. *Everyone* loves clowns. Well, except for Stephen King's creepy murdering dude." He shuddered. "Those teeth gave me nightmares for weeks."

Rick ignored Luca and laid his hand on Angelo's arm. "We can discuss the reception when we know where it's going to be held, right? Finding a venue is the first task on the list."

Elena looked bewildered by the proceedings, not that Rick could blame her.

Angelo let out a growl. "You people are bloody *crazy*, do you know that?"

"Down, boy," Rick murmured, giving Angelo's arm a gentle squeeze. "Play nice."

Angelo inhaled deeply and then sagged into his chair. "Rick's right. We can talk about this once we've found a venue for the wedding."

"Then you'd better get a move on," Vincente said with a frown. "We're already in March, for God's sake. If you're serious about getting married in August, you don't have long left."

It occurred to Rick that they might have bitten off more than they could chew, but there was no going back now. *We wanted control of the wedding and now we've got it.*

Heaven help us.

It was either going to be the most wonderful wedding—or that three-ring circus he'd predicted a couple of weeks ago.

As they cleared away the cups and plates from the table, Angelo whispered to Rick, "It's no use. We have to set her straight on a few things."

"And there you have the crux of the matter," Rick muttered. "She's thinking straight, all right, only *we're* not." Angelo was right: they'd let things go on far too long.

They went into the kitchen and Rick shut the door behind them. Angelo went over to his mother and took her hand.

"Leave the coffee things for a minute, Mum. We need to talk to you."

She stiffened. "What, again? Didn't you say enough in there?"

Angelo pulled out a chair from the kitchen table and gestured for her to sit, before joining her. "Mum," he began, his voice gentle, "you know, don't you, that there's no way we can get married in a church?"

Her eyes widened. "Of course you can! Why would you think that?"

Angelo let out a heavy sigh. "Because we're gay?"

She narrowed her eyes. "I'm no idiot. I know that. And gays get married nowadays."

"Not in a Catholic church, they don't." He cocked his head. "You know that, right?"

She stared at him, her lower lip trembling. Finally she sighed too. "I don't know what I could have been thinking."

"I do," he said quietly. "You wanted a big, traditional Italian wedding for your baby boy, but traditional equals Catholic, and gay and Catholic just don't fit together." He smiled at her. "What was your plan? To make us wait until the Pope declares marriage equality is fine by him? Because I think you'd have quite a wait on your hands. And as for all our relatives you're dying to invite, just how many of them would come to a gay wedding? Hmm?"

"I know some who would," Rick interjected. "I met some of your cousins when we were over there, and they were fine about us. They'd be over here in a heartbeat."

Angelo turned to look at him, nodding in agreement. "And they'll be at the top of the list." He turned back to Elena. "Trust me, there will be lots of people at this wedding, people who are every bit our family as if they were our flesh and blood. People who love us and accept us, just like you do."

Her lip quivered. "But if this Franco is a priest, surely he can't marry you either. The church wouldn't allow it."

"If he was still a priest with a parish, probably not. But he can give us a blessing, right? As long as we have someone there to make it legal, it's all good."

She nodded slowly. "That makes sense, I suppose." Angelo kissed her cheek and she smiled. "You are a good boy. You said these things to me where the rest of the family cannot hear."

"No one blames you for wanting the best day for us," he told her. "It's not your fault you see life through rose-coloured spectacles. But now that you see things as they really are, you understand why we should organize the wedding?"

"Yes, *tesoro*. On this matter, you know best." Her eyes sparkled. "*This* matter."

Angelo laughed. "Meaning that where everything else is concerned, Mama knows best?"

"Of course!"

Angelo pulled her to her feet, encircled her with his arms and hugged her tightly.

Rick shook his head. *Mothers.*

"Hey, it's good to hear you." It had been some time since they'd spoken, but Angelo remembered that voice.

"Maria told me I should give you a call."

Angelo smiled to himself. "She didn't waste any time." Across the room, Rick looked up from his laptop and gave him an inquiring glance. *Franco*, Angelo mouthed. Rick gave a single nod and went back to his e-mails.

"If what she tells me is correct, you don't have time to waste. So, you'd like me to perform the ceremony? Well, perform a blessing, at any rate."

Angelo liked Franco's no nonsense approach. "Yes, if you can fit us in."

"I don't know if Maria told you, but my circumstances have changed recently. I no longer have my own parish."

"Yes, she said something about you being a prison chaplain? Bit of a change there."

There was a brief pause. "Let's just say a lot of things came to a head, and I decided a move was required. I've been working with the prison service for the last six months."

"Which prison do you work in?" Angelo thought it odd that Franco hadn't mentioned it in his last Christmas card.

"Belmarsh."

"Wow." Angelo was familiar with the type of prisoners that resided within the walls of Belmarsh. "That sounds like it might be a tough job at times."

"Sometimes, yes. But we can talk more about this when we meet. I presume that's what you'd like? A meeting to discuss the wedding? Seeing as time is a factor."

No beating about the bush with Franco. It made a refreshing change. "That would be good. When can you fit us in?"

"Evenings work best for me. I could be there tomorrow evening, if that's convenient? The sooner, the better, really."

"Perfect." Angelo felt better already. *Finally we're making steps.*

"There's one thing I should say at this point. Maria said you don't have a venue booked yet."

"This is true." That was the next headache to overcome.

"I might be able to help you there. Leave it with me. I'll let you know tomorrow if I've been successful."

"Oh wow, that would be fantastic." Angelo didn't believe their luck.

Franco chuckled. "No promises, mind. Just pray everything comes together, all right?"

Angelo could do that. "We'll see you tomorrow then. Do you want to come for dinner?"

"Sorry, I have plans. Thanks for the invitation, though. I should be there by eight-thirty if that's okay." Angelo assured him it was fine and they finished the call.

"That sounded very positive," Rick said with a smile.

Angelo put his phone on the coffee table and held his arm wide. "What are you doing all the way over there?"

Rick chuckled and closed the lid of his laptop. He put it aside and got up from his armchair to sit beside Angelo on the couch. Angelo put his arm around him and drew him close.

"You're right, it was very positive. Franco's coming here tomorrow evening at eight-thirty. And get this—he says he might be able to help with the venue for the ceremony."

"Aw, great!"

Angelo laughed. "Let's wait and see what he comes up with before we say that, okay?" He loved sitting like this, the two of them with their arms around each other. It was a feeling that never grew old.

Rick craned his head to look up at him. "Apart from knowing we get a card from him every Christmas, I don't know much about Franco, except that he's your friend."

Angelo sighed and snuggled Rick against him. "He's the reason I turned up at Trinity that day, armed with a sonic screwdriver." He chuckled as he recalled Ed, fists clenched, fiercely protective of Rick. *Thank God for Blake's calm manner.* If it hadn't been for him, Angelo wouldn't have got past Karen's desk at reception.

Rick's eyes widened. "Franco was? You never told me that."

Angelo nodded. "He told me I had two choices—obey my father and probably be miserable for the rest of my life, or decide for myself who I was going to gift my heart to."

"Wow. And he's a Catholic priest? Since when does the Catholic church condone homosexuality?" Rick narrowed his gaze. "Ah, I get it. He's gay."

"That, he would neither confirm nor deny. He said it didn't matter because he'd taken vows to lead a life of celibacy."

Rick snorted. "As did all the gay priests we read about in the media."

Angelo cupped Rick's chin. "What I'm telling you is, Franco is a good man. He's the reason we're together right now. He made me see sense. So regardless of your feelings about organized religion—and I am more than aware of them after all this time—this is someone who deserves our attention."

Rick laid his head against Angelo's shoulder. "I never said anything, but when your mum decided she was going to arrange the wedding, I... wasn't happy."

Angelo froze. "What?"

Rick sighed. "I knew she'd want a big church wedding, and the thought made me uncomfortable. I just figured we'd end up getting married in a Unitarian church or some other denomination that doesn't think all gays are going straight to hell. You know I'm no fan of churches, but equally I know it's how you were brought up. It was important to you, so... I said nothing."

Angelo was stunned. There was a heavy feeling in the pit of his stomach. "And you would have gone through with it, wouldn't you, despite it not being what you wanted?"

Rick nodded. "If it made you happy, then yes."

Angelo grabbed hold of him and tugged him into his lap, Rick straddling him. "Don't ever do that again." He locked gazes with Rick, his heart pounding. "I mean it, Rick. This is our wedding. *Ours.* Don't keep your feelings from me. That's no basis for married life."

Rick swallowed. "I promise, from now on, I'll share everything."

Angelo stared at him, his heart aching with love for the man who was his whole world. He cupped the back of Rick's head and slowly drew him closer into a kiss. It was soft, tender and full of love.

It didn't stay that way, of course.

Hands roamed, stroked and caressed. Lips and tongues got in on the act. And when Rick climbed off his knee in silence and stood before him, hand outstretched to lead him to their bed, Angelo was more than happy to go along.

Chapter Six

"Colin, do you have a minute?"

Colin glanced up in surprise at the sound of Simon Wilson's voice. It was rare for the senior partner to turn up unannounced, and yet there he was, standing at the door to Colin's office.

Something's up.

"Sure. Your office?"

To his even greater surprise, Simon came into the room and closed the door behind him.

Oh, this is not good.

He waited until Simon had seated himself in the chair facing his desk. "I was about to pour myself a coffee. Would you like one? Or tea, perhaps?"

Simon smiled. "Thank you, but no. And I'm not staying long. I just wanted a quick word, that was all."

Colin had always thought of himself as a positive thinker, but to his dismay his heart was hammering and the only thought in his head was *what have I done?*

Simon leaned forward, his clasped hands on the desk. "I'll come straight to the point. We're very pleased with the work you've done since you started with us at Wilson & Beckett. You're punctual, efficient, and you consistently produce excellent results."

Oh my. Colin was lost for words. He swallowed and reached out to straighten his pen on the desk.

Simon chuckled. "I think that's the first occasion where you've been speechless." He tilted his head to one side and gave Colin a keen glance. "Let me guess. You were racking your brains, trying to work out where you'd screwed up."

"Something like that," Colin admitted.

Simon laughed. "God, no. Although I have had a couple of conversations like that so far this morning. It makes a nice change to have something positive to say." He sat up, hands resting on his knee. "The main point of this conversation is to ask if you feel up to heading the CAD department." He regarded Colin steadily.

Colin blinked. "But... I mean... that's Emily Parson's job."

Simon nodded. "Emily will be leaving us. I'm telling you this in confidence, mind. She's decided she needs to be nearer to her daughter in the West Midlands. I'm not going to go further into the reasons for the move. Needless to say, when we thought about who would replace her, you were first on our list."

"You... didn't want to advertise the position?" When Simon quirked his eyebrows, Colin hastened to elaborate. "Not that I'm not flattered, you understand. I'm just... surprised."

"I understand. And no, if we're going to recruit, it will be designers just starting out, people we can train to work with us. We want someone at the helm that we can trust, in whose work we have absolute faith." He smiled. "You fit the bill perfectly. So... do we go ahead and announce your promotion?"

Colin grinned. "As if I could turn down such an offer. Yes, and thank you for the trust you're placing in me."

"Thank *you*," Simon said, rising to his feet and extending his hand to Colin. "Your work helped us win the RIBA award, after all. It's only fair that we recognize your contribution." They shook hands. "There will be an e-mail later today, informing the staff. Congratulations, Colin." Simon walked towards the door.

Colin had a feeling his face was going to ache from smiling by the end of the day. "Thank you," he said when Simon paused at the threshold. Once the door had closed, he sank into his chair, warmth spreading through him.

Wait until I tell Ed.

He knew better than to call him at work. It had been different when they'd first got together—they'd managed to indulge in phone sex on more than one occasion—but not now that Ed was the CEO. Besides, Ed tended to worry if Colin called him at the office.

It can wait until tonight. Colin planned to call in at the local supermarket on the way home to buy a bottle of champagne, because this was certainly a situation that called for it.

The office was about an hour from closing when the e-mail finally came through. The fluttery feeling in his belly was back again as he saw his name on the screen. Somehow that made it all the more real. His phone pinged as he read it, announcing the arrival of an e-mail to his personal account, and still smiling, he opened up the folder—and stopped at the sight of Ray's name.

It had been three weeks since Ray had called, and Colin had assumed whatever he'd wanted to share couldn't have been all that important. He opened the e-mail entitled *News* and began reading.

Cold spread out from somewhere deep inside him, and his hands grew clammy. *Oh my God.* He stared at the screen, as if that would somehow change the words that seemed to move on the virtual page. Shaking his head, his fingers gripping the phone, he re-read the long message, hoping to God he'd got it all wrong.

Except he knew, somehow, that it was all too real.

Colin,

I'm sorry I hung up on you so abruptly during our phone conversation. To be honest, I'd thought I could do this over the phone, but when it came down to it, I lost my nerve. Phone calls are so immediate, aren't they? You say the words and they're out there, and you can't take them back, rephrase them... Far easier to draft and redraft an e-mail.

Only then, the hard thing is hitting Send.

Okay, I'll be brief. I've been HIV+ for a number of years now, and unfortunately time seems to have run out for me. I now have AIDS and I'm in the end stage, or pretty close to it.

Why am I telling you this?

Maybe because it still feels like you and I ended too soon. Whatever the reason, you were one of the most important people in my life. Maybe that's why I've stayed in touch all these years. I didn't want to lose you.

I don't know how much longer I have left. I don't want your pity, by the way. There is no one to blame here but me. I made some bad decisions in my youth, and now I'm paying for them, so yes, the responsibility is all mine.

I suppose in some way I feel that I wronged you. Whether you agree with that or not, I'm asking you to forgive me for leaving the way I did. I was never one for goodbyes.

Thank you for the years we shared. You were wonderful. I will always be honoured that I was the one who got to show you how great it can be to love another man. Only time in my life when I was someone's first, and believe me, you left some pretty big shoes to be filled.

Love you, Colin.

Ray.

It didn't get any better the second time of reading. Or the third. Or even the fourth.

With a start, Colin realized that the office had grown quieter. He glanced at the clock on his desk and knew why—an hour had passed and it was time to go home. Slowly he stood, automatically switched off his monitor and the lamp on his desk, and then removed his jacket from the back of his chair.

All he felt was numb.

Ed would be the first to admit he wasn't the most patient of men, but he tried his hardest when it came to Colin. It always astounded him how much he'd changed in the four years since Colin entered his life. Apart from the obvious fact that he'd changed lanes, of course.

Ed liked to think Colin brought out the best in him. He loved how Colin always saw the positive side to everything, which was usually right after Ed had blurted out something negative.

We fit, don't we? Opposites attract, an' all that.

Which was why he'd said nothing when Colin had walked in the front door, clearly subdued. He figured it was easiest to wait until Colin was ready to share about his obviously crap day.

But when Colin had showered, helped cook the dinner and dish it out, all the while saying very little, Ed figured his lover needed a gentle push in the right direction.

Except Ed was never one for using a feather when a sledgehammer would get the job done far quicker.

He paused halfway through their meal and cleared his throat. "So what 'appened at work today to piss *you* off?"

Colin snapped his head up, his brow furrowed. "Nothing. Why?"

Ed snorted. "Why? You've barely 'ad two words to rub together since you got 'ome."

Colin put down his fork. "Actually, something did happen today, but it was a good thing. I got promoted." He smiled.

Ed would have believed he had it all wrong, except Colin's smile didn't make it as far as his eyes.

What—wait—what was that last part?

Ed put down his knife and fork. "You mean to tell me, you've been in the 'ouse for *two hours*, an' you're only tellin' me this *now*?" He tried to ignore the flare of pain in his chest and the fact that his stomach was suddenly rock hard. *Something is really wrong.*

Colin's face tightened. "I'm sorry. I didn't phone you at the office because I know you have a lot on your plate during the day. And I was going to buy some champagne because I was over the moon about it. But then, something else happened that put a damper on my elation, and I guess I found it hard to shake off my mood."

The knot of tension in Ed's belly writhed like a tangled mass of snakes.

"Okay. I'll come back to your mood in a sec. What was the promotion?"

"You're looking at the new head of the CAD department."

Ed nodded. "Sweet. Now tell me what was so bad that you're not celebratin'. Because to my mind, you should've come through that door singin' an' dancin'."

Colin pushed his half-eaten meal away from him. "I received an e-mail, that's all."

"That 'ad to be some e-mail, to take your mind off a whoppin' great promotion." Something fired in his brain. Someone asking for Colin's e-mail address. Ed opened his eyes wide. "Ray sent it, didn't he?"

The way Colin stiffened was all the answer Ed needed. Words were superfluous.

"Yet another thing you 'aven't mentioned. Why is that?"

Colin stared at the remains of his dinner. "I was going to tell you when I'd figured out how *I* felt about it. I'm still processing."

"Was it bad?"

Colin winced. "Not for me."

Ed huffed. "Aren't ya gonna tell me what he wrote?"

Slowly Colin raised his head. "It doesn't matter." His voice was a monotone.

Ed was doing his level best to remain calm. "'Ow can you say it doesn't matter? If it affects you, it affects me."

Colin lifted his eyebrows. "Look, I know you're concerned, but please, don't leap in with both feet. Me sharing what Ray sent me is only going to make things worse. And besides, I'm right. It doesn't affect you. He's part of my past."

A cold wave rolled over Ed. "So what? Your past matters to me." They'd had disagreements in the past, but Colin had never spoken in such a lifeless, hopeless tone. Just hearing it sent shivers down Ed's spine.

Colin gave a weary sigh. "Ed, telling you what he shared with me wouldn't make it any more palatable, believe me. But I promise, when I've gotten my head around all this, I'll tell you everything. It's not a secret, it's just... a little overwhelming."

Something in his voice sank in, and Ed finally got it. Colin was hurting, and knowing that made his heart ache.

"Fine," he said. "I'll leave it alone then. But I'm 'ere if you need me, okay?"

Colin nodded, the first hint of a smile playing about his lips. "Thank you."

Ed gestured to Colin's plate. "An' now I'll heat this up. You're not goin' without yer dinner." When he reached for it, Colin grabbed his hand.

"You know I love you, right?"

Ed smiled. "That's the one thing I'm bleedin' certain of." He bent down and kissed Colin on the lips, and then headed for the kitchen. While he waited for the microwave to do its stuff, he did his utmost not to think about that e-mail.

He'll tell me when he's ready.

Ed could wait until then. He hoped.

Ed stared at the ceiling. They'd been in bed for over half an hour, and he knew by the sound of Colin's breathing that he wasn't asleep. Ed rolled onto his side and shifted across the mattress to curl up around Colin.

As soon as his chest came into contact with Colin's broad back, Colin became rigid. "Not tonight, Ed, all right?"

For some reason, the assumption cut him to the quick. "I wanted to cuddle ya. I thought maybe you needed a cuddle right now." Ed rolled away onto his side, facing away from him, his stomach churning. This wasn't like Colin.

The sheets rustled behind him, and then Colin's warm arms came around him. "I'm sorry," Colin whispered. "I had no right to speak to you like that."

Ed reached over to click on the lamp, and then turned to look him in the eye. "For Gawd's sake, Col, what is it? Can't I 'elp ya?" He knew what was really eating away at him, and he couldn't hold it back any longer. "Why can't you tell me what Ray wrote? Was it something personal? Because if that's the case, I don't know what to say to ya. I didn't think we kept secrets from each other." Every fibre of him hoped to God that wasn't the case. The thought that Colin felt he couldn't share something with Ed made him feel sick.

Please, Col.... Just talk to me.

Colin groaned. "God, I *swear*, it's not like that, it's just..." He sighed. "I know this will sound crazy, but... it felt as though just saying it out loud somehow made it real, and fuck, I don't want it to be. I want to wake up tomorrow and find it was all a bad dream, that Ray really isn't dying..." He gulped.

Ed gaped. "What?" His head was spinning. *Ray, dyin'? What the fuck?*

Colin sighed again. "See? I told you it didn't make sense." He regarded Ed in silence for a moment, before stretching out his hand toward the bedside cabinet for his phone. He scrolled through and then handed it to Ed. "Here," he said simply. "Read it for yourself."

Ed scanned the e-mail, his heart plummeting. It took two attempts for the words to sink in, and when they did, his throat tightened and his chest ached to realize what Colin had been going through. "Oh wow." He raised his eyes and stared at Colin. "Aw, love, I'm so sorry. I know you two were close."

"I still can't believe it, to be honest." Colin seemed so tired. "And I can't get past the feeling that I need to do something."

"Such as what?"

Colin hesitated before replying. "I want to see him. Not yet, maybe, but at some point."

Ed handed him the phone. "Unfinished business?"

"Something like that."

"What did he mean, about leavin' the way he did?"

Colin sat up and stuffed pillows behind him. "You know I said he got a job offer in Edinburgh? Well, I found that out when I came home from work one night—I'd been working in a restaurant during the summer—and received a text telling me about the job, and that he'd already left for Scotland. I messaged him back, asking why he hadn't told me. I got what you see here: he hates goodbyes."

"That must've 'urt." Ed could only imagine the pain Colin had gone through. To spend three years of your life with someone, only to have them discard you so quickly.

"It stung, all right. So when I got the Christmas card that year, I was surprised. I thought he'd wanted to break off all contact. Apparently not. And the cards kept on coming, giving little away about his life in Edinburgh." Colin swallowed. "Seems like he kept a great deal from me."

"An' you want to see 'im, to get some answers. I understand that." Ed reached out to stroke Colin's thigh, covered by the soft sheets. "Take yer time before you make plans to go dashin' off, okay? It's like you said—you need time to process it all. An' for all you know, he might not want visitors."

"Fair point."

Colin's pained stare was too much for Ed. "Listen, why don't I switch off the light, an' then hold yer until you fall asleep? I know you probably don't believe you *can* fall asleep right now, but it can't 'urt." He caressed the firm thigh. "I just want to 'old ya."

Colin smiled. "Right now, being held is exactly what I need."

Ed swiftly turned out the light and lay down, snuggling around Colin's body, his arm draped over Colin's waist, hand lying protectively over his heart. *Not that it'll stop 'im from 'urting.* He lay in the dark, listening to Colin breathe.

Ed had never felt so useless in his entire life.

Chapter Seven

Rick gave the apartment a last glance to make sure everything was neat and tidy before Franco arrived.

Angelo chuckled as he came up behind him and put his arms around Rick's waist, his chin resting on Rick's shoulder. "Yes, it looks lovely."

"Ha!" Rick turned his head and kissed Angelo soundly on the cheek. "If I left things up to you, we'd be knee deep in crap."

Angelo released him and took a step back, eyes wide in an affectation of innocence. "I have no idea what you're talking about."

Rick let out a loud snort. "Pull the other one. I always marvel how you keep the studio so spick and span, with a place for everything, and everything in its place, and—"

"Hey, that's common sense. We're talking chisels, hammers, saws..."

Rick nodded, grinning. "So what is so wrong with extending the same courtesy to our apartment? I mean, what about your piles of magazines that you leave everywhere, the folders with your sketches for pieces, shoes—my God, I counted *ten pairs* of your shoes around this place. Ten! I don't think I even *own* ten pairs."

Angelo narrowed his gaze. "So basically, you're implying I'm a slob."

"Implying? Who's implying?"

Angelo let out a long sigh. "Oh well, looks like the honeymoon is over."

Rick chuckled. "I believe it's customary for the honeymoon not to start until after the wedding?" He moved closer to wrap his arms around Angelo. "I'm feeling pretty confident that I can get you to change your slobbish ways. I might need the rest of our lives together to do it, but I'll do it. I can be pretty tenacious. It might take me until you're in your eighties, but I'll get there."

"Tenacity is a good quality in a husband," Angelo said softly, rubbing his thumb along Rick's jawline. "The ability to hold onto something is always good."

Rick knew that tone. It was the one that was usually a prelude to sex. "Is there something I should be holding onto?" he asked with a smile.

Angelo nodded deliberately, his eyes gleaming. "My shoulders, while I lift you up and fuck you against the bedroom wall."

Rick groaned and let go of Angelo to adjust his hard on. "This is not fair. Not when we have a visitor arriving at any second. *Especially* one who's a priest." He gestured to the bulge in his jeans. "I mean, what am I supposed to do about this now?"

The intercom buzzed, and they both jumped.

"Might I suggest," Angelo said as he headed toward the door to the apartment, "a strategically placed cushion?" Rick could hear him laughing all the way down the stairs into the studio.

He shook his head. Angelo's libido was truly amazing. Rick glanced down to his visible erection and groaned silently. *Bloody Angelo.* He just had time to sit on the couch and yank a cushion into his lap before the door opened and Angelo walked in, followed by a guy in maybe his late forties, bearded, with glasses, and wearing a black leather biker's jacket over a tight black T-shirt, jeans and heavy boots.

Rick blinked.

Franco laughed. "You must be Rick. Let me guess—I look nothing like a priest."

Beside him, Angelo snickered. "See? It's not just me. No one expects a leather-clad priest with muscles."

Rick started to rise, but Franco waved his hand and sat next to him. "It's good to finally meet you."

"Yeah, it's only been, what, ten years?" Angelo observed with a chuckle.

"I send Christmas cards, what more do you want?" Franco grinned. "And seeing as I might be here for a while, is there anything to drink around here? Non-alcoholic—I'm on the Harley."

"You ride a Harley?" Rick shook his head again. "Nope. Definitely not what I expected. And we *have* to introduce you to Ed at the wedding."

"Ed?"

Angelo smiled. "Rides a Harley." He left them to go into the kitchen.

"Ah, right." Franco leaned forward and removed his jacket, placing it over the arm of the couch. He sat back and studied Rick, thick arms folded across his chest. "So, you work for a publishing house?"

Rick nodded. "Trinity." He met Franco's thoughtful gaze. "And you work with some bad-ass convicts."

"Guilty as charged." He winked. "Excuse the pun."

"So what do you do all day? I mean, once you've conducted a service on Sundays, what's left?"

Franco chuckled. "You'd be surprised. The Chaplaincy is an important part of the prison. For instance, a new prisoner has to meet with one of the team within twenty-four hours of arriving."

"Really?" Rick drew his legs up onto the couch and tucked his feet under him. "What for?"

"We invite them to register as a specific religion, although they can change it at any time. We do stuff you might not expect, such as lending radios, musical instruments or typewriters."

"Listening to you, anyone would think your job is a walk in the park, but I know different," Angelo said as he came back into the lounge, carrying a tray with three glasses of juice. "Belmarsh takes care of Category A prisoners, isn't that right? The ones that pose the greatest potential risk?"

Franco nodded, his expression sobering. "I haven't been there all that long, but from conversations with my fellow chaplains, it's clear things have changed a lot."

"In what way?" Rick sat up and rubbed his forearms briskly, where goose bumps had formed.

"About one in every five prisoners is converting to Islam, but we're talking those who follow Muslim extremism here."

"Wasn't Belmarsh where they detained that famous Muslim cleric, the one who was inciting violence?" Rick asked.

Franco snorted. "More like *infamous*. He's gone, but what he left behind..." He shook his head. "This is where the Muslim chaplains—the Imans—come in. They take part in a daily battle to counter the jihadist interpretation of Islam, running programmes that attack the Islamic justification for terrorism." Franco's expression was sad. "We are under no illusions. The task is monumental, but we are determined to show these men that there is another way and that their ideology is wrong."

"Is it working?" Angelo asked, handing Franco a glass.

"If I had a way of reading minds, then I could answer that question. We can but hope that through our efforts, through prayer, we can lead them away from the path they've chosen and onto the path that leads to self-improvement." He took a sip of juice. "But enough about me. Let's talk weddings. That's why I'm here, after all."

Rick fought the urge to shiver. "Now you *sound* like a priest."

Franco flashed him a smile. "Don't let the talk of prayer put you off. I'm basically an okay guy." He winked.

Rick couldn't help snorting. He could see why Angelo liked him.

"You mentioned you might have an idea about the reception venue," Angelo said.

Franco's face lit up. "What if I told you I'd found a venue where you could hold both the reception *and* the wedding ceremony? One that would please even your mother?"

Rick stared at him. "Wow. If you can do all that, I'll believe in miracles."

Franco took a longer drink and then set his glass down on the coffee table. "Hever Castle is about thirty-five miles from central London, just north of Tunbridge Wells. It was Anne Boleyn's childhood home, and it's stunning, set in beautiful gardens and surrounded by a moat. I've visited it several times, and I swear, it gets better every time. It's run commercially as a tourist attraction, along with offering *very* high class bed and breakfast facilities." He paused, smiling. "And... I happen to know the man in charge of the whole operation."

"*Knowing* him is one thing," Angelo interjected. "It's late in the day to hope they have a date available."

Franco nodded, his face straight. "You're right, of course. Does that mean you wouldn't be interested to learn that Friday August 19th is temporarily booked in your names? Including accommodation for the wedding night?" He flashed them a wide grin.

Rick gaped. "And what did you have to promise the guy in charge to pull *that* off? That you'd sleep with him?" It was only when Angelo began to cough violently that he remembered Franco's profession. "Shit. Oops, sorry. I mean, wow, that's fantastic."

"That mouth of yours always gets you into trouble," Angelo muttered, followed by a rough chuckle.

To Rick's surprise Franco didn't laugh. For one brief moment his face turned ashen and he stared at Rick with wide eyes. Then he regained his composure and cleared his throat. "Is that date okay with you?"

Rick's chest tightened. *I've upset him.* He gave himself a mental kick up the backside. *Since when do you ask a priest if he's sleeping with a guy?* No wonder Franco had looked shocked. "I... Let us check the diary, okay?" He fired Angelo a look, and his fiancé launched himself up off the armchair and across the room to his phone.

Franco appeared to have gotten over his shock. "While Angelo is checking the diary, why don't you have a look online? You can see the gardens and the house, even the accommodation."

Rick nodded and grabbed his laptop from the coffee table. "Hever Castle, you said?" It wasn't long before he pulled up the site and—

"Oh my God. Angelo. *Please* tell me that date is free." He stared at the images in disbelief before turning to Franco. "Seriously? We can have our wedding here?"

Angelo came across to peer at the screen. "Why? Does it look good? It—" His eyes widened.

Franco's chuckle rumbled out of him. "I gather you like what you see."

"Like?" Rick shook his head in amazement. ""It's beautiful."

"Mum is going to have kittens when she sees this," Angelo murmured, apparently unable to tear his gaze away from the screen.

Rick tugged on his sleeve impatiently. "Well? Does that mean you have no jobs booked for that date?" He knew Ed would be fine about whichever date they chose. Most likely Trinity would close for the day anyway, because all the staff would be at their wedding. But Angelo had a number of projects on his books.

Angelo's smile warmed Rick inside. "It's clear so far." He turned to Franco. "And we're definitely booked in for August 19th?"

Franco held up his hand. "I said temporarily, but all that's needed is a deposit and it's a firm booking. Although you'll have to get a move on, organizing the caterers. Anthony said he could help there too if needed. They have a lot of weddings, and he has contacts in the catering world."

"Anthony. He's the guy in charge?" Rick asked. Angelo sat on the floor in front of the coffee table and clicked through the site.

Franco nodded. "Actually, he and I go way back. We were friends at university, before I entered the priesthood. We reconnected about a year ago. When Maria mentioned you needed a venue for the reception, he was the first person I thought of calling. We met for dinner this evening to discuss it. I hadn't even considered the possibility of holding the wedding there—that was Anthony's suggestion."

"Oh wow."

Angelo's soft cry broke through their conversation. He twisted to stare at Rick over his shoulder, his eyes shining.

Rick peered at the laptop screen and his jaw dropped. "Is that the accommodation you were telling us about?"

"Yes. They have several rooms and suites."

"Look at that four poster bed." Angelo's voice was laced with awe. "And that gorgeous carved ceiling and all that wood panelling. It's wonderful."

Rick kissed the top of his head. "Now *that* is a perfect room for a wedding night." He turned back to Franco, grinning. "Where do we sign?"

Franco reached for his jacket and fished out his phone. A moment later, he smiled. "Hey." He laughed. "Yes, I know I only just left you. I'm here with Rick and Angelo." He paused. "Oh, definitely. They love it. In fact, I think they're busy choosing their room for their wedding night as we speak." He listened intently. "Sure. I'll pass that on. Oh, and they'll need to talk about catering for the reception. Yes, we have to set the ball rolling on that one ASAP." Another pause. "And thank you again. You really have saved the day for them." His smile widened. "Yes, let's do that." He said goodbye and disconnected. "Anthony says to use the Contact link on the website. When he sees your message, he'll email you details about the booking. He also suggests that you might want to visit the castle for a look around, to decide on where to hold the ceremony, and to make a firm choice of room."

"That's a great idea." Rick was buzzing with excitement. "Can we go next weekend?"

Both Angelo and Franco laughed loudly.

"You are such a big kid sometimes." Angelo gazed at him fondly.

Rick speared him with a look. "Hey, come on, you're the one who plucked August from out of nowhere. We don't have time to waste, do we, Franco?"

Franco held up both hands. "Whoa, leave me out of this. I know better than to come between a soon-to-be-married couple." He pulled a notepad from his jacket pocket. "Now, can we talk about the ceremony?" He grinned. "That *is* why I'm here, right?"

Angelo closed the laptop and sat next to Franco on the couch. "Quite right."

"Do we need to have a civil ceremony first?" Rick asked. "Before you bless the marriage, I mean?"

"I wish you could take the whole ceremony," Angelo said quietly. "But we know that's not possible. We've already explained to my mum that the Catholic Church wouldn't recognize our marriage."

Franco regarded him in silence for a moment, before putting his notepad on the floor and then sitting back. "I suppose I need to be honest with you."

Rick straightened, the hairs on his arms standing on end for some inexplicable reason.

Franco clasped his hands together and stared at them. "What I told you is true. I'm a chaplain at HMP Belmarsh. What I neglected to tell you is that I'm not the Catholic chaplain."

Angelo blinked. "What?"

"I'm no longer a Catholic priest. The Church and I parted company six months ago. I still preach, but for the Unitarian church."

Angelo appeared stunned. "When we last talked, you seemed perfectly happy. What happened?"

Franco shrugged. "I supposed it came down to a difference in ideology. I wasn't prepared to preach something that I didn't believe was right, so I made the decision to leave the church." He sighed. "It wasn't an easy decision, by any means. But I'm happy in my new position. And today, when you talked about me not looking like a priest, I thought I could... bluff it out, say nothing. I couldn't."

"Sounds like it had to be something pretty huge for you to take this course of action." Rick observed him keenly. Franco said nothing, and Rick realized whatever had brought about this change, he was not about to share it.

"Does this mean you can conduct the ceremony?" Angelo asked, his expression brightening.

Franco sighed. "I'm what is referred to as an Authorised Person, meaning that the ceremony would be legal, but that applies *only* if it's conducted in the Unitarian chapel. And I should point out here that my status there is a fairly recent thing. As yet, I haven't conducted any weddings. For *your* wedding, you'd still need an authorized person from the General Registrar's office present to hear those all-important two sentences that make it legal."

"Two?" Rick was intrigued. "You mean, the whole wedding could take a couple of minutes? Have you *any idea* how many boring weddings I've had to sit through, that felt like they went on for hours?"

Angelo snorted. "Try a Catholic wedding. It's like a wedding and a Mass, all rolled into one." He tapped Franco's thigh. "But you've got me thinking. Which two sentences?"

"The one where you declare that there's nothing lawful to stop you getting married, and the other where you say you take your partner as your lawful wedded whatever." He grinned. "You two would be my first same-sex marriage ceremony." Franco seemed to relax for the first time since his confession. "So, what do I need to know about you two to make this a more personal service?" He waggled his eyebrows. "I'm sure you both have things to share about your relationship during the past ten years."

Rick coughed and Angelo snickered. "Some things are definitely not for sharing, especially with *my* family."

Franco grinned. "Gotcha." He reached down to pick up his notepad. "Let's start then."

Chapter Eight

March 21st

   "Come in." Ed glanced up from his desk and smiled at the sight of his PA. "Oh, Mandy, I love ya."

   She chuckled as she placed the large mug of coffee in front of him. "Yeah, yeah. Heard it all before. And we both know it's the coffee you love."

   Ed laughed. "Well, duh." He often joked that Mandy had only been given the job because she made good coffee. "You only 'ave one strike against ya."

   Mandy grinned. "We've discussed this. It's not my fault your sister named her little girl Mandy, okay? My parents got there first."

   "Yeah, okay." Ed sniffed the rich aroma. "'Ow did you know I was ready for a coffee?"

   She guffawed. "Oh, I don't know. Maybe because there's a *y* in the day?"

   Ed frowned. "Eh? All days end with a—" He broke off and gave her a stern look. "Oh, very funny. Out."

   Still laughing, Mandy exited his office, closing the door behind her. Ed ignored the siren call of the coffee and stared at his monitor. Blake was due any minute for their monthly meeting, and Ed wanted to have all the facts at his fingertips. Not that he was concerned: the company was doing fine, amazing though that was in the present climate.

   Well, it was doin' fine, until last night. He knew Blake would want to talk about the news that had rocked the publishing world the previous evening.

   He gazed at the framed photos on his desk. One was of him and Colin, taken in the restaurant the night Colin had proposed. Colin's face bore bruises, the result of an incident at the end of a football match, one which had ended up with Ed spending a few hours in a police cell. Another was one of Colin that Ed had taken the previous summer, his face lit up by the sun, his expression relaxed and happy. It was Ed's favourite photo, not only because Colin looked wonderful, but also because of the memories it brought back to him. They'd spent a week on the south coast, when Colin had roped Blake in to make sure Ed took a holiday.

It had been his New Year's resolution to spend less time at the office, and it was already beginning to look like an epic fail.

His intercom buzzed. "Ed? Blake's here. And he's not alone."

Mandy's delighted tone told him instantly who else had accompanied Blake. He got up from his desk and walked to the door. He could already hear the *coos* and *ahhs* from some of his female staff.

"Are you distractin' my staff again, Mr. Davis?" he said loudly with a grin as he strode along the hallway to the reception area. Sure enough, Blake and Will stood in front of Karen's desk, Nathan wrapped up and held against Will's chest in a grey sort of sling. Ed shook his head. "My, aren't we trendy?" Beth, Karen and Mandy were gazing at the baby and making cute noises, not that Nathan noticed—he was fast asleep.

Will lifted his chin and smiled. "These carriers are all the rage. It's actually pretty comfortable."

Ed snorted. "Babies went around in carry-cots in my day."

Karen stared at him. "Yes, but that was back when the earth was cooling." Her eyes twinkled with amusement.

Blake laughed. "I see nothing changes around here. Still the same respectful working relationships that I remember so fondly." He met Ed's gaze. "How about we leave Will with Nathan's fan club, while you and I go into your office?"

Ed nodded, pleased. It was good to know Blake was still the same efficient businessman he'd always been. "Mandy, can you bring through some coffee for *Mr.* Davis?" He grinned.

"No problem."

Blake followed him along the hallway, the noises behind them not dimming in the slightest. Blake closed the door. "I take it you've spoken with Lizzie?"

"Yeah." Ed's good mood submerged beneath a fleeting dark cloud. "Don't get me wrong. I'm really 'appy for 'er, but I'd only just got 'er to work part-time. We'll 'ave to see if Thomas can come back an' work for us again full-time. At least he's familiar with the set-up 'ere." Thomas had run the translation department once Lizzie had become a full-time mum.

"Good idea." Blake sat in the chair facing Ed's desk. "You saw the news yesterday?"

Ed had known it wouldn't take long. "You mean that Real Romance went tits up?" he scowled. "Angel sent me an e-mail last night. A heads-up would've been nice. The site goes dark in less than two days." The online site sold e-books and had sent out a shock announcement that it was folding. "I'm puttin' out notices to tell readers that if they've bought our titles via the site an' subsequently lost 'em, they can just send us a copy of their receipt an' we'll replace the books. Least we can do." He hadn't begun to calculate the effect it would have on the writers' royalties.

Blake sighed. "Time to look for alternative sites, I think. That was top of my list for discussion this morning. It's bound to affect business. Our job now is keep our heads and keep the company going." He pulled his tablet from his briefcase. "Okay. Let's see what we can do with this mess."

Ed nodded. It was times like these that he was glad Blake was around.

Their meeting lasted an hour, and by the time they were done, Ed's head ached. It was probably the most testing time he'd experienced since taking over the running of the company, but he knew Blake wouldn't have entrusted him with the task if he hadn't felt Ed was up to it.

Blake got up and stretched. "And now I'd better go see what my husband is up to," he said with a wink.

"Are things settlin' down at 'ome?"

Blake paused at the doorway. "Nathan is nothing like Sophie was as a baby. She was forever gurgling, making those cute little noises, remember? Nathan is so quiet in comparison. He's such a placid baby."

Ed snorted. "For Gawd's sake, don't say it like it's a bad thing! Enjoy the peace while it lasts. Because the time will come when you're complainin' about 'ow much noise 'im an' all 'is mates are makin' in his room."

Blake laughed, but then his face straightened. "Don't even joke. I think about Sophie and how the past four years have flown by. Let me hold on to Nathan as a baby for as long as I can."

They left the office together and walked through the hallway in search of Will and Nathan. They found Will in Rick's office, the pair of them deep in conversation. From the sound of it, the topic under discussion was the wedding, not that *that* was any surprise. Nathan was lying on a pile of cushions that Ed recognized immediately.

"Excuse me? Those are from my couch!" he said, pointing at them.

Rick frowned at him. "Shh, not so loud. You'll wake Nathan. And are you saying you begrudge that sweet little baby a few measly cushions?" His eyes sparkled with mischief.

Ed narrowed his gaze. "You can be a right pain in the arse sometimes." He gave Nathan a glance, but the baby was still sleeping soundly. "Gawd, that kid can sleep through anythin.'"

Will quirked his eyebrows. "Don't let this blissful state fool you. We always know when he's hungry or tired, and of course, when it's time for Blake to change his nappy." His gaze went to Blake, and Ed bit back a chuckle. Will loved to bait his husband.

"Still keepin' you up nights?" Ed asked them both.

"Less now, I guess." Will gave Blake an inquiring glance. "Are you done?"

Blake nodded. "Time to get this young man home before he wakes up to tell us very loudly that it's time for his lunch."

Ed couldn't resist. "Do you still 'ave to 'ide the pots of chocolate puddin' from Will?" It had been a standing joke around the office when Sophie was very small that Will was addicted to baby chocolate pudding.

Blake snorted. "Oh, we've moved on. *Now* it's the Rusks. I keep finding them on his desk, hidden where he thinks I can't see them."

Will glared. "They're good to nibble while I'm writing." It was noticeable, however, that there was no trace of malice when Blake helped him to wind the grey sling around Nathan's sleeping form, securing it over Will's shoulders and around his back while Will held their little boy against his body. Ed never tired of watching his friends together, of seeing the love they shared.

"Did you mention next weekend to Ed?" Will inquired, his arms supporting Nathan. "Rick says he's in, and that Angelo will be by the time Rick's finished working on him." His eyes sparkled.

"What about next weekend?" Ed gave Blake a keen glance. "Something you've forgotten to mention?"

"We wondered if you'd like to come and stay with us for the weekend. We're having a... garden party."

Ed arched his eyebrows. "I know today's the first day of spring, but a *garden party*? It'll be bleedin' freezin'!"

Rick snorted. "It's not that sort of a party. For one thing, you'd need to bring a pair of wellies and a warm jacket."

Ed stared at Blake, who gave a quick shrug. "We decided it was time to start work on the garden. We haven't done a thing since we moved in, and there's a lot that needs clearing. So—"

"So you thought you'd use your friends as cheap labour," Ed interjected, grinning.

"That was the first thing I said when he came up with it," Will piped up.

Blake gave him a hard stare before returning his attention to Ed. "We'd value your opinions as to what we do with it. And you'd be well fed, I can guarantee that. Mostly we thought it would be nice to spend the weekend with you four."

Ed liked the sound of that. "Lemme talk to Colin, see what he thinks, before I commit meself."

"Of course. Just let us know either way." Blake leaned over and kissed Will's cheek. "Come on, let's get you home." He turned back to Ed. "And *you* are doing a great job. I know things aren't easy right now."

Ed waved a hand. "Pfft. We'll manage. It's good to know you're there if we need ya."

"Always." Blake's intense blue eyes focused on him. "You only have to ask."

"Glad things are finally looking up on the wedding front," Will said to Rick with a smile. "I'll go online and check out this venue when we get home." When Blake's jaw dropped, Will grinned. "No, Blake Davis, you are *not* going to ask him questions now. I'll tell you all about it on the way home. I know what you're like when you get talking. You can be such a gasbag sometimes." He exited Rick's office, chuckling quietly.

"He likes livin' dangerously, doesn't he?" Ed commented to Blake with a nod of his head toward the door Will had just taken.

Blake gave him an evil grin. "We'll see how mouthy he is when I've put Nathan to bed after I've fed him." He followed Will.

Ed shook his head. He caught Rick's gaze. "I wouldn't wanna be Will tonight."

Rick waggled his eyebrows. "Ha. I have no sympathy. If you ask me, Will knows exactly what he's doing."

Ed had to admit, Rick had a point.

He went back into his office and shut the door after him. He pulled his phone from his pocket, debating whether or not to call Colin during his lunch break. It had been a week since he'd received Ray's e-mail, and although he hadn't mentioned it, Ed knew it had to have been on Colin's mind. Colin had been quieter, more thoughtful, and even though Ed was doing his damnedest to be patient, he was dying to say something—*anything*—that might help.

When his phone vibrated, startling him out of his reverie, he wasn't surprised to see Colin's name flash up. It was a common occurrence, almost as if they could read each other's minds.

"Hi. You on yer lunch break?"

"Yes, thank God. It's been quite busy here this morning. I've told Marion absolutely no calls."

"Then I'm 'onoured." Ed waited, but Colin didn't respond. "You okay, Col?"

"I've been thinking."

"Oh, careful. Your brains will over'eat." When no laughter, not even a chuckle ensued, he gave a sigh. "Let me guess. Ray?"

"Yes."

"Do you still want to see him?"

Colin's breathing hitched. "Why—do you think I shouldn't?"

"I think," Ed said carefully, "that you need to do what you believe is right. Ray's e-mail was askin' ya to forgive 'im. Do you need to see him to do that?"

"It's like you said. Unfinished business."

"An' maybe you want to see 'im for one last time. You were close once." Ed got that. "So what next? Are you gonna call 'im?"

"I think so. Then we'll see what happens." Colin sounded so deflated, it tore at Ed's heart.

"Listen, I've got an idea. 'Ow about I stop off on me way 'ome an' get us a takeaway from our favourite Indian? No need to cook, an' after we've eaten, we can cuddle up on the couch an' watch a film."

"Right now that sounds absolutely wonderful." A note of genuine pleasure had crept into Colin's voice, and it did Ed good to hear it.

"In that case, I'll get off the dog 'n' bone an' make sure I don't finish too late tonight."

Colin chuckled. "And there was I, thinking I'd weaned you off all those Cockneyisms."

Ed snorted. "You what? I'm an 'ackney lad, born 'n' bred. You can take a man out of the East End, but—"

"—but you can never take the East End out of the man, yeah, yeah, I know," Colin finished for him. "And I wouldn't have you any other way, my little Cockney sparrow." Another chuckle.

"Hey! Who you callin' little?" In that moment Ed felt light, almost giddy with relief. "Now get off this phone, before I decide to paddle your arse later for that last remark."

"You and whose army?" Colin joked. "I'll see you tonight." He disconnected the call.

Ed placed his phone on the desk and stared at it, unseeing. *At least I made him laugh.*

Something that had been in short supply lately.

Colin came back to his desk with a fresh cup of coffee. He pulled up Ray's e-mail on his phone and sent a short reply.

Can we talk? I don't have your phone number.

Then he leaned back and drank his coffee. When thirty minutes had passed with no reply, he began coming up with reasons why Ray hadn't come back to him immediately.

He's not got access to his e-mails.

He's busy.

He tried to ignore the one reason that made his chest tighten. *He doesn't want to talk to me.*

The phone's ping announced the arrival of an e-mail and he pounced on it.

I wasn't sure you wanted to talk, especially after I heard nothing for a fortnight after the e-mail. I'd resigned myself to not hearing from you again.

Want me to call you? Or if now's not a good time, here's my number.

Colin stared at the screen, his stomach clenching. *You wanted this, remember?* Except now he was here, on the point of phoning, he had no clue what he wanted to say. Everything had changed since that last call. *Now I know he's dying. What the hell do I say to him?*

More importantly, could he talk without that knowledge cracking his voice? Without a whole wealth of emotions taking over?

Only one way to find out.

Colin tapped in the number and waited. Ray answered after two rings. "Hi."

"Hi." For a second he was stumped. *What do I say next? How are you? Sorry you're dying?* Colin gave himself a mental slap. "I've not caught you at a bad time, have I?"

Ray chuckled. "I was dozing when your e-mail arrived, but I take a lot of naps. It's good to hear you again, especially as I... well, I said as much in my reply, right?" He paused. "I *am* glad you called, though."

Colin had to say something. "I was sorry to hear your news."

"Yeah, well. It is what it is. I was in two minds about contacting you, but like I said..." Another pause. "Christ, this is just as hard as last time. I thought it would be easier, now that I'd told you, but..."

"Can I see you?" Colin blurted out.

Silence.

"Ray?"

Ray cleared his throat. "Sorry, you sort of caught me off guard there. You really want to see me?"

Colin had done a lot of thinking about this. "Yes. I can't put everything in my head in an e-mail, and talking about this over the phone just seems wrong. So... I'd like to come up to Edinburgh and see you. If that's okay with you."

"When... when were you thinking of coming?"

That sounded hopeful. "Maybe in a couple of weeks? Just for the weekend. I could fly up there. That would be fastest." He might need to finish early on the Friday, but he didn't think the partners would begrudge him a few hours off.

"On your own?"

That stopped him for a second or two. "Yes." He hadn't once considered the possibility of taking Ed with him. Ed had enough on his plate without adding Colin's woes as well. When Ray fell silent again, Colin's heartbeat sped up. It wasn't until that moment that he realized how much he wanted this. *I need closure. I need to say goodbye to him.*

"Ray?"

"Okay. You can visit. Just... don't be too shocked when you see me, all right? I'm not exactly pretty right now."

Colin couldn't resist the urge to lighten the conversation. "Since when were you ever pretty?"

"Bitch." Ray laughed. "Okay. Let me know your ETA when you have the details. I look forward to seeing you. From the look of that photo about your company, you appear to have gotten... bigger." He chuckled. "I always did like muscular men."

That was one titbit Colin would *not* be sharing with Ed. "That's what playing rugby does for you. I'll e-mail you my travel details when I have them." He paused. "Take care, Ray."

"Doing my best, but I think that ship has sailed." Before Colin could respond, Ray forged ahead. "I'll see you soon. Bye, Colin." The call disconnected.

The winking light on his desk phone put paid to any time Colin might have spent playing the conversation over and over in his mind. Right then it was time to work.

Plenty of time to recall Ray's words in the middle of the night when he couldn't sleep. He hadn't slept well since the e-mail's arrival.

Ed's gentle foot massage was melting him into a puddle of goo. Which was probably what Ed had intended. "You're really good at that, you know?" Colin was pleasantly full of chicken Korma, lamb Tikka Masala, pilau rice and peshwari naan bread. The beers Ed had brought had his head buzzing nicely. A mellow, absolutely perfect end to his day.

Ed dug his thumbs into the arch of Colin's left foot. "I never did 'old much with that reflexology crap, but maybe there's somethin' in it after all." He paused. "So, wanna tell me about it?"

"You know, we'd make a fortune on the stage if we ever decided to do a mind-reading act," Colin joked.

Ed chuckled and rubbed his thumbs in slow circles over the ball of Colin's foot. "We just know each other, that's all. I knew when you came in tonight that there was something on your mind. I wasn't gonna push ya." His gaze met Colin's. "I knew you'd tell me, sooner or later. An' besides, I'm tryin' to cut down on my bull-at-a-gate impressions." He grinned.

Colin smiled. "Okay, where is Ed? What have you done with him?"

Ed stopped his massage and shifted along the couch until he was sitting at Colin's side. He leaned in slowly and kissed him on the lips. "I just like keepin' you on yer toes." He sat back and regarded Colin steadily. "Well?"

Colin recounted the conversation with Ray. "I figured I'd go up there the first weekend in April. That's only a couple of weeks off."

"Do you want me to go with ya?"

Colin blinked. "Ray asked me that too, if I was going alone." He thought best about how to frame his answer. "Maybe not. It'll just be for two nights, after all."

"An' maybe you'd feel awkward 'avin' me there. Ray bein' your ex an' all."

Is that it? Colin considered Ed's suggestion. "You know I have no secrets from you," he began, but Ed cut him off with a finger to his lips. When he withdrew it slowly, his eyes were kind.

"Look, it's understandable, all right? This is your first boyfriend we're talkin' about. You an' Ray have got things to say to each other, an' you don't need me around for that. I only asked in case you felt like you wanted moral support."

"And I do appreciate that, really." Colin reached for Ed's hand and squeezed it. "Knowing you're here, waiting for me to come home, that means a lot."

"'Ave you spoken to anyone at work about this? Will you need any time off?"

"I haven't looked at flights yet—I was going to do that tonight—but there shouldn't be a problem."

Ed chuckled. "It's a good thing you didn't tell him you'd go this weekend, 'cause we're gonna be a bit busy."

"We are?" Colin racked his brains. "I didn't think we had anything planned."

Ed got up and held out a hand. "I'll tell you all about—in bed." He hoisted Colin to his feet.

Colin followed him from the lounge, smiling to himself. If he knew his Ed, the talking wouldn't last long.

Chapter Nine

March 26th

"Okay, lunch is over, back to work." Will cracked the whip that snapped through the air, sharp and loud. He laughed when all five men jumped, their heads swivelling in his direction, mouths falling open.

"Where the 'ell did you get that?" Ed yelled, lurching from his garden chair and striding over to where Will stood by the French door, the whip now hanging down by his side. "On seconds thoughts, do I really 'ave to ask? I always knew you were a kinky bleeder."

Blake coughed loudly. "It's a good thing Sophie's in the bathroom right now, because—"

"Yeah, I'm sorry, but it's all Will's fault," Ed remonstrated. "I mean, look at that thing!"

Will coiled up the whip and placed it on the patio table. "I find it comes in very handy for keeping husbands in order," he said with a grin. Blake merely arched his eyebrows. "But if you all want to eat my wonderful lasagne for dinner, then it's time to put in some work."

Angelo shook his head. "You're a hard task master. Just look at what we've accomplished in one morning!"

Will couldn't deny the six of them had already made a huge dent in the work. Ed and Colin had cleared away all of the rubble that had been left at the top of the garden, and the skip Blake had hired was nearly full. Angelo and Rick had cut back the masses of buddleia shrubs that had seeded themselves all over the place. Will and Blake had spent their time making pots of coffee and tea for their workforce, trying to curb Sophie's enthusiasm for digging up the flower beds, and keeping an eye on Nathan who lay in his pushchair, bundled up against any sudden chill winds and protected from the sun by a huge parasol. The weather so far had been kind and it had been a mild, sunny day.

"So what's the plan for this afternoon?" Rick asked as he collected the mugs from the table.

"And put that away," Blake instructed with a nod toward the whip. "I don't want Sophie getting her paws on that."

"Fair point." Will grabbed the whip and took it into the house, stuffing it into a nearby drawer. When he returned, the men were standing by the table, surveying the garden.

"I was just telling them what we'd discussed about what to do with the garden," Blake told him. "Maybe a pergola at the top end where it gets the most sun. We could pave under it and use it as a dining area."

"No ponds," Will added. "Not with the kids. It's too dangerous."

Ed nodded. "Yeah, I don't blame ya." He shivered. "You 'ear too many 'orror stories about kids drow—"

"Is it time for me to plant some flowers yet?" Sophie asked in her clear voice.

Will smiled at her. She really did look adorable in her dungarees worn over a pale blue sweater, sun hat and flowered wellington boots. "We told her she could plant something," he explained to the others.

"Hey, princess, why don't you find me a nice spot for this?" Ed held up the potted shrub he and Colin had brought, 'to start them off,' he'd said.

Will caught Blake's eye. "I'm sure she can plant that. It might change positions once we get the garden design worked out, but it would be better off in the ground than in its pot."

"Good idea." Blake picked up a trowel. "Here you go, Sophie. Use this. Uncle Ed will help."

Will watched as Ed and Sophie walked slowly around the garden, looking for a good place to plant it. He loved how their friends adored their daughter and clearly liked spending time with her.

"You know, you might want to think about hiring a landscape designer," Angelo suggested. "How big is this garden? Eighty feet by about sixty? I know that's not huge by any means, but it's a big enough space that you can do a lot with it."

"Yeah. I read about this one garden designer who divided up a two hundred foot long garden into different 'rooms,'" Rick added. "A path connected all of them, but each room had a different look, different types of plants." He grinned. "Mind you, if Blake wanted to hire *him*, he'd pay a lot for it. Travis McConnell is famous. The famous ones always cost an arm and a leg."

Will chuckled. "I think we can handle our humble little back garden, thank you very much."

He walked over to Nathan's pushchair and crouched beside it. Nathan was asleep, his little hands covered by mittens knitted by Lizzie. Only a couple more months and he'd be crawling around on a blanket in the sunshine. If he *did* crawl: Sophie hadn't. Their precocious daughter had been walking at nine months' old.

Blake came over to him and gazed at Nathan. "He's such a good baby."

Will had to agree. At six weeks old, he was sleeping through the night, awaking only when his nappy needed changing or if he was hungry.

A loud shriek pierced the air and Will jerked his head up instantly. "What's wrong?" he said, leaping to his feet and rushing over to where Sophie was clinging to Ed's legs and shaking.

Ed smiled. "Nothin's wrong. Sophie saw a huge spider, that's all." He stroked her hair. "It's okay, princess. He won't 'urt ya. An' spiders are our friends."

Will bit back his laugh at the look of horror on Sophie's face. "Ew. I don't want a spider for a friend. Spiders are icky. And they have too many legs."

He smiled. "Spiders like it if you leave them alone," he advised her.

"Will."

The urgent tone in Blake's call had him turning immediately. One look at Blake's expression was enough to have him hurrying over to where he knelt beside the pushchair. "What is it? What's wrong?"

Blake inclined his head to where Nathan lay, his eyes closed, no change in his position.

Will frowned. "What?"

Blake lifted his chin and locked gazes with him. "Sophie's scream didn't wake him. Don't you think that's a little strange?" He kept his voice low.

Will opened his mouth to say no, but he halted. The hairs on the back of his neck stood on end. "Now you mention it, yeah." He joined Blake, kneeling at the other side of the pushchair and taking Nathan's hand in his. He rubbed it gently and the baby opened his eyes, blinking. "Hi there, gorgeous," Will said softly.

"I want to try something," Blake said quietly. He rose to his feet and glanced around the garden, clearly seeking something. He picked up two trowels from the ground and walked back to the chair, standing where Nathan couldn't see him. "Watch him," he instructed Will, that same urgency in his voice from a moment ago.

Will focused on Nathan. He gave a start when Blake brought the trowels together in a loud *clang*.

Nathan didn't react. At all.

"Well?" Blake demanded.

"Do it again," Will urged. Blake repeated the action and Will watched Nathan closely for any sign, even the minutest flicker.

Will swallowed. "Nothing. No reaction." Blake's face was suddenly ashen. "Blake, move closer and do it one more time."

Blake came forward until he was standing right behind the parasol, holding the trowels as close to Nathan's head as possible. He brought them together, the clang loud as it resounded around the now quiet garden. By now the others were walking toward them, and a hush had fallen over the group.

"What's goin' on, guys?" Ed called out. Sophie was in his arms, her arm flung around his neck.

Will ignored him and spoke to Blake in a low voice. "Some reaction, but I can't tell if it was to the sound or the vibrations, because I could feel those."

"Blake?" Rick was at Blake's side, staring at the trowels in his hands with obvious bemusement.

Blake's gaze met Will's and the flash of pain was all too real, as were the unspoken words. *Not now.*

"We'll tell you later, okay?" Will didn't want to talk about this in front of Sophie. Hell, he didn't want to discuss it at *all*, as if just saying the dread words that lay on his heart would somehow make them real.

The expression on Blake's face said enough.

Is our little boy deaf?

Dinner had been a subdued affair, with no one talking much. Their friends weren't stupid: Blake knew they'd picked up on the silent conversation between him and Will. When Will took Sophie upstairs to bed, after copious hugs, Blake went over to the drinks cabinet and lowered the hinged door. "Drink, anyone?" He felt numb.

It can't be true. We've got it all wrong. We're overreacting.

"'Ow about you tell us what's wrong first?" Ed said.

"When Will comes down," Blake assured him. He poured himself a large Scotch and then faced them. "Anyone going to join me?" Four grim faces met his, and Blake pulled down five more glasses from the shelf. "He won't be long. She's been yawning her head off for the past half an hour." He poured out more of the smoky looking liquid and handed the glasses around, placing one beside the couch where Will had sat with Sophie in his lap.

"You're worrying me," Rick said, his face tight, his fingers laced with Angelo's, whose expression was equally troubled.

"Yeah? Well, join the club." Blake said recklessly, before taking a long gulp of Scotch that hit the back of his throat. The fact that Nathan had shown some reaction gave him hope that maybe they did have it all wrong.

He sat on the couch, aware for the first time of the awkward silence that had fallen. "I'm sorry," he said quietly. "I'm just a little shaken. And it's probably just Will and I being a right pair of drama queens."

"Speak for yourself, *honey*," Will said from the doorway. He closed the door and made sure the baby monitor on the wall was switched on. Blake patted the seat cushion next to him and Will flopped down onto it, his head back, eyes closed.

"*Now* will you tell us what the fuck is goin' on?" Ed demanded. "Because it feels like someone died."

Will opened his eyes and gave Blake an inquiring glance. He nodded. "Tell them." Blake took a drink from his glass while Will told them what they'd noticed.

"Wait—you think he's deaf?" Rick sat up on the couch next to Angelo. "There are any number of things that might cause hearing problems in kids—if that's what he's got."

"Like what?" Blake straightened, his heartbeat speeding up a little. There was a flutter in his belly and his breathing quickened. He latched onto Rick's words. *Maybe it's not deafness.*

"Maybe his ears are blocked by wax or something?" Rick suggested.

"There's that condition, glue ear," Angelo added. "My cousin had that when he was very little. They did a procedure and he's fine."

"What procedure?" Will asked.

"They put these tiny plastic tubes—grommets, I think they're called—into his ears. They stop the fluid from building up."

"Hang on a minute." Colin sat up and leaned forward, his arms resting on his knees. "One, I thought glue ear only occurred after something like a heavy cold, and Nathan hasn't had one, has he?" He glanced at Blake, who shook his head. "And two, if it *is* glue ear, the first thing the doctors will do after testing is make you wait a while to see if it clears up on its own, which it may well do. And 'waiting' means anything from three months to a year, because it can clear up on its own."

Ed turned to face Colin, his eyes wide. "'Ow come you know all this?"

Colin smiled. "It's amazing what you pick up by osmosis in a staff kitchen. One of my colleagues was talking about his little girl." He returned his attention to Blake and Will. "Even if they diagnose Nathan with glue ear, they will wait to see if it clears up on its own. That was what was frustrating my colleague, Den. He was complaining that while they were waiting, his daughter's education and speech development were suffering. Granted, she's older than Nathan, so that's not such a worry right now. But Rick's right. It might not be as bad as you think."

"First thing Monday morning we're taking him to the paediatrician," Will said, his tone resolute.

"What I don't understand is how quickly this has developed," Blake said, staring into his glass. "He was tested when he was born and everything was normal. And he's been in perfect health."

Will's hand covered his. "Worrying about it isn't going to achieve a single thing, except waste our energy. We wait and see what the doctor says, all right? We stay hopeful." He gave a half smile. "And we act less like drama queens."

"Do you want us to go?" Ed asked.

Blake widened his eyes. "God, no. Right now we could use some good company. Right?" He looked to Will for agreement.

Will nodded. "And please, don't think you have to rush off tomorrow. Stay in bed as long as you like, and I'll make us all a leisurely brunch. We were going to have a quiet Sunday, and we hoped you'd share it with us."

Rick glanced at Angelo, who nodded. "You can have us until late afternoon. That's when we need to see my mum." Angelo smiled. "Wedding plans."

"Rather you than me, mate," Ed said with a snicker. He peered at Blake. "An' what exactly is your definition of 'quiet'? More garden clearing?"

Blake smiled. "I was thinking more along the lines of taking a walk by the river after brunch, helping Sophie feed the ducks, not to mention the squirrels in the park, stuff like that."

Colin let out a quiet sigh. "That sounds like a great way to spend a Sunday." He squeezed Ed's thigh. "When was the last time you fed ducks?"

Ed guffawed. "Never. I don't feed the bloody things, I *eat* 'em. Preferably crispy, in those little pancakes." Colin rolled his eyes and smacked Ed's leg.

Will glared at him. "You do *not* say that anywhere near Sophie, do you hear me?"

Ed gave him a pained look. "As if I would." He gazed around the room at the men seated on the three couches laid out in a U shape in front of the fireplace. "You know what we need right now? A distraction. Anything to stop us dwellin' on something we can't do anything about." He looked over at Will. "Got a pack of cards?"

Blake arched his eyebrows. "Cards? Seriously?"

"Hey, strip poker! Now there's an idea." Rick gave an evil chuckle.

Blake shook his head. "No. Worst case scenario: we're all naked or semi-naked and Sophie strolls in, clutching Mr. Bunny, and complaining that she can't sleep."

Will chuckled. "Wouldn't you like to be a fly on the wall when she tells her nursery school teacher about that?" He got up from the couch and went over the drawers below the bookcases. When he came back to them, he placed three black boxes on the table. "Cards Against Humanity, anyone?"

"I've never played this." Colin peered closely at the boxes.

"I have." Will grinned. "I went to a readers' convention last year in Chicago, and one night another author suggested playing this. There were about eight or ten of us in the bar, and it was hilarious. Although I will say, it's not for the faint hearted." He came over to where Blake sat, and knelt beside him. "Ed's right. There's nothing wrong with a little distraction, right?" he said in a low voice, his eyes focused on Blake's face. Will swallowed. "Because I'd rather not think about worst case scenarios right now."

Blake knew that feeling all too well.

Will pulled back the sheets and climbed into the bed, moving immediately to curl up around Blake's body. He kissed Blake's neck and shoulders. "All quiet. I've just looked in on Sophie and Nathan. Both fast asleep."

Blake turned in his arms to face him. "Who drew the short straw for the sofa bed?"

Will smiled. "Rick and Angelo, except that it was more a case of them suggesting Ed and Colin take the king size bed. Rick figured they needed the room."

Blake chuckled. "One of these days Rick will push Ed too far with one of his remarks, and then stand back." He stroked Will's chest, his touch gentle. "Are we making too much of this?"

The iron fist squeezing Will's heart that he'd done his best to ignore all evening, was back with a vengeance. "I keep thinking about how quiet he's been. No little cute noises like Sophie made, no gurgling or anything. When you add that to what we saw today..." He shivered. "I meant what I said earlier. I don't want to think about what *might* be until we have all the facts. We'll get the doctor to test his hearing again, and then we'll see where we stand."

"The one thought that won't leave me alone is that somehow we missed this. We didn't pick up on the signs."

Will couldn't miss the pain in Blake's voice. "Now stop that. We don't know right now that we've missed anything, do we? Let's just wait and see, okay, babe?" He kissed him on the lips, his hands on the warm skin of Blake's back. "Is it wrong that I just want to block this out for a while? I keep turning things over and over in my head, until I can't think straight anymore."

Blake kissed the tip of his nose. "I have news for you, Will Davis. You never could think straight. Gay, remember?"

Even Blake's attempt to use humour wasn't enough to pierce the layers of dread and fear that surrounded him. Will grabbed hold of him and rolled onto his back, taking Blake with him. He reached up to hold Blake's head between his hands, and gazed into those azure eyes he loved so much. "Make the world go away for a little while? Please, babe?" He swallowed. "I need you."

Blake nodded slowly. "I need you too."

Will brought his legs up to wrap them around Blake's waist and held onto him. "Show me," he whispered. "Show me how much you need me."

Blake did just that, employing his lips, tongue, fingers and cock, and for a short while they rocked together in a bubble of sensuality that sent Will soaring.

A temporary bubble that burst when he awoke in Blake's arms, his fears assaulting him in a fresh wave.

Chapter Ten

Angelo stared in dismay at the A4 sheet of paper in his hand. *Didn't she listen to a word we said?* The sheet was covered in her small, neat handwriting—*thank God it only covers one side*—and contained a list.

A very, very long list.

"Mum," he began, after meeting Rick's agonized gaze and returning it with his own, "We can't invite all these people." There had to be three hundred names, easily, and he didn't recognize most of them.

"Why not?" Mum sat facing him across the dining table, her lips pressed together, her jaw set. "There will be plenty of room at the venue. I looked at it on Maria's laptop. And I read what it said. They can cater for large weddings." She stiffened. "I know you have organized this, but I assumed I was going to pay for this. You think I cannot afford to have so many guests? Is that it?"

Whoa. What?

"Mum, who said anything about you paying for any of this?" Angelo glanced at Rick beside him, who was looking as baffled as he felt. "You didn't pay for Vincente's wedding, or Paolo's. Why should you feel you have to pay for mine?"

"Their weddings were paid for by the families of their brides, and you're..." She broke off, her teeth worrying her lip.

Angelo arched his eyebrows. "Do I look like a bride to you?"

Rick snickered. "I did say it was time to get rid of the long, curly hair."

Angelo gazed at him with narrowed eyes. "Not helping," he muttered. He returned his attention to his mother. "Seriously, Mum, we don't expect you to pay for our wedding. Rick and I both have a good income, we can take care of this ourselves." He gave her what he hoped was a gentle smile.

Mum sighed. "This wedding confuses me." She stared at the table's varnished surface.

This was new. "In what way?"

She raised her chin and met his inquiring gaze. "Will Rick's father walk him down the aisle to give him away? Or will you walk to meet him?"

The penny dropped. "This whole two grooms thing is what's confusing you?"

"Yes!" she wailed. "I have no idea who will be doing what!" She lowered her gaze to the table again.

Quickly Angelo fired a glance at Rick, who had stuffed a handkerchief into his mouth, and tears of laughter sparkled in his eyes. It didn't help that he knew exactly what Rick was thinking.

There are so many ways to take that last statement.

Angelo regained his composure. "Okay. Yes, there will be an aisle of sorts, and we *will* be walking down it—together. No one is giving anyone away. And when the ceremony is at an end? Franco will pronounce us spouses for life, Mr and Mr... etc... "

Rick grinned. "I rather liked, 'I now pronounce you happy and in love.'"

Warmth filled him. "I liked that one too." They'd had a few giggles with Franco when they'd discussed vows. Angelo cleared his throat. "Anyway, back to you. Are you okay with us paying, Mum?"

She levelled a firm stare in his direction. "Would it matter if I wasn't? You will go ahead and do what you want anyway. *So* like your father."

Angelo wasn't sure if he was appalled or flattered by that remark. He tapped the sheet with his finger. "Let's get back to this list. I've never heard of half these people. Who are they?"

"Family."

Angelo arched his eyebrows. "Whose family? Ours?" He sighed. "Mum, let's whittle this list down to less than a hundred people."

Her mouth fell open. "Are you serious? Think of all the people we will offend if we don't invi—"

"I guarantee that the vast majority of these people have never even heard of me," Angelo stated flatly. "And I am *not* having Sicilians taking over our wedding."

"Here comes the mafia," Rick whispered. Angelo reached under the table and gripped his thigh—hard. Rick's stifled yelp was cute.

"You speak as if being *Siciliano* was a bad thing." Mum's eyes flashed.

Angelo met her stare. "And you and I both know how scary *Nonna* can be when she's in full flow." When his mother opened her mouth and then snapped it shut, he grinned. "See? You know I'm right."

"This would make a great film, you know?" Rick gave him a wicked smile. "My Big Fat Italian Wedding."

Angelo leaned closer to whisper in Rick's ear. "And if you carry on, when we get home, it will be my Big Fat Italian hand across your pale, smooth, bare arse."

Rick's eyes gleamed. "Promises, promises." He nodded toward Mum. "But, er... not in front of the children, eh?"

Mum's cough claimed his attention. "When you two have finished... " She leaned across the table and picked up the sheet. "I will try to do as you ask."

"Thank you, Mum. We do appreciate it." Angelo gave Rick a meaningful stare. "Don't we?"

"Oh, sure." Rick nodded enthusiastically.

"Now can we discuss the reception?" Her face lit up. "I had an idea. I would like to put a miniature olive tree on every table, with little lights all over them."

Angelo stifled his groan. *Out of the frying pan...*

"I hope there's nothing seriously wrong with little Nathan," Rick said as he undressed for bed.

"They're doing the right thing by getting him checked out as soon as possible." Angelo hoped with all his heart that it turned out to be something simple. Nothing as heart-breaking as Nathan being deaf.

"At least we accomplished something today with your mum," Rick noted. "If she chops that list of hers down to a manageable size, that's one thing less to worry about."

Oh yes. His mother. Rick wasn't forgiven yet.

Angelo removed his jeans and briefs and stood by the bed, letting Rick get a good, long look at his body. "I do believe I owe you a spanking."

Rick's gaze jerked from Angelo's groin, where his cock had already begun to fill, to Angelo's face. "Er, excuse me?"

Angelo wagged his finger. "Don't come the innocent with me. All those muttered remarks this afternoon. It's a good thing Mum didn't hear any of them."

"Oh, come on." Rick chuckled. "You have to admit, even *you* thought that comment about not knowing who does what was funny. I could see it in your face!"

Angelo nodded. "Yup. Not denying it. But the cracks about cutting my hair? Our big fat Italian wedding? 'Here comes the mafia'?" He grinned. "Yes. They call for a spanking." Not that he'd ever spanked Rick before. That was something for the porn videos they watched together sometimes.

Maybe it's time to try it. See what all the fuss is about.

Rick stared at him for a moment. "Oh my God. You're serious. You... you want to spank my arse?"

Angelo waggled his eyebrows. "Might be hot." The thought of Rick, stretched out across his lap, his arse firm and round and ripe for Angelo's hand... His dick jerked upward.

And Rick noticed. "So I see," he said with a hint of a smile. He stood up from the bed, unfastened his jeans and shoved them past his hips, taking his boxer briefs with them. One look at his stiffening dick told Angelo he wasn't the only one who thought it might be hot.

Angelo climbed onto the bed, stuffed pillows behind him and leaned against them, patting his thighs. "All aboard."

Rick snickered and got onto the bed, his cock bobbing. "We're really doing this?"

"Why not? Those guys in the videos seem to enjoy it. They make enough noise about it. Why don't we see if it's as good as they make out?"

Rick gave a shrug and stretched himself out over Angelo's lap. Angelo could feel his hard dick against his thigh. Rick twisted to glance over his shoulder. "So... we just... start?"

Angelo laughed. It felt so weird to be doing this. He rubbed the firm globes of flesh before him and smiled. "Here goes." He brought his hand down with a loud smack as it connected with Rick's arse cheek.

"Ouch!" Rick stared at him over his shoulder. "That smarts!"

"Aww, poor baby." Angelo rubbed where the blow had landed, and then tried another, aiming for a different spot. To his surprise, Rick giggled. "That was funny?"

Rick snickered. "Sorry. I'm just finding it hard to take this seriously. Go on, do it again."

Angelo smacked him, harder this time, and Rick laughed. Another strike, and Rick was laughing harder. Angelo stopped and stared at him. "Why are you laughing?" He landed another couple of smacks, but Rick's laughter didn't diminish. Angelo gave up. "Okay, this is a waste of time if you're not going to take it seriously." He had to admit, he wasn't finding the experience as much of a turn-on as he'd anticipated.

Rick sat up, still chuckling. "I'm sorry, babe. It sounded so hot, and it always *looks* hot when you see it on screen, but if I'm honest? It just feels ridiculous. Maybe it's just not for us."

Angelo sagged against the pillows. "I'm going to have to agree with you on that."

Rick moved across the bed to lie next to him, his head on Angelo's chest. "Now I'm all disillusioned. There goes a hot fantasy out the window."

Angelo laughed quietly. "Any other hot fantasies I should know about?"

Rick craned his neck to peer up at him. "Why? Do you think we need to spice things up a bit in the bedroom?"

Angelo shrugged. "Nothing wrong with a little experimentation. I'm sure there are lots of, er, bedroom activities that we haven't tried yet. Just because spanking wasn't for us, doesn't mean there won't be others that are more to our taste."

Rick's eyes gleamed. "Such as?" He prodded Angelo's belly with his finger. "Go on, you started this. What have you seen that you thought might be worth a try?"

Angelo shifted, getting comfortable. "The obvious seems to be bringing in a third person. Ever wanted to have a threesome?" He hadn't even once considered it, but knowing Rick's history, he was curious to hear his thoughts on the subject.

"Nope." There was no hesitation in Rick's voice whatsoever. "We don't need anyone else. Just you and me."

The declaration warmed Angelo's heart. "Okay then. Your turn."

Rick giggled. "Ever wanted to suck on my toes?"

Feet? Angelo shuddered. "Not my first choice, no." He searched for a suggestion to elicit a similar reaction from Rick. "There's always bondage. I could tie you to the bed. Maybe borrow some of Will and Blake's toys?" Their toy box was no secret among their closest friends.

Rick guffawed. "Hell no. You are not tying *me* to the bed while you have your wicked way with me."

Angelo chuckled. Tying each other up didn't do it for him either.

"Ooh!" Rick grinned. "I could be your puppy!"

"Excuse me?"

Rick got up on all fours and wiggled his arse. "You know! I could get a puppy tail butt plug, and you could put a leash on me. Hey, I could wear one of those dog masks, the leather ones."

Angelo burst into laughter. "If I want a puppy, I'll go to a kennel or a rescue centre." Then another idea came to him, and he grinned. "There's water sports."

Rick grimaced. "And you can *keep* your golden showers, you got that? Ew."

He laughed out loud. "You're safe, babe. Definitely not my scene." But this was getting to be a fun conversation. He thought quickly. "Ooh, how about I fist you? That seems a pretty kinky thing to do these days." He held up his hand and waggled his fingers. "You think your tight little arse could take my hand?"

Rick smiled sweetly and held up a fist. "You think your pretty face could take my fist? Because that's the only fisting you'll get if you try *that*, mister." He grinned. "But if we're talking kinky, I could always get one of those metal sounds and slide it up your slit."

"Okay, that's enough," Angelo yelled with a shiver. "You just hit the red zone on my gross-o-meter." Rick dropped onto the bed beside, him, howling with laughter. He sighed and tugged Rick into his arms. "Let's face it. We're vanilla, through and through."

Rick kissed him slowly, pulling on his lower lip and sucking it. When he broke the kiss, he stared into Angelo's eyes, his pupils dark. "There's nothing wrong with vanilla. Lots of kissing, licking, sucking and touching. And what follows lots of kissing, licking, sucking and touching?" His voice was husky with desire.

Angelo cleared his throat that had tightened. "Making love. With the man I love."

Rick smiled. "Now there's an idea."

Angelo shifted lower on the bed, until Rick was lying on top of him, straddling Angelo's thigh. He gazed up at Rick's face hovering above him, and smiled. "I believe you mentioned kissing," he whispered.

Rick's eyes lit up. "Oh yeah, gotta have kissing." Their mouths met, and Angelo parted Rick's lips with his tongue while he caressed and stroked down his back to the swell of his arse. Angelo spread his legs and rocked gently, rubbing his balls against Rick's thigh. Rick propped himself up on his arms and deepened the kiss, low grunts of pleasure escaping his lips when Angelo reached lower to squeeze his arse, fingers digging into the firm flesh. Angelo kept up that slow rocking motion, his full dick now rubbing against Rick's belly.

"Oh, now what do we have here?" Rick said with a grin, before shifting to his side, his lips reconnecting with Angelo's in a sensual kiss. Angelo's cock jerked up and then smacked down on his belly with a dull thud. Rick chuckled. "Someone's eager." He moved slowly to grasp Angelo's dick around its base, before taking it carefully and deliberately into his mouth, all the way to the root. No hurry, no urgency, just the slow worship of Angelo's shaft. Angelo lay there and accepted it, his hand stroking over Rick's shoulder, maintaining their connection, while Rick stroked across his inner thigh to his balls, a whisper of skin on skin.

God, it was heaven. Slow, languid passes of Rick's tongue down his cock, lower, lower, until Angelo's balls were gently sucked into wet heat, wringing a groan from Angelo's lips. Then a gasp as Rick shifted again, once more above him as they kissed again and again, before he began a leisurely path down Angelo's torso, laying a trail of kisses to his dick. Angelo closed his eyes and lost himself in the feel of Rick's lips and tongue on his body. When he could take it no more, he opened his eyes.

"My turn," he said, licking his lips.

Rick knelt up. "What did you have in mind?" He pumped his heavy cock.

Angelo smiled. "Sit on my face? I want to get you ready for my dick."

Rick let out a sigh of sheer contentment. "I thought you'd never ask." He moved to straddle Angelo's head, affording him perfect access to the tight pucker. Rick rested his body on the mound of pillows and gripped the headboard, knees far apart as he awaited Angelo's tongue.

Angelo wasn't about to make him wait long.

He reached up to spread Rick's cheeks, and chuckled when Rick reached back to help him. Angelo licked over his hot hole, loving the shivers that ran through Rick's body, morphing into shudders when he pushed insistently with his tongue, the tight muscle loosening further for him with each attempt.

"Oh, yeah, that's it," Rick moaned, rocking gently above him.

Angelo was in no hurry either, fully engaged in the worship of Rick's hole. When Rick began to writhe, his moans gaining in frequency, Angelo rolled onto his belly and knelt up behind him, sliding his thick cock between cheeks damp with his saliva. It never grew old, the sense of joy and fulfilment he got every time they made love. There was still that same awe, that the man before him was his, truly his, mind, body and soul.

"God, I love you." The words came from his heart.

"Love you too, but I'll love you even more if you get inside me right this second," Rick gritted out.

Angelo laughed and stretched out a hand to grab the lube from its usual place on the bedside cabinet. A swipe of slick fingers through Rick's crack and over his cock, and he pushed inside him, a slow, insistent penetration until he was fully seated.

"Oh." Rick's breath left him in a long sigh. "Yeah. God, yeah."

Angelo grabbed hold of Rick's hips and began the sensual in-and-out that always made his body sing, his heart beat faster, and his blood pump harder. He rocked into him, the motion fluid and regular, loving the familiarity of it all, how Rick pushed back to meet his thrusts, both of them breathing faster now.

"You still feel as amazing... as you did... that first time," he ground out between thrusts, hips rolling, alternating long, deep, slow glides into that tight channel with short, quick plunges. "God, you feel so good." He pulled his cock free and dropped onto the bed on his back. "Sit on my dick."

Rick turned quickly and sat astride him, reaching behind him to guide Angelo's shaft inside him. It wasn't long before he was bouncing on Angelo's hard cock, their lips locked in kiss after kiss while he clung to Angelo's shoulders, feeding him loud gasps and groans of pleasure.

Gone was the desire for slow, leisurely, unhurried lovemaking. Angelo's blood pounded in his ears, his skin tingled and his body raced toward its climax. Rick leaned on his arms and held himself still while Angelo thrust up into him, dick sliding faster, pistoning into him.

"Fuck, so deep inside you," Angelo moaned, trying to get deeper still, the slap of flesh against flesh growing louder.

"Let me," Rick demanded, his hands flat on Angelo's chest. He rocked back and forth, moving faster, Angelo's cock sliding in and out of him like a well-oiled piston, Rick's own dick as hot as a firebrand against his belly, slippery with precome. He leaned back, hands now on Angelo's thighs while he rocked faster, faster, Angelo powerless to do anything but take it, staring up at the beautiful man fucking himself on Angelo's cock. When Rick bent over him to kiss him, Angelo seized his chance to fuck him harder, the two of them see-sawing as one gave way to the other, their moans and grunts growing louder with each thrust into Rick's arse.

Except Angelo wasn't ready to accept orgasm, not yet.

He lifted Rick and grabbing him around the waist, shifted him onto his back. Angelo pulled out of him and tugged him toward the edge of the bed. Rick nodded, his eyes wide, and drew his knees to his chest. Slowly, so slowly, Angelo pushed inside him for what he knew would be the finale. He leaned between Rick's legs to kiss him, a leisurely exploration with his tongue while he began to slide deep into him, until his dick was buried up to the hilt.

"Fuck, you're still so tight," he murmured. "Feel me deep inside you? Filling you slowly?"

"God, yes," Rick moaned.

"Nice and slow," Angelo breathed, "so deep inside you that I could almost feel your heartbeat. "

"Oh my God," Rick groaned. "I have ... no fucking complaints... whatsoever... about vanilla sex... not when it.... it feels this fucking good."

Angelo grinned. "You said it." He began to pick up speed, his cock sawing in and out of that tight hole, both of them clinging to each other as they rocked together, gaining momentum. Rick's hands were on his back, his shoulders, his neck, on his hair as Angelo fucked him, face buried in Rick's neck as he slammed into him now, flesh slapping loudly against flesh.

Angelo reached between their bodies to wrap a hand around Rick's dick, tugging hard, working the hot shaft as he pushed him closer to his climax. When Rick stiffened and cried out, his cock sending an arc of come past his shoulder, Angelo groaned with joy. He pulled out and lay down beside Rick, holding him through his orgasm, kissing him, and stroking his damp chest and belly. When Rick's breathing grew more regular, Angelo kissed him on the lips.

"Love watching you when you come," he murmured into his ear. Rick smiled. "I love that feeling too." He got up and crawled across the bed until he was poised above Angelo's still rigid shaft. His gaze met Angelo's as he bent over his groin to take Angelo's cock between his lips and suck the head, hard.

That wet heat was all it took to have Angelo spurting into his mouth, his body trembling as he arched up off the bed, Rick taking every drop, until Angelo collapsed, panting. Rick cleaned his dick with a slow tongue, making him shudder.

Rick chuckled after giving his cock one last lick. "Funny. You don't taste of vanilla."

Angelo held his arms wide and Rick didn't hesitate. He crawled up Angelo's body and gave a happy sigh when Angelo held him close while they kissed.

Angelo broke the kiss and looked Rick in the eye. "Would you change the way I taste?"

Rick grinned. "Only if you could somehow make your come taste like chocolate."

Chapter Eleven

March 28th

Dr. Rollins sat down behind her desk and gazed at them, her eyes kind. "I'm glad you came to see me. It's always best to seek medical advice as soon as possible. I know you've probably been worrying about this, and I understand that completely, but after running the test, everything checks out."

Will stared at Dr. Rollins. "But that can't be right." Nathan was in his arms, sucking on the dummy that had kept him peaceful during the test. Will stroked up and down his back, keeping the motions soothing.

"What are his hearing levels?" Blake asked. "Are they normal?" Blake looked as tired as Will felt. Neither of them had slept well the previous night, and Will could hear the strain in his voice.

Dr. Rollins regarded him calmly. "This test doesn't give us hearing levels."

"Then what the hell does it do?" Will blurted out. Blake laid a hand on his thigh, and he took a deep breath. "Sorry. I shouldn't have spoken to you like that."

She smiled. "It's okay. Like I said, you've clearly been worrying about this. Let me explain. The procedure is called an OAE—Otoacoustic Emission—and it's the same test they would have done when Nathan was born. It looks at the function of the outer hair cells in the ear."

"A test which he's passed both times," Blake commented. "And none of this explains why he's obviously having difficulty hearing." He clicked his fingers to the side of Nathan's head. When Nathan didn't turn toward the sound, Blake returned his attention to the paediatrician. "Now don't tell us that's a normal reaction." They'd watched as she had conducted similar tests, and Will's heart sank when Nathan showed no reaction to the noises produced.

We're not imagining this.

She looked from Blake to Will, and finally to Nathan. "Ordinarily, I'd recommend that we monitor his reactions and do a follow-up with behavioural testing when he's six months old. Because based on our examinations, his ear structures appear healthy."

Will straightened in his chair and stared at her. "You said 'ordinarily.'" That one word gave him hope that she wasn't going to sit on her arse and do nothing. *Why else do we pay for private healthcare?*

She nodded. "What makes me consider the alternative is the fact that I am acquainted with you two. I've been Sophie's paediatrician since she was three months old, and I know you two don't go running to a doctor at the first sign of a temperature."

"So what is your recommendation?" Blake asked, a touch of impatience creeping into his voice.

Dr. Rollins gazed at the monitor on her desk and moved the mouse over the pad. "I'm going to refer you to an otolaryngologist for the recommendation of an ABR." She raised her head and gazed at them. "This is the next level of testing. The ABR, or Auditory Brainstem Response test, will measure Nathan's brainwave responses to sound so we can get a complete picture of his auditory system. Once Nathan is given the go-ahead for testing, then you need to see an audiologist." She peered at the screen and smiled. "You won't be surprised if I tell you there are at least five of them on Harley Street."

Will glanced at Blake and raised his eyebrows. Private healthcare was one thing, but *Harley Street*, famous for its large number of private medical and surgical specialists? Blake met his gaze with a shrug. Will knew that look. It was Blake's '*I don't care what it costs because we're doing it anyway*' look.

Will addressed Dr. Rollins. "Who do *you* think we should see?"

She moved the mouse. "I've made a few referrals to Alan Donovan. He's an audiologist and he's good. I have no idea how long you'll have to wait for an appointment, so I'd call as soon as possible. You might be lucky and he can fit you in promptly." Dr. Rollins returned her attention to the screen. "Deborah Michaels is good, as is Eric Taylor." She looked up at them. "I have no idea what their waiting lists are like either, but you never know. There are always cancellations. Start calling them and see if one of them can fit you in." Blake cleared his throat and she sighed. "Or, you two can take Nathan out there to the waiting room where there are some toys that might interest him while *I* make a few calls."

Will smiled. "Thank you. We really appreciate this." He got up and carried Nathan out of the office, Blake following. When the doctor's door was closed and they were alone in the waiting room, Will gave Blake a hard stare.

"You shouldn't bully her."

Blake widened his eyes. "That wasn't bullying! All I did was cough."

Will arched his eyebrows. "Mm-hmm. And you knew exactly how she'd react."

Blake gave a shrug. "I figured she would have more luck if she'd already referred people to these guys." He sat on the couch next to Will and reached into the large toy box beside it. When he held up a brightly coloured, soft cloth rabbit, Nathan's face lit up and he made a grabby hand for it. He squeezed it and a loud squeak filled the air.

Will's chest constricted. *He can't hear that.* "What's wrong with him, Blake?" he said softly. "He's passed that bloody test twice."

Blake put his arm around Will's shoulders. "Then they obviously need to conduct different tests, okay? It doesn't matter about this latest result. We saw what happened when she rang the bell and clapped her hands. Nothing." He leaned over and kissed Will's cheek, before kissing Nathan's forehead. "We are going to get Nathan seen by someone who specializes in this, and we *will* get to the bottom of it."

The door to the doctor's office opened and Dr. Rollins came out to them, a sheet of paper in her hand. "Okay, this was the earliest appointment I could get for you. Deborah Michaels will see Nathan on Thursday morning. The pre-test instructions are here, and it's important that you go through them, because Nathan will be sedated."

Will blinked. "Sedated? Why?" That one word was enough to set his heart racing.

"Because the ABR will only run properly when he's asleep." She gave them a half smile. "Don't worry. This will explain everything you need to do. Let's get some answers for you."

Will nodded. "Thanks, Dr. Rollins."

Blake stood and took the sheet, folding it and placing it in his jacket pocket. He held out his hand to her. "Thank you, and thanks again for calling them."

She crooked her eyebrows. "You knew I would, didn't you?"

He smiled. "I had an inkling, yes."

She paused, Blake's hand still in hers. "Once we have the results, we'll be able to make the best recommendations for Nathan's needs."

Both Blake and Will nodded again, Will's throat tight. He didn't want to think about some of the possibilities.

They said goodbye and left the clinic, Will pushing Nathan in his pushchair as they walked to the car park. Blake was quiet, and Will could understand that. If Blake's mind was anything like his, right then his thoughts were in overdrive.

He sighed. "The last thing I feel like doing is heading home to write. I've never felt less like writing in my life."

Blake halted in the middle of the pavement. "Then don't. All I want to do right now is spend time with you and the kids. So, how about we go to Sophie's nursery, pick her up, and the four of us can go to the park or the zoo or something? And then tomorrow let's pack some bags and go away for a couple of days. Maybe to the seaside. Anywhere."

Will stared at him. "You're going to let Sophie miss school?"

Blake snorted. "Why not? It's not as if during those two days she's going to miss lessons on brain surgery, is it? She isn't even *four* yet, for God's sake!"

Will shrugged. "I thought brain surgery was last week. *This* week it's nuclear fusion." He smiled. "I love the idea though." *Because if we're keeping ourselves occupied, we're not thinking about Thursday.* As much as he wanted answers, Will was scared he wouldn't like them when he got them.

March 31ˢᵗ

Blake's heart was hammering so hard, he was certain Will could hear it. They stood beside the medical couch where Nathan lay on a blanket, sleeping. Nathan had seen the ENT for a medical check and Dr. Michaels, the audiologist, had already performed two tests. One to ensure that Nathan's middle ear system was working properly, and a more familiar second test when she'd tried to get Nathan to turn his head toward various sounds. But this last test, the ABR, was what Blake been both looking forward to and dreading since their appointment with the paediatrician.

Keeping Nathan awake as late as possible the previous night, stopping his feeds after four-thirty in the morning, no liquids after seven, keeping him awake during the drive to the clinic.... It was all scary as hell and Blake wanted it to be over.

A nurse had come in a few minutes ago to give Nathan the sedative via an oral syringe, and it hadn't taken long before he'd fallen asleep in Will's arms. Dr. Michaels was in the process of cleaning the skin on Nathan's forehead and behind each ear. She'd explained that was where the electrodes needed to be placed to measure Nathan's responses. She attached some little sticky pads to each site, secured the cables, and inserted the tiny earphones into Nathan's ear canals.

She'd already gone through exactly what would happen during the test and how long it would last, so they knew what to expect. Blake's gaze was focused on the laptop screen where the results would be displayed. He and Will were silent, watching as the doctor went through the test. Blake didn't think time could possibly move any slower as he watched the screen fill with a series of lines. Periodically Dr. Michaels would click something on the screen and the tracings would start all over again.

Nearly an hour and a half later Dr. Michaels turned toward them. "We're finished."

Blake exhaled shakily.

She nodded, and he got the feeling she was used to this reaction. "Okay, let's clean off this little man, and then we'll talk." Dr. Michaels spoke softly as she removed the insert headphones, unclipped the electrodes and carefully removed the pads from Nathan's delicate skin. Nathan made an unhappy noise while she wiped his face, and Blake wanted to pick him up and hold him against his heart.

"I'll take him," Will said quietly, scooping him up and wrapping a blanket around him, the one they'd brought from his cot at home. Will had figured the familiar scent would provide Nathan with some comfort. They followed Dr. Michaels from the small room into her office, where they sat on the couch where they'd previously discussed the tests. The doctor retook the armchair, a tablet on her lap.

Will cradled Nathan in his arms, his gazed flitting from him to Dr. Michaels. Blake said nothing but waited for whatever was coming at them.

"Well, the ABR test ran with great accuracy, and I'm now able to give you a diagnosis." Her cool blue eyes focused on Blake. "Nathan has Auditory Neuropathy Spectrum Disorder, or ANSD for short. The previous tests didn't pick up on it because with ANSD most of the structures of the ear are healthy."

She paused there, and Blake was glad of the breathing space. Because she'd just dropped a bombshell that he was finding difficult to take in. *He has a disorder. There really is something wrong with his hearing.* Not that Blake hadn't known that, deep down, but hearing their fears confirmed left him with a sour taste in his mouth and a dull ache in his chest.

In desperation he latched onto her last words. "You said most."

She nodded. "The simplest way to describe it is that there's a disconnect between the inner hair cells of the cochlea and the auditory nerve, or there's a malformed nerve altogether."

"How bad is it?" Will blurted out. Blake stretched out his hand to lay it on Will's thigh, needing the connection.

Dr. Michaels didn't break eye contact. "Nathan's case is severe." She scrolled over the tablet screen and then held it up for them to see. "This is an example of an ABR with normal hearing."

Blake stared at the lines, a series of jagged waves with peaks and troughs.

She scrolled again, and then turned the screen once more. "This is Nathan's ABR. As you can see, other than this brief response at the very beginning that originates from the inner ear itself, which we call the cochlear microphonic, the lines are basically flat or at best slightly wavy. That's because there's no response from the auditory nerve."

Cold spread out from Blake's core, sending icy tingles through his body. "He's deaf?"

She nodded, her eyes kind.

In that second it didn't matter to the logical part of Blake's brain that there would most likely be solutions to improve that situation. All he could think was that his son would never hear his dads' voices.

Blake wanted to weep.

With that one statement, a numbness descended over Will as he saw Nathan's life change before his eyes. Then the numbness ebbed away as a shockwave of grief crashed over him. His chest ached and his body felt cold. *Oh my God. He's a baby. He isn't even two months old and this changes* everything.

"Now tell us the solutions." The tremor in Blake's voice betrayed what he was clearly trying not to show. Will was glad one of them had their wits about them. "Are we talking hearing aids?"

Dr. Michaels cleared her throat. "For severe ANSD our options are more restricted than with other forms of hearing loss. One thing we know is that a traditional hearing aid is not very effective. They are designed to make sounds louder, but for someone who can't process sound, all it gives them is loud noise—*not* communication."

"So what's the bottom line?" Blake demanded.

Dr. Michaels spoke softly, exuding a calm Will certainly did not feel. "There is the option of teaching him sign language, using cochlear implants, or a combination of the two."

Will widened his eyes. "Implants? That would mean surgery." His gaze dropped to Nathan and he shivered. "He's just a baby." His eyes met Blake's. *This isn't happening.*

Blake opened his mouth to say something but Dr. Michaels cleared her throat again. "I know this is hard to take in, so let me give you some examples. I have several patients with ANSD who use different approaches. One little boy's parents decided not to use hearing aids or go down the CI—cochlear implant—route, and he communicates via BSL—British Sign Language."

"What about a patient similar to Nathan?" Will demanded. "With similar hearing loss?" He would deal with grief later, because that was exactly what it felt like. Blake was correct: right then they needed solutions.

"I have a little girl who has a severe case of ANSD. She wears an implant. With it on, she can communicate with relative ease. I am not saying she can hear perfectly, but it's efficient. Without it, she's deaf."

There it was again, that one word that made Will want to cry.

"What would be your suggestion in Nathan's case?" Blake wanted to know.

Deborah studied her tablet for a moment. "If it were *my* little boy, I'd go down the CI route *and* teach him sign language. Yes, the implants are expensive, but I'd be recommending them whether I worked on Harley Street or not." She met their gazes. "Do you have any questions?"

"What caused this? How come Nathan has this ANSD in the first place?" Will's voice shook slightly.

"That's a good question. However, although a lot of research has taken place during the last decade, we still don't completely understand what causes it."

"Then how can you be sure he has it?"

Her calm manner didn't change. "There are a number of common causes of hearing loss in infants, none of which apply to Nathan. He hasn't had a virus like Meningitis. He doesn't suffer from a genetic disorder. And he wasn't born prematurely, so we can rule out the side effects of medications used to treat complications in immature organs." She placed the tablet on the small table beside her. "That leaves us with ANSD. The results from the ABR confirm the diagnosis." She leaned forward, her elbows on her knees. "Is there anything else you want to ask me?"

Will glanced at Blake. "I... I just need to get my head around all of this." It was too much. His head was spinning, and all he wanted to do was get home, bar the door and hide away from the world with Blake and their kids.

"That's a common reaction, believe me," she said kindly. "I know this is a shock, but we need to act quickly in Nathan's best interests. The sooner we set wheels in motion to give him the tools he'll need to communicate, the better."

Will knew she was right, but he didn't want to think about the options.

In that moment, he didn't want to think at all.

"Is there any information you can give us to take away and digest?" Blake asked. "Because I don't think either of us is in any fit state of mind to be making decisions right this second."

Will swallowed and looked to Blake, nodding in agreement. *I can't deal with this right now.*

Dr. Michaels nodded too. "I will give you leaflets and links to various sites where you can find out more, but I'm going to stress that you don't leave it too long before you get back to me. And unlike a first consultation, you don't have to wait long for an appointment. When you call me and tell me you're ready to discuss Nathan's treatment, I will see you within forty-eight hours. *That* is how importantly I view this." She paused. "It's a lot to take in, I know. The leaflets will tell you about the implantation procedure, and the links show examples of children who've been through it." She smiled. "And when you see some of the videos, I guarantee you will feel better about the whole process."

Will focused on Blake. *I need to get out of here.* His mind had slipped into overdrive.

Blake nodded, as if he'd heard the unspoken words. He gave Dr. Michaels his attention. "We'll take the information, and then we'll discuss it at home. I promise you, we won't leave it too long. Neither of us wants to see Nathan suffer any more than he has to."

Will didn't want to consider the possibility of Nathan suffering for *one fucking second.*

Chapter Twelve

Will was a mess.

Ever since they'd arrived home, his emotions had been all over the place. For one thing, he had no appetite whatsoever, and judging by how Blake had pushed his food around his plate, neither did he. Will had done his damnedest not to let Sophie pick up on his state of mind, but when she'd run to him with one of her favourite books, demanding that he read to her, the words wouldn't keep still on the page, and he'd felt sure he was on the point of losing it.

Thank God for Blake, who'd taken one glance at his face and come over to the couch where Will and Sophie were seated, his arms wide, pleading for a Sophie hug. Will flashed him a grateful look and escaped to the kitchen. He'd leaned against the sink, staring out into the garden beyond the window.

This still doesn't feel real.

It felt like it was happening to someone else. Not them. Having a deaf child was something that happened to *other fucking people*, damn it!

When he'd regained his composure, he drank a glass of water and walked into the lounge to spend time with his family.

Thinking could wait. Right then he had a daughter to read to.

Blake had no idea what had awoken him. He rolled over to look at the alarm clock beside the bed—Will's side of the bed, except Will wasn't there. Blake rubbed his eyes. It was three in the morning. He hadn't had all that much sleep to begin with: he recalled seeing midnight come and go.

Not all that surprising, really. There was way too much on his mind to sleep.

He swung his legs over the side of the bed and reached for the robe he'd left on top of the covers. April was definitely not warm enough for walking around the house naked in the early hours. He pulled it on, got up and walked over to the bathroom door. One peek inside told him Will wasn't there. As he left their room, he peered into the children's bedrooms. Sophie was fast asleep in her usual position, on her tummy, knees drawn up under her, bottom in the air, making a little blanket-covered mound. How she managed to sleep like that, Blake had no idea.

Nathan lay on his back, the blankets still on top of him, his small arms above his head as though he had thrown them up in protest in his sleep. His night light was on, an LED-lit baby bunny that sat next to his cot, a soft glow emanating from it. Blake crept into his room and stood at the foot of the cot, gazing at his infant son.

I promise you, I will do whatever I can for you, so that you'll have the best chance in life.

He blew his baby a silent kiss and then crept out of the room, pulling the door closed behind him.

Now to find Will.

Blake padded down the stairs, noting the blueish light that slid under the door to Will's writing cave. He pushed it open and poked his head around. Will sat at his desk, his head in his hands, and the air of dejection that clung to him was almost tangible. The light came from the computer monitor.

Christ, look at him. He looks like I feel.

"Baby?"

Will jerked his head up, blinking. "What are you doing up?" he whispered.

Blake came into the room. "I could ask you the same question," he said softly. "What are you looking at? How long have you been here?"

Will sagged into the swivel chair. "An hour or so. I couldn't sleep. You'd finally dropped off and I didn't want to wake you with all my tossing and turning, so I came down here." He gestured to the leaflets on the desk next to the keyboard. "I was reading them again."

Blake's chest tightened. "Oh, love." They'd spent all evening reading and re-reading the information, and yet Blake felt like he'd retained only a fraction of it. Underlying that thought was the knowledge that Dr. Michaels didn't want them to delay, which only added to the pressure. Not to mention the churning in his stomach.

"Then I started doing some research into cochlear implants." Will shook his head. "I feel like Alice and I've just fallen down the rabbit hole."

"Why? What did you find?" Blake walked over to where Will sat and crouched beside him, gazing at the bright screen.

"I found plenty about the risks involved in the surgery, but we'd already read about those. No, what shook me was reading messages on a forum." Will flicked his head toward the chair behind Blake. "Pull up a seat. You're going to need to be sitting down for this."

Blake had the feeling he wasn't going to like what Will had found.

Will scrubbed his fingers through his hair. "Okay, we can forget about the hearing aids vs cochlear implants arguments, and believe me, that's a good thing, because there are huge threads on that topic alone. I came across a forum where parents were asking questions about implants. Usually parents whose child had just been diagnosed, and they wanted advice from people who'd been there."

"Okay." Blake could understand that. Once the shock had worn off, he'd had about three million questions of his own. *Who better to ask than people who've already been where we're about to tread?*

Will clicked on a link. "A lot of parents on this site believed their doctors were prescribing treatment by implants because they're in it for the money. Not that I think that for one second about Dr. Michaels."

"I agree." Blake trusted Dr. Rollins's recommendation.

"There were quite a few of these people who were saying how highly invasive the surgery was, how the risks were more severe than the docs made out, how in some cases the surgery didn't work. There's probably some truth hidden in there. Dr. Michaels said it wasn't perfect, right?" He took a deep breath. "The kicker was this message from a woman who was deaf."

Will shivered, and Blake grabbed his hand. "Carry on."

Will's face glowed in the cool light from the screen. "Her whole tack was anger that these parents had reacted as if being deaf was a disease, a bad thing, something that should make them sad. She was challenging the way they saw their child's hearing loss. Basically she was saying that there is nothing wrong with being deaf. What was wrong was how people perceived it as a terminal illness."

"I think terminal illness is a bit overboard." Blake was genuinely puzzled. "But I can totally understand those parents. They're facing a future where they can't communicate with their own kids, and in this world, communication is vital."

Will nodded. "Her argument was that parents are too quick to jump on the implant bandwagon, and too lazy to be bothered to learn sign language. She said the parents should embrace their child's deafness, and not brush it off." He swallowed. "Because she said the child would remember this as he or she grows up."

It was Blake's turn to take a deep breath. "We talked about this, right? We're going to learn sign language, and we are going to make sure Nathan learns too, as soon as he can." He cocked his head to one side. "That *was* what we decided, wasn't it? The implants *and* sign language?" When Will didn't respond, Blake sighed. "Okay, you need to tell me what you're thinking here."

Will pulled his hand free and clicked the mouse to close the link. He swivelled in his chair to face Blake. "There's this whole Deaf culture out there, Blake. There are people who argue that while we might be shocked by the diagnosis, shocked that our 'perfect' baby isn't perfect after all, that's just us judging the situation by the standards we're used to. They argue that deafness isn't harmful, and that yes, our baby is *still* perfect, and that our job as parents is to make him or her *feel* perfect." He shook his head. "I learned some new words today. Audism. Audistic. Being audistic is being prejudiced based on hearing status. These people claim that doctors ignore the option of raising a child as culturally deaf."

Blake stared at him. "What?"

Will nodded. "They claim doctors believe that speaking is the be-all end-all. There was a huge discussion about how society places a lot of emphasis on hearing and speaking, to the point where many hearing people see it as the only way to truly have language. So along comes a hearing parent, with little or no knowledge of the Deaf community, and they panic, thinking they're not going to be able to communicate with their child. The experts recommend implants and they go along with it, because deep down they want to hear their child's voice, they want their child to hear *their* voice."

"So in going down the CI route, we're just being selfish?" Blake asked incredulously. Will nodded, and Blake set his jaw. "Fine. Then call me selfish, because I want that. I *want* Nathan to know what we sound like. I want him to be able to communicate by signs *and* by speech." He rubbed over his face.

Will regarded him in silence for a moment, before sighing. "How about I make us some hot chocolate? We can talk while it cools, but it might help us to get some sleep." His gaze returned to the screen. "This is making my head ache."

"That doesn't surprise me." Blake's head was in a mess too, and he'd had far less time to make sense of all the stuff Will had been wading through. He could see why it had affected Will so strongly. *Who wants to think they're acting out of purely selfish reasons, and perhaps agreeing to a procedure out of fear and prejudice?*

Will got up from the chair and left the room. Blake half-listened to the familiar sounds as his husband went about the task of heating milk in the microwave. On an impulse, he shifted into the chair Will had vacated, and typed a few words into the browser. He read down the list of posts and then clicked on a link. He was so immersed in what he read that he jumped when Will placed a mug in front of him.

"Sorry. You were miles away." Will stood next to Blake's chair, his mug in his hands.

Blake gestured to the monitor. "Did you read this article? It was one of the links Dr. Michaels suggested."

Will peered at the screen. "Uh uh. I didn't get that far. I got side-tracked by the whole Deaf community thing."

"Then take a seat, because *you* need to hear *this*." He scanned the first paragraph. "It says here that most kids are implanted at the age of twelve months, although they can have the procedure sooner. That wasn't what caught my attention, however. It also says here that babies start to hear in the womb when they're around twenty-four weeks along. So for a twelve month old child who's being implanted, they are actually sixty-eight weeks behind their normal hearing peers in terms of being able to identify sounds." He peered at the screen and read aloud from it. "'Now, that might not sound like a lot, but keep in mind the cerebrum of the brain is responsible for our development of everything, from our ability to learn, to creating the capacity to recall memories.'"

"And there you go, emphasizing speech."

Blake shook his head. "Listen to this. 'In the first three years of life, a child's brain will contain nearly twice as many synapses'—that's when—"

"I know what synapses are," Will said quickly. "Neural connections forming, right?" When Blake stared at him, Will shrugged. "I had to research it for a book. Keep talking." He took a sip of chocolate and winced.

"Where was I? Oh yes, the brain will contain nearly twice as many synapses as they will once they achieve adulthood. So where DNA provides the blueprint for the brain, a child's environment and experience make up the construction. Now, there's any number of events or circumstances in a child's life that will affect the number of synapses formed. But the loss of a natural sense? The loss of a child's ability to connect to their environment through sound?" Blake shook his head. "Can you imagine the number of synapses that a Deaf child will not form compared to a hearing child, simply because they lack the ability to form a bond with a parent by the sound of their voice?"

Will stilled, his gaze locked on Blake. "You're saying that by not giving Nathan the opportunity to hear us, to form a bond with us, we're actually harming his development?"

Blake nodded slowly. "And now I see why Dr. Michaels didn't want us to leave it too long before we proceed with implants."

Will hadn't broken eye contact. "You're also saying we need to agree to the implants, aren't you?"

"Yes, babe. And I'm not saying this to be selfish. I'm thinking of Nathan, about how we need to take care of his needs. Because Dr. Michaels was right. We need to act in his best interests."

"I *was* thinking of Nathan," Will said quietly, placing his mug on the desk.

Blake clasped both his hands. "I know that." He was so tired, it was unreal. "Look, now it not the time for this discussion. How about we try to get some sleep? We can talk more about this in the morning, after I've dropped Sophie off at the nursery."

Will nodded. "You're right. My brain is addled with all this." He rose to his feet. "Come on. Switch everything off and let's finish the hot chocolate in bed."

Blake shut down the PC and turned off the monitor. He followed Will from the room, and they crept upstairs as silently as possible.

Maybe sleep will make things clearer.

Because right then, 'things' were as clear as mud.

Will stirred in Blake's arms, his head on Blake's chest as he listened to the comforting beat of his husband's heart. "You know, what you said just now, downstairs? It wasn't quite true."

Blake's hand trailed softly up and down his back. "Hmm? Which part? And I thought we were switching off our brains too."

It wasn't that easy. "You said *we'd* decided on the implants and sign language." That wasn't how Will remembered it. He recalled Blake saying it, and him being too lost in his own grief to respond.

Grief.

Will shuddered. "They were right, weren't they, on that forum? We're grieving. We got the news about Nathan and we're grieving. We heard that one word, Deaf, and we only saw the negative."

"That's natural," Blake murmured. "There's always a grieving process when any challenge presents itself. It takes time to digest and come to grips with it all. And of *course* we perceived that news as being negative."

"Yeah, but are they right? Did we see it that way because we don't know anyone who's deaf? Because we know so little about Deafness that we automatically see it in a negative light?"

Blake shifted in the bed and seconds later, Will blinked in the warm light of the bedside lamp. Blake lay on his side, his head propped up in his hand. "I understand where you're coming from. Those comments opened your eyes, and mine too, if I'm honest." His face tightened. "Our whole world just changed, and right now we're struggling to deal with a ton of different emotions." He took a deep breath. "And for the record, yeah, I'm grieving too."

Fuck. Like Will didn't know that with every fibre of his being. The problem was, words wouldn't take away the pain they were both obviously dealing with.

Will pushed down on the ache inside him and laid his hand on Blake's chest. "There were positive things on that site too. There was this one guy who's deaf. He said that being deaf isn't the end of everything. He's never heard a word in his life, but he's been to university, got his master's... " He recalled something else the commentator had written. "He said every deaf child is unique."

Blake nodded. "Exactly. And while I'm beginning to understand these parents who don't see Deafness as being something negative, I'm looking at *our* situation, *our* son. I'm looking deep within myself to work out what I really want to do here, which way I want us to go." His gaze met Will's. "Which way *we* want us to go. Because we need to be together on this. This is no one's decision but ours." Blake reached out and cupped Will's cheek, and Will leaned into the touch. "So forget for a minute everything you've read, all those posts that have your mind in turmoil, and tell me. What do *you* want for Nathan?"

Will swallowed, aware of the fluttery feeling in his chest, the way his heartbeat sped up.

"You said before that you wanted Nathan to know what we sound like. You wanted him to be able to communicate by signs *and* speech. You also said that made you selfish." Will's eyes glistened in the lamp light. "Then I guess that makes me selfish, because *God*, I want that too." He shifted closer, needing to feel Blake's arms around him. "Is it wrong that we want to do this now, when he's too young to make the decision for himself?"

Blake sighed. "That's the us being selfish part. It could be argued that we're doing this for us, not Nathan. But I want him to have every chance of success in the future, and to me, that means being able to communicate as fully as possible." He stroked down Will's arm. "I think those people in the forum were right: being deaf is not the end of the world. That being said, our world is built with people who hear in mind. I don't see it as selfish if you make it possible for your child to function as well as possible in that hearing world. In fact, I can almost make a case for the opposite argument."

Will frowned. "Go on."

"You could argue that it's selfish to refuse your child the implant just because you feel to do so would be making deafness into something negative. In fact, *not* embracing all the opportunities available feels almost akin to refusing blood transfusions or vaccinations against measles, and stuff like that."

Will widened his eyes. "Oh wow. I didn't think of it in those terms. And that makes sense to me."

He pulled Will against his body. "Then we're agreed? We tell Dr. Michaels to go ahead and get the ball rolling for implantation?"

Will nodded against his chest, his arm across Blake's waist. "Yes. And then we find classes in sign language." He sighed. "They say you're never too old to learn a new skill. I guess we're about to find out if that's true."

"Yes, it won't be easy, and yes, it will require a significant investment of time and energy, but think about this," Blake said quietly, his lips moving against Will's hair. "We learn sign language, and then we teach Nathan and Sophie. That sounds like a great way to develop a nurturing, positive relationship with our children."

When he looked at it that way, the tightness around Will's heart eased off a little.

Just a little.

Chapter Thirteen

April 1ˢᵗ

"Come in," Ed called out when he heard the soft rap on his office door. He beamed when Colin stuck his head around it. "Hey! What are *you* doin' 'ere? You're supposed to be on yer way to bonny Scotland." They'd said goodbye that morning before Ed had left for work, not without some sadness on Ed's part. Since they'd become a couple, there had been very few occasions when they'd spent time apart. The prospect of two nights without Colin—not to mention the whole of Saturday—was not a welcome one.

Not that he'd share that information with Colin.

He grinned at Colin. "I thought I'd got rid of you. I was lookin' forward to 'avin' some time on me tod." He winked.

Colin came into the office, smiling. "Mm-hmm. Is that why I spied a pile of rugby DVDs near the TV? *And* the flyer from that new Indian takeaway that you tried to hide in the tea towel drawer?"

Ed gaped. "Gawd, you don't miss a bleedin' trick, do ya?" He got up from his chair and went over to Colin, who'd dropped his bag to the floor. "Is that why you're visiting me at work? To let me know you've 'ad cameras installed all over the 'ouse?"

Colin gave a mock gasp. "Don't tell me—you saw the brochure from the surveillance company." He chuckled. "Can you blame me for wanting another chance to see you before I catch my flight?"

"I'm not gonna complain about that," Ed said quietly, before stepping closer to take Colin in his arms. "Another chance to kiss this gorgeous mouth? Bring it on." He loved the way that Colin didn't hesitate for a second before bringing their lips together in a deep kiss. When they parted, Ed shook his head. "You know I'm gonna miss ya, don'tcha?"

Colin nodded. "No more than I'll miss you, but it's only two nights. It'll be Sunday before you know it." He glanced around him. "It's not often I get to see you with your CEO hat on."

Ed released him and stepped back. "It's a nice office, innit? It used to be Blake's." He gazed at his surroundings and snickered. "If these walls could talk. Blimey."

"What do you mean?"

Ed grinned. "There's a rumour around 'ere that Blake an' Will nearly got caught in 'ere once with their trousers down." He nodded toward the desk. "I bet *that* saw some action."

Colin gaped. "They fucked in here?"

Ed gave a slow nod. "An' the way some of these guys tell it, that was just par for the course with those two." He tut-tutted. "Dirty little fuckers."

"Oh, I don't know." Colin waggled his eyebrows. "I can totally see why they would. The thrill of someone walking in on them... "

Ed snorted. "That's what locks are for."

Colin stared at him. "And of course, you *always* lock *your* door when I call you during my lunch hour so we can—"

"Hey!" Ed covered Colin's mouth with his hand. "Walls may not 'ave ears, but PAs certainly do, an' mine is right through that door." Slowly he removed his hand.

"So it's okay for her to hear you talking about Will and Blake fucking over the desk, but not about you and I having"—he dropped his voice to a whisper, "phone sex?" Colin's eyes gleamed.

Ed laughed. "You're a wicked man, you know that?" His breathing quickened when Colin leisurely slid a hand down his side before trailing his fingers over Ed's hip and eventually his crotch. "And where do you think you're going?"

Colin grinned and leaned closer to kiss Ed's neck just below his ear. "Lock the doors, Ed. Both of them."

"What the 'ell are you playin' at?" Stupid question really, when Colin was stroking the outline of his burgeoning erection.

"Indulge me," Colin said softly. "I'm going to be away from you for two nights. Let me go away with something to remember when I'm up in cold Scotland in a strange bed."

It was Ed's turn to gape. "I don't give a shit what Will an' Blake did in 'ere, we are *not* fuckin'." His gaze flickered toward his outer door. "I wouldn't put it past that lot to 'ave their ear'oles pressed up against the door."

Colin opened his eyes wide. "Who's talking about fucking? All I want to do is get my mouth on you." He licked his lips. "Suck you. Lick you. Hear that gasp I fucking love when I make you come." Ed's cock jerked beneath his hand and Colin locked gazes with him. "Ed? Lock. The. Doors."

Like Ed was going to turn down the chance to get Colin's mouth on his dick.

He moved swiftly to turn the lock on the connecting door between Mandy's office and his, and then moved even quicker to lock the outer door. When he turned around, Colin was standing by the leather couch below the huge window. "Do I close the blinds?" he asked with an innocent air.

"Too bloody right you do," Ed growled. "I'm not 'avin' every Tom, Dick 'n' Arry feasting their beady little eyes on us gettin' off." He walked across the room, his fingers busily employed in unfastening the button on his pants. The thought of Colin sucking him off in the office already had him hard as a rock.

Colin chuckled. "You don't believe in wasting time, do you?" He pulled the vertical blinds across the expanse of glass.

Ed shrugged. "I figured you 'ad a plane to catch. No time to dick around." He snorted. "Pun intended." He stood in front of Colin, his pants undone, and cupped his bulge. "Now, where were we?"

Colin brushed Ed's hand aside and pressed his palm against his zipper. "Oh, I do like it when you're eager." He gripped Ed's length and Ed couldn't repress the little shiver of anticipation that trickled through him. Colin slid his fingers under the soft cotton of Ed's briefs and when they came into contact with skin, Ed's shivers multiplied.

Colin brought his lips to Ed's ear. "I love that about you. All the times we've done this, and yet your body lights up every time, like it's the first time." He wrapped his fingers around the solid length and Ed bucked into his hand. "You like my hand on your cock."

"No shit, Sherlock," Ed ground out, placing his hands on Colin's shoulders. "I'd like it even better if it was yer *mouth* on me cock." He applied pressure, steadily pushing Colin until he was kneeling before him. "Take it out." The words tumbled from his lips in a hoarse whisper.

Colin slowly lowered the zipper, grasped his pants and briefs firmly, and pulled them down past Ed's hips in a sharp tug. Ed's dick sprang up, swollen and dark. Colin grasped it firmly around the base and brought the head to his lips, parting them to let him in.

Ed was too far gone to take this slowly. He thrust, filling Colin's mouth with his cock that throbbed to feel Colin's tongue wrap around it. Ed cupped the back of Colin's head with both hands and rocked back and forth, going deep. "Fuck, yeah, that's it. Use your tongue. Love it when you push your tongue into me slit."

Colin groaned around his length and sucked harder, Ed's dick sliding fluidly between his lips as he thrust deeper, hips rolling as he gained momentum. Ed couldn't take his eyes off Colin's face, the way his lips tightened and relaxed around his shaft, the way his cheeks hollowed, and *Holy Mother of God*, the way Colin gazed up at him, the usually pale blue eyes darker, his pupils huge.

"Gonna go balls deep," he growled, watching Colin's face as he always did for a sign to let rip. Colin gave him the merest nod and that was it. Ed thrust all the way in until he felt the head of his dick bump against the back of Colin's throat. "Oh, Gawd, yeah." His cock dripped with saliva as he slid it in and out, holding Colin's head steady while he fucked his face. When Colin pulled away, Ed wanted to howl in frustration, until Colin pushed him back onto the couch, Ed dropping like a stone, his pants around his knees.

Colin shoved his clothing down until it was bunched around his ankles, then he grabbed Ed's knees and spread them wide. Ed's cock pointed up to the ceiling, wet and hard. Colin leaned over and took it deep, his head bobbing faster and faster.

Oh shit. Ed felt his orgasm blossoming inside him, swelling, sending out tendrils of pleasure that he knew were about to overwhelm him, and he couldn't keep a lid on it. His heart hammered and his body jolted as he filled Colin's mouth with his come, groaning to hear the sweet sounds his lover made as he swallowed every drop. Ed stroked Colin's hair, holding on tight when Colin licked a path from his balls to his slit.

Little by little he relaxed, aware of Colin's hands on his thighs, reaching under his shirt to stroke his belly, fingers tugging gently at the furry trail that led to his pubes. Ed gazed at him, his body warm and sated, his hand caressing Colin's head.

Colin gazed at him with a broad smile. "Now *that* is a memory worth holding onto."

Ed sat up and grabbed him, pulling him closer so that their mouths connected, Colin's lips crushed against his own, the taste of his come on Colin's tongue. When he broke the kiss, Ed fell back against the seat cushions and regarded Colin sadly. "You didn't get the chance to come."

Colin shook his head. "And it doesn't matter. I loved watching you come. I'll get off tonight, when I'm recalling how you looked, your taste, your smell." He grinned. "I might even call you while I do it."

Ed chuckled. "I'm gonna 'old you to that."

The door handle rattled, and both of them jerked their heads up.

"Oops," Colin said with a wicked grin, getting up off his knees. "I think we just ran out of time."

Ed lurched to his feet and pulled up his pants. As he tucked his limp dick into his briefs, he shook his head. "You're a bad influence, you know that?"

Colin laughed. "Yes, and that's why you love me." When they were both standing, Colin leaned forward and pressed a lingering kiss to his lips.

Another door handle rattled, this time from Mandy's room.

Ed snorted. "I think they're onto us." With one last glance at his office, he walked over to the connecting door and unlocked it. Rick and Mandy stood on the other side, both smirking.

Ed cocked his head to one side. "Yeah? Did you want something?"

"I was about to pour myself a coffee and wondered if you wanted one while I was at it." Rick snickered. "Except when I came to ask, *you* were at it." Beside him, Mandy covered her mouth and gave a smothered gasp.

Ed levelled a hard stare at Rick. "I 'ave no idea what you're talkin' about. But a coffee sounds good. Give me a minute while I say goodbye to Col."

Rick's eyes twinkled. "Take as long as you need, boss. Shall we lock the door again?" He grinned. "You might want some privacy while you, er, talk."

"An' you might be 'eadin' for a smack, so watch it," Ed warned him, before closing the door on both of them.

Colin had already picked up his bag. "I'd better go. It's already past midday and I need to catch the Gatwick Express. The flight leaves at 15.10." He crooked his finger. "Last kiss."

Ed chuckled and went over to Colin to wrap his arms around him. "Nah. We've got loads more kisses left to come."

Colin laughed. "Why is it everything that comes out of your mouth usually sounds dirty?"

Ed gave another snort. "Duh. That's because it usually is." He leaned forward and kissed Colin one more time. Then he patted him on the backside. "Now get out of 'ere. The sooner you're gone, the sooner you're back where you belong."

"In London?"

Ed smiled. "In my arms." For a man who'd always hated excessive sentiment with a passion, he was frequently astounded by how often such thoughts passed through his head when it came to Colin. *He's turned me into a big ball of mush.* The thing was, Ed didn't mind it one bit.

"I'll be landing about half-four on Sunday," Colin said as Ed walked him out of the office and along the hallway to the reception area.

"D'you want me to meet you at Gatwick?"

Colin shook his head. "Just have something nice planned for dinner, a bottle of wine chilling in the fridge, and you waiting with open arms when I come through that front door."

"You got it." Ed gave him a peck on the cheek. "Now get your gorgeous arse to Gatwick."

Colin grinned and left him standing by Karen's desk. Ed watched him walk away through Trinity's glass doors. When he was no longer in sight, he turned around to find Karen and Rick observing him.

Ed put his hands on his hips and scowled. "Well? Neither of you got any work to do? And where's this coffee you were goin' on about?"

"Be right with you, boss," Rick said before he darted off in the direction of the kitchen. Karen was still staring at Ed, a soppy smile plastered all over her face. When Ed folded his arms across his chest and cleared his throat, she lowered her gaze and made a show of shifting papers around on her desk.

Ed shook his head and strode down the hall to his office. When he got inside, he sniffed the air. *Damn it.* Ed went into his private bathroom and snatched the can of lavender air freshener from the cabinet under the sink. He sprayed into the air above the couch and then returned the can to its usual position.

"A bit late for that," Rick commented as he came through the door with two mugs of coffee. He flashed Ed an evil grin. "It's already all around the office."

Ed glared at him. "*Your* doin', I suppose." When Rick gazed back at him with an innocent expression, Ed guffawed. "An' you can knock *that* off for a start. It's been an 'ell of a long time since *you* were innocent." He held out a hand for his coffee. "Now, 'ow about you change the subject an' tell me 'ow things are progressin' with this weddin' of yours?" He sat at his desk and leaned back, his hands wrapped around the mug.

Rick perched on the chair facing Ed. "It's going well. Angelo's mum Elena has finally cut down her list of Italians, and the invites are going out this week. I still don't think many of them will turn up, but I could be wrong. I hope so, for her sake. Apparently, when Angelo's brothers got married, there was a huge Italian contingent. I'd hate for her to be disappointed if a lot of the invited guests decline the invitation."

"The gay thing?" Ed hazarded a guess.

Rick nodded. "I know her attitude had changed over the years, but I think she's expecting a bit much of very traditional Sicilians."

Ed shook his head. "I 'ave to say, I'm not a fan of big family weddings. If it was me, I'd do it as quiet as possible, an' with as little fuss as possible."

Rick leaned forward. "Does Colin know this? I mean, I'm assuming you two have talked about it."

Ed sipped his coffee before speaking. "Colin 'asn't got a lot of family to invite, an' I get the impressions those he *has* got wouldn't be keen to come an' watch two blokes gettin' 'itched. So I'm not about to invite a load of people, 'cause it would only make 'im feel bad." He grinned. "There's a lot to be said for elopin'. Just sayin'."

Rick clutched his chest in mock horror. "Elena would kill us." He sat back in his chair. "So, what are you going to be getting up to this weekend? While the cat's away, and all that." He waggled his eyebrows. "We could have a boys night round at your place. You, me and Angelo, Will and Blake. Alcohol, takeaway... porn."

Ed gave a loud snort. "I don't think so." Though he had considered going to spend some time with Will and Blake on Saturday. He'd spoken on the phone with Blake that morning, and something was... off. It was just a feeling, but Blake had sounded strained. But when Ed had suggested the idea, Blake had said they had plans.

Ed wasn't convinced, but there was little he could do about it. If his mate needed to talk, he knew where to find Ed. He'd just have to find something else to occupy his time, so that he wouldn't be forever watching the hours tick by until Colin came home.

Look at me. He's going to be away for two nights *an' I'm already dreadin' the idea of being without 'im.* Further proof, as if he needed it, that Colin was the centre of his world. Not that Ed told him that often enough. *I sometimes think he has no clue just how much he means to me, how much I need 'im.*

Maybe it was time Ed did something about that.

He glanced across his desk at Rick and it was then that it hit him. A lightning bolt, if ever there was one.

"Rick? You got a minute to talk a bit longer?"

"Sure." Rick smiled. "Anything for the boss."

Ed gestured with a flick of head. "Then close the door."

Chapter Fourteen

Colin's first thought as he stared out of the taxi window was that he'd come to the wrong address. Ray had told him over the phone that he lived in a top floor flat on the centre of Edinburgh, and for some reason Colin had expected a block of flats, maybe dating back to the sixties or seventies.

But not this. Not a five-story, gorgeous building in red and grey stone, more like some ancient university than the exterior of people's homes.

"This is Well Court?" Colin asked the driver, who laughed.

"It's a beauty all right," he said, smiling. "I wouldnae mind livin' in Dean Village maself. And that'll be nine pounds."

Colin paid him and climbed out of the taxi, his bag in one hand and his coat over his arm. Sunset wasn't that far off, and he was starting to get hungry. He crossed a stone courtyard, heading toward the main door. To the left, a clock tower stood, tall and majestic, and in front of him the gable of the building climbed in old brick steps to its peak.

This is beautiful.

He walked into the large entrance lobby and began to climb the stairs, thankful for the rugby that kept him fit. Except that only made him wonder how Ray coped; Colin himself was slightly out of breath by the time he reached the top floor and apartment 29.

He stood still for a moment, both to get his breath back and to quash the butterflies in his stomach. He had no clue what awaited him on the other side of that heavy front door, and now that he was actually there, the prospect of seeing Ray after all these years made his heartbeat quicken and his mouth dry.

For fuck's sake, just ring the bloody doorbell.

Then it occurred to him. *Even my inner voice is beginning to sound like Ed.* The thought made him smile.

He raised his hand, took a deep breath, and pressed the black button set into a small white box beside the door. A minute later, it opened and Colin fought the urge to react to the sight that met his eyes.

Ray had got old.

He looked a damn sight older than his fifty-four years, and a hell of a lot thinner than Colin remembered. His short, brown hair had thinned out dramatically, and there were more lines in that face, especially around the eyes. There were a few sores around his lips that looked painful, and an air of fatigue clung to him. But despite the change in Ray's appearance, there were faint glimmers of the man Colin had known thirteen years ago. Ray's smile hadn't changed a bit, and the sight of it brought back memories that rolled over Colin in a slow tide. Memories of loving Ray with all his heart.

"Hey, stranger." Ray's face lit up and he held out his hand. "You made it then."

Colin ignored the outstretched hand. He stepped into the hallway, dropped his bag, and enveloped Ray in a careful hug. Ray froze and then relaxed into the embrace. Colin held onto him, his heart breaking just a little to see his ex so changed. "Hey yourself," he whispered, before releasing Ray and taking a step back.

Ray closed the door behind him. "Here, give me your coat." He helped Colin out of the long wool coat Ed had insisted he bring along, for which Colin was now profoundly grateful. April had burst onto the scene with a cold snap in Scotland, and he'd tightened its warm layer around him as he'd made his way down the steps from the plane.

"Are you hungry?"

Colin opened his mouth to reply, but his stomach got in there first with a loud grumble. He gave Ray a sheepish glance. "I guess I don't have to answer that one."

Ray chuckled. "I've got a couple of ready meals in the fridge, unless you want to relive the good old days and get a pizza." He tilted his head and his gaze roved up and down Colin's athletic form. "Except you don't look like you eat a lot of pizza." Colin couldn't help noticing how he appeared to be fighting for breath.

Colin shook his head. "You *had* to say that, didn't you? You *had* to make me think about chicken supreme pizza."

Ray's eyes widened. "My God. You remembered."

Colin snorted. "How could I forget? It was the one we ordered every time we went to Pizza Hut on a date."

"Then that does it. Chicken supreme pizza it is. There's a Pizza Hut in Raeburn Place that delivers." He grinned. "Potato wedges, garlic bread, coleslaw and a bottle of Pepsi to go with it?"

Colin laughed. "*Now* who has the good memory?" He didn't get to eat pizza that often, although Ed would give him an argument every weekend that it was the sixth food group. *The things I have to do to keep that man of mine on the straight and narrow.* He grinned to himself. Right then Ed was probably digging into a very large Indian takeaway and loving every mouthful.

"And what was that?" Ray paused in the middle of scrolling over his phone screen.

"What was what?"

"That look."

Colin smiled. "I was thinking about my partner. Right now he'll be sitting in his favourite armchair with a plate of Beef Madras, a naan bread, poppadums with mango chutney, and a can of beer, while he watches rugby matches on DVD." He laid a hand on Ray's arm. "Let me order this." When Ray arched his eyebrows Colin shrugged. "For old times' sake. Not to mention thanking you for putting me up this weekend."

Ray smiled, but then his smile faded as he thrust a hand into his jeans pocket to pull out a folded handkerchief. He coughed into it, the hacking sound loud and harsh, and Colin was alarmed to see a flash of red when Ray wiped his mouth.

"Are you okay?" No sooner had the words left Colin's lips than he berated himself. Stupid question.

Ray nodded, his breathing erratic. "Let's... let's get dinner organized, yeah? We can... talk later."

Colin had a feeling it was going to be a long conversation.

While Ray poured out a glass of wine for Colin and some juice for himself, Colin took a quick tour of the flat. It was small, with sloping ceilings on both sides and wooden floors that gave the rooms a warm glow. Small, square windows were set into the roof. One room comprised a kitchen and living room, and Colin estimated the compact space probably measured fourteen feet by ten. One door led off it to the bedroom. The bathroom was all done in white tiles, with a shower over the bath. Despite the flat's diminutive size, there was a light, spacious feel to it.

"I love your flat," he said as he went back into the living room. Ray was placing two glasses on the coffee table. He glanced at Colin and smiled.

"I've been here for a few years now. Tomorrow I'll take you down to the river which flows past the rear of the building. I walk along it once a day—if I have the energy, that is." Ray sat on the small two-seater couch and patted the cushion. "This is your bed tonight, by the way. And before you ask how I can expect you to fit that muscled physique on here, it opens out into a bed."

Colin grinned. "Thanks for that. I had visions of sleeping with my feet sticking out the window." His attention was drawn to the sores around Ray's mouth, and he couldn't help wondering about his state of health.

Unfortunately Ray caught his glance. "Yes, I know, I've looked better."

"Can we talk about your health?" Colin asked hesitantly. He was conscious of not wanting to overstep any boundaries.

Ray snorted. "Health? I always think that sounds like such a positive word, don't you? And one that doesn't really fit this situation." There was a bitter edge to his voice that made Colin's stomach clench. "Anyway, we can talk about me tomorrow. Right now I want to hear all about you."

Colin gave a start when a loud buzz came from near the front door.

"And that will be the pizza," Ray said with a grin. "You can get the door, seeing as this is your shout."

"No problem." Colin got up from the couch and reached into his jeans pocket for his wallet. He took the large box and the plastic bag from the delivery guy, paid him, including a tip, and then brought the items through into the living room. Ray had plates and cutlery waiting.

The smell of the pizza had Colin salivating. The last thing he'd eaten had been breakfast. Then he gave an inward chuckle. *Not quite the last thing.*

Ray shook his head at the sight of the food that filled the table. "I hope you're hungry, because my appetite isn't what it used to be."

"Just eat what you can," Colin told him. He'd wait until tomorrow to get answers.

"There's still some garlic bread left."

Colin groaned. "God, no. I feel like that character in the Monty Python sketch, when the waiter tries to get him to eat a wafer thin mint. Any more and I'll explode." He knew he'd overfaced himself, but that was partly due to not wanting Ray to feel bad about the meagre amount he'd eaten. "I can't remember the last time I felt this stuffed."

Ray laughed. "You put more food away than you did as a student, that's for sure."

Colin had to admit, the food had taken him on a trip down Memory Lane. "Oh, I don't know. Remember that Indian restaurant you took me to, the *all you can eat* one?"

It was Ray's turn to groan. "Oh Lord, yes. You had chicken Korma and Lamb Tikka Masala coming out of your ears, you ate so much. Where did you put it all?"

Colin snorted. "You had a theory, as I recall. You said I had a tape worm." It was as if the intervening years had simply melted away and they'd slipped back into the same comfortable conversations they'd shared as lovers.

Some things had changed, however. Ray had eaten little of their takeaway.

Colin gazed at the remains on Ray's plate. "Apparently one of us was hungry."

Ray sighed. "That's pretty common nowadays, I'm sorry to say." He cleared his throat. "Anyway. Enough about me. Tell me about this job of yours. That piece I read about the award was very impressive."

Colin spent the next ten minutes telling him about the company, his promotion and the kind of projects he got to work on. Ray settled against the seat cushions and listened, although it seemed to Colin that more than once he was finding it difficult to concentrate. He said nothing, but filed it away, one more thing to ask Ray about when they finally got around to discussing his health.

"So... your partner, Ed. What's he like?"

Colin smiled. "Ed? He's a bear."

Ray chuckled, but his laughter died as another fit of coughing overtook him. When Colin caught sight of yet more blood on Ray's handkerchief, it sent a shiver through him that he did his best to suppress.

"That makes sense. You always did lust after the hairy guys who came into the bars on Canal Street."

Colin gave a mock gasp. "I have no idea what you're talking about. I only had eyes for you." That was true enough. He vividly recalled the heady feelings of first love, of being totally smitten with the handsome lecturer, the feelings of disbelief that Ray had wanted to date *him*. He gazed at Ray, his emotions warring within him. He'd loved Ray with all his heart, and had thought that love was returned. But Ray's abrupt departure had left him with doubts. *Did he ever really love me?*

Colin pushed aside such thoughts and poured himself another glass of wine. "I met Ed when I joined a local rugby team. Not that anything happened between us for a long time, over a year in fact."

"Playing hard to get, was he?" Ray said with a snicker.

"More like, playing it straight." Colin smiled. "I was the catalyst for him owning up to his hidden desires. And once he gave up trying to label himself, he was happy to accept that he was in love with a man."

"You're head over heels, aren't you?" Ray's voice was soft. When Colin blinked, he smiled. "It's obvious when you talk about him. I'm glad about that, truly."

Colin studied his glass. "We're engaged. And one of these days, I'll swap that ring for a wedding band." Maybe it was time to start putting plans in motion. *You never know what's around the corner.* Seeing Ray in his present state had reinforced that.

"That's wonderful." There was no doubting the sincerity in Ray's voice. "I'm so happy for you." He sighed. "I wasn't that lucky. Then again, I made some wrong decisions, so it's no surprise things turned out the way they did." Whatever else he'd meant to say was lost in another fit of coughing, which left him fighting for breath. Colin waited until the colour in Ray's cheeks had returned to normal before attempting a conversation.

"Maybe we should—"

"Look, would you mind if we called it a night? To be quite honest with you, I'm exhausted. And we do have the rest of the weekend to talk, right?"

Colin nodded. "Sure. I'm feeling tired myself." It was a lie, but Ray didn't need to know that. "I'll call Ed before I go to sleep, but I'll keep the noise down, okay?"

Ray gave a weak smile. "The way I've been lately, I'll be sound asleep as soon as my head hits the pillow. I doubt I'll hear you." He paused, a frown creasing his forehead. "There is one thing. I'll try not to wake you, but I tend to go to the bathroom a lot during the night."

"That's fine. I'm a sound sleeper too."

Ray eased himself gingerly up from the couch. "Then let's clear this lot away so I can move the table for you to set up the bed."

Colin was on his feet in seconds. "I can do that. You just get yourself ready for bed." He picked up the pizza box and the polystyrene boxes, and placed them on the kitchen worktop. Ray walked through the door into his bedroom and returned with sheets, pillows and a folded blanket.

"These should keep you warm enough, but to tell the truth, this flat is pretty warm all year round." He pointed to the cabinet above the sink. "There are glasses for water in there, and the blue towel on the rail in the bathroom is yours."

"Thank you." Colin took the bed linen and proceeded to remove the seat cushions. By the time he'd opened out the bed and made it up, Ray had finished in the bathroom and was standing in his robe by the couch.

"Sleep well." Ray gave him a tired smile. "And tomorrow we can go for a walk."

Colin nodded. "You sleep well too." He waited until Ray had disappeared into his bedroom and the door was closed behind him before getting out his phone. He undressed quickly and went into the bathroom to brush his teeth. Once he was under the sheets, he called Ed, his earphones in place.

"Hey." The note of genuine pleasure in Ed's voice sent warmth rushing though him. "Where are you?"

Colin chuckled. "On a sofa bed, in a flat, in Edinburgh, where do you think?"

"Blimey, you're in bed already?" Colin caught the soft rustle of crisp cotton. "'Ang on a sec."

He smiled to himself, knowing exactly what Ed was doing. "Please, take your time." He reached into his bag at the side of the couch and pulled out a clean handkerchief that he laid on the pillow next to him.

"Okay. I'm in bed." Ed sighed. "Wish you were 'ere with me though."

"I know." They weren't used to spending nights apart.

"Tigger's taken to sleepin' on your side of the bed when you're not 'ere." Ed huffed. "Even the cat misses ya." He paused. "So, how's Ray?"

It was Colin's turn to sigh. "We haven't talked that much since I arrived, although that will change tomorrow. But right now I'd rather talk about something else." He smiled. "Like the last time I saw you."

"Oh. Funny. I was just thinkin' about that."

"Were you indeed?" Colin slid his hand over his chest and tweaked his nipple. "And what were you thinking, exactly?"

"Your mouth on me dick."

All thoughts of Ray slipped from his mind. Colin reached under the sheets and wrapped his hand around his cock, stroking it leisurely. "I love that, you know. Sucking you off, making you shudder." He kept his voice low. Ray didn't need to hear this.

"Are you gettin' 'ard?" Colin could hear the change in Ed's breathing, how it quickened.

He tugged at his stiffening length. "Oh yeah."

"Bugger off, cat!" Colin caught the soft whump of Tigger landing on the floor. "Sorry 'bout that, but I draw the line at 'avin' the bleedin' cat watch me while I 'ave a wank."

Colin laughed quietly, trying to imagine Tigger staring at Ed while he...

Oh yeah.

"What are you thinkin' about?

Colin closed his eyes. "What I'm going to do to you when I get home on Sunday," he whispered.

"Tell me," Ed demanded.

"Only if you tell me where your fingers are right this second."

"Fuck, 'ow did ya know? They're in me arse."

Colin chuckled. "I know you, baby."

Ed growled. "'Ow many bleedin' times do I 'ave to tell ya? Don't call me baby." He would have sounded more believable if not for the breathless quality that told Colin exactly what he was doing.

"You're not fooling me for a second, Ed Fellows. You like it."

"Like fuck I do." Another low growl. "Do I look like I'm anyone's baby?"

"Do your fingers feel good while you fuck yourself with them?" he whispered. "Do you wish my fingers were inside you right now?"

"Gawd, don't you know it," Ed moaned. "Wish it was yer cock, an' you balls deep in me."

"That... can be arranged," Colin said, stroking his now rigid dick. In his mind he could picture Ed, lying on his back, knees pulled up to his chest, his hole stretched and waiting for Colin. "Want to be in bed with you right now, making love to you."

"Yeah, fuck, yeah." Ed's breathing sped up. "Col, soon."

"I hear you." Colin tugged harder, already aware of the tingle in his balls that heralded his climax. "Me too. Next time, though... I'll be coming inside you."

The loud groan that filled his ears signalled Ed's orgasm, and it was enough to push Colin over the edge. He stifled his own moans as he shot his load into the handkerchief, his body shuddering through the wave of pleasure that broke over him. "Oh wow."

"Wow is right." Ed chuckled. "I 'aven't come like that in a while. You'll 'ave to go away more often."

Colin laughed quietly as he wiped himself clean. "I see. Trying to get rid of me, are you?"

"Nah, but think about the welcome 'ome sex that's comin' your way," Ed said with a snicker.

Colin tried not to groan. "You're not helping," he whispered.

"We could always do it again tomorrow night." The hopeful tone to Ed's voice made Colin want to laugh.

"You're a wicked man."

"Does that mean yes?"

God, Colin wanted to laugh out loud right then. "It means we'll see. And now I'm going to end this call before Ray opens his bedroom door and demands to know what on earth I'm doing out here." Lord knew he'd tried to be discreet.

"Thank you," Ed said sincerely. "I did miss ya tonight. Call me tomorrow? And we don't have to, you know..."

Colin chuckled. "You are such a paradox. One minute you're telling me in graphic details what you want, and the next? You're as shy as anything." He smiled to himself. "I love you."

"Love you too. I was only thinkin' this morning that I don't tell you often enough 'ow I feel about ya. Maybe those need to be the first words out of my mouth every morning when I wake up with you beside me, because Gawd knows, I'm grateful for every fuckin' day that I 'ave you in me life."

For a moment Colin was lost for words. Ed wasn't usually given to voicing his emotions, and just hearing him baring his soul brought tears to prick the corners of Colin's eyes.

"That is quite possibly the sweetest thing you have ever said to me."

Ed chuckled. "Yeah, well, don't get used to it. I'm not the mushy sort."

"No, but when you speak from the heart, you turn *me* to mush." Colin sighed. "Good night. Only two more sleeps until I'm back."

"Thank Gawd for that. Not lettin' you go away again," Ed said gruffly. "Now get some sleep." He disconnected the call.

Colin removed his earphones, still smiling. He stared up at the small window, through which the night sky was visible.

What will tomorrow bring?

What disturbed him was the uneasy feeling that thought brought with it.

Chapter Fifteen

April 2nd

Colin leaned on the green metal bridge that crossed the Water of Leith. "This is stunning." Beside them rose Well Court, the rear of the buildings as imposing as the front, with turrets that overlooked the water. "When was this built?"

"1886, I think." Ray rested his forearms on the railing.

Colin observed him closely. "Are you sure you're up to this?" Ray didn't appear rested after a night's sleep, and still seemed to have difficulty breathing.

Ray sighed. "Trust me. This is as good as it gets." He turned his head toward Colin. "I try to get out here once a day because there's going to come a time, and I don't think it's that far off, when I won't be able to do this anymore."

Colin froze. "You're really... dying?" There had been part of him that had hoped Ray had been exaggerating, that it wasn't true.

Ray swallowed. "Lung cancer. Well, that's the part that's killing me. There's a list."

"I thought you said AIDS..."

"Look, we can talk about this later, all right? For now, let's just go for a walk along the water's edge, and enjoy the view." His gaze met Colin's. "Dwelling on the subject does not make it any more palatable, believe me. All I want to do is spend some time with you, and not think about it." He huffed. "Which is easier said than done, I know, but let's give it a try, okay?"

"Okay," Colin agreed.

They spent about forty minutes strolling along the Water of Leith Walkway, and Colin had to admit, it was a beautiful place to live. They passed old stone cottages, complete with metal troughs hanging from iron railings, which were filled with flowers. Above the trees that lined the walk, a grey stone church tower rose up. Their route alternated between stone pavements and a path that ran close to the water's edge, cool and peaceful, with overhanging trees and ducks that swam along, quacking loudly. It was such a tranquil scene, and yet its beauty was marred by the knowledge Ray had shared.

He really is dying.

By the time they returned to the flat, Ray looked pale and haggard, his breathing laboured. When Colin offered him an arm as they climbed the stairs, it seemed at first that he might refuse, but then he relented and took it. They made their way up slowly, pausing now and again so that Ray could catch his breath. Once inside the flat, Colin helped him onto the couch.

"In… my bedroom…. Oxygen tank and mask," Ray wheezed, before breaking into a coughing fit.

Colin dashed into the room and found them beside the bed. He brought them to Ray who looped the mask over his head and turned on the air. Colin sat beside him, his stomach churning as he watched Ray's pallor diminish. When Ray was finally breathing normally, or as normal as Colin had seen thus far, Colin fetched him a glass of water.

Ray took several careful sips before placing the glass on the table. "I suppose… now would be a good time to talk."

Colin nodded, his chest tight.

"There have been numerous infections during the last few years," Ray admitted. "They're what the docs call 'opportunistic infections.'"

"What kind of infections are we talking about?" Colin's heart sank to think Ray had been so ill, and hadn't been in touch before this point.

"Herpes simplex, for one." Ray gestured toward his mouth. "As you can see. I've also had pneumonia and TB."

"TB?" Colin recalled reading something about TB making an unwelcome return to the UK.

Ray nodded. "They treated that. But there are a whole host of other nasties that are part and parcel of my daily life now."

"Such as?"

He shrugged. "Night sweats. I get them a lot. Then there's severe diarrhoea." He grimaced. "I did say nasty, right? Plus the meds mean my appetite isn't what it used to be, as if I can eat that much with all this going on." Another gesture to his painful looking mouth. "Hence the weight loss."

"How long have they given you?" Colin asked, his heart aching.

Ray squared his jaw. "Now you listen to me. I'm not about to wallow in a pity party, so neither are you. I'm doing okay so far, living here. I can manage. And when the time comes that I can no longer do that, then I'll check myself into a nice little hospice somewhere." He gave a sad smile. "I'm not an idiot. I know I'll need palliative care eventually. Just, not yet." He sagged against the seat cushion. "I'm sorry, but that walk has wiped me out. I need to take a nap." Ray expelled a long breath. "And that's another thing. I seem to be sleeping more."

"Listen, if that's what your body is telling you, then that's what you do." Colin patted Ray's knee. "Go put your head down for a while. I'll be fine. I've got my phone and my tablet, and I'm pretty sure I have e-mails to answer. When you've rested, I'll make us something for lunch, okay?"

"Okay." Ray rose unsteadily to his feet. "Could you do me a favour and bring the oxygen tank through for me?"

"Of course." Colin picked it up along with the mask and followed Ray into his bedroom. He waited until Ray had lain down on the bed before placing the tank next to the headboard where he'd found it. Colin gazed down at his ex. "Now get some sleep. You won't even know I'm here."

"But I'm glad that you are," Ray said quietly.

Colin unfolded the blanket from the foot of the bed and covered him with it. Then he crept out of the room and closed the door behind him.

Once he was sitting on the couch, Colin leaned forward, his head in his hands, his thoughts full of the man Ray had been, the lover who'd taken a shy nineteen year old boy and showed him love. Whatever happened, Ray would always be a part of Colin's life.

Then he sighed. *He's not dead yet.*

Colin reached into his bag and found his tablet. He needed distracting.

✦ ✦ ✦

"So what do you want to do for dinner this evening?" Ray asked, his feet propped up on the coffee table. He grinned. "Indian takeaway?"

Colin snorted. "Absolutely not. I had my year's quota of fast food last night. How about I see what's in the fridge, and I rustle up something healthy for us?"

Ray sighed. "You sound like the nurse who comes here to do my check-ups. She gave me a leaflet all about the beneficial effects of various herbs and spices, for people living with HIV/AIDS."

Colin eyed him speculatively. "And have you followed any of the advice?"

Ray's eye roll was answer enough.

Something had been niggling away at the back of Colin's mind ever since their conversation that morning. "I've been meaning to ask you. I thought once someone received a diagnosis of HIV+, that it could be decades before AIDS developed, if it did at all."

Ray stilled. "What's your point?"

Colin gave a shrug. "Only that this all seems to have happened so fast. I mean, when did you first get the diagnosis?"

To his surprise, Ray suddenly avoided his gaze. "A while ago."

"Fine, but what's 'a while'? Five years, ten?" When Ray steadfastly looked in the opposite direction, the hairs on the back of Colin's neck stood on end. "Ray? What's going on?"

Silence, and now the skin on his forearms erupted into goose bumps.

Colin took a deep breath. "Ray? When did you find out you were HIV+?"

Slowly Ray turned his head to meet Colin's gaze. "March 18th, 1992."

It was as if an icy hand had plunged into his heart. "What?" He blinked. Swallowed. Stared. "But... that would mean... " Colin gaped at him and fought hard to maintain his composure. "You knew... when we got together in 2000... you knew you were positive?"

Ray nodded, his eyes wide and focused on Colin, his hand rubbing the leg of his jeans.

"But you didn't say a word." Colin couldn't believe it. "How could you be with me for three years—three years, Ray!—and not say a bloody word?"

Ray's breathing hitched, and another coughing fit overtook him. Colin watched him, waiting until it had passed, the questions piling up in his head. "I never saw you take any meds. Not once."

"When they first gave me the diagnosis, they told me I had seven to ten years, max. But then they said I wouldn't need to start taking medication until I got sick." Ray shuddered out a breath. "I felt healthy. It wasn't until after I took the job here that I began showing signs of sickness."

A wave of cold crashed over Colin. "Fuck. Oh my God. That party."

Ray flushed. "What party?" His gaze wouldn't meet Colin's, however.

Colin felt sick. "You know damn well what party. The one your friends organized the last year we were together, just before the end of term. The one where we both got very drunk. The one where we went back to your place and you said I 'took advantage of you.'" He shivered. "The night—the one and only night—when you fucked me raw." He lurched to his feet. "How? How could you have unprotected sex when you were fucking HIV+? Of all the irresponsible—"

"That was down to you, remember? You wouldn't take no for an answer." Ray's jaw trembled. "And I wasn't sober enough to stop you."

"Then you should have told me the truth!" Colin yelled.

"How could I? How the hell could I have told you?" Ray's eyes were wild. "And it was because of that night that I ended us. I could never have stayed with you after that, always thinking that I might have infected you too."

"That's why you took the job here? As a way of ending us?" Now it all made sense.

Ray nodded miserably.

Something still didn't add up.

"Then why the fuck did you keep in touch? Why send me Christmas cards? Why not make a clean break of it?"

"Because I fucking *loved* you," Ray shouted, only to start coughing again, and this time there was blood.

Colin balled his fists. "You don't fuck someone bareback and not reveal your status."

"I sent you cards because I had to make sure you were safe," Ray whispered. "It was my only way of checking that you were still healthy."

Colin took a couple of deep breaths and then walked into the bathroom. He plucked his toothbrush and toothpaste from the shelf above the sink, and thrust them into the toiletries bag he'd left next to the shower. Then he walked back into the living room and grabbed his sweater from the back of the couch and stuffed it and the toiletries into his overnight bag.

"What... what are you doing?" Ray stared at him, aghast.

"Getting out of here. I cannot be around you right now," Colin gritted out.

"Your flight isn't until tomorrow."

"Then I'll get on the first flight I can organize." Colin pulled his coat from the hook beside the front door.

"Please. Colin. Don't go like this," Ray pleaded.

Colin picked up his bag from the floor and threw his coat over his arm. "I... I don't trust myself to be here right now. I'm leaving before I do something I'll regret." And with that he went to the door, opened it, and walked out of Ray's flat and his life.

By the time he reached the main street, he was shaking. He stood at the curb, watching for a taxi, his mind still reeling from Ray's revelations, his heart still stinging from the betrayal. The ride to the airport went by in a blur of passing traffic, and when he got there, he went through the mechanics of changing his flight, his mind on autopilot. There were a few hours to kill before he was due to leave, and Colin retreated to the bar.

He sat by the window, gazing out at the tarmac where the planes lined up at their respective gates, but he didn't see them. He drank absently from his large glass of white wine, craving some measure of numbness that didn't come. He knew it would eventually, but right then his emotions were too close to the surface, too raw.

I just want to go home. To Ed.

Ed switched off the TV with a sigh. There was nothing worth watching anyway, and it was getting late. He glanced at the clock on the mantelpiece. 11.30 p.m. and still no call from Colin. Ed could have called, but he didn't want to disturb Colin if he and Ray were in the middle of a serious conversation. He suspected there might be a few of those occurring over the weekend.

Might as well get into bed. At least he'd be comfortable when Colin called to say good night. He went around the lounge, and smiled when Tigger stretched before dropping gracefully from the couch to the floor. "Yeah, it's your bedtime an' all, kitty." Tigger ignored him as usual, strolling past him into the kitchen where his basket sat next to the fridge. Colin often joked Tigger had chosen that spot while he planned how to develop opposable thumbs to get into the fridge on his own.

Ed switched off lamps, vaguely registering the sound of a car pulling up outside the house. When he heard a key in the front door, Ed strode into the hallway, just in time to see Colin enter the house and drop his bag onto the floor with a weary sigh.

"What the 'ell are you doin' 'ere? You're not due back until tomorrow."

Colin arched his eyebrows. "Tell your bit on the side to leave, then. He's not needed tonight." He removed his coat and placed it on the chair beside the hall table.

Ed guffawed. "You what? I 'ave quite enough on me plate with you. What makes you think I could cope with two fellas?" He stopped when he got a closer look at Colin. "Hey. Are you all right?"

"Not really." Colin opened his arms. "Come here. I need you."

Like Ed could refuse him anything.

He walked into Colin's open arms and slid his hands around his waist. There was the faintest whiff of alcohol on his breath. "Are you drunk?"

Colin kissed his cheek. "No, but I wish I were. I had a glass of wine at the airport, and another during the flight."

That was enough to set Ed worrying. "Col? What's wrong?"

Colin released him. "I'm tired and I'm ready for bed. How about we talk there?"

Ed nodded. "You go on up. I'll grab a glass of water. Do you want one?"

"Please." Colin picked up his bag and headed for the stairs.

Ed went into the kitchen and filled two glasses. After a last look around to make sure everywhere was locked up tight, he climbed the stairs to their bedroom.

Colin was sitting fully clothed on the edge of the bed, staring at his reflection in the mirrored wardrobe door. There was such a dejected air about him that it sent shivers through Ed. He said nothing but placed the glasses on each side of the bed, and then commenced undressing. When Colin had still made no move, Ed padded barefoot around to his side of the bed and grasped the hem of his sweater.

"Come on, let's get you outta these clothes."

Colin gazed up at him. "Taking care of me?"

Ed stopped and bent over to kiss him softly on the lips. "Don't I always?" Then he resumed his task, pulling the sweater up and over Colin's head. Colin slowly undid his jeans, moving like he was in a dream or something. Ed knelt at his feet, removed his shoes, and then tugged his jeans and briefs until they were off. Colin climbed under the sheets and laid his head on the pillows, his arms folded beneath. Ed followed suit and got in beside him, lying on his side, his head resting in the palm of his hand.

"Okay," he said quietly. "Tell me what 'appened." He listened intently while Colin told him of Ray's physical state. "Aw, the poor bloke." Colin's jaw tightened, and Ed stared at him, his scalp prickling. "What is it?"

Colin gazed at him, his eyes empty and distant. He began to speak in a flat, monotone voice, and Ed listened in growing dismay and horror. When the implications hit him with full force, Ed sat bolt upright in bed, his fists tight.

"I'll fucking kill him." Blood pounded in his ears and his pulse raced.

"No need," Colin said wearily. "Time will accomplish that feat for you."

Ed gaped at him, his mouth open. "'Ow can you be so fuckin' *calm* about this?" He scanned the room for something with which to vent his rage, and his gaze alighted on the glass beside the bed. He picked it up and hurled it at the wardrobe where it shattered into pieces, the mirror cracking along half its length. "Tell me! Because I don't fucking *get* it." His whole body trembled with impotent rage.

Colin stared at him with wide eyes. "Hey. Listen to me. You need to calm down." Before Ed could retort that he wasn't about to calm down *any fucking time soon,* Colin laid a gentle hand on Ed's thigh. "I know how you feel. Believe me, a few hours ago, I felt the same way. The only difference is, I've had time to think, to reflect." His voice shook. "I had to move past the feelings of betrayal, and the only thing that helped me do that was the knowledge that it could have been a lot worse. I'm negative, Ed. Yes, he could have infected me that night, but he didn't. I was lucky."

"Lucky?" Ed didn't believe what he was hearing. "He could've given you a fuckin' *death sentence!*"

Colin said nothing but knelt up in bed, facing him, his arms slipping around Ed's trembling body. "Ed? Babe? I need you. God help me, I really need you right now."

The hurt and pain in Colin's voice pierced through the layers of anger and hopelessness, and Ed took several long, deep breaths. Colin lay down again and held out his arms, an invitation Ed could not refuse. He joined Colin, stretching out his body on top of him, their mouths fused in a long, lingering kiss. When they parted, Colin looked him in the eye.

"Make it go away? Please?"

Ed nodded and pushed his knees between Colin's thighs. Colin wrapped his legs around Ed's waist and held onto his shoulders while Ed began to move, slowly rocking against Colin's dick in a leisurely, sensual grind.

"I've gotcha," Ed said, his voice suddenly husky. "An' I'll take care of ya too."

He meant those words with every cell in his body.

The broken glass and shattered mirror could wait. Right then he had something much more important to take of.

Chapter Sixteen

Rick nudged Angelo in the ribs with his elbow. "Go on, she's on her own in the kitchen. Now's the perfect time."

Angelo sighed. He knew Rick was right. It had been obvious all the way through Sunday lunch that something was wrong with Mum. She'd been quiet, answering questions with the barest response, and judging by his siblings' expressions, he wasn't the only one who'd noticed.

"Do you want me to come too?"

Angelo was on the point of telling him no, when he reconsidered. "Yes. I might need your wisdom."

Rick arched his eyebrows. "Wow. I have wisdom? When did that develop?" He grinned. "Must be a bi-product of living with you. I was never wise before we met."

Angelo smiled and leaned over to kiss him on the lips, ignoring Luca's instant imitation of retching. Angelo merely glanced over Rick's shoulder at his brother and glared.

Rick twisted his neck to gaze at Luca. "You're just jealous. Rachel's clearly not kissing you enough." He chuckled to hear Luca's explosive snort.

Angelo tugged his arm. "Ignore the brat. Let's go talk to Mum." He got up, Rick joining him, and they went into the kitchen.

Mum stood at the sink, her back to the door. Angelo walked over to her and put his arm around her shoulders. "Anything we can do to help?"

She shook her head and continued doing the washing up.

"I could dry for you," Rick suggested, picking up the tea towel from its hook beside the cutlery drawer. When she didn't respond, he got right into the task anyway, taking plates from the rack and drying them.

"Mum, what's wrong?" Angelo asked in a quiet voice.

"Wrong? Nothing is wrong," she replied briskly.

Patiently, Angelo placed his hand over hers and stilled it. He took the washing up brush from her and placed it in its receptacle next to the tap. Then he handed her the towel. "Dry your hands and come sit at the table."

Her blue eyes focused on his. "Angelo, please, just let me get on with—"

Angelo shook his head. "I'm not listening, because it's obvious something is wrong. And neither of us is leaving this kitchen until you tell us what's going on."

Mum sighed heavily. "You are as stubborn as your father, do you know that?"

Angelo flashed her a quick grin. "Breaking News. *You're* as stubborn as Dad was, so it's no surprise I inherited that particular trait." He pulled out the chair and inclined his head toward it. "Now sit."

Mum raised her eyebrows and glanced at Rick. "Is he this bossy with you, too?"

Rick laughed. "No, he's worse."

She shook her head and sat in the chair. Both Angelo and Rick joined her, and Angelo reached across the table for her hand, enfolding it in both of his. "All right, Mum. We're listening."

For a moment she said nothing, but simply stared at their clasped hands. Then Angelo's heart sank when tears welled up in her eyes and slid down her cheeks. "No one is coming," she whispered.

Angelo's chest ached. "What do you mean?" Across the table, Rick stared at her in obvious dismay.

"I-I sent out all those invitations, and no one is coming." She swallowed. "There will be no one at your wedding."

Angelo didn't believe that for one second. "Have you got the list you made? Of all the family members you've invited?" She nodded gloomily. "Then would you get it for me, please? I'd like to see it."

Mum sniffed, got up from the table and left the kitchen.

"No one?" Rick frowned. "That can't be right?"

Angelo heaved a sigh. "I'll believe it when I see it. I think she's blowing it all up out of all proportion myself, but let's see." He clammed up when Mum came back into the kitchen and handed him an A4 notepad. Angelo opened it up and glanced down the list. "You sent out one hundred invitations?"

She nodded.

"So we're talking two hundred guests, if they all bring a plus one."

"No, we're *not*," she said huffily, "because they don't want to come."

Angelo scanned the list. "Well, it says here that my cousin Paula and her husband are coming."

Rick's face lit up. "Paula? Didn't I meet her on our trip? She was nice."

Angelo nodded, his attention going back to the list. "Mum, you've noted about twenty replies here from people who have said they're coming. I don't understand. How is that no one?"

From the pocket of her apron, she pulled out a bundle of envelopes, tied together with a ribbon. "These are some of the replies I received."

Angelo held out his hand. "Can I see them?" After a moment's hesitation, she placed the bundle in his palm. Angelo opened up the first and scanned it. His Italian was very rusty, but he knew enough to get the gist: the words *omosessuale* and *deviante* were enough of a giveaway. Angelo placed them on the table. "Are they all like this one?"

Mum shrugged, an affectation of nonchalance, but Angelo knew better. His mum was hurting. "Mostly, yes."

Rick was watching him, his brow furrowed.

Angelo gave him a tight smile. "It's pretty much as we knew it would be."

"Ah." Rick took Mum's hand. "Elena, this isn't a surprise to us."

Her eyes flashed. "But it is to me."

Now Angelo got it. "Mum," he said softly, "you expected a lot more people to come, didn't you?" When she nodded, he picked up the towel and gently wiped away her tears. "I know twenty to forty people doesn't sound like a lot, not when you'd invited a potential two hundred, but it really is okay."

She jerked her head up and gaped at him. "How can you say that?"

Angelo searched for the right words, but he knew there was little chance of making her understand. "You've spent the last nine years getting to know your gay son. You accept me—us—for how we are. You don't see being gay as anything wrong—do you?"

Her mouth fell open. "No," she said vehemently. "This is how God made you. I believe that now."

Angelo nodded. "But that's not how the majority of people feel over there in Sicily. They think like Dad did, before he got to know me better. But like I said, you've had nine years to get used to the idea that you're going to have a son-in-law instead of a daughter-in-law. You cannot expect the rest of the family to come to the same decision in five minutes flat."

"Then..." She studied the notepad in Angelo's hands. "You think I should be pleased that these people are coming? Even though there are so few of them?"

He nodded.

"And there will be lots of people at the wedding who love us, Elena," Rick added. "People who have been waiting to see us married. People who support us, as you do." He squeezed her hand. "Don't worry." He grinned. "People will come, Elena. People *will* come."

Angelo rolled his eyes.

The kitchen door pushed open and Vincente stuck his head around it. "What does a man have to do around here to get some coffee? I'd hate to cross a desert with you two." He chuckled. "Now stop gassing and put the coffee on." With that he disappeared as promptly as he'd arrived.

Mum heaved a heavy sigh. "How about he gets off his fat backside and makes the coffee himself, instead of sitting around waiting for someone else to do it for him, the lazy so-and-so?" she muttered.

Angelo's jaw dropped. Rick's jaw dropped.

Mum looked from Angelo to Rick, and shrugged. "Well? If you two can speak your minds, why shouldn't I?" She nodded toward the door. "Besides, if he gets any fatter, he's going to split his costume next Christmas." She bit back a smile. "The seams are already straining."

"Mum!" Angelo burst into a peal of laughter. "You're a wicked woman."

She smiled. "Didn't you know? Rick taught me all I know." She winked at Rick.

Angelo lifted her hand and kissed the back of it. "Mum, everything will be fine. If we have twenty or so family members coming from Sicily, then that's wonderful. It's going to be a fantastic wedding." He gazed across the table at Rick, his heart swelling with love. "Because I'm going to be marrying the most wonderful man in the world."

Rick's face glowed.

"You see? *That* is what my family cannot see—the love in your voice and in your eyes when you look at Rick." Mum grabbed both their hands and held on tight. "But I see it, *tesoro*. And I shall be the proudest woman alive to watch you make your vows to each other." She released them and got to her feet. "I had better make the coffee for your *grassone* of a brother." She left them to set up the coffee percolator.

Rick sidled up to Angelo. "*Grassone?* I've not heard that one before. What does it mean?"

Angelo stifled his laughter. "Basically?" He lowered his voice to a whisper. "Fat slob."

Rick's look of astonishment was comical.

April 7ᵗʰ

Dr. Michaels sat back in her chair and regarded Will and Blake with a smile. "I'm glad you came to this decision. There are a few more tests I'll have to run before we go any further, but they won't be problematic."

"So what happens next?" Blake asked, reaching for Will's hand across the arms of their chairs. Will laced their fingers together.

She shifted her mouse across the pad and peered at the screen. "The first thing to do will be to set a date for the surgery. The implantation age for infants is typically around twelve months."

"But... I saw a video on YouTube," Will said, frowning. "A little girl on her activation day. She was about eight months old."

Dr. Michaels smiled. "You've been doing your homework."

"Does that mean you can do the procedure earlier?" Blake wanted to know.

"There are some cases of earlier procedures, yes, but I must stress they are not the norm." She gazed at Blake. "I take it you'd prefer the surgery to be done as early as possible." He nodded, and she peered at the screen. "We could be talking October, if all goes well, but that will depend on the results of our tests."

"How long will the surgery take?" Blake wished he was taking notes. He wanted to remember all this.

Dr. Michaels moved the mouse again, and the printer behind them whirred into life. "I'm printing out a leaflet I give to parents, providing all the key information, but I'll go through it now. The surgery is performed under general anaesthetic, and typically takes three to four hours. Then Nathan will stay in hospital overnight so we can monitor him." She smiled. "I'm not going to go through the procedure now. We can discuss that nearer the time. Now is the time for questions."

Will flashed Blake a look. "We need to know about the risks."

She nodded. "Of course." Her voice was calm, and this more than anything went some way to quelling Blake's own feelings of panic. He was glad they weren't going to hear all the ins and outs of the surgery, because he didn't think he could take that. Just the thought of Nathan, sedated, in an operating theatre... It sent shivers through him.

"As with any surgical procedure, there are risks," Dr. Michaels continued. "And I know they can sound very scary when your little boy is the one undergoing surgery, but they are for the most part rare or temporary, if they do occur at all."

Blake steeled himself, aware of Will's hand tightening around his. "So let's hear them."

"The facial nerve runs through the middle ear and is very close to where the surgeon will be working. An injury to it could result in partial weakening. And of course, anaesthesia can cause adverse reactions, but generally the incidence of this is very low. Then there's cerebrospinal fluid leakage."

Will stilled. "Oh God."

Dr. Michaels gave him a gentle smile. "I can't sugar-coat it, but again, the incidence is very low. There is also the risk of meningitis, but that usually only occurs in higher risk surgeries where the patient also has a malformation of the cochlea."

"Can the surgery have any lasting effects?" Will's voice was quiet.

Dr. Michaels nodded. "The nerve that provides taste to the tongue also goes through the middle ear, and there's always the potential risk for injury during the surgery. There are a few more common risks, such as Tinnitus—a ringing in the ears?—dizziness, infections from the wound, and even numbness in the area around the ear." She clasped her hands in front of her on the desk. "What's important here is to think about the benefits. You've chosen to go down this route because the benefits far outweigh any provided by a hearing aid. We won't simply be amplifying sound and relying on a damaged system to process the information. The implant will bypass the impaired areas and directly stimulate the nerve. Nathan will be able to perceive soft, medium and loud sounds. He'll be able to distinguish different types of sounds, and correctly discriminate language."

"He'll be like a normal hearing child?"

She hesitated. "He'll have access to information much like a child with normal hearing, but I want to make sure you're aware of and understand realistic expectations. I've also included a leaflet with that explained and we'll talk more about those points in detail as this process continues. Something else you might want to consider is bilateral implantation."

Blake blinked. "Both ears?"

"Yes. Hearing with both ears can improve speech understanding in noisy settings, because let's be honest here, how many children will live in a quiet world? And feedback from bilateral patients indicates that volume and tone sound better than with only one implant." She met Blake's gaze. "Would you have mono when you could have stereo?"

"When you put it like that..." Blake glanced across at Will, who appeared dazed.

"One important point to consider also is that generally speaking, listening and communicating with hearing loss is exhausting on any given day. Having bilateral processors will lessen the strain."

"How long after the op will he be able to hear?" Will demanded.

"Activation day occurs typically three weeks later, and I will warn you now—it's a very exciting but also very stressful day. For Nathan it will be scary, confusing, and funny as he hears sounds for the first time. Now, it does take a few sessions to fine tune the processors. Basically we hook up the processor to our computer and play a series of beeps that only Nathan will hear. It's a more difficult task with babies because we're watching for any recognition of the sound. Then we activate the speech feature." She grinned.

For the first time since they'd entered her office, Will smiled too. "I saw some of those videos on YouTube. They were amazing."

Dr. Michaels relaxed into her chair. "And that's when the hard work begins. Nathan will have to participate in an aural rehabilitation programme, either with speech pathologists or audiologists. Essentially we'll be teaching him how to listen. How to make all this noise he suddenly hears, have meaning."

Will gave a rueful smile. "Our hard work begins now." When she tilted her head to gaze at him inquiringly, he squeezed Blake's hand. "We're going to start learning sign language."

"And what we learn, we'll pass on to Sophie."

Dr. Michaels nodded approvingly. "You'll be amazed how much you will be able to communicate to Nathan by your facial expressions and gestures. He should start to pick things up within a few months. Children learn so fast." She grinned. "Sophie will probably be better at sign language than both of you. From what you've told me, that little girl is quick."

Blake chuckled. "We'd already worked that one out." He glanced at Will. "We'll be the ones with 'Could do better' while she goes to the top of the class."

Dr. Michaels got up from her desk and walked over to the printer. "Don't underestimate yourselves, gentlemen. She takes after *one* of you, after all." She handed the sheets to Will. "We'll set up the tests and then fix a date for the surgery. In the meantime, try not to stress about it, okay? Nathan will certainly pick up on that. And one last question. Does Sophie know that Nathan is deaf?"

Blake shook his head. "It's a conversation we've been meaning to have." He'd hesitated because he was unsure of how Sophie would react.

She nodded. "Then now might be a good time."

Will regarded him steadily. "Tonight."

Blake wasn't looking forward to that conversation at all.

Chapter Seventeen

"So, what did you do in school today?" Blake asked as he placed a bowl filled with sliced apple and grapes in front of Sophie. He sat at the kitchen table, Sophie in her chair. Will was pouring out two mugs of coffee and a glass of milk. He'd already prepared their dinner, and once Sophie was in bed, they'd eat. Nathan was already asleep in his room, and tiny noises filtered through the baby monitor on the wall.

Sophie deliberated between a piece of apple and a fat green grape. "We learned a song about a spider." She shuddered. "Spiders have lots of legs."

"A song about a spider?" Blake was intrigued. "Can you sing it for me?"

Sophie nodded, beaming. When she burst into a very tuneful and loud rendition of Incy Wincy Spider, Blake had to smile too, especially when she added gestures to accompany the lyrics. Will stopped what he was doing and watched her, his face creased into a smile. When she reached the end, they both applauded her, and her face lit up.

"Can I go and sing it to Nathan?" Sophie asked, before biting into an apple slice.

Will chuckled. "Talk about perfect timing," he murmured. He brought over Sophie's glass, placed it near her and then sat facing Blake.

"Nathan is asleep, sweetheart." Blake pointed to the monitor. "Can you hear him?"

Sophie paused in her attack on her fruit and cocked her head to one side. She smiled. "He sounds funny."

Blake laughed. "When you were a baby, you made noises too." He indicated the fruit. "Do I get a grape?" Sophie plucked two from the bowl and dropped them into his palm. Blake gazed lovingly at his generous daughter. "Thank you. I'll give one of those to Daddy." He handed it to Will. "Sophie, Daddy and I need to talk to you about something important, about Nathan."

She frowned. "Is he all right?"

Will's gaze met his, and Blake swallowed. "Nathan is fine, sweetheart. We're going to talk with him in a different way, that's all.
"

"Why?"

"Because Nathan is deaf," Will said quietly. "He can't hear us when we talk."

Sophie regarded him with obvious surprise. Then she gave them a confident smile. "But if I sing my song to him, very loud, he will hear that."

Blake's chest tightened. *If only.*

"Sophie, it doesn't matter how loud you sing. Nathan can't hear you." Will peered intently at her. "You know how sometimes, when Papa is telling you to put your toys away, and you put your fingers in your ears? Can you hear what Papa says like that?"

She giggled. "Silly Daddy. No."

"Well, that's what it's like all the time for Nathan. His ears don't work the same way yours do."

"Why is Nathan deaf?" Her usually cheerful smile disappeared, and she stared at them, a faint frown furrowing her brow.

"People become deaf for many reasons. Sometimes, babies—like Nathan—are born like that. Some people might become sick. Some may begin to lose their hearing as they get older."

She studied them for a moment, and then her forehead smoothed out. "Oh. You mean, like when you shout at Papa from the kitchen to fetch something for you, and he says, 'I can't hear you,' in that singing voice?"

Will smirked and glanced at Blake. "That's just Papa being silly. Papa hears everything."

"I know. He hears you when you are in the kitchen, eating his chocolate."

It was Blake's turn to smirk.

Will ignored him and continued. "But Papa and I went to see a special doctor, and she's going to help Nathan hear us."

"How?"

Will glanced across at Blake. "Where are your reading glasses?"

Blake got where Will was going with this. He rose from the table and went into the lounge to retrieve the glasses case from the small table. When he rejoined them at the table, Blake opened the case and put on the rimless glasses.

"You know how Papa wears glasses to read the newspaper?" Will asked her.

Sophie bit her lip. "Not all the time. Sometimes he says things like, 'there's nothing wrong with my eyes', and he holds the newspaper really far away."

Will glanced at Blake, his eyes sparkling. "Yes, well, Papa needs those glasses to help him see. And it doesn't matter that he hates how he looks in them, because I think Papa looks very—" He paused. "Very pretty when he wears them." Sophie giggled. "But what I'm trying to say is, just like the glasses help Papa see, this doctor is going to give Nathan something to help him hear."

"Like glasses?" She stared at him, her eyes wide.

"Not quite, sweetheart. They're going to put something on his head that will help him to hear."

"Good," Sophie declared emphatically. "I want to sing to him."

Blake had a brainwave. "You know all those actions you did when you sang about Incy Wincy Spider?" he asked her. "Well,

Daddy and I are going to learn how to talk to Nathan by using our hands."

Sophie burst into a peal of laughter. "Hands can't talk, Papa."

Blake stared at her, grinning. "Is that so? What do I mean when I do this?" He laid a finger on his lips.

"That means I have to be quiet."

"And what do you think this means?" He rubbed his belly.

Sophie watched him for a second, and then she nodded enthusiastically. "You're hungry!"

"Good girl," Blake said, beaming at her. "Well, some deaf people talk with their hands. It's called sign language. They use different shapes for different words. That was how to say hungry."

"Papa and I are going to learn how to use sign language, so we can talk to Nathan," Will added.

Sophie bounced on her chair. "Can I learn too?"

"Of course you can. That way, we can all talk to each other."

Sophie's little face glowed. She picked up Mr. Bunny from the chair next to her. "I'm going to learn sign language," she told him proudly.

"There will be no sign language for you if you don't eat all your fruit, young lady," Blake told her, his voice firm.

Sophie put down her rabbit immediately and went back to eating her apple and grapes. Blake's gaze met Will's. "And when she's asleep, you and I will start looking for ways to learn."

Before Will could respond, Sophie nodded. "We have to learn together. We're a family."

Blake stared at her, his heart full of love. "Yes, we are, sweetheart."

"Will, come here. I think I've found something."

Will caught the edge of excitement in Blake's voice instantly. He hung the towel over the heated rail and went into the bedroom. Blake was already in bed, a pile of pillows stuffed behind him, the laptop balanced on his knees and a pair of earphones lying against his chest. He glanced up as Will entered, his eyes shining.

"Come take a look at this."

Will climbed onto the bed and sat beside him. "What have you found?"

Blake pointed to the screen. "This is the website for the NDCS—the National Deaf Children's Society. There's so much on here."

"I thought you were looking up where we can find classes on sign language."

"I was. Did you know you can take qualifications in BSL?"

Will sighed. "I don't give a fuck for qualifications. I just want to learn how to communicate with our son."

Blake put the laptop to one side, and then extended one arm. "Come here." Will shifted closer until his face was buried in Blake's neck. He inhaled deeply, drawing Blake's warm scent into his nostrils. "I know, babe." Blake's voice was gentle. "And I have no plans for us to take exams in British Sign Language. But what I found will help our situation."

That got Will's attention. "Oh?" He shoved his pillows against the headboard and sat up next to Blake. "Show me."

Blake picked up the laptop. "They have a section here: Communicating with your deaf child. It talks about the different methods, using sign language as a first language—"

"Whoa. Wait a minute." Will stared at him. "*First* language?"

Blake nodded. "Basically they group the different communication methods into three types of approaches. There's listening and speaking, which will work well with the implant. Then there's sign language as the first language, and spoken English as the second." He stared at Will. "Do you get the implication? At home we'd *all* use sign language around him, all the time."

"You said three approaches." Will's head was spinning. The idea that sign language would become the norm was such an incredible concept that he couldn't quite grasp it.

Blake nodded. "Finally, they talk about using a combination of different methods, the key point being that there is flexibility, that there is no *one method* which should be considered better than another. It all boils down to what would work best for Nathan and us. So we'd use signing, speech and hearing, fingerspelling—"

Will chuckled. "That would be the 'back to school' part, right?"

"Uh huh. We would also use gestures, facial expressions and lip-reading, the idea being that we don't rely on just one method, but a combination of all of them." Blake scrolled through the site. "There's a section on learning sign language as a family too. It says the level is pretty basic, but I figure Sophie could learn with us. And you can learn online too. That would be great for us." He closed the laptop and placed it on the bedside cabinet. "We could start with the basics, then you and I could move onto level 1."

"There are different levels?"

Blake nodded. "The way I see it? The more Nathan can communicate, by whatever means, the better his chances in life." He sighed and shifted on the bed, until his head was on Will's chest. "I know it's going to be a lot of work, and it's not going to be easy, but there's plenty of help out there."

His words reverberated against Will's chest, tickling him. Will closed his eyes, enjoying the feeling of Blake's warm body against his, the way Blake gently stroked his belly, his fingers moving inexorably toward Will's cock that jerked in anticipation. The last few weeks had brought with them levels of stress that had taken their toll.

But things are looking better. There's a light at the end of the tunnel.

Will smiled to himself. Things would look even better in a moment...

He kissed Blake's forehead. "Hey," he said softly. When Blake craned his neck to gaze up at him, Will smiled. "Lock the door, Blake."

The speed with which Blake dived across the bed was gratifying. And just watching Blake's dick harden as he walked slowly toward Will, did wonderful things for his libido. Will rolled onto his belly, tilted his hips and offered himself, sighing with delight when Blake's body connected with his, Blake's weight pinning him to the mattress, his shaft hot and thick as it slid between his cheeks.

Will closed his eyes and awaited the pleasure he knew was coming.

April 20th

Colin put away the last of the plates and gave the sink one final swipe with a cloth.

"We're a good fit, you know that?" Ed said from the doorway.

Colin glanced at him and smiled. "Oh?"

Ed gave an emphatic nod. "You're the Yin to my Yang."

Colin snorted. "What you mean is, I'm the tidy freak who counteracts your inner slob. Except sometimes it's not so inner."

"Hey!" Ed gave him a mock glare. "Don't you go insultin' my inner slob." He grinned.

Colin folded the cloth and placed it next to the tap. "So, do you have any work to do this evening, or do I have you all to myself?"

Ed came into the room and pulled open the fridge. "I was gonna have a beer. You want one?"

Colin shook his head. "Anything on TV worth watching?" Not that he felt much like vegging out on the couch. He was... restless. "You know what? Scrap that idea. I might go for a run instead."

Ed studied him in silence, a beer can in his hand.

"What?" Colin retorted. "Can't a man go for a run? Exercise is good for the body, especially when we haven't had a match for a while." He missed rugby. The team was in transition mode right then. Several players had quit due to other commitments, and with no replacements lined up, their numbers were severely depleted.

Ed took a drink before speaking. "I was thinkin' you an' me might 'ave a chat."

"About what?" Like he didn't know. Ray had been the elephant in the room ever since Colin had got back from Edinburgh. That was due in no small part to Colin. He didn't want to *think* about his ex, let alone talk about him. Those moments when Ray came to mind, Colin was aware of the fluttery, empty feeling in the pit of his stomach. Ray hadn't called, emailed, texted—not that Colin was at all surprised by that. But Ray was still there, in the back of his mind, a constant niggling that wouldn't go away. And while he wasn't in their conversations, Colin felt his presence in other ways.

He and Ed hadn't made love since that night. It wasn't that he'd made a conscious decision to avoid sex, it was just that the desire wasn't there. Something was eating away at his insides, and Colin had a pretty good idea what.

He felt... guilty. The way he'd left, the way he'd made no attempt to contact Ray... Then a wave of fresh resentment would crash over him, as he recalled Ray's revelations, his betrayal. That only led to more guilt. He needed to move on, leave it all behind him, but Ray couldn't do that. Ray's past was slowly killing him.

"Come an' sit with me on the couch," Ed suggested.

Colin regarded him for a second or two, before reaching into the fridge for a bottle. *Fuck it.* If they were going to discuss Ray, maybe a glass of wine might make him feel better. He poured himself a glass and followed Ed into the lounge. Tigger sat on the window sill, staring out into the front garden. *It's a bit dark out there for spotting birds*, Colin told the cat silently.

Ed sat down and patted the seat cushion next to him. "Park that fine arse 'ere."

Colin had to laugh. "Don't ever change, Ed."

Ed lifted his eyebrows. "An' what would I change? Granted, me looks will fade, but that's the same for all of us. The way I speak? Pfft. I'm too long in the tooth now to give a fuck. People take me as they find me. That doesn't mean I can't lay on the charm when I 'ave to—you catch more flies with 'oney, an' all that—but I see no reason not to be meself with those who know me."

Colin put down his glass, leaned across and kissed Ed on the lips, a warm, fleeting connection that felt good. "Exactly. I wouldn't have you any other way."

Ed leered. "You can 'ave me any way you want me." Then his face straightened. "Okay, I've been thinkin' about Ray."

"And why would you want to do that?" Colin reached for his glass and took a long drink, relishing the crisp white wine. "The last time we spoke about him you were all for killing him."

Ed snorted. "Yeah, well, I've slept since. I'm a few weeks older an' I've cooled off. The last three weeks 'ave given me time to think, to put things into perspective."

"Perspective?" Colin gazed frankly at him. "Nothing has changed. He still—"

"Yeah, yeah, I know what he did. An' yeah, he was an arsehole not to tell ya. I'm not gonna argue with ya on *that* score." Ed paused. "But being an arsehole doesn't mean he doesn't deserve some compassion."

Colin blinked. It was the last thing he'd expected to hear from Ed.

Ed drank from his can, and then cradled it in his hands. "Who visits Ray?"

"I don't understand."

"Who goes to see 'im? Anyone?"

Colin racked his brains. "He spoke about a nurse who goes there to do check-ups."

"'As he got any friends?"

Colin had to think for a moment. Ray hadn't mentioned anyone.

Ed was nodding. "See, this is what I'm askin'. Does he 'ave anyone who's there for him?"

For the life of him, Colin couldn't answer.

Ed leaned forward, put his can on the table and then clasped his hands together, elbows balanced on his knees. "I can't get 'im out of me mind. I don't mean I'm thinkin' about 'im non-stop, it's just that he's... there, like an itch I can't reach. An' the one thing I keep comin' back to, is when all's said an' done, Ray 'asn't got that many days left to 'im, 'as he? An' that doesn't feel right. He contacted you in the first place to ask forgiveness for the way he left, right?"

Colin nodded, stunned into silence.

"So you can't leave it like this." Ed's gaze met his. "You've gotta ask yerself a question—do you forgive 'im?"

Oh God. Now *there* was a question.

Colin finally found his voice. "Do you think I should?"

Ed shrugged. "Not my place to say, Col. Only you can answer that. But these last couple of days, I found meself thinkin' about 'ow he must be feelin'. He wanted forgiveness, an' he only made matters worse. An' the thought of 'im spendin' his remainin' days alone an' feelin' like shit 'cause he messed up again... "

Colin swallowed. Ed's words conjured up an unpleasant picture. More than that, they gave him a clear insight into the man he loved. "You have a large heart, don't you? You hide it well under a layer of gruffness, but there's a soft core to you that can't be denied."

Ed fixed him with a hard stare. "You go spreadin' it around that Ed Fellows 'as a soft 'n' mushy side, an' I will tan your arse so 'ard, you won't sit down for a week." His eyes twinkled. "I've worked too long an' 'ard on me rep as a curmudgeon to 'ave you ruin it for me." He reached out for Colin's hand. "An' *you* can talk. You've got an 'eart as big as the Atlantic. That's why you went to see Ray in the first place." He lifted his chin and locked gazes with Colin. "An' that's precisely why you'll do what's right. I know ya." He leaned over and kissed him, slowly and thoroughly, and Colin melted at the intimate gesture.

Ed got to his feet. "An' now? I think I'll 'ave an early night."

Colin glanced at the clock. "Er, Ed? It's only eight o'clock. You can't be sleep—" The penny dropped.

Ed grinned. "Who said anything about bein' sleepy?"

Colin laughed, his heart lightening a little. "I might join you and not be sleepy too." It had been too long, after all, since he'd lost himself in Ed, in the heat and passion they created between them. He paused. "I... I just have to make a call first."

It was easier to breathe once he'd made the decision.

Ed nodded slowly in approval. "I'll be waitin' for ya in bed." His eyes glittered. "I'll be the one on all fours with his arsehole lubed up."

Colin put his hand to his chest. "Don't *say* things like that, not before I have to make a phone call. How do you expect me to think clearly when you torment me with images like that?"

Ed sauntered out of the lounge, waggling that firm arse. "It's in me job description—'Keep Col on his toes.'"

Colin stared after him, shaking his head and laughing quietly. When all was quiet, he picked up his phone from the table and scrolled through. He paused to take a couple of deep breaths, not entirely sure of what he was going to say.

When the number had rung six or seven times, Colin was ready to call it a night.

"Hello?" Ray sounded drowsy, cautious.

"Hi. Did I wake you?" Colin kept his voice low.

Silence for a moment. "Yeah, I'd fallen asleep on the couch." Ray paused. "I didn't expect to hear from you again."

"To be honest? I didn't expect to be calling you, but I've been talking with Ed. This was his idea."

"I guess I owe him, then." A pause. "I *am* sorry, you know. I'm sorry I didn't tell you, I'm sorry we drank too much that night, I'm—"

"You know what?" Colin was on his feet, pacing. "It was stupid what we did, yes. And although I will never be okay with the risk you took with *my* life, in the end *I* lucked out." He caught his breath. "So I forgive you."

"You... you do?"

"I don't know if I'd be saying the same thing if *I'd* become infected, but let's not go down that road. I dodged *that* bullet. You were less lucky."

"I... I don't know what to say."

Colin reflected on Ed's words. "Ed asked me a question tonight, and I couldn't answer it. He asked if anyone was there for you."

In the pause that followed, he heard Ray's breathing, harsh and erratic. "No," Ray said at last. "There's no one."

The knowledge made Colin's heart sink. "But... why? You've been living there for thirteen years. You must have had relationships, grown close to people."

Ray's sigh filled his ears. "I made a decision, when I first moved up here. I decided never to have another relationship. I kept everyone at arms' length." He let out a wry chuckle. "I think I see the boy who delivers my groceries more than anyone else. You were my last relationship, Colin."

"Why?" The thought of Ray alone, no one to share his life, and later, knowing he was dying... Colin fought back the tears.

"Why? I couldn't take the chance of putting someone I loved at risk. And I did love you."

That knowledge didn't ease the ache in his heart.

"This Ed of yours. Sounds like he's pretty fond of you."

"He loves me." The simple truth, plain and unvarnished, sent warmth through Colin. "Just like I love him."

"Then make the most of every day you get with him, all right? Life's too fucking short." Ray's voice rose. "Promise me that?"

"I promise."

Whatever else Ray had intended saying was lost in a fit of coughing. Colin waited until he'd stopped. "Are you okay?"

"Sorry, Colin, but it's time I was in bed. Thank you for calling. You have no idea how much it means to me. Good bye, and good luck." The dull click signalled the end of the conversation.

Colin stared at the phone. *Is that it? Am I going to leave it like this?*

Then he realized Ed was upstairs, waiting for Colin so they could make love.

The questions would wait until the morning. Right then he had a man to love.

Chapter Eighteen

May 5th

When his phone rang, Colin was *this* close to ignoring Marion completely. In fact, it crossed his mind to pull the cable from its box on the wall. His own phone was on silent.

Except he wouldn't do that, of course.

With a sigh, he picked up the handset and pressed the blinking red button. "Marion, what can I do for you?"

"You have a visitor in reception."

He stifled his groan. "No. I'm sorry, but you'll have to tell them to call back later." Colin's lunch hour was sacrosanct. Apart from a much needed break, it was the only chance he had throughout the day to call Ed, and right then he had some making up to do.

"He's very insistent." What puzzled Colin was the amusement he could plainly hear in her voice. There followed a muffled conversation, and then Marion was back on. "He says to tell you, if you won't see him now, then there will be no... foot rub for you tonight." She giggled.

And just like that, the tide of Colin's day turned. "Send him up, please, Marion." He put down the phone and gave his office a glance. The last thing he wanted was for Ed to walk in and find a mess. He would never let Colin hear the last of it.

When Ed poked his head around the door, Colin didn't waste any time. He tugged Ed into the room, pushed the door closed behind him and pulled him into a hug.

Ed chuckled against his neck. "Someone's pleased to see me."

Colin kissed him on the lips. "If it had been anyone else, they wouldn't have got past Marion."

"Funny. She didn't look like a Rottweiler to me." Ed grinned. "Does she make a good guard dog?"

Colin laughed and pushed him down onto the chair facing his desk. "Now, tell me why you're here."

Ed gave a mock gasp. "I need a reason to visit ya? Yeah, I'm really feelin' the love."

Colin gave him a stern glance. "I can count on less than the fingers on one hand the number of occasions you've been to this office." His lunch could wait. This was more important.

"I was waitin' for ya to tell me what's goin' on, but seemin' as I've been doin' that for two weeks now, with nothin' 'appenin', I'm takin' matters into me own 'ands." Ed speared him with an intense gaze. "So what's on your mind, Col?"

Inwardly Colin groaned. *I might have known I couldn't hide it.* "Is this about last night? I was going to call you today to apologize. I wasn't in a good place last night, that's all." It hadn't been Ed's fault.

Ed snorted. "That was obvious. I don't think you strung more than ten words together all night. But like I said, it's not just about last night. You've been like this for a couple o' weeks." When Colin stared at him, him stomach churning, Ed gave him a fond glance. "You thought I wouldn't notice? You've not been yerself. You've been quiet, distracted... Maybe others might not pick up on those things, but I'm not others. I know ya too well."

Colin's throat tightened.

Ed cocked his head to one side. "Is it Ray?"

"Why would you say that?" Ray hadn't been a topic of conversation since Colin had called him.

"Maybe because he's been on *my* mind too."

Colin blinked. "Oh? In what respect?"

Ed got up from his chair and walked over to Colin's window. He put his hand to the frame and stared down at the busy London street below. "I think you need to pay 'im another visit."

Colin almost choked, he caught his breath so fast. Ed's words mirrored his own thoughts with eerie precision. "I'd thought about e-mailing him or calling him." That much was true.

Ed shook his head. "Nah. He can lie his arse off in an e-mail or in a call. It's trickier to do that when you're face to face."

Colin shook his head. "Okay, when did you develop clairvoyant abilities?"

"Eh?"

Colin reached across the desk for his phone. "I e-mailed him, a week ago."

"Did he reply? What did he say?"

Colin scrolled through his e-mails. "It's not so much what he said, as what he didn't say." He found the e-mail and passed the phone to Ed. "I'd said I hoped he was still getting out for his walk once a day."

Ed peered at the phone. "Sort of a generic reply, ain't it? 'Thanks for touching base.'"

"Yes, I noticed that too. But look at how he refers to my question."

Ed read aloud. "'Those days are behind me.' What the 'ell does that mean?" He scanned it again. "He doesn't give much away, does he?"

Colin sighed. "Exactly." The thought that Ray had possibly worsened but didn't want to share that knowledge, made his heart ache.

Ed handed back his phone. "Then go see him. Tomorrow."

"Just like that? Do I tell him I'm coming?"

Ed shook his head. "Nah, he'll only try an' put you off, if this e-mail is anything to go by. Can you get off early tomorrow? Assumin' there's a flight, of course."

Colin reached for the mouse. "There's only one way to find out." Ed shifted to stand at his side while he pulled up the website. When he bent down to kiss Colin's head, Colin raised his chin and smiled. "What was that for?"

"That was for 'avin' a big 'eart." Ed peered at his desk. "Where's your lunch?"

"I was going to skip it, while you were here."

Ed growled. "Oh no, you don't. Go get whatever you're eatin'. I'll stay 'ere an' look for flights."

Something occurred to him. "Why aren't you at work?"

Ed gazed at him, his eyes warm. "I told 'em I 'ad somewhere important to be, an' that I'd be gone for a couple of hours."

Colin stood up and kissed him. "Then I'll bring lunch for two."

Ed's eyes gleamed. "Is this a workin' lunch or...?" He leered.

Colin shook his head, laughing. "Get those ideas right out of your head this minute. For one thing, there are enough people in and out of this office to make whatever you're thinking, extremely impractical."

Ed pouted like a little kid. "Spoilsport." Then he grinned. "Well, go on, then. Get yer arse into gear. We've got lunch to eat an' a flight to book." He sat in Colin's chair and swivelled around on it. "Pity, though. We could get up to all sorts in this."

Colin was still laughing when he reached the staff kitchen.

It was beginning to feel like a case of déjà-vu.

Colin paid the driver, got out of the taxi and walked across the courtyard to the main door of Ray's building. It had been good of Simon Wilson to give him the time off: he hadn't even batted an eyelid when Colin had made the request. The only difference had been no visit to Trinity to see Ed—there hadn't been enough time.

He climbed the stairs, his mind already on what awaited him at the top. He hoped Ray wouldn't be pissed off that he'd come unannounced, but Ed was right: Ray would have prevaricated.

Colin pressed the doorbell and waited. Surprisingly, the door opened quickly and a young woman stood there in a pale blue uniform. She blinked.

"Are you here to see Ray?" she asked in a soft voice.

He nodded. "Is this a bad time?"

She huffed. "Where are ma manners? Come in." She stood aside to let him enter, and then closed the door quietly behind him. "Here, let me take your jacket." She helped him out of it, before hanging it on a hook. "Ray is asleep right now."

"Oh."

She studied him for a moment. "I was about to make maself a cup of tea. Would you like one?"

"Make it a coffee, then yes," he said with a smile. "And the name's Colin."

Her eyes widened. "Ah. I *was* wonderin'. Nice to put a face to the name. I'm Kelly, by the way."

They walked into the living room/kitchen and she filled the kettle. "So Ray has mentioned me?" He kept his voice low.

Kelly nodded, her back to him as she put out two mugs. "He told me you were payin' him a visit, back in April. But when I asked how it had gone, I got the impression I'd asked the wrong question." She turned around and leaned against the sink. "Which I thought was sad, seein' as you're the only person he's ever mentioned since I've been doing his check-ups." She tilted her head. "I also got the impression that you were important to him."

Colin's chest tightened. "Once, a long time ago." He gazed at Ray's bedroom door. "How is he? Or are you not allowed to divulge that information?"

Kelly's gaze flickered in the same direction briefly. "I cannae comment on that. But what I *can* tell you is that the next time you pay him a visit, it probably won't be here." She pressed her lips together.

There was a lump in Colin's throat that made it difficult to swallow. He took a deep breath. "Palliative care." Kelly didn't respond, but that told him everything he needed to know. His eyelids grew hot and his vision blurred a little. Colin rubbed his eyes. "How long before he has to consider that?"

"We're already trying to find a place for him."

Another thought struck him. "Does... does he know that?"

She gave a slow nod. "It might be a few weeks, or a couple of months before space becomes available. But he cannae carry on here. Not now." Another glance toward his bedroom door. "To be honest, if his condition worsens, hospitalization is our next option."

The sound of coughing erupted from behind the closed door, and Kelly didn't waste time. Colin made himself useful and finished making the drinks, his thoughts on Ray. Clearly his condition had deteriorated a lot since the beginning of April. Kelly was right: living on the fifth floor of an apartment building was out of the question.

She appeared at the door. "He wants tae see ya." She smiled at the sight of the tea. "Aw, you nice man."

Colin handed her the mug and then entered the bedroom. Ray lay in bed, his head propped up on a mound of pillows, an air mask in place, connected to the oxygen tank. His eyes focused on Colin and he wagged a finger in the air.

Colin sat on the edge of the bed beside him. "And what's that for?" he asked quietly, struggling not to reveal his emotions. Ray had lost more weight, and there were dark circles around his eyes.

Ray pulled the mask away a little. "You... didn't tell... me you... were coming. Sneaky." The breath wheezed out of him.

Colin took his hand. "Didn't you know? Sneaky is my middle name. And besides, you'd have only said no." He cocked his head toward the door. "Kelly seems a good sort."

Ray nodded. "She's a... little treasure. Comes here... three times a day... now." He put the mask back in place.

More confirmation, as if it were needed, of the state of Ray's health. Colin rubbed his thumb over the back of Ray's hand, and he could see instantly that the motion soothed him.

"Colin?" He glanced toward the door. Kelly held out his mug. "Thought you might want this." She brought it over to him.

"Thanks. Are you here for much longer?"

"Until I've finished ma tea. I'm just writing up ma notes for his doctor. I'll talk to you before I go." She smiled and left them alone.

Ray was breathing more easily, and as Colin watched, he drifted off to sleep. He eased Ray's hand from his, before getting up carefully to leave the room. Once outside, he joined Kelly on the couch.

She observed him for a moment, her hands wrapped around her mug. "When we first broached the subject of palliative care, the doctor told him it may be given at home, in a hospital if home care wasn't possible, or in a hospice. He was adamant about not wanting to go into hospital. He was asked at the time if there was anyone else who could be part of that discussion. He said there was no one."

Suddenly Colin felt very tired. "I asked him a few weeks back if there was anyone. I got the same answer."

"Where do you live?"

"London." Which right then seemed a million miles away.

"Ah, I see." Kelly took a drink from her mug. "Not exactly next door, is it?"

"Not really, no." He glanced at Ray's bedroom door. "He looks worse than the last time I was here."

She nodded. "He's relying more and more on the oxygen, and now there are other factors to consider. The pain is increasing." She bit her lip. "I'm not supposed to be talking about him, but you're the only visitor he's had, and you obviously wouldnae be here if you didnae care about him. Palliative care won't treat the lung cancer, but it can help to reduce symptoms like the pain, the fatigue, and of course the emotional issues." Kelly smiled. "He seemed happy to see you. I gather he had no idea? The look on his face when I told him you'd arrived... " She drained her mug and glanced at the watch attached to her uniform. "I need to go. Do you want to give me your details? If we need to... get in touch with you, for any reason. It would help to have a point of contact."

Colin nodded. That much he could do. He gave her his number, and Kelly scribbled it in her notepad. He finished his coffee while she put her things together. When she was ready, Colin walked her to the door.

"You said it might be weeks before space becomes available in a hospice?"

Kelly nodded. "Do you want us to let you know when we find something?"

"Please." Finding Ray in such a poor state had taken the wind right out of him, but Colin was finding his breath again. He let her out and then went back into the kitchen to wash his mug. He quietly opened Ray's door, so as not to disturb him, but Ray was fast asleep.

Colin sat on the couch and got out his phone. "Hi there," he said in a low voice when the call connected.

"Col? You all right?"

The sound of Ed's voice, full of concern and so vital, brought a wave of sorrow that rolled over him, leaving him feeling exhausted. "Oh, God, Ed."

There was a brief silence. "I take it Ray hadn't told you the 'alf of it."

Colin filled him in, relating what Kelly had told him. His heart ached when he spoke of how Ray looked. Ed listened in silence.

When Ed didn't speak for a few seconds, Colin cleared his throat. "You still there?"

"Who says he 'as to look for an 'ospice in Edinburgh? Those places are everywhere, right?"

"Er, yes." Colin wasn't sure where Ed was going with this.

"An' there are *bound* to be 'ospices in London, right? Prob'ly more than there are up there."

"Ed? What are you saying?"

Another pause. "I'm sayin' don't leave 'im on 'is own. No one deserves to be alone when they're like that. Bring him 'ome."

Colin's heartbeat raced. "Okay, try that again, slowly."

Ed sighed. "I think you should pack a suitcase with essential stuff, an' then call round a few rental car agencies an' 'ire a car. Drive back to London, an' bring Ray with ya."

There was a heavy feeling in his stomach. "And do what, exactly?"

"Ray can stay with us, while we find 'im an 'ospice. I'll make up the guest room for 'im, an' then I'll start lookin'. I might ask Blake. That man 'as so many contacts, it wouldn't surprise me if he knows of a place or two."

Colin closed his eyes and thanked God for the day he'd met the wonderful man on the other end of his phone. "And you say *I've* got a big heart?"

Ed huffed. "I just 'ide mine better."

"One thing I don't get. Why drive back? Surely it's faster to fly."

"Nah. Not if he's 'avin breathin' difficulties. He wouldn't cope with the cabin pressure. No, this way is better. You can take it slow." Colin heard the clatter of keys. "It's a seven to eight hour journey with no stops, but you can't do that. Start as early as you can tomorrow morning. Take all day if you 'ave to. Put Ray in the back with pillows, make 'im as comfortable as you can. An' send me regular updates so I know where you are." Colin's phone pinged. "That's me. I've just sent you the route."

"I love you." They were the only words that could fully convey what Colin was feeling.

"Love you too. I'll get the room ready, then I'll do some shoppin'. An' if I 'ave time, I'll go see Blake. Might as well get the ball rollin', eh?"

"Bless you."

Ed chuckled. "I'm already blessed, thank you very much. I've got you, remember? Now, 'ave you eaten yet?"

"No, not yet. The nurse has only just left."

"Right. Then order a takeaway and get yerself fed. While you're waitin' for the food to arrive, 'ave a look around for what you need to pack. Just take what Ray needs. We can deal with what to do with the flat another day."

"And tell Ray what's happening. You forgot that part. You know he's going to disagree."

Ed snorted. "Like he's in any position to do that. We're thinkin' of what's best for 'im, and that *does* not include stayin' in a lonely flat with no visitors while he waits to find a place to die in. Sorry, but no fuckin' way."

"I might not use those exact words when I talk to him." Colin shook his head. "You're amazing."

"You can tell me that again tomorrow night when you're 'ere in me arms where you belong."

"Are you sure you know what you're letting us in for?" Colin tried a last-ditch effort to be practical.

"We're not talkin' long, are we?"

Colin had no idea. "That depends on how quickly a place becomes available."

"We'll manage, Col. If we can put up with *all my family* for three days at Christmas, we can survive Ray stayin' with us." He laughed. "He'll be a bloody sight quieter than them, that's for sure."

Colin coughed. "But the same rules will apply." He waited for the penny to drop.

"Oh. Oh yeah." Ed sighed. "That does it. I'm buying a gag."

Colin laughed so hard, he thought he'd rupture something.

Chapter Nineteen

Blake stood in the doorway to the lounge, his heart swelling with love at the sight that met his eyes. Will and Nathan were on the floor, Nathan on the brightly coloured quilted blanket that Lizzie had given him. Will was holding up a toy that didn't appear to be anything but a collection of coloured hoops, all linked together, and Nathan lay on his back, stretching up to try and grab it. His little legs were in the air too.

"Is he trying to grab it with his fingers or his toes?" Blake asked, coming into the room.

Will laughed. "You're just in time. I was about to call you."

Blake glanced around the room. "Where's Sophie?"

"In her room. She said she had a surprise for us, and she's working on it." Will grinned. "I was told most definitely to stay out of her room."

Blake laughed and joined Will and Nathan on the floor. "So why were you going to call me?"

Will leaned over and kissed Nathan's belly, and Blake loved how Nathan's face lit up in a smile. "Because we have a surprise for Papa, don't we, beautiful?" Carefully he rolled Nathan onto his tummy, his arm tucked under him, and then grabbed hold of his teddy bear, placing it a short distance from him. Nathan made grabbing gestures as he tried to reach it.

Will rolled him onto his back, and then repeated the action. After three or four times, he placed Nathan on his back and moved the teddy out of his reach. "Ready to dazzle Papa?" He grabbed the teddy bear and made it dance. "Come on, you know you want Big Ted. You can do it."

Blake watched, mesmerized as Nathan stretched out one chubby little hand but couldn't quite reach. "God, I remember doing this with Sophie. Once she got going, she moved so fast!"

Will chuckled. "I've got news for you. This little one would probably beat her. Oh my God, when he starts crawling we'd better watch out."

Nathan had clearly grown tired of not being able to reach his favourite teddy. When using both hands yielded no results, he rolled, first onto his side, and then finally onto his tummy, his hands grabbing hold of Big Ted's back paws.

Will picked him up and cuddled him. "Yay! You did it." His gaze met Blake's. "And one day he'll hear me say that."

Blake nodded, swallowing. Then he did a face palm. "Damn. I should have been videoing you while he did his first roll."

Will smiled. "I don't think that's the only time he's going to do it. You'll have other opportunities." He widened his smile for Nathan. "Yeah, who's a clever boy?"

Blake knew exactly what he was doing. They'd read on a website how important it was to use facial expressions to show moods.

"Papa! Daddy!"

Blake arched his eyebrows. "We've been summoned to Her Highness's chamber." Laughing, he left the room and headed up the stairs, Will behind him with Nathan in his arms. Sophie's door was partly ajar. "Can we come in now?"

"Yes."

When they entered, Sophie was sitting at her little table by the window, her face alight. In front of her was a pile of cards, and Blake could just make out the drawing of a car on the top one.

"Sit down," Sophie instructed them.

"God, she takes after you," Will whispered as he carefully lowered himself to the carpet, Nathan between his crossed legs, leaning back against him, his head supported.

Blake chuckled. "With that hair? She is *so* your daughter." Sophie's long brown hair was almost the exact shade of Will's.

Will lowered his voice. "Not denying that, but there's no doubting she's your daughter too. It's that bossy Davis streak."

"Okay, you need to stop talking now." Sophie fixed them both with a firm stare.

Suitably chastised, Blake straightened both his body and his face. "Okay, we're all yours."

Sophie leaned across the table, picked up the cards and began to spread them out in front of her. "At school last week, I told my teacher about Nathan being deaf."

"You did?" Will asked in surprise. Then his eyes widened. "That explains the sympathetic looks I got when I picked Sophie up from school."

"My teacher showed us something on the TV, about sign language."

Blake shook his head, smiling. "That's wonderful. What did you see?"

Sophie smiled too. "We have been learning all week how to say some words using sign language."

Will peered at the cards. "Did you make these?"

She nodded proudly. "Every word we learned, I made a card for it so I could practice. Then when Nathan is bigger, I can teach him too."

Blake stared at her, gobsmacked. *Our little girl is amazing.*

Sophie pointed to the cards. "Daddy, choose a card. I have to do the sign for it."

Blake scanned the cards. "Ah, you did transport? How many signs did you learn?

"Seven. Now, Daddy, pick a card."

Will perused the cards and then pointed to the drawing of two feet. "Is that walking?"

Sophie nodded. She curled one hand over and then brushed her fingers twice over her upturned palm.

"That's wonderful. Do another," Blake demanded.

Will pointed to the car. "How about this one?"

Sophie held out her hands as though clasping a steering wheel, and moved them as though turning it. One by one they went through the cards, and each time Will and Blake applauded her.

Sophie frowned at the end. "That's not how you do it. Teacher showed us." She clapped her hands twice and then held them up in the air, waving them both. Then she held up her index finger and placed it against her ear. "That's how you say deaf in sign language." She grinned. "What have you learned to say?"

Blake laughed. "Daddy and I have been learning a different way of using our hands." They'd been watching videos on fingerspelling, and it had been Will's idea to turn it into a competition. *Yeah, that may have been a bad move.*

"Show me!" Sophie demanded, bouncing on her chair.

The sound of a car door slamming had Blake rising to his feet. "We can't right now, because we have a visitor."

"We do?" Will gave him a puzzled glance.

"I was coming to tell you, but you distracted me with Nathan." Blake smiled and then winked at Sophie. "Uncle Ed is here."

"Yay!" Sophie was up off her chair and flying past them out of her room and down the stairs before they could say another word.

"Wait for us!" Will yelled. "You know the rules." Sophie wasn't allowed to open the front door.

"Then hurry up, Daddy!"

Blake followed Will down the stairs at a far more sedate pace than their daughter, shaking his head. "I am *not* that bossy," he muttered under his breath.

"Save it for someone who doesn't know you like I do," Will said as he reached the front door where Sophie was still bouncing. He let

Ed in, Nathan balanced in the crook of his arm. Ed smiled when he saw the baby, but before he could greet Will, Sophie was holding up her arms, clamouring for a hug. Ed scooped her up and gave her a cuddle.

"Hey, Princess. How's my favourite girl?"

Blake chuckled. "One of these days you'll say that in earshot of one of your *other* favourites, and then there'll be hell to pay."

"Nah." Ed kissed Sophie's cheek. "This little madam 'ere will always be my favourite girl. I was there in the 'ospital the night you were born," he told her.

Sophie wrinkled her nose. "Yes, and Papa said you were all dirty."

Ed gave Blake a hard stare. "Oh he did, did he?"

Sophie nodded. "And Uncle Colin." Ed put her down and she tugged on his hand, pulling him toward the lounge. "Do you know that Nathan is deaf?"

Ed nodded, the humour leaving his face. "I do, yes, Princess. Your daddies told me an' Uncle Colin." For a second his gaze alighted on Blake and Ed gave him a brief nod.

"Why don't you show Uncle Ed the sign language you learned at school?" Blake suggested.

Ed's eyes widened. "They're teachin' sign language nowadays? Blimey. Things 'ave changed since my day. Then it was French or German."

"If you think about it," Will said as they followed Ed and Sophie into the lounge, "you're more likely to meet someone who's deaf or hearing impaired in this country, than someone who speaks French or German. Makes perfect sense."

"Can I get you something to drink?" Blake asked Ed, who was already on the couch watching Sophie sign.

"A coffee would be good, if you've got any going." Ed brought his attention back to Sophie. "That's a plane, right?" Sophie's delighted squeal was adorable.

Blake smiled to himself as he went into the kitchen to put on the coffee machine. He could envisage Sophie teaching everyone she knew to sign. Then he thought about it. All their friends had been part of Sophie's life so far, and therefore would be part of Nathan's. He didn't think for one minute that they would balk at the idea of learning a few signs.

We never saw this coming, but we're adjusting to our new reality. They had to, if Nathan was going to get the most out of life in the future.

When the coffee was ready, he carried the mugs through into the lounge. Ed was leaning forward, copying Sophie as she showed him her signs. Will sat in one of the arm chairs, Nathan on his lap, clutching his teddy bear.

"So, to what do we owe this unexpected pleasure on a Saturday morning?" Blake sat on the arm of Will's chair, gently stroking Nathan's head. "You didn't say anything on the phone."

"Didn't Colin want to come?" Will inquired.

"Col's in Edinburgh, but as we speak, he's hirin' a car to drive back 'ere. I'm 'ere to pick yer brains, Blake." He stopped talking when his phone rang. "Talk of the devil," Ed said with a grin. He answered and sat back against the cushions. "Good mornin', gorgeous." His brow furrowed. "Okay, say that again."

Blake's arms came out in goose bumps as Ed's frown deepened, his expression one of intense concentration.

"What the fuck? You're kiddin'. When did you speak to 'im?" A pause. "What, no way at all?" Ed sighed heavily. "Well, fuck. So what are yer gonna do?"

Will sat up, his gaze flickering to Blake.

"Yeah, well, I suppose. So when are yer comin' 'ome?... Fine. I'll 'ave yer dinner ready.... Yeah, I love you too." He disconnected and sat there, staring blankly at the phone.

Sophie giggled. "Uncle Ed said a bad word."

Ed blinked and then paled. "Gawd. I forgot where I was. Sorry, guys."

Will addressed Sophie. "Sweetheart, Papa and I need to talk to Uncle Ed. Can you go to your room and make some new signing cards for us? We'll come up in a minute and see them."

Sophie beamed. "Yes!" She scrambled to her feet and dashed from the room, calling out, "Don't be long, Daddy."

Blake waited for a minute until all was quiet before clearing his throat. "Ed? Is everything all right?"

Ed regarded him, blinking. "Sorry, guys. I came 'ere on a mission, only that call sorta makes it null 'n' void." He drank some coffee before continuing. "Okay, I'd better start at the beginning. Col's ex, Ray, got in contact with 'im. To cut a long story short, Ray 'as lung cancer, an' a whole load of other things, 'cause he 'as AIDS. Col went to visit Ray twice in Edinburgh, but this second time, it was obvious Ray was in a bad way. Rather than let 'im look for an 'ospice up there, I suggested Col brings 'im back to London, an' that he could stay with us until a space turned up. I was comin' to ask Blake if he could recommend an 'ospice, 'cause I think Justin was in one, right?"

Blake nodded. His dad had spent some time in a hospice after his stroke.

"But it seems me plan ain't gonna 'appen. Colin went to see Ray's doctor this mornin', to check on what medication Ray might need, an' the doc told 'im categorically that Ray was in no state to travel, not even in an ambulance."

"Hell." Will stared at Ed. "So what now?"

Ed huffed. "Col says he's coming back tomorrow. After that, he'll try to get up there every few weeks. It's not ideal, but given the distance involved, what else can he do?" He took another drink from his mug. "Anyway, that's enough about me. Tell me what's new."

"If you want to talk about it, you can, you know," Blake said softly.

Ed gave him a half-hearted smile. "Nah. It won't solve anythin'. This is a shitty situation an' I think we all know 'ow it's gonna end, right? So all I can do is be there for Col when he needs me. All any of us can do, really." He gazed at Will who was holding up Nathan's teddy bear and making it dance for him. Nathan was smiling and trying to grab it. "Back to you guys. Are you learning to sign too?"

Blake knew Ed was avoiding thinking about his situation, not that he blamed him. *I've wanted to run away from our situation more than once.* Except of course he wouldn't do that.

Will smiled. "We're learning to spell with our fingers, as well as a few new signs each day. Blake decided it would be good if we made it a little more... interesting."

Ed grinned. "Do tell."

Blake snorted. "All I said was that every day we had to sign to each other. If I sign and Will understands, I get a point. But if he doesn't get it because my sign wasn't clear enough, he gets the point, and vice versa."

"I gotcha, a bit of competition." Ed looked from Blake to Will. "Who's winnin'?"

Blake sighed. "He is."

Will arched his eyebrows. "It's early days, right? You'll get the hang of it." His eyes gleamed. "I mean, you've already improved since you—"

"Don't," Blake warned. Like Will would listen to that.

Ed cackled. "Go on, *one* of yer tell me."

"We were learning some basic signs," Will explained, "And Blake did this." He formed a right angle with his thumb and index finger, positioning his hand at his chin.

"Yeah? Whass 'at mean?"

Will's gaze met Blake's and his warm, chocolate brown eyes held sympathy. "It was an easy mistake to make. He was supposed to be signing 'policeman.'"

Ed widened his eyes. "'Supposed to'?"

Will chuckled. "Only one small problem." He sat his chin in the corner of the L-shape formed by his fingers. "*This* means policeman." He altered the angle slightly, reverting to his earlier position. "*This* means 'lesbian.'"

Ed gaped briefly, before bellowing with laughter. "Priceless. Yeah, it don't really pay to get *those* two words confused."

Blake had known Will couldn't keep quiet about it, given such ammunition. "Okay, okay. Enough laughter at my expense, I think." He gave Will a Look that promised retribution when their guest had departed. In fact, he was sorely tempted to save his revenge for when Will was naked and tied up.

Handcuffs were a wonderful invention.

"You're not *still* sulking, are you?" Will asked as he undressed for bed. Blake was already under the sheets, his back facing Will.

"Who says I'm sulking?"

Will would have been more convinced if Blake's words hadn't been directed toward the wardrobe. "Don't think I don't know what this is about. You're pissed off at me for telling Ed about your little sign mishap." When Blake didn't reply, Will lifted the sheet and climbed into the bed behind him, spooning around him, his hand snaking over Blake's waist to rub his belly. He kissed Blake's shoulder. "Hey," he said quietly. "You can't be good at everything."

Blake inclined his head. "No harm in trying."

Will nuzzled into his neck. "I'm serious. Do you know what an amazing man you are? I can count on one hand the number of things you've attempted in your life and have met with failure. That's why your staff thinks you're Superman, you *do* know that, right? Why do you think they come to you when they need advice? You fix things."

"Not everything can be fixed that easily."

Will kissed his shoulder again. "Maybe not, but you'll give it a bloody good try."

Blake gave him a sweet smile, and Will's tension eased—until he felt something cold and hard snap around his wrist. "Blake, what are you playing at?"

Blake's smile morphed into a wicked grin. "Payback time." Before Will could respond, Blake rolled over and pulled Will's right arm above his head, fastening the other half of the cuff through the headboard. Then he pushed Will onto his belly and sat astride him, pinning him to the mattress. From beneath Blake's pillow emerged another set of handcuffs.

Will's heartbeat sped up. He loved it when Blake got kinky. "Help, help," he whispered.

Blake snorted. "Oh, please. We both know you have a huge smile all over your face right now."

Will had nothing to say on that subject.

When Blake had secured both his hands to the bed, he shifted position and gripped Will's arsecheeks, spreading them.

"Oh, fuck, yeah," Will groaned into the pillow at that first touch of Blake's tongue to his hole. He pulled his legs under him, knees to his chest, and tilted his arse, eager for more. Blake chuckled against his puckered entrance, and went right back to licking *so fucking slowly* over his hole, even though Will rocked back, letting him know exactly where he wanted Blake's tongue.

Blake obviously hadn't read the same script because he kept up the sensual tongue bath, not once pressing insistently against the tight ring, although Will felt as if his whole body was screaming at Blake to just *take* him.

When his hole was penetrated not by Blake's tongue but by two slick fingers that pushed deep inside him, Will knew the message had gotten through.

He was about to be well and truly fucked.

A hot, bare cock slid into him, and he reared back his head to moan at the exquisite pleasure. He ached to touch his dick, but that was out of the question. All he could do was take what Blake had to give. He grabbed hold of the headboard, his fingers curling around the cut out vines and leaves, and waited, his body tight around Blake's thick cock that filled him to the hilt.

Blake curved his body around Will's, his breath hot on his shoulders. "How long do you think it will take me to fuck the come out of you?" Blake's voice was husky, raw with desire. He eased his dick out of Will, until just the head remained. "How long do you think you can last before you shoot all over the sheets? Five minutes? Less?" Blake grabbed onto his shoulders, his hands firm and warm.

"Stop talking and fuck me," Will gritted out, desperate to feel that long shaft fill him again and again. When Blake didn't move, he craned his neck to stare back at him. "Blake, come on."

Blake covered him once more with his body. "I might not be good at everything," he whispered, "but I'm very, very good at some things." And with that he thrust all the way into Will, fast and deep, and Will groaned. "And one of those things...." Blake withdrew again, only to spear Will with one long push of hot flesh. "Is knowing what makes your body sing for me." Another painfully slow retreat. "Knowing what makes you want to cry out my name because I make you feel so good." Blake filled him, and they both exhaled. "Knowing how much you love it when I bury my cock deep inside you. Knowing I can take your breath away when you take all of me." Blake began to move faster, sliding in and out of his body, hands anchored to Will's shoulders. Blake groaned. "God, it feels so good to fuck you."

"Please," Will begged. "Make it last. I want it to last." He knew the truth, however, with each glide of that long, hot dick inside him. The handcuffs bit into his wrists, only adding to the spiralling heat and passion. The edges of the carved wood dug into his fingers. Blake slammed harder into him, Will's body jolted by the impact as Blake snapped his hips faster. Every thrust of Blake's cock brought him perilously close to the edge.

When Blake wrapped his fingers around Will's dick and gave it one, two, three hard tugs, that was all it took to have Will cover his hand with warm come. Will shivered, closed his eyes and let his orgasm wash over and through him in a slow pulse of sensual joy. Blake was still inside him, and as the last of Will's climax ebbed away, he began to move again, quickly building to his former pace.

"Let me feel you," Will whispered. "Come on, love."

Blake let out a low cry and Will rejoiced to feel Blake's cock shudder inside him, the tell-tale throb that told him Blake had come. Blake held onto Will, laying a carpet of tender kisses across his shoulder blades, the fierce and impatient lover replaced by the gentle and tender lover once more. Carefully, Blake unlocked the handcuffs and rubbed over Will's wrists, all the while still buried inside him. When he eased his dick from Will's body and rolled Will onto his back, Will held up his arms and Blake filled them. They lay together, bodies slick with come and perspiration, hands still touching, exploring, while they kissed and caressed, Will not wanting to let go of the moment.

When Blake finally lay still beside him, Will took hold of his hand, brought it to his lips and kissed Blake's fingers. Then he placed it over his heart and covered it with his own.

"I am in total agreement."

Blake raised his head to give Will an inquiring glance.

Will smiled. "You are very, very good at some things."

Chapter Twenty

June 4th

"This is beautiful!" Elena exclaimed as they crossed the wooden bridge into Hever Castle, the placid waters of the moat reflecting the early morning sunshine. Ahead of them was the portcullis, and through an archway lay the main door. As they drew closer, Rick caught sight of a tall, slim man dressed in a dark blue suit.

"That must be Franco's friend, Anthony," he whispered to Angelo. "Damn."

Angelo glanced at him. "And what does that mean?"

Rick widened his gaze. "It means he's hot." He stroked Angelo's back. "I can still look, right?"

Angelo chuckled. "Of course. Looking is allowed. And you do have a point. Franco has good taste in friends."

Anthony smiled and walked toward them. "Welcome to Hever Castle. I'm Anthony Calderfield, and I'm in charge of bookings. Franco might have mentioned me."

"He did, yes." Angelo indicated Elena. "This is my mother, Mrs Tarallo, I'm Angelo and this is Rick."

Anthony extended a hand to Elena, and when she held out hers, he clasped it and kissed the back of it. Elena's face flushed.

"You may call me Elena."

Anthony smiled as he straightened. "So, my first question is, are you aware of our wedding venues, and do you have a preference?"

"We've looked on the website," Angelo informed him, "and although the Astor wing and the Castle are truly magnificent, I think what appealed to both of us was the Italian garden." He grinned. "Not to be *too* stereotypical, you understand."

Anthony laughed. "To be honest, if it were me getting married in August? That would be my choice too." He winked. "And maybe that was why I pencilled you in for that particular venue. So shall we take a look?"

Angelo nodded, and reached down to grasp Rick's hands. They walked back across the bridge, Elena at their side.

"As I told you on the phone, I've taken the liberty of organizing a sampling session for you today, as part of your visit. There'll be the canapés that will be served during the drinks reception prior to the wedding, then the menus for the wedding breakfast, and finally a selection of dishes for the evening. Are we closer to agreeing on a final number of guests?"

Angelo nodded. "At the moment, we've reached nearly a hundred, but there shouldn't be many more than that."

"That's great. The limit on the Italian Garden weddings is one hundred and eighty."

Rick gazed across at the landscape. "It's such a beautiful venue," he commented, squeezing Angelo's hand. "We're so glad you were able to accommodate us."

Anthony smiled. "When Franco told me about the two of you, it was obvious he cared for you. I was just happy I was able to help." He pointed ahead to a large expanse of water. "This is the lake, and your wedding will take place overlooking it."

Rick stared at the stone arches of the loggia that he'd seen online. "There?" The warm coloured stone reflected the sun's rays, giving the spot a peaceful appearance.

Anthony nodded. "We'd use the piazza for the drinks reception, so your guests can look out at the lake and the fountain." He led them through the loggia and down toward the lake.

"Such a beautiful place," Elena said quietly. "Your father would have loved this."

Angelo's hand tightened around Rick's. "I'm sure he would have."

They walked through a rose garden, Anthony talking with Elena about the history of the place while Rick drank in their gorgeous surroundings. The fragrance was sublime.

"Happy?" Angelo asked him in a low voice.

Rick nodded. "I still can't believe it's finally going to happen."

Angelo chuckled. "We're not there yet. Don't go counting any chickens."

Rick wasn't worried. After all they'd gone through to arrive at this point, nothing was going to stop this wedding, short of a natural disaster wiping out all off Kent and its environs. Then he reconsidered and sent up a silent plea. *Make sure You have nothing on the books for August nineteenth, okay? Because You know I have nothing against You personally, right? I think You did a great job, especially when I look around me right this second. It's just that assholes have made a mess of it, and usually in Your name.*

He had to smile to himself. *I'm having a conversation with God, asking Him to make sure our wedding is catastrophe-free.*

Anthony led them into a Palladian style building, with vaulted ceilings and full length arched windows. The atmosphere inside was light and airy, and the lake and gardens could be seen through the windows.

"This is the Guthrie Pavilion," Anthony told them. "This is where your wedding breakfast would take place."

The room was already laid out for a wedding, with round tables covered in snowy white tablecloths, displays of creamy, fragrant flowers in the centre of each.

Elena regarded the centrepieces. "You will not need the flowers," she declared emphatically.

Rick had a sinking feeling he knew what was coming, but he kept a straight face. "Oh?"

She nodded, smiling broadly. "I have already arranged for the miniature olive trees."

Anthony blinked. "Olive trees?"

"Yes. They have been grown specially. Each tree will have little white lights in them."

Rick snuck a glance at Angelo, who was staring at his mother. "I thought this was just an idea."

Elena opened her eyes wide. "A very good idea. Which is why I went ahead and spoke with the garden centre months ago. They should be ready in time for the wedding."

Oh hell.

Anthony nodded slowly. "I see. Well, that is certainly different. Is it an Italian custom?"

Elena beamed. "No, but I saw it on Pinterest."

Both Rick and Angelo gaped.

"Since when did you go on Pinterest?" Angelo demanded.

"Since Paolo showed me on his laptop. He wanted to give me some ideas for the reception."

"I'll just bet he did," Rick muttered. Angelo reached behind him and gave him a light tap on his backside. Rick gave him an innocent look. "What?"

"Behave," Angelo whispered. He returned his attention to Elena. "That sounds like a lovely idea."

"Could you give me the details of the garden centre?" Anthony asked. "That way I can liaise with them directly about delivery times and setting up on the day."

"Of course." Elena's face glowed. "They will look so beautiful."

One look at her delighted expression, and Rick knew Angelo wasn't about to argue.

"So, if you're happy with the Pavilion, let's go into the castle where I've arranged the menu samples. They should be ready for us by now." Anthony held out his arm to Elena, who took hold of it, still smiling. They walked ahead of Rick and Angelo at a steady pace, Anthony leaning in to talk to her, Elena nodding and listening intently.

"He's a very charming man, isn't he?" Rick said quietly. "He has Elena practically purring."

"This is his job, right? He has to deal with the public all the time, so it makes sense that he'd have good people skills." Angelo grinned. "He'd make some lucky man a wonderful husband."

Rick gave a mock gasp. "I hate it when you read my mind. How do you do that?" Anthony's suit and the way it fitted the contours of his body, his manner of speaking, the confidence that permeated his words... Rick could easily see Anthony as gay.

He gave himself a shake. "I really must stop doing that. Not every good looking man is gay. And for all I know, he might be highly offended that I'm even considering him as such."

Angelo squeezed his hand. "I won't tell him if you won't." He leaned closer. "So, what are the odds that Mum wants Italian food on the menu?"

Rick wasn't about to take that bet. He had a feeling Elena wanted their wedding to have a traditional Italian feel to it. That gave him pause.

What do Italian grooms wear?

It was official. Angelo was in Food Heaven.

"Oh, my God, these are delicious!" He took a bite of another canapé, this time a slice of spicy naan bread spread with smoked chicken mousse, delicately flavoured with coriander.

Rick eyed him with amusement. "Do you *have* to moan like that when you eat?"

Angelo thrust the remainder of the canapé into his hand and Rick ate it in one bite. He rolled his eyes and let out a soft moan that was an exact duplicate of Angelo's. "Oh my God!"

Angelo nodded enthusiastically. "See?" He turned to Anthony. "And all these can be available?"

"Yes. You simply need to choose how many canapés per person, four, six or eight."

Angelo snorted. "Well, that will be an easy choice. Forty Italians plus Rick's family and all our friends? Better make it eight."

Rick smacked his backside. "I'll tell Maggie you said that."

Angelo did an eye roll. "Oh, come on, Christmas Day at your parents' house? It's like a feeding frenzy. Last year I vividly recall having to arm wrestle Maggie for the last of the roast potatoes."

Anthony laughed. "This sounds like it's going to be a very interesting wedding." He handed Angelo the list of canapés. "This is all of them, including the hot ones." There was a variety of toppings, from duck to salmon, to roast beef, and two or three vegetarian options. "We'd need your final list a week before the wedding at the latest. Shall we move on to the wedding breakfast and the evening menus?" He led them over to another table where covered dishes awaited them.

"We choose one starter, one main course and one dessert, right?" Rick asked.

Anthony nodded. "Plus one vegetarian option. But to be honest, there are five or six options for each course, so it shouldn't be too onerous a task to choose something."

Mum was perusing the list. "There is no soup on this list," she declared. "Angelo, you need to have soup."

He sighed. "Mum, I don't think they have Italian wedding soup as an option."

"Wedding soup?" Anthony tilted his head to one side.

"It's a soup with green vegetables and meat, usually meatballs," Angelo explained. He and Rick had tried it at a wedding in Sicily when they'd visited his family. He gave his mum a smile. "What about the chicken terrine? Chicken is usually a good choice. And the baby tomato salad for the vegetarians."

She pursed her lips. "If you say so."

Angelo stifled his groan. So far it had been plain sailing. He supposed he should have expected the shoe to drop at some point.

"Oh wow, they have roast beef and Yorkshire pudding." Rick was practically drooling.

Apparently that was the wrong thing to say.

Mum widened her eyes. "Could it *be* any more English?"

Angelo regarded the list of courses. "The desserts are more Continental." There was a cheesecake, a sorbet, a summer berries fruit salad and... He smiled. "Mum, there's a Frangipane tart."

She huffed. "That's an improvement, I suppose."

Angelo couldn't miss the way Rick's face tightened. They'd known there might be issues with the reception, but Angelo had kept his fingers crossed that Mum would be okay with their choices.

"There is pasta on the evening menu," Anthony said with a smile.

Mum jerked her head toward him. "Pasta?"

He nodded. "Spinach and Ricotta Tortellini, with a garlic and cream sauce. Plus there is also Sea Bass."

Angelo could have hugged him. Mum's smile was back as Anthony opened one of the covered dishes to let her taste the pasta. She turned to him and Rick, and beamed. "This is really good. You need to try this." She went back to tasting the pasta.

Angelo caught Anthony's eye and mouthed *thank you*. The man was a godsend.

When they'd hummed and hawed about the choices, Angelo and Rick made the final selection and Anthony made notes. Then he consulted his watch. "The last detail I need from you is your choice of room for the night of the wedding. With the Italian Garden weddings, I recommend the Anne Boleyn wing." His eyes gleamed. "In fact, I think I have the perfect room for you two." He turned to Mum. "I'm going to borrow Angelo and Rick for a moment while I show them the accommodation. We shouldn't be long. Please, try some of the other dishes."

Mum gazed at Angelo. "Can I come too?"

Rick bit his lip but said nothing.

Angelo cleared his throat. "Mum, you really don't need to see our room, do you? Why don't you stay here and try some more of the samples?" Anthony nodded in agreement.

"If you say so." She gazed at the dishes. "I may have a little more of the pasta."

Angelo kissed her cheek. "Save room for your lunch," he told her. "We've still got an afternoon trying on suits, remember? And we're seeing the bakers at four."

They left her in the castle and Anthony led them through the grounds to the Anne Boleyn wing.

"Your mother seems to be a formidable character," he commented.

Angelo snickered. "Tactfully put. I'm sorry, but I had to draw the line somewhere. I didn't want her seeing where Rick and I would be spending our first night as a married couple." He stared at the building ahead of them. "Is that it? Wow. That looks... old." The leaded windows were beautiful.

"To be honest, my first thought was the Edward VII suite. It has a seven foot bed." Anthony smiled. "Definitely a room fit for a king. But then I had another idea." He opened the wide wooden door and led them into a large hallway with oak floors and panelled walls. When they reached another door, Anthony paused. "Let's see if what you think of this."

He opened the door and they stepped into a suite, the bathroom off to the left and the main area dominated by a wide bed and windows that filled one wall. The fittings were modern, but somehow did not seem out of place. Oak beams ran across the ceiling, and in the bathroom was a roll top bath big enough for two.

Angelo couldn't stop smiling. "This is perfect." Rick's hand found his, and they gazed at the luxurious room. "And that bath. Won't that be wonderful, to take a long bath at the end of what promises to be a very long day?"

"There will be champagne waiting for you," Anthony added. "That will be from me." He winked. "Franco said I am to take special care of you."

Based upon everything they had seen so far, Angelo figured they owed Franco—big time.

It was official. Rick was in Wedding Suit Hell, and Angelo was right there with him.

He stared at the row upon row of suits that lined the walls of the upstairs room. Elena had brought them to the men's outfitters that several family members had recommended, and if the selection he was seeing was anything to go by? Some Italians had no taste in clothing whatsoever.

Rick leaned in to whisper to Angelo. "She's kidding, right? Tell me she's kidding."

Angelo shuddered. "I'm beginning to get a very bad feeling about this."

Elena was moving along the rows, pulling out jackets and exclaiming enthusiastically about them.

"What did your brothers wear?" Rick wanted to know. He couldn't really see Luca in any of the garish colours on offer.

"Vincente wore a royal blue suit," Angelo said in a low voice. "Paolo's was sage green, I think."

Sage green? Rick wanted to throw up. "Tell me you don't want me to wear *any* of these, and I will love you forever."

Angelo chuckled. "I thought that was a given."

Rick pulled out a jacket in light blue and shivered. "Ugh. No. Just.... No."

"Angelo!" Elena held up a shiny silvery-grey suit. She beamed. "What do you think?"

"*Say something*!" Rick hissed. "Please. If you love me."

Angelo laughed quietly. "Now, would I let you marry me in a shiny silver suit? Hmm?" He gave Elena a patient smile. "Not sure that's really me, Mum."

"Ya think?" Rick muttered.

Elena glared at him. "It would be more helpful if you pointed out suits that you like, rather than making comments."

Angelo nudged Rick in the ribs with his elbow, and Rick coughed. "I'm sorry, Elena. I know there are lots of suits here, but so far I haven't seen one that makes me go, 'Yes! That's the one!'"

"Then maybe I might be allowed to make a few suggestions?"

Rick glanced over Elena's shoulder at the tall, slim man who'd shown them to the room. He walked over to them, looking both Rick and Angelo up and down.

Elena's face lit up. "Thank you. That would be most welcome."

The sales assistant studied Angelo for a moment. "With your colouring, you could go with either a very dark suit or a very pale one, like cream."

Rick snorted. "I can't see you in a white suit, babe. Just saying."

The assistant pursed his lips and gave Angelo a keen glance. "Do you trust me?"

Angelo smiled. "I don't even know you, but yes, I'll trust you."

"I'm Harry, and I'm about to make you look amazing." He grinned at Rick. "And then it's your turn." He beckoned Angelo with a crooked finger. "Step into my fitting room."

Angelo gave Rick a flash of a smile before disappearing into the changing room after Harry. Rick stared at the door. Angelo might trust Harry, but Rick trusted his gaydar. And right then it was pinging like crazy.

I trust Angelo. Harry? Not so much.

"Harry seems like a pleasant young man," Elena commented. She peered intently at Rick. "Can I ask you something? Do you think he might be... gay?"

Rick laughed and impulsively he hugged her. "Hey, your gaydar is working!"

Her brow furrowed. "My what?" She didn't release him, however. Her frown smoothed out and she hugged him back. "You make Angelo very happy. This is why I love you like one of my own sons."

Rick's chest tightened. It was possibly the sweetest thing she had ever said to him. He kissed her cheek. "I love you too, Elena." It was the truth. While Vittorio had taken his time warming to the idea of Rick as part of the family, Elena had been far quicker to accept him.

"So... what do you think?"

Rick jerked his head in the direction of the fitting room—and stared.

Angelo wore a three piece suit in a rich ivory/cream colour. The waistcoat fitted his slim form, and the white shirt and gold tie went perfectly against his olive skin. The contrast of pale suit and black curls was so striking that Rick was stunned.

"You look... beautiful," he said simply.

Angelo's face glowed, and next to him, Harry beamed.

Elena's breathing hitched. "Oh, Angelo. You look wonderful."

Rick walked slowly over to where Angelo stood, and grasped both his hands. "How the hell do you expect me to remember my vows when I'm standing there, looking at you?"

Angelo smiled, leaned forward and kissed him. "I have only one word to answer that. Ditto."

Harry cleared his throat. "Wait until you see what I have in mind for *you*. When I'm done, you'll have GT magazine wanting to do a spread on your wedding."

Angelo groaned. "Do *not* give my mother ideas, okay?" He patted Rick's backside. "Go let Harry work his magic."

Rick smiled and followed Harry into the changing room. As Harry pushed open the door, Rick caught Elena's whisper.

"What is... GT magazine?"

The air was filled with the sweet aroma of cake and chocolate and other delicious smells. Angelo stared at the display of wedding cakes. "I didn't realize it was going to be so difficult a choice."

"I know," Rick murmured. "Do we go for traditional, or modern, or something totally different?"

Elena huffed. "I have already taken care of this."

Angelo blinked. "You have? But I thought we were here to decide on a design."

Mum gave him a wide smile. "I emailed Patricia the recipe for your cake weeks ago. We are here to make sure everything will be on time."

Rick darted a glance at Angelo. "I thought the same as you."

The door at the rear of the shop opened and a young woman appeared. "Mrs. Tarallo? Glad to finally meet you." She greeted Angelo and Rick with a smile. "And you two must be the bridegrooms-to-be. I'm Patricia Merton. I own the bakery. Would you all come this way?"

They followed her into an office with chairs set out. "Please, sit down," she said, before sitting at the desk and reaching for a sketch pad. When they were seated, she placed the pad on her knee. "Thank you for coming today. Based on the information Mrs Tarallo gave me, I've put together an idea for your cake."

Elena frowned. "Didn't you receive my email?"

Patricia gave her a sweet smile. "I did, yes, and thank you for that. I hadn't seen a recipe for Italian wedding cake."

Angelo groaned inwardly. *I might have known.*

"Is that the one I tried when we were in Italy?" Rick asked. "The one with crushed pineapple and nuts in it, with cream cheese all over it?"

Angelo nodded.

"Unfortunately, I tend not to use recipes that contain nuts. Too many people with allergies. And although it looked like it was a delicious cake, it was very... impersonal for a wedding cake. So I took the liberty of designing one that reflected the two of you." She flipped open the pad and handed it to Angelo.

Rick leaned in to get a better look. "Oh, wow."

Angelo swallowed. "This is beautiful." It was a drawing of a large, round cake, the base of which was deep, and whatever covered it had been grained to look like wood. At one point, part of it curled off, and there was a chisel beside it, looking for all the world like part of the covering had been carved away. On top of the base was a large open book, and on the left hand page was gold lettering, announcing their marriage. On the right...

He had to smile. "I was going to ask if we would be having those," he said, pointing to the two figures in black suits who stood together side by side.

"Your mother had asked if we could do that."

Elena sighed. "I was upset that you were not going to make the cake I asked for, but now that I see this?" Her gaze met Angelo's. "It is perfect."

Patricia beamed. "I wanted it to be something that reflected your lives."

Rick leaned against him. "And it does."

Angelo put his arm around him. "Is it August yet?"

The day couldn't come soon enough.

Chapter Twenty-One

June 18th

Colin plumped up the pillows and Ray leaned back, the air mask in place. His breathing was more laboured than it had been during the day, and Colin was doing his best to make him comfortable. In the last six weeks, he'd managed two visits, and it was depressing to see the changes in Ray. The breathlessness was getting to be a serious problem, and Colin suspected it wouldn't be long before more medical intervention would be needed.

"In case I... forget to say... thank you." The mask muffled his words, but Colin could make them out.

"For what? Coming to see you?" Colin forced himself to smile, determined to be as positive as he could. "You don't need to thank me for that."

Ray pulled the mask aside. "So... what have you... been doing... since your last... visit?"

Colin gently eased the mask back over his mouth and nose. "Less talking, please. I'll do enough talking for both of us." He shifted on the bed so that he was facing Ray. "I've been putting together a new project. The company has been asked to submit a design for a new government building, and we're really excited about it. London has its fair share of innovative designers, and we want to do something that will really stand out."

Ray smiled. "So proud of you."

Colin took hold of Ray's hand. "Do you remember when we were dating? I used to drag you around so many buildings, and you just went along with it. You had the patience of a saint."

Ray chuckled. "I remember... your reaction... when you saw... the Lowry... and the Imperial... War Museum North."

Colin nodded. "They're amazing!" He and Ray had gone to the opening of the theatre and gallery, not two months after their first date. Then he scowled. "How could they have demolished the Hacienda? I mean, it was a fucking *icon*, for God's sake!"

Ray wheezed out another laugh. "Still talking... about that?... It was over... fourteen years ago.... Give it a rest."

"You have to admit, when it comes to architecture, Manchester has a somewhat chequered portfolio."

Ray grinned. "There's always... Urbis." He closed his eyes.

Colin sighed. "There is." The glass building that had arisen after the IRA bombing in 1996 was still one of his favourites.

It took a moment or two for it to occur to him that Ray's breathing had changed, and he quickly gazed at Ray's chest to check on its rise and fall. When he realized Ray had fallen asleep, Colin gently placed Ray's hand on the bed and got to his feet as carefully as possible. He stood by the bed, gazing down at the sleeping figure, his heart heavy.

Colin knew what was coming, although he did his best not to think too far ahead. The last two times he'd flown to Edinburgh, all the way there he'd felt... leaden. What dispelled that feeling was the obvious happiness he saw in Ray's eyes when Colin walked into the flat. That brief respite was tempered by the knowledge that Colin now had a key: Ray was unable to get up easily and let him in.

It was time to move him.

"Hey."

Ray's whisper pulled him back into the present, back into a world where it hurt to gaze upon what had become of the man he'd once loved.

"Do you need anything?" he asked Ray softly.

To his surprise, Ray blinked back tears, and Colin knelt by the side of the bed. "Hey, what's wrong?"

Ray pulled the mask away from his face just a fraction. "Would... would you hold me... for a minute?"

Hot tears pricked his own eyes, and Colin wiped them away. "Of course." He climbed gingerly onto the bed beside Ray, who leaned on one elbow, waiting for him to settle. Colin sat back against the pillows and held his arm wide. Ray leaned against him, his head on Colin's shoulder. Colin held him gently, aware of his breathing, of how much weight he'd lost, unconsciously comparing with the last time they'd held each other, all those years ago. Then, it had been him in Ray's arms, Ray taking his weight.

Colin closed his eyes and remembered the days when the man in his arms had meant the world to him.

Let me hold him while I can.

He recognized the pattern of his thoughts. *I'm mentally preparing for his death.* He tried to occupy his mind with lists of what would need to be done, and his throat tightened when he realized the first item would be to decide Ray's final journey.

I guess there are some conversations that need to take place.

He knew there was no one else. Ray's parents were dead, and there were no siblings. It grieved him sorely that so few people would mourn him.

Colin knew the day Ray passed, there would be one person who cried.

Colin walked through the glass doors into the Arrivals hall at Gatwick airport, feeling weary and low. It didn't help that all around were smiles of joy as his fellow passengers greeted those who awaited them. What he wouldn't give right then to see Ed's beautiful face, see that familiar smile...

That same familiar smile from the bear of a man who stood near the coffee shop, holding two large cups...

Colin resisted the urge to walk up to Ed and kiss him long and hard, but God help him, that was a tough decision. He walked over to Ed, unable to stop smiling. "What are you doing here?"

Ed's smile was so full of love that it made his heart ache to see it. "Dunno. Something told me you might need a friendly face right now."

Fuck it. Colin ignored the cups, cupped Ed's face between both hands and kissed him, drinking him in. Ed didn't bat an eyelid, but closed his eyes and sighed. When Colin broke the kiss, Ed murmured, "Well, if that don't set tongues waggin' around 'ere, nothin' will." He grinned.

Colin laughed, and *God*, it felt good. "Do you think we might have offended some delicate soul's sensibilities?"

Ed snorted. "Fuck 'em. An' besides, let's face it, these days there are more likely to be more people who get off on seein' two guys kissin'." He waggled his eyebrows. "Thank God for Torchwood, eh?" He handed Colin one of the cups. "Now get that down yer neck, 'coz you won't be able to drink it on the way 'ome."

It took a moment for Ed's words to register. Colin stared. "You came on the Harley?"

Ed grinned. "When's the last time you took a ride on me bike?" He leered. "As opposed to ridin' anything else, of course." He glanced down at Colin's bag. "That'll squash in the box, once I've taken out your 'elmet." He leaned forward and kissed Colin on the lips. "Love ya. So glad you're back. And when we get 'ome, I've got a nice surprise waitin' for ya."

"If it involves cuddling up with you, I'm in." Right then the idea sounded wonderful.

Ed smiled. "There might be a bit of cuddlin' involved. Now drink up."

Colin gave a mock salute. "Yes, sir."

They walked through the airport toward the exit, Colin sipping his coffee. The prospect of a fast ride on the back of the Harley, his arms around Ed's waist, was a pleasant one. Conversation would be non-existent, which was fine by him. He wasn't in the mood to talk, but maybe by the time they reached their home in Sutton, he'd feel differently.

The thought sent a shiver down his spine.

I have Ed. Ray has no one.

Yeah, it wasn't a good thought.

"Are you 'ungry?" Ed opened the fridge and peered inside. "I wasn't sure if you'd 'ave something on the plane."

Colin snorted. "You're kidding, right? Have you seen what's on offer? But to answer your question, I'm not really hungry."

"'Ow about a beer?" Ed stuck his head around the door. "Wine?"

Colin chuckled. "Why, Mr. Fellows, are you trying to get me drunk?"

Ed cackled. "Nah. You're easy. Don't need alcohol to get into *your* boxers." When Colin gave a mock gasp, Ed stared at him. "What—you denyin' it?"

"Enough. I'll have a glass of wine."

Ed pulled out a bottle of white wine, closed the door and studied Colin for a moment. "So, 'ow is he?" He reached into the cabinet for two glasses.

"As you'd expect."

Ed didn't need to be looking at Colin to know his demeanour had changed. He could hear it in Colin's voice. He poured out the wine and shoved the bottle back into the fridge. "'Ad he changed much since the last visit?" Ed handed Colin a glass.

Colin nodded. "He's relying more and more on the oxygen, but I think the pain has increased too. There were some heavy duty pain killers lying around."

"When do you plan on goin' there again?"

Colin took a long drink of wine before answering. "Maybe in a couple of weeks." His eyes had a faraway look in them that Ed didn't get to see that often. It was a look he didn't like very much.

He put down his glass and took Colin's from him. "I think you need to switch off for a while."

Colin sighed. "Easier said than done, at this point." His gaze met Ed's. "I guess I'm having a hard time coming to terms with the fact that he'll be gone before the year is out."

That did it. Ed couldn't stand to see Colin in pain.

"Come with me." He took hold of Colin's hand and led him out of the kitchen and up the stairs.

"A little early for bed, isn't it?" Colin commented dryly.

Ed squeezed his hand. "Time for your surprise." He pushed open their bedroom door and entered, standing aside to let Colin see the bed laid out with towels, the bottle of massage oil warming in a bowl of water, and the oil burner that stood on the bedside cabinet.

Colin sniffed the air. "Okay, you're going to think I'm crazy, but... can I smell custard?"

Ed chuckled. "*That* is Ylang Ylang, an' I'm prob'ly sayin' it all wrong, but I wanna smell it, not pronounce it. The girl in the shop said it was good for relaxin' yer." He sniffed up. "There's a whiff of rose, too."

Colin stilled. "You went shopping for this... for me?"

Ed chuckled. "Yeah, an' I won't be doin' *that* again in an 'urry. I got some right weird looks from some people. You'd think they'd never seen a bloke shoppin' for aromatherapy oils before."

"Maybe not a bloke that's built like you," Colin suggested with a smile, his eyes shining.

That hint of a smile made it worth all the amused glances he'd received.

"Okay, you, get yer kit off." Ed flexed his hands. "An' I'll get the 'ole magic fingers ready."

That got him more than a flash on a smile. Colin snorted. "Always did like what you do with your fingers."

Ed gave him a mock glare. "'Ey. Mind out of the gutter, if you please. I'm about to give you the most professional massage I can manage."

Colin looked suitably abashed. "Right away, Mr. Masseur." He unbuttoned his pale blue shirt down to his waist, and then tugged it out to finish. Ed stepped in to help, unzipping his jeans and kneeling to remove them, along with Colin's socks.

He pointed to Colin's briefs. "Off with them, too. Then lie face down on the bed an' get comfy."

Colin did as instructed. "When did you set up the oil?" he asked as he climbed onto the bed and moved onto the spread towels.

"While you were on the phone to Ray." Ed stripped off his own clothing, and Colin arched his eyebrows. Ed huffed. "What—you want me to get oil on me clothes? I like these jeans." He waited until Colin had lowered his head onto the pillow, and then he straddled Colin's arse. The oil was within his reach, and Colin lay quiescent beneath him. Ed leaned forward to kiss across Colin's shoulder blades. "Now, all I want you to do is switch off yer brain for a bit. There'll be plenty of time for thinkin' tomorrow, an' the day after, an' the day after that. Now is the time for you to let me massage away your cares, if only for a little while." Another soft kiss, this time to Colin's neck. "Ready?"

"Ready." The pillow muffled the word.

Ed opened the bottle and poured out a palm full of oil. After replacing the bottle in the bowl, he rubbed his hands together and proceeded to move them gently over Colin's upper back and shoulders, keeping the movement leisurely and even. He dug his thumbs into the warm flesh, moving them in a circular motion, and was rewarded with a low moan of pleasure.

"Thass' it," he crooned. "Feels good, don't it?"

"You have no idea," Colin said with a sigh. "I love your magic fingers."

Ed chuckled. "An' I've only just gotten started." He worked Colin's shoulder blades, kneading the flesh, careful not to exert too much pressure as he edged lower. Colin appeared to have melted into the mattress, and that was fine by Ed. He pushed hard at the solid muscles above the curve of his arse, using his thumbs again to manipulate the flesh and loosen it.

"God, yes, there," Colin groaned. "So stiff there."

"That's what you get for doin' a lot of sittin' on a plane." Ed applied a little more oil and worked harder, shifting back to dig his fingers into the firm globes. "Playin' rugby is definitely good for your arse."

Colin turned his head to the side and chuckled. "You're biased. You have a thing for my arse. Don't bother denying it."

Ed leaned over him, brushing his lips over Colin's ear. "Never 'eard you complain," he whispered.

Colin clenched his buttocks, pushing against the mattress, and Ed laughed softly. "You got a problem there?"

"You're making me hard," Colin whispered.

Ed lifted his leg over to kneel beside him. "Roll over an' show me." His own dick was already filling. Slowly Colin rolled onto his back, his cock rising into the air, thick and heavy. Colin lifted his head from the pillow to gaze at it, before peering at Ed.

"Well, don't just sit there. Do something."

Ed laughed quietly, before wrapping oil-slick fingers around the stiff shaft, moving them languidly up and down, enjoying the feel of silken skin sliding over a hot core of solid flesh. Colin dropped his head back onto the pillow with a heartfelt moan, and Ed moved a little faster, listening to the change in Colin's breathing. His own cock curved up, hard and wanting, and he tugged at it, smearing precome over the head where the skin was stretched taut and shiny.

"How does this oil do as lube?" Colin asked him, his gaze focused on Ed's face.

Ed caught his breath. "Why don't we find out?" He straddled Colin's groin, reaching back to slide his fingers up and down the slick shaft. With his other hand he rubbed between his cheeks, spreading a little oil over his hole. It had been a week since they'd made love, and he anticipated the burn to come. Gently he guided Colin's dick into position, feeling its heat against his pucker.

Colin locked gazes with him. "Sink down on it. Want to be balls deep inside you."

Ed nodded, feeling the blunt head press against his ring, feeling it stretch him as his hole let him in, as he sank all the way down, until Colin's heat filled him to the hilt. "Oh, Gawd," he moaned, relishing the sensation of being full. He became still, waiting for the burn to fade, waiting to give Colin a sign that he was ready.

Colin's gaze hadn't shifted. "Tell me I can move. Tell me when you're ready," he asked breathlessly.

Ed's breathing sped up, and his heartbeat raced. He leaned forward, until his face was inches from Colin's. Their lips met in a gentle kiss that belied the urgent desire building slowly inside him. "Love you," he whispered.

Colin reached up to caress his cheek. "Love you too." He began to move, tilting his hips to slide in and out of Ed's body. It was a slow motion, so fucking gentle that Ed wanted to say something, to demand that Colin fuck him—until he realized what was happening.

This was no lightning fuck, no desperate, frantic coupling, no race toward orgasm.

This was his lover, his beautiful man, making love to him.

"Oh, yeah," Ed sighed, sitting up and leaning back, his weight on his arms as he lifted himself up and down, shuddering as Colin's long, thick shaft filled him. He reached back to touch it as it slid into him, feeling how his hole was stretched around its girth. Reaching further, he cupped Colin's sac, gently squeezing his balls. Colin's low cries spoke of how much he was loving this.

Ed bent over him to kiss his furry chest, before laying a trail of kisses to his pits, nuzzling there, letting Colin's scent fill his nostrils. "Fuck, you smell good." Colin's hands were on his head and back, stroking him, all the while moving in and out of him at a languid pace, Ed rocking back and forth on that hard cock. Colin cupped his nape and drew him into a kiss, still caressing him, one hand sliding down Ed's body to squeeze his arse.

Their foreheads touched, and Colin closed his eyes. "Love how it feels to be inside you, to feel like we're totally connected."

"We *are* connected." Ed sat up, his hands on Colin's chest, and rocked a little faster. "You're inside me, an' I'm not talkin' about yer dick." He placed over his heart. "You're in 'ere." He touched his temple. "An' 'ere. There's no place I could go to get away from yer, because you never leave me. An' I wouldn't want it any other fuckin' way."

Colin shifted, sitting up, his cock slipping from Ed's body, and kissed Ed's chest while he slid his hands over Ed's arse. He paused and locked gazes with Ed. "I don't tell you enough how much I love you. How glad I am that you're in my life. How happy it makes me to know you're going to be my husband."

"An' that makes those times when you *do* tell me, all the sweeter." Ed held Colin's face between his hands. "You don't 'ave to be forever tellin' me you love me for me to know it." He held up his left hand, where Colin's ring gleamed on his finger. "This tells me. Every single day."

That earned him a kiss, one that started out slow and tender, but then Colin plunged his tongue deep, and Ed groaned into the kiss. Colin parted them and smiled. "Face down."

Ed responded swiftly, lowering himself to the mattress and grabbing hold of its edge. He spread his legs wide and Colin moved to lie between them, guiding his dick between Ed's cheeks to penetrate him once more. Colin slid his arms beneath Ed's body, anchoring himself, and began to rock into him, gently at first, but then building momentum, until loud moans poured from bother of them. The only sound in the room was their combined breaths, harsh and erratic, as Colin pushed into him, driving his cock deep into Ed's channel.

"Gawd, yeah." Ed pushed back against him, the two of them moving together, keeping pace. Colin sank all the way into him and Ed bucked beneath him, rising to meet each thrust, until his balls tightened and he knew they were there.

Colin grabbed hold of his waist and held on as he rose to his knees, bringing Ed with him, his dick still wedged inside him. Ed groaned as Colin reached around him to grasp his cock, tugging it, working it, all the while sliding into him, one hand gripping Ed's hip.

"Now," Ed gasped as he came, body shaking, his dick sending out creamy ropes of spunk over the sheet. Colin kissed his neck and shoulders, his hips still moving, only now more erratically. "Come on, Col. Wanna feel you come."

Colin gave a harsh groan and thrust deep, his fingers digging into the fleshy part of Ed's hip. He shivered, his body tight against Ed's, every ripple through him easily discernible.

They knelt like that for a while, Colin's arms wrapped around Ed's waist and chest, the pair of them locked together while their mutual orgasms melted away. Ed turned his head for the kiss he knew awaited him, and Colin's lips met his, warm and soft. "It's a good thing you're 'oldin' me up," Ed said with a chuckle. "I'm as limp as a wet rag."

Colin kissed his neck and trailed his fingers over Ed's nipples, making him shudder. "And I'm hungry."

Ed laughed. "Well, you won't get fed if you don't take yer cock out of me arse."

Colin eased out of him, and as always, Ed felt its loss instantly, as if part of him was no longer there. He shuffled on the bed until they faced each other, and pulled Colin into his arms, holding him close.

"We have all night to hold each other," Colin whispered. The loud grumbling of his stomach was a comical addition to the statement.

Ed gave him one last kiss on the lips. "I'm gonna 'old you to that."

A night of snuggling on the couch sounded perfect. Just what both of them needed.

Chapter Twenty-Two

July 1ˢᵗ

"Hey, time for a break," Blake called from the kitchen. "Lunch is nearly ready."

Will saved his work and then stretched his arms up high above his head. The book was progressing well—at least, that was what Blake told him. Much as Will loved his husband, he was more inclined to listen to his beta readers, who were also reading it chapter by chapter. He knew Blake would always tell him if something stank, but he *was* inclined to be a little blinkered sometimes. His betas always shot from the hip. They loved his books, but they told him what he *needed* to hear, not necessarily what he wanted to hear. Will had no time for readers who told him everything he wrote was 'lovely': he wanted readers who could be honest with him, even if the truth hurt.

He closed the file and then got up from his desk. "Are you going to try again?" Two days previously they'd given Nathan his first taste of pureed vegetables, mixed with a little formula. Judging by the look on his face, Nathan hadn't been impressed.

When he got to the kitchen, Nathan was already in his high chair, waving his little arms at Blake, who was stirring something in a bowl. Will sat at the table next to Nathan and kissed his head. "So what's he having this time?"

"Pureed sweet potatoes." Blake filled the small plastic spoon and then held it up to Nathan. "You'll like this, sweetheart." He ate the puree, smiling the whole time. "Actually, this tastes really good. It reminds me of that roasted sweet potato soup you make—you know, the one so thick you can stand a spoon upright in it?" Blake grinned, before taking another mouthful.

"Hey, it's Nathan's lunch you're eating," Will protested.

"There's plenty. And besides, watch him when I eat."

Will watched the way Nathan's eyes followed Blake's every move.

"See that?" Blake gazed at their little boy, his blue eyes warm. "Remember how Sophie used to try and steal the spoon from us when we did this?"

"Especially if it was pureed fruit," Will added, smiling. After two or three more mouthfuls, Nathan was gesturing toward the spoon, his forehead creased. "Better give him some, Blake." When Nathan slapped his hands on the plastic tray in front of him, Will laughed. "I think that was Nathan-speak for 'Feed me, Papa!'" A wave of sorrow overtook him, and his throat tightened.

"Babe? What is it?"

He should have known Blake's eyes missed nothing.

Will got up from the table and went over to the sink to pour himself a glass of water. He took a long drink before facing Blake, making an effort to appear normal. "It's nothing." He forced a smile. "Now feed our ravenous little boy."

Blake quirked his eyebrows. "One, he's hardly ravenous, and two—and a far more important point in my book—why are you lying to me?" He held the spoon to Nathan's lips, a faint smile crossing his face when Nathan sucked it into his mouth, making a cute little noise. "I think sweet potato gets the thumbs up." He raised his chin to regard Will. "I've put a quiche in the oven for us. If you could rustle up a salad, that would be good."

Will nodded, relieved to have something with which to occupy himself. "Sure." He went over to the fridge and pulled out all the ingredients. As he tore off handfuls of lettuce and dropped them into a glass bowl, he tried to push aside his earlier reflections, hoping that Blake would forget whatever it was he thought he'd seen in Will's expression.

Yeah, right.

"So, are you going to tell me what's wrong?" Blake spoke quietly.

Will closed his eyes, his fingers wrapped around the knife handle. The ache in his heart was still there, try as he might to escape its reality. "Sometimes I forget," he said softly.

Blake remained silent for a moment, and the only sounds in the room were the whirr of the electric oven and Nathan's low hums of appreciation as he ate. "Don't stop," Blake urged him at last.

Will swallowed. "I wake up some mornings and I go into Nathan's room. I stand there, staring at him while he sleeps, and he's so fucking beautiful it makes me ache inside. I see the mobile hanging above his cot, and I stretch out my hand to turn it on, so it can play that little tune. Because I've forgotten that Nathan can't hear it." He opened his eyes and stared out at the garden beyond. "How can I forget that? And then it all comes flooding back, and I remember that I have to smile and let him see my face. I think about the months to come, and how I'll have to start using signs for things like milk and eat and sleep, and..." He ground to a halt, unable to get out another word.

Blake's soft sigh brought him back into the kitchen, into the present.

"It isn't easy, is it? To think of him as being normal? I know, babe, believe me."

Slowly Will turned to face him, shocked to see Blake's eyes glistening.

Blake looked from Will to Nathan. "Sometimes I just want to forget what's coming and simply enjoy him as a baby."

Relief crashed through Will, and he nodded, his eyes wide. "Yes. Oh God, exactly." He strode across the kitchen to stand behind Blake's chair, bent over and wrapped his arms around Blake, crossing them over his chest, his face buried in Blake's neck. "I just feel like I should be doing something every day to get ready, whether it's learning to sign, or reading up on how to communicate with a deaf child, or listening to experts... Just... something."

Blake's hand covered his. "And the next time you feel like that, you tell me, okay? Because we are *both* in this—together. And there's Sophie, and Ed and Colin, and Rick and Angelo, Lizzie and Dave, Peter.... Fuck, babe, there are so many of our friends who want to be a part of this little boy's life." Blake grasped Will's hand and brought it to his lips, kissing his fingers. "We can do this, Will. You got that? We *can do* this, but only if we work together." He locked gazes with Will. "You're my strength, sweetheart. You're my sanctuary, my refuge, but it works both ways. I'm all those things and more—for you."

Nathan let out a gurgle that made them jump. Blake laughed and wiped his eyes. "And *that* was Nathan-speak for 'Why has the food stopped, Papa and Daddy?'

"Let me feed him?" Will asked. "You can finish the salad."

"Okay." Blake handed him the spoon and gave up his chair. Will sat down, before scooping up some of the puree. As he chugged it toward Nathan, like a little train, Will opened his mouth wide, trying not to laugh when Nathan copied him. "Good boy," he praised as Nathan emptied the spoon. He smiled broadly, and Nathan's smile matched his.

Will glanced at Blake, who stood watching them. "He's going to be a fast learner."

Blake nodded slowly. "And we'll be ready for him."

Will regarded their son. "Yes, we will."

Of that, he was suddenly in no doubt.

"So everything is moving along swimmingly?" Franco helped himself to another glass of water. "Venue sorted, cake ordered, suits bought, rings bought—"

"Oh fuck," Rick said weakly. He gaped at Angelo across the dining table. "I knew there was something we'd—"

"Will you relax?" Angelo rolled his eyes. "They're ordered. They just need picking up. Don't you remember? I told you I'd take care of that."

"You did?" Rick shook his head. "This wedding is addling my brain."

Franco chuckled. "As long as you remember to turn up on the right day, everything will be fine."

Angelo laughed. "Seeing as there'll be none of this 'not seeing the groom before the wedding because it's bad luck' crap, I'll make sure of it."

Franco tut-tutted. "Oh, now, I can't say I approve. After all, you're both virgins, right?" He gazed at them innocently, before bursting into laughter when they stared at him. "Relax, you two. I have no such illusions about either of you."

Rick snorted and Angelo fired him a warning look. "You wouldn't be reacting like that if Mum was here. You're a virgin, I'm a virgin, remember?"

Franco widened his eyes. "Surely she can't believe that. I mean, you're nearly forty. What does she think—you have separate bedrooms? You don't have sex?"

Angelo huffed. "To be honest, I have no idea what she thinks, and I have no desire to find out." He shuddered. "I mean, come on. Did you like discussing sex with *your* mother?"

Franco stilled. "Actually, I was the one to bring up the subject. Not one of my better ideas, as it turned out." He shrugged. "But that was a long time ago." Then he grinned. "And I still have the scars." He gave an exaggerated shudder, and Angelo laughed.

"It must be difficult doing your job sometimes," Rick interjected. When Franco gave him an inquiring glance, he continued. "You must hear a lot of prisoners talking about all kinds of things, and I'm pretty sure sex is on the list of topics."

"Why must that be difficult?" Franco asked, a slight frown creasing his forehead.

"Well, you being celibate."

Franco chuckled. "I may be celibate, but that doesn't mean I'm a complete innocent." When Rick stared at him, he laughed. "What is it, Rick? An ex-priest who is also a sexual being is not dreamed of in your philosophy?"

Rick flushed. "I'm sorry. I guess I shouldn't make assumptions."

Franco's smile was gentle. "No need to apologize. You're not the first to do so, and I doubt you'll be the last. And to answer the question you didn't quite get around to asking me, yes, the men I work with do tend to talk a lot about sex. Sometimes I think they try to shock me, others because it's a release for them. I sit there and listen, and try not to react, but sometimes I admit it is difficult." He cleared his throat. "Enough about me. Everything is going well?"

"It is," Angelo assured him. He was finally beginning to see the light at the end of the tunnel. "And we really must thank you for putting us onto Anthony. That man is a godsend." Suddenly the word seemed inappropriate. "If you get my meaning," he hastened to add.

Franco's gentle smile didn't alter. "On the contrary, I think it's the perfect word for him. Though there are occasions when I wonder exactly what God's purpose was in letting our paths cross after so many years."

"Isn't God sharing that titbit?" Rick teased.

To Angelo's surprise, Franco's smile faltered. "Let's just say he's keeping quiet on this one."

Angelo wasn't sure what to make of the enigmatic reply. "Well, he certainly charmed Mum. She must have mentioned him at least twice in recent calls."

Rick snickered. "If it wasn't for the fact that you're marrying me in—" He consulted his phone. "—forty-eight days, I might be concerned that she had designs on setting you up with him." He gave Angelo a mock glare. "So don't go getting any ideas, okay? He might be hot but you're all mine."

Angelo laughed. "I think you're safe. I have my hands full with you." He gave Franco an apologetic glance. "Sorry about that. Rick's first impression of Anthony was definitely X-rated."

Franco raised his eyebrows. "I'll be sure to pass that along. But Rick will have to join the queue. There are quite a few men interested in Mr. Calderfield."

Rick gave a low whistle. "Damn. My gaydar is apparently working just fine."

"And here we go again, off on a tangent." Franco gave them a hard stare. "Do you two always get distracted by sex?"

Angelo snorted. "Only if there's a y in the day." Then he sighed. "My apologies. You came to dinner so we could finalize the ceremony, and all we've done is distract you."

"Again, no apologies needed." Franco gave them an amused glance. "Although I should point out that as hosts, you leave a lot to be desired. There was some mention of coffee, I believe?" He winked and glanced pointedly at his watch. "That was only half an hour ago."

"Oops." Rick got up from the table. "You two talk ceremony, I'll go make the coffee." As he passed behind Angelo's chair, he kissed the top of his head. "No more distracting our guest, you." He darted out of reach before Angelo could smack him.

Franco laughed. "I always enjoy coming here. You are a very entertaining couple."

Angelo was glad of the chance to be alone with him. "I promise not to distract you anymore, but to be honest, I think you arrived here in that state. And when I come to think about it, you were pretty much the same your last visit. Is everything okay?" Franco was a genuinely nice guy, and Angelo got the impression he had something on his mind. "I mean, if there's something you want to get off your chest, we're good listeners."

Franco bowed his head for a moment, and Angelo was dismayed at the aura of sadness that seemed to cling to him. When he raised his chin, however, his eyes were calm. "You're a good man, Angelo. I am so glad we met, and even happier that I was instrumental in bringing you and Rick together. And I promise you, if I ever have need of your advice, I *will* ask." Then he smiled. "So, have you given any thought to the music you'd like played as you enter? What about best men? I'm assuming you both want someone to stand with you?"

"Glad you brought that up," Rick said as he entered the room, carrying a tray laden with coffee pot, milk jug, sugar bowl, cups, and a plate of *biscotti*. "We've been talking about that very thing."

Angelo smiled. "Rick wants to ask his friend, Will. I can't see him saying no, as both he, his husband and their two children will be at the wedding anyway. But my choice is a little... different."

Franco's eyes sparkled. "I'm sure Maria will say yes in a heartbeat."

Angelo gaped. "How did you know I was thinking of my sister?"

Franco laughed. "Knowing how close the two of you are? It was the obvious choice." He folded his arms across his wide chest. "Well, that was easy. What about the music? We need to think about hymns. It's traditional to have them during the service."

"No hymns," Rick said in a firm voice. Angelo glanced across at him, and Rick shook his head. "And don't you look at me like that. I don't care if it upsets Elena. I'm not budging on this one."

"Hey, I'm with you on this, remember?" Angelo kept his tone soothing. "But I do like the idea of some music during the ceremony."

"Fine," Rick said emphatically. "Then we find a friend who can sing, give them a couple of songs that actually mean something to us, and voilà. I'd much rather that, than have everyone singing along to something just for the sake of it."

"You're not getting married in a church," Franco reminded them. "The ceremony is pretty much what you wish to make of it. As long as the legalities are met, you can do whatever you want." He grinned. "Within reason."

Angelo guffawed. "Don't look so worried. We're not about to do anything that would embarrass my mum, not after all the effort she's put into making this wedding perfect."

"There's something else we have to talk to you about," Rick said. "But it can wait until after the coffee."

"That sounds mysterious." Franco regarded him quizzically. "Something important?"

"Let's just say there's one other detail we need to tell you about," Angelo said with a smile. He glanced at Rick. "Forty-eight days? Really?"

"I have a countdown app on my phone." Rick got up and came across to sit on Angelo's lap, his arms looped around his neck. "August the nineteenth will be here before we know it."

Angelo kissed him and wrapped his arms around Rick's waist. "Then we'd better make sure we're ready for it." He looked into Rick's eyes. "Still sure you want to marry me?" he joked. "There's still time to change your mind. After all, there's always Anthony." He waggled his eyebrows.

Rick laughed softly. "I think I'll take my chances with you. Besides, I've already invested several years in training you to get you just the way I like you. Do you think I'm likely to chuck that all away over a hot guy?"

Angelo gave him a mock glare. "*Trained* me?"

Rick slid off his knee and made a run for the kitchen. "Franco, tell him how bad it will look if I'm hobbling on crutches at my own wedding!" he called out.

Franco laughed. "I'm staying out of this."

Angelo joined in with his laughter. "I always said you were a very wise man." He picked up the coffee pot and held it out to Franco. "Coffee?"

Franco proffered his cup. "You're not going to take revenge?"

Angelo snickered. "He'll keep. After all, I know where he sleeps."

Chapter Twenty-Three

July 14th

Colin disconnected the call and placed his phone on the coffee table. *Disconnected. An apt word for how I feel right now.* He'd known it was coming, of course, but anticipating the event and actually having it happen were two very different animals. He felt detached somehow, clinically observing it all take place, as if from a distance.

"Col?"

He gave a start. "Christ."

Ed sat beside him. "I brought you a coffee," he said, pointing to the mug. "Wasn't sure if you 'eard me come in. You looked miles away."

"That's probably because I was," Colin admitted. He sank back against the cushions. "That was Kelly, Ray's nurse, on the phone."

"Oh Gawd. Is he...?"

Colin shook his head. "Not yet. She was calling to let me know he's in a hospice. They moved him there this morning." He picked up the mug, glad to have something to do with his hands. That disconnected sensation was still with him.

"In Edinburgh?"

Colin nodded. "He's in a Marie Curie hospice. It's not a big place, according to Kelly. There are only twenty-five beds. She also says visiting hours are flexible." His phone pinged the arrival of a text. "That'll be from her. She was going to send me the contact details for them." He sipped his coffee, his mind already going over flight times. The mental distraction was a blessing right then. Anything not to have to think about Ray...

It took him a moment to realize Ed was no longer sitting beside him.

Hell. Distracted was one thing—fucking *oblivious* was another.

To his relief, Ed came back into the lounge, Colin's laptop bag in his hands. He handed it over, and Colin gazed at him inquiringly.

Ed did an eye roll. "I'm not stupid. You wanna book a flight, right? 'Cause I assume you're goin' to see 'im." He flopped down onto the couch and reached for his coffee.

Colin put the bag aside and stopped him in mid action. He kissed Ed on the mouth, wishing the simple kiss could convey just how much he loved this man. Ed made a soft noise, before shifting closer to hold the back of Colin's head, deepening the kiss. When they parted, Ed didn't let go.

"Listen," he said quietly. "I know this prob'ly feels like a shit deal right now, but you don't 'ave to go through this on yer own."

Colin kissed his forehead. "I'm glad I have you to come home to."

Ed straightened, his hand falling to his lap. "See, thass' what I wanted to talk to you about." He met Colin's gaze. "Let me come with ya."

"What?" Colin frowned. "Why would you want to put yourself through that?"

Ed widened his eyes. "Oh, so it's all right for *you* to go back an' forth to bleedin' *Scotland* every couple o' weeks, but not for me to come with ya one time?"

Colin took a deep breath. "You've never met Ray. You're never going to, at this rate. And if you do, you'll be seeing—"

"Someone who loved ya," Ed interrupted. "Ray cared for ya. That makes 'im worth a visit, right? An' besides, I'd rather be at yer side, supportin' ya, givin' you someone to 'old onto when you need it, instead of waitin' 'ere, wond'rin' what the 'ell you're goin' through." He cocked his head to one side. "You gonna turn me or that offer down?"

A wave of fatigue rolled over him, and Colin sagged back once more. "Sounds like I'd be a fool to refuse, doesn't it?"

Ed leaned in, his warm eyes focused on Colin's. "Like I said, no one says you 'ave to do this on yer own. An' I wanna do this, Col. Don't shut me out, please."

Colin's throat seized up and he swallowed, but his mouth was dry. He hurriedly drank some coffee, grateful for the liquid. He couldn't ignore Ed's plea.

"We'll need to book a hotel for the night. I don't want to go there and back in a day."

Ed nodded. "Then we'll fly up there on Saturday, an' come back Sunday. I'll book us somewhere near the 'ospice, shall I?"

Colin shook his head. "If we're going to do this, find us somewhere in the city centre. Where there's noise, and light, and—"

"An' distraction," Ed finished for him. "I gotcha."

In that moment Colin truly knew he did. He opened up the laptop and switched it on. "I'll get going on the flights then."

Ed got out his phone. "An' I'll search for an 'otel."

Colin laid his hand on Ed's arm. "Thanks. I'm just sorry you're getting to meet him in these circumstances."

"I figured it would do 'im good to see another friendly face." Ed smiled. "An' I'll be sure to share lots of stories about you."

"Oh God," Colin groaned. But even as he pondered what on earth Ed would find to tell Ray, he couldn't help but be thankful that he'd be there at Colin's side.

Because I really need him now.

"When did you last see Ray?" Julie, the Staff Nurse asked them. The three of them were seated in her small office, and from beyond her door came the low hum of voices. She'd met him and Ed at the reception desk.

Colin did a swift mental calculation, and realized to his horror that he'd stayed away longer than he'd intended. "Nearly four weeks."

She nodded, her face kind. "I'm asking because if it wasn't a recent visit, then I need to prepare you. Since he arrived two days ago, we've had to intervene medically."

Colin became aware of Ed's hand at his lower back, a comforting touch.

"What does that mean?" Ed asked.

"We had to insert a tube into his chest to drain off the excessive fluid that was causing his breathlessness. If we don't see a significant improvement, then we may have to consider laser treatments to open up the blocked airways." She paused for a moment, studying Colin's face. "Helping relieve Ray's shortness of breath and his pain is the first step we often take with patients who have lung cancer, but there are other needs that we must address too. We have to treat his anxiety and nausea. Plus there are other physical symptoms related to AIDS that have to be taken into account."

"Is he in a lot of pain?" Colin's chest tightened as an iron hand squeezed his heart. It sounded as though Ray's condition had worsened considerably.

"His pain management regimen includes anti-inflammatory medications and opioids. We try to encourage patients to participate in determining doses of the pain meds, because the amount needed to block the pain will vary from day to day."

"Is he awake?" Ed asked.

She hesitated. "Yes, although we've been giving him medication to help him sleep. That's normal at this stage. The lack of sleep, combined with anxiety, often leads to depression, and this is the case for Ray. We're treating that too."

"You said other physical symptoms." Colin didn't want Ray to see his and Ed's reactions if they were surprised or shocked by his appearance.

She nodded. "There are a few lesions on his face and neck. He's developed Kaposi's sarcoma, which again is often seen in late stage AIDS patients. And he now has a catheter." Another pause, and this time she leaned forward, her voice gentle. "He knows you're here. We told him when you called us. What you must prepare for is Ray's changed mental state."

The hand around Colin's heart became like ice. "Okay," he said slowly.

"Ray is starting to shows signs of having trouble concentrating and thinking. And you may see evidence of mood swings."

"'Ow much longer does he 'ave?"

Colin was grateful for the touch of Ed's hand right then.

Julie was silent for a moment. "It might be three weeks, or closer to six. But no longer than that." She addressed Colin. "Do you want us to call you when his condition deteriorates? We would understand if you couldn't be here, given where you live. But if we think there's the possibility that you could make it here before he passes, do you want to be told?"

Colin's face tingled and he had difficulty swallowing past the lump in his throat. He wanted to say *No*, that he didn't want to be at Ray's side when he shuffled off this mortal coil, but he couldn't. Not when he knew beyond a doubt that Ray had no one.

"Call me," he said at last.

Julie nodded, her eyes warm and so kind. "I'll make a note of it. Would you like to see Ray now?"

There it was again, that knee-jerk reaction to flee, to say *no*, he didn't want to see what the last four weeks had reduced Ray to. He took a couple of deep, calming breaths, before meeting Julie's gaze. "Yes, please."

"We're *both* gonna see 'im," Ed confirmed, his hand slipping around Colin's.

Julie smiled. "It will do him good to see some friendly faces. I understand he's been on his own a lot." She got up from her chair, they did the same, and then she led them out of the office and along a long corridor. "Ray's room overlooks the garden," she told them as they walked. "It's a peaceful spot, and sometimes there are red squirrels in the trees." She stopped at a door. "I'll come in with you and see if he needs anything, then I'll leave you alone. Would you like some tea? I can have some brought to you."

"If there's any coffee goin', that would be great." Ed gave her a grateful smile.

"Sure." She pushed open the door and entered the room with them following her.

Colin fought the urge to weep at the sight that met his eyes. Ray was propped up in bed, with various tubes emerging from beneath his gown, and an air mask over his nose and mouth. An IV stand was beside the bed, and on a small table sat a heart monitor, along with a small grey console, from which came a long cable that ended in a fat plug with a button on top. Connected to the box was a plastic container, and Colin figured this was the infusion pump that delivered Ray's pain relief. The plug lay on Ray's bed within reach.

Ray turned his head carefully as they approached him. His faint smile lifted Colin's spirits a little. "Hey," he said weakly, the sound muffled by the mask. His brow furrowed when he saw Ed. "Do... do I know you?"

Ed stepped forward and grasped his hand that lay on top of the covers. "Nah, mate. I'm Ed, Colin's other 'alf." He winked at Colin. "His better 'alf."

When Ray let out a little chuckle, Colin thanked God for Ed. *I should trust his instincts more.*

He joined Ed and squeezed Ray's shoulder. "I leave you alone for five minutes and you go and get yourself a room with a view of squirrels."

Ray smiled. "Little buggers are always running around out there." He sounded better, less breathless. "So... how did you two meet?" He pointed a finger at Colin. "This one told me a little, but I figured he was being economical with the truth."

Ed sat on the bed, and Colin took the high backed chair beside it. Ed grinned. "Well, I'm not surprised. He took advantage of me after plyin' me with copious amounts of alcohol."

Colin gasped dramatically. "It's a lie."

Ed fixed him with a hard stare. "That *was* you, right, on me couch? I 'ave one thing to say to you—leather boot lace." He gave Colin an evil grin.

Ray chuckled. "Oh my God, the mind boggles." He regarded Colin with a smile. "I like him."

Colin gazed with love at Ed. "I'm pretty fond of him too."

For the next hour they sat with Ray, chatting, although he and Ed did most of the talking. Ray appeared to be concentrating, and Colin was glad of that. They drank coffee and helped Ray drink his water through a straw. When Ray asked them what day it was, that was the first indication that he was tiring.

Julie came in to do her checks. "Why don't you two go and have some lunch while Ray has a nap? The Stable Bar pub is right around the corner, and they serve good food." She smiled. "You need a break too."

Ed patted Colin's arm. "Sounds like a plan. Come on, I'm buyin'."

Julie chuckled. "Can't say fairer than that, can you? Get in there before he changes his mind. My other half always manages to leave her purse at home. It's obviously a gift." She left them after changing Ray's urine bag. Ray had already fallen into a light sleep.

Once they were outside the hospice, Colin inhaled deeply, and Ed put his arm around him.

"She's right. You need a break. We were both up bleedin' early this mornin' to get to the airport. Let's go find this pub, 'ave somethin' to eat, an' then we can go back later an' see Ray again." His gaze met Colin's. "It's my turn to take care of you."

He looks knackered.

Ed knew it was more than just the early start. Ray's condition was clearly weighing heavily on Colin. One look at him as he sat at their table, his eyes so far away, and all Ed wanted was to get him as far away as possible from Edinburgh and its associations.

Colin rose to his feet. "I need to find the bathroom." He pushed back his chair and went in search of it.

Ed put his head in his hands, his elbows on the table. He'd done his best to remain positive, because that was what Colin needed right then, but *fuck*, he was tired. He'd slept badly the previous night, and all he wanted was a long, hot shower, preferably with Colin in there with him. He'd knead away Colin's tension with a good rubdown.

Ed pulled his phone after checking there was no sign of Colin returning imminently. He scrolled through to Rick's number. "Hey. You got a minute?"

"Sure. I'm only doing the laundry. Angelo's in his workshop. What's up?"

"I've only got a sec. I'm just checkin' that everything's in order." He kept his eyes peeled the whole time.

Rick chuckled. "Stop panicking. Everything's fine. I've sent you an e-mail with the details, okay? Now go back to enjoying your weekend."

Ed sighed. "I wish. Not that kind of a weekend."

There was a pause. "Are you okay?"

"Not really, but it's a long story. Go back to washin' yer smalls."

"See, this is why we all love you," Rick said with a chuckle. "For your way with words. See you Monday." He disconnected.

It was perfect timing. Colin came into view, and Ed hastily stuffed his phone back into his jeans pocket.

"Have you ordered yet?" Colin asked him.

"Nah, I was waitin' for you." He handed Colin the large laminated menu. "See what you feel like. An' don't tell me you're not 'ungry, because you're gonna eat anyway."

Colin shook his head. "You meant what you said about taking care of me."

"Always." Ed forced a smile. "Now, what do ya fancy?" He studied Colin as his lover perused the menu. *I would do anything to take this from you.* All he could do for now was to be there for Colin.

*   *   *

"That better?" Ed asked him as they held each other in the middle of an extremely comfortable king bed.

"Much." Colin's head still buzzed pleasantly from the wine with dinner, but he had an idea that was all part of Ed's plan to make Colin feel boneless and relaxed. The shower had been the first clue. Colin had been rubbed and pummelled until all his tension had bled away, down the drain with the swirling water. The feel of Ed's body curved around him, that wide, furry chest pressed against his back, those strong arms holding him, supporting him... Sheer bliss.

There was also the magic of Ed's tongue, which had caused more than a few cries of pleasure to rebound around the bathroom.

Dinner had been delicious, but this was what he'd looked forward to all day—the moment when the world was outside their bedroom door, the bolt drawn, and it was just the two of them.

He closed his eyes, not surprised when Ray came instantly to mind. The second half of their visit had provided a glimpse of reality.

"You're thinkin' about 'im, aren't ya?"

Colin sighed. There was little point in trying to hide it. Ed knew him too well, not that Colin would change that for the world. It comforted him that he lay in the arms of a man who truly knew him, understood him, balls to bones.

"I was thinking about when we got back after lunch. He didn't know where he was. And for a minute, I got the impression he didn't know me."

Ed's arms tightened around him. "Julie mentioned that, though. She said he can get confused."

Colin sighed again. "You can say that again. He didn't know if he was on this earth or Fullers."

Ed arched his eyebrows. "What the 'ell does that mean?"

Colin snickered. "Oh dear. I forgot I'm talking to a Cockney sparrow. That's something my grandmother used to say when I was little. She came from Yorkshire, I think. Anyway, Fuller's Earth was a type of clay they used to spread over floors to absorb oil and grease in environments such as garages."

"Ah." Ed nodded. "So a wise men would know which earth he was standin' on." He peered at Colin. "You don't talk like you come from up North. I mean, I knew you did, but there's no trace of it in your accent."

He laughed. "Thank you. That would please my mother immensely. She put me through grammar school for precisely that purpose."

Ed stroked up and down his arm, a languid, sleep-inducing motion that lulled him into a warm state of contentment. "Do you know 'ow often we've talked about your family in the last four years?"

Colin snorted. "I'm going to go with *never*." Ed had asked the usual new couple questions when they'd first got together, but Colin hadn't given much away. Eventually Ed had gotten the message: *don't ask about Colin's family.*

When Ed fell silent, Colin realized that he couldn't keep him in the dark for ever. It wasn't fair, not if they planned to marry. Because *wedding* implied *family*.

"There's not much to tell. Just the usual story of parents who weren't happy with their son's life choices. Let's leave it at that." He didn't want to think about them. Such thoughts always left a sour taste in his mouth.

Another moment of silence. "Do they know you're engaged? I feel stupid askin' ya, to be honest, because I feel it's somethin' I should know about the man I share me life with."

Colin heard the hint of rebuke, and his stomach clenched. Ed had a point.

He took a deep breath. "I'm sorry. You're right, of course. I should have told you all of this a long time ago. After all, I know everything about your family."

It was Ed's turn to snort. "Only because I'm like an open book. I don't hide anythin'. I can talk about the ins and outs of a cat's arse."

In spite of his heavy heart. Colin had to chuckle. "And you say *I* come out with funny phrases?"

"Don't change the subject."

Colin huffed. "I wrote them a letter, telling them all about it. I didn't want them to find out somehow and use it as an excuse for more unpleasantness."

"What did they say?"

Colin shifted until he was on top of Ed, gazing down at him. "I wouldn't know, because they never replied. *Now* can we change the subject?" He brought his lips to Ed's in a lingering kiss.

Ed reached up to stroke his cheek. "Any particular topic you'd like?"

Colin leaned into his touch. "I don't want to talk about Ray, because right now, it feels too... raw. I just want all the thoughts in my head to shut the fuck up for one night."

Ed nodded. "I can 'elp with that." He wrapped his arms around Colin's body and gently rolled them both until Colin lay beneath him.

Colin let out his breath in a long exhale. "Yes. Let's make love."

Then Ed's lips were on his once more, and that was just perfect.

Chapter Twenty-Four

August 6th

"Blimey, this looks different!" Ed stared at the garden, beaming. "'Ow did you find time to write *an'* do all this?" He gazed around them at the patio, done in warm terracotta tiles that seemed to soak up the sun. The table and six chairs were perfect for long summer days.

Blake had to admit, the garden did look good. The lawn was smooth, and the air was permeated with subtle perfumes from the flowers that filled the beds around it. From one corner came the musical trickle of water, and in various spots dotted here and there were places to sit and look and contemplate.

He'd been doing a lot of contemplating recently.

Will snorted. "There's this wonderful new invention. It's called the Internet. And when you type 'gardeners near me', all these names start appearing on the screen."

Blake whacked him on the arm. "You're supposed to lie and say it was all our hard work. Have you learned *nothing* from me all these years?" He grinned.

"That is really cute," Angelo said, pointing to the lawn where Nathan was sitting on a blanket under a dark green canopy stretched out between four poles. Rick was under there with him, not to mention a large assortment of Nathan's toys. Judging by the laughter that filtered across the grass, Rick was busy entertaining Nathan.

"Have you noticed?" Will said proudly. "He's sitting up on his own."

Blake chuckled. "I hate to break it to you, but if you haven't got kids, a baby sitting upright for the first time is not the thrill you think it might be." Angelo snickered. Blake scanned the garden for Sophie, and caught sight of her at the far end, walking with Colin while she watered the flowers with her own little green watering can, decorated with ladybirds. She appeared to be doing all the talking.

"Is Colin all right?" He'd seemed quiet when he and Ed had arrived.

Ed followed his gaze to where Colin stood. "Not really." His face tightened.

Will poured a glass of punch and handed it to him. "Is everything okay with you two?"

Ed didn't reply straight away, but took a sip of his drink. "This is nice." He relaxed into his chair. "To be honest, when you first called to ask us round for lunch, I think Col was gonna refuse. I told 'im this was just what he needed. A couple of hours with friends, when he doesn't 'ave to think about... " He sighed heavily. "I know what's goin' on. When he's at work, his mind is occupied, but when he gets 'ome, it's another matter." He regarded the three of them. "We're expectin' a call any day now, tellin' us that either Ray's not got long left, or that he's already passed on. I think once that 'appens, things will get back to normal." His gaze flickered back to Colin. "He can put it behind 'im."

"Is the hospice nice?" Will stilled. "That doesn't sound right, but you know what I mean."

Ed nodded. "They seem like a nice bunch of people, an' it's good that Ray's not on 'is own anymore." He cleared his throat and then took another drink. "Anyway, enough maudlin talk." He peered at Angelo. "Less than two weeks to go, mate. You ready to put on the ol' ball an' chain?" He winked.

Angelo laughed. "Don't let Rick hear you say that."

"Say what?" Rick was walking toward the table, Nathan in his arms. He held him out gingerly to Will. "I think you need to deal with this young man," he said, wrinkling his nose.

Will cackled. Nathan held out his arms to Will, who took him, smiling widely. "Aw. Don't you want to change his nappy?"

Rick's eyes opened wide. "No, I bloody don't." He shuddered. "Ugh. Baby poo. That's stuff's part toxic waste, part Velcro—it sticks to everything."

Angelo and Blake guffawed.

"I'll be right back," Will said as he walked toward the French doors with Nathan in his arms.

"Have you two discussed kids? Because it doesn't sound to me like Rick is all that keen." Blake grinned.

Rick's eyes met Angelo's, who shrugged. "Go ahead."

Rick joined them at the table and helped himself to punch. "As it happens, we *have* talked about this. We'd like to adopt. And we don't mind if it's a baby or a little kid. As long as we can give them a happy home, that's all we want."

Blake nodded. "I think that's wonderful. Heaven knows there are enough children in the UK who need a family. Any kid who gets you two will be very lucky."

"Papa!" Sophie came running across the garden, waving her watering can in the air, Colin walking behind her at a more sedate pace. "Me and Uncle Colin found a snake!"

Colin smiled. "Not exactly. It's a slow worm." He held out his hands, bending over so that Sophie could see it again. "I think this one is a girl, Sophie. See that dark stripe down its back?" He held it gently, letting it undulate over his fingers. "She'll be getting ready to sleep for the winter soon. Isn't she pretty?"

"Can I touch her?" Sophie pleaded.

"Okay, but stroke her gently with one finger." Sophie did as instructed, her gaze locked on the smooth-skinned, golden-grey lizard. She turned to Blake with a wide-eyed stare. "She's not slimy at all, Papa."

Colin laughed. "Lizards aren't slimy. Neither are snakes." He lifted his chin to regard Blake. "She was sunning herself on that pile of logs over in the far corner. I take it you put them there deliberately, as part of the habitat?"

Blake nodded. "How come you know so much about slow worms?"

Colin gave him a sad smile. "Someone I know was really into nature and making his garden a haven for all kinds of wildlife."

Blake hazarded a guess. "Ray?"

Colin blinked. "Yes. He used to have frogs that spawned in his pond, and hedgehogs that lived in this crate he made into a house for them." He smiled. "I remember one night, we got back late to his house, and there was this strange snuffling noise from the back garden. There were two hedgehogs. It was the weirdest thing. The female was standing still, and the male was circling her, over and over again. It was obviously a mating ritual."

"What's... mating?" Sophie gazed up at Colin, her eyebrows scrunched up.

"It's what happens when animals want to have babies," Blake explained. "The boy hedgehog was trying to get the girl hedgehog to notice him. Then if she likes him, they'll make babies."

Blake steeled himself for the questions he felt sure would come, but Sophie merely nodded and went back to stroking the slow worm. Colin's gaze met his, and they both bit back smiles.

"I think I'll go and put the slow worm back where he belongs," Colin said, straightening.

Sophie addressed his hand. "Bye! Don't get eaten!" The others laughed, and Colin left them, the slow worm cupped gently in his hands. Sophie watched him go, and then gazed at them. "Where's Daddy?"

"He's changing Nathan." Blake peered closely at her face. "And you, young lady, have caught the sun. Where's your cap?" Her cheeks and forehead were pink.

"I left it in my room."

"Then go get it. And when you come back, I'll put on more sun cream."

"Yes, Papa." Sophie ran into the house, narrowly avoiding tripping over the step.

Blake shook his head. "One of these days, she'll catch her foot and fall."

"Then she falls," Ed said practically. "You can't wrap 'er up in cotton wool, Blake. Kids learn by makin' mistakes. Blimey, the number of falls *I* 'ad as a kid is nobody's business. An' once she *does* trip over 'er own feet, she'll know next time to be more careful. Right?"

"You're right," Blake agreed. It didn't mean he was happy about it. If he had his way, Sophie would never know what it meant to feel pain.

"An' that was a close one," Ed added with a grin. "I was dyin' for 'er to ask if you an' Will mated so you could 'ave 'er an' Nathan." He winked. "I can just picture you an' Will, tryin' to explain the birds an' the bees."

Angelo and Rick laughed, but Blake scowled. "I'd like her to stay a little girl for as long as possible. Some of the things she hears other kids say at nursery school fill me with horror." He sighed. "Don't get me wrong. If she asks questions, we always try to answer them as honestly as possible. I mean, for God's sake, she already knows what a penis is!"

"You were great just now," Rick said earnestly. "She was curious, and you satisfied her curiosity. If she'd wanted to know more, she'd have asked. And from what you've already told us, it's obvious you've treated the subject like it's a normal, everyday topic." He paused.

"Has she asked yet why she has two dads, and not a mum and dad like her school friends?"

"No, but then again, she thinks it's normal. There are at least four children in her class that have same sex parents." Blake smiled. "Thankfully, times are changing."

Will came through the French doors, pushing Nathan's buggy, Sophie at his side. "I think he's ready for a nap. I was going to put him in the shade while we have lunch. He's already had some formula."

"I gave Nathan his bottle," Sophie announced, beaming.

"That's because you're a wonderful big sister," Blake said, opening his arms wide in invitation. Sophie ran into them and he lifted her up onto his knee. He kissed the top of her cap. "Good girl. Daddy and I would be unhappy if you got sunburn."

"Here you go." Will passed over the bottle of children's sunscreen, before moving the pushchair against the wall, where it would be in plain sight.

Blake squirted cream into his palm and applied it to Sophie's face while she screwed her eyes tight shut, lips firmly pressed together. He made sure the cream went on her neck and every other place where her skin was exposed to the sun. Then she slid off his knee and went over to Angelo, grabbing his hand. "Come on, Uncle Angelo. I want to show you the lion."

Laughing, Angelo allowed himself to be dragged toward the rear of the garden. "I hope it's not going to eat me," he said over his shoulder to Rick, grinning.

"There's a lion?" Ed snorted. "I dunno, snakes, lions... this place is turnin' into a bloomin' menagerie."

"The feline in question is a stone lion's head with water trickling from its mouth," Blake told him. He glanced to where Colin walked toward them, his previous good humour vanished as he stared out over the garden. Ed followed Blake's gaze and held out his hand to take Colin's. "You okay, Col?"

Colin clasped his hand briefly and then released it. He sat in the empty chair next to Ed. "I'm sorry. It just feels so... surreal. I'm sitting here, surrounded by friends, chatting about inconsequential things like slow worms and wildlife, and all the while, Ray is..." He swallowed. "I'm just finding it difficult to act like everything is normal, when it really isn't."

Blake's throat tightened. "Oh, believe me, I know exactly what you mean." He gazed at Will who walked over and stood behind him, his hand squeezing Blake's shoulder. "We both do. You get on with... stuff, the minutiae of daily life that keep your brain occupied, because it's when you *stop* doing things that your mind defaults to other things. Not that they ever really go away. They're always lurking in the background."

"That's why we're grateful you all accepted the invitation," Will added. "You have things going in on your own lives too." He glanced at Rick. "Some pretty big things, actually. But having you here... We need our friends, now more than ever."

"I suppose it must take some getting used to," Colin mused. "The knowledge that Nathan is deaf."

Blake covered Will's hand with his. "It's true that the first thing to cross your mind is 'Oh my God, this is terrible.' But then you start to see things differently. For us, it was a case of not thinking of this as a disability, but simply as this is *Nathan's reality*. We'll do what we can to help him succeed in life, hence the implants, sign language, whatever it takes."

"That doesn't mean we're not worried," Will added. "We look at the calendar and count off the weeks until October."

"This operation," Ed began, speaking hesitantly. "Is it dangerous? I mean, I know people 'ave implants fitted all the time, but still, Nathan's just a baby."

Blake scanned the garden quickly. Sophie was still in sight, Angelo crouching down beside her. "We'll tell you what's involved, but not now. Little ears, guys. We don't want her hearing this."

"Can you stay for dinner?" Will asked. "I don't know if you have plans for this evening, but you'd be most welcome to eat with us. We can talk when Sophie's gone to bed."

"Angelo and I have no plans. We're seeing Elena tomorrow for Sunday lunch. I'm sure Angelo won't mind."

Ed glanced at Colin. "You wanna stay?"

Colin smiled. "Actually, I think that's a good idea."

"It helps, doesn't it, being around others?" Blake said quietly.

Colin nodded, and to Blake's mind, he relaxed a little.

"Er, never mind about dinner." Ed gave Will a mock-glare. "We 'aven't 'ad so much as a sniff of lunch yet." He flicked his head in Nathan's direction. "At least *he* got a bottle."

Will laughed. "It's ready. And if you're that hungry, you can help me bring it out."

Ed got to his feet and followed Will into the house, muttering under his breath, "What did your last slave die of?"

Blake shook his head, smiling to himself. *Never a dull moment with Ed around. Thank God.*

"Okay, then what's the sign for this?" Ed asked, pointing to Sophie's glass of milk. She mimicked pulling a cow's udders, and he laughed. "Really?"

"Yes, that's right," Blake said, standing up from the couch, "and it's time for our little sign language teacher to go to bed."

"I want to stay up with you and Daddy." Sophie pouted. "Can't I stay up?"

Blake gave her a hard stare. "And since when do you argue? You're going to be staying up late when we go to Rick and Angelo's wedding, right?"

"Yes, Papa. But—"

Blake said nothing but regarded her steadily, unblinking.

Sophie stood up. "Yes, Papa."

Will smiled to see this interaction. "Good girl. Now say good night." She went to each of their friends, arms wide for a hug. Will had watched her spend at least half an hour teaching them all the signs she'd learned, and it was good to see how they took her seriously.

He gave her a big hug and kissed her on the cheek. "Sleep well, precious."

"Good night, Daddy. Love you."

"Love you too."

Blake scooped her up into his arms and lifted her onto his shoulders. Will had to smile. Sophie loved it when he did that. He could hear her giggling as they went upstairs. Nathan was already asleep in his cot, the baby monitor switched on. Will closed the door to the hallway and sighed.

"Okay, who's for another glass of wine, or maybe something stronger?"

"You got any brandy?" Ed inquired.

Will nodded and went over to the drinks cabinet. "Anyone else for brandy? On second thoughts, I'll just bring over the bottle and some glasses.

"Something soft for me," Angelo said. "I'm driving."

Will saw to their guests, and then sat on the couch, a glass in hand.

"'Ave you written yer speech yet?" Ed asked him with a cheeky smile.

Will laughed. "No one word." He winked at Rick. "Not worried, are you, about what I'm going to reveal?"

Rick snorted. "Put it this way. I think I've got less to worry about with you, than Angelo has with Maria." He rubbed his hands together gleefully. "I can't wait to hear all her tales about him growing up."

Angelo stared at him. "She wouldn't embarrass me—would she?" Rick merely arched his eyebrows and he groaned. "Of course she would." The others laughed.

"How's Lizzie doing? She must be on maternity leave by now. Is she still coming to the wedding? It must be close to her due date."

"She's due at the beginning of September," Ed told Will. "She's been on maternity leave since the end of June." He chuckled. "The last time I spoke with her, she was complainin' about Dave. Seems he's not up to speed with gettin' the baby's room ready."

"Do they know the baby's sex?" Will asked. He felt a flush of guilt that he hadn't been in touch with her or Dave for a while. Then he reasoned that there had been quite a lot going on in their lives to account for that.

"Yup. It's a girl. An' Lizzie wanted Dave to repaint the room, seein' as he'd painted a racin' car on the wall for Justin." Ed snickered. "This one took 'em by surprise."

Blake poked his head around the door. "They're both asleep." He peered at the coffee table. "Shall I bring some snacks through?"

Will smiled. "Thanks, babe. Great idea." Blake retreated and Will got up to check the baby monitor's volume level. There was no sound from Nathan's room. He sat down again and picked up his glass.

"So, tell us about the op," Ed said quietly. "Will Nathan 'ave to stay in overnight?"

Will nodded. "The surgery takes about three to four hours usually." Blake came in with bowls of crisps and snacks, and placed them on the table. He sat beside Will and then picked up the glass of brandy Will had poured for him. Blake sat back and reached for Will's hand, their fingers intertwined on Will's thigh.

Will tapped behind his ear. "This is where they'll go in. It contains a honeycomb of air pockets, and they use a drill to open these up to go in deeper."

Blake sighed. "We've read up on this so many times, not to mention watched videos of the procedure, that we know what happens step by step." Will tightened his grip on Blake's hand, and Blake gave him a grateful glance. "The short version is they make a hole from one to one and a half millimetres wide through the bone of the cochlea, and that's where they insert the electrodes."

"Electrodes." Rick shuddered, and then gave Blake an apologetic look. "Sorry. It just seems hard to connect that word with the little boy I was playing with in the garden."

Will huffed. "You get an idea of how we feel, then. I keep telling myself that the end result will be worth it, because Nathan will have a much better chance of communicating once he has the implants." He met their gazes. "He's going to have two implants. We've discussed it with Dr. Michaels and we've decided that's the way to go."

"There's a receiver part, isn't there, that fits onto the electrode?" Colin asked.

Blake nodded. "They create a slight indentation in the bone further back on the skull, which is where the receiver stimulator part sits at the end of the operation. Then the wound is sutured closed and on go the bandages."

"And three weeks after that is activation day," Will concluded. His gaze met Blake's. "When the hard work really begins."

Blake nodded. "And we'll be ready for it."

"Any time you want an 'and with anything, you only 'ave to ask, you know that, right?" Ed said, his tone earnest. Beside him, Colin was nodding.

"And that goes for us too," Rick added. "Babysitting, shopping, whatever. If there's things we can do to make it easier for you, name them."

"There's one thing we can all do," Colin said suddenly. "You can e-mail us the link for those online lessons in sign language. Just watching Sophie this evening was an eye-opener. She knows so many signs, and she's only four." He smiled. "All four of us have been a part of her life, and I see no reason why we won't be part of Nathan's. So that means we need to communicate with him too."

Will's throat tightened, and he turned his head to gaze at Blake. "You do realize this gives us a problem?"

Blake blinked. "What problem?"

Will gestured to their four friends. "How the hell do we choose which of them is going to be Nathan's godfather?" It was a joke between them that while Sophie hadn't had a church baptism, she did have several people who considered themselves to be honorary godparents.

Blake grinned. "That's easy. All of them."

Chapter Twenty-Five

August 11th

Colin put down the phone and made a few notes in the file on his screen. The sheer scale of this project was impressive, but he relished the challenge. When the new building was finished, it would be eye-catching and maybe even a little controversial, but innovation always pushed boundaries in his opinion.

The phone buzzed. "Ready for your coffee now?" Marion asked.

Colin glanced at his watch. Ten-thirty and the day already showed signs of being long but productive. "I think I can manage a coffee break."

"I'll be five minutes."

He stretched, his spine popping. Outside the temperature was climbing, but in his office the air con kept the room at a far more reasonable temperature. He gazed at the brilliant blue sky above the line of buildings, not marred by a single cloud, and the first thought that came to mind was Ed on that beach the previous summer, lying face-down on a towel, while Colin leisurely applied sun screen to his back and legs.

I think I need a holiday.

Not that it was an option right then. Not while Ray...

Colin leaned on his desk and put his head in his hands. The previous night, Ed had been on the phone with Rick, talking about the wedding. Colin had half listened, not really taking anything in. He couldn't drum up any enthusiasm for the event, but he put that down to current events. He hoped that by the time the big day arrived, he was in a better frame of mind. Because if he still felt the same, he was half inclined not to go. Rick and Angelo didn't need him and his poor mood spoiling their wedding day.

When his personal phone rang, one look at the screen sent his stomach plummeting. It was the hospice. Colin stretched out his hand toward it, but it was as if he was reaching through treacle, a thick sludge that impeded his every movement. The call connected and he recognized Julie's voice, quiet and lilting.

"Colin? Hi, it's Julie, the Staff Nurse from the hospice. Is this a convenient time to call?"

Seeing as there were only two possible routes their conversation could take, he resisted the urge to tell her that this was always going to be a bad time to call. He steeled himself for the inevitable. "It's fine. How is he?" What surprised him was that he *wanted* Ray to still be alive, for them to have the opportunity of one last conversation.

"How soon can you get up here?"

Shit. They were apparently down to the wire.

"This afternoon if I get my skates on." *And if my boss is willing to grant me a leave of absence for a few days...*

"I think that would be a very good idea. I don't think Ray has long left, and he's asking for you."

"Then I'll do my best." He said goodbye and disconnected the call, all the while trying to decide who to talk to next—his boss or his fiancé. *Get the practicalities out of the way. I can call Ed later when I'm en route.*

Two minutes later he was peering around the office door at Simon's secretary. "Is he busy?"

Trish smiled. "You're in luck. He's just this minute finished a conference call. Go right in."

Colin pushed open the door and stepped into Simon's light, airy office that occupied a corner of their building. Behind his desk was a tall cabinet containing all their awards and press releases. Simon glanced up from his desk and smiled. "Good morning." Then the smile faded. "Are you all right?" He gestured to the deep chair facing his desk. "Sit down."

Colin did as instructed. "I'll come straight to the point. You know I've been spending a few weekends in Scotland these last couple of months."

Simon nodded. "A sick friend, I think you mentioned once."

"By the way, thank you for those occasions when I was able to finish work early to catch a flight."

Simon's smile made a brief appearance. "Don't mention it. I like to think of everyone who works here as being part of a family. And isn't that what you do with family? You help them when they need it?"

It fitted Colin's experience so far of working in the company. "Yes, but not every business treats its staff as you do." He paused. "Ray was my ex. I've been visiting him because I recently discovered he has lung cancer."

Simon drew in a sharp breath. "Oh, I'm so sorry. I take it by your expression that the news isn't good?"

Breathing, speaking—both acts were a real chore right then.

"I've just received a call from the hospice where he's—"

Simon held up his hand. "You don't have to say another word. That told me all I need to know. Would you like a leave of absence?"

Colin's throat threatened to seize up, and he coughed. He got his breath back. "I'm sure I'll only need a couple of days."

Simon shook his head. "You take as long as you need, okay? And if there's anything I can do, please don't hesitate to ask."

Colin stood and extended a hand over Simon's desk. "Thank you," he said, gripping Simon's hand tightly. When he released it, he stepped back. "I'll go and arrange a flight."

Simon nodded. "My thoughts will be with you."

Colin gave him a grateful smile and hurried from the office. Once he was back at his desk, he took a moment to regain his composure before calling Ed.

"Nice timin'," Ed announced as the call connected. "I'm just 'avin' me coffee break."

"Julie called," Colin said quickly.

Ed's manner changed in a heartbeat. "When are ya going?"

"On the first flight I can get a seat," Colin told him. "There's one around one-thirty, I think."

"Right. You 'aven't got time to go 'ome, so go as you are. You can buy toiletries at the airport. Get your arse to Gatwick an' I'll meet you there. Leave the tickets to me. 'Ave you got yer passport?"

"It's in my laptop bag. Wait—*you're* coming too?" His head was spinning.

Ed sighed. "You didn't think I'd let ya go there on yer own, did ya? I figured you'd need me." He went quiet. "Was I right?"

God bless Ed. "Like you have to ask. Thank you." He hadn't realized until then just how much he dreaded the journey to Edinburgh, for what was in all likelihood the last time.

"Thank me when you see me. We're wastin' time. I'll meet ya outside the North Terminal, all right? I'll text when I've got the flight times. Just get there as fast as you can." He hung up before Colin could say another word.

Ed's brisk manner broke through his dazed state, and Colin packed up his laptop, grabbed his coat, and headed out of the office, trying not to think about what awaited him at the end of his journey.

The speed with which Julie led them to Ray's room was enough to set Colin's heart racing. She'd met them at the door when they got out of the taxi, greeting them with a few words.

"We told him you were on your way," she said as they walked briskly through the hallways. "I'll show you in then I'll leave you alone. There's a buzzer to call me if you need me." She stopped outside his door. "Just so you know? He signed a DNR order this morning. He said he's ready." She patted Colin's arm. "It won't be long now." Julie held the door open for them, and Colin walked slowly to the bed.

Ray was breathing laboriously, the air mask fogged with condensation. His eyes were closed. The only sounds were the monitor beside his bed and the torturous rasp of his breathing. Colin gazed down at him, conscious of Ed's hand on his back, a comforting presence.

"Hey there," he said softly.

Ray's eyes flickered open, and he smiled. "You're here."

Colin sat on the bed and took Ray's hand in his. "You knew I'd come, right?"

Ray grasped the air mask and pulled it aside. "Something... you have to know.... Saw... a solicitor... this morning."

"Please, put the mask back on," Colin begged.

Ray gave a slight shake of his head. "Important. You'll get.... a letter... naming you as... executor... "

"You want me to take care of things for you?"

Ray gave a slow nod. "Not got... much.... Just the... flat. Sell it. Proceeds to go... to an AIDS charity... Trust you to... pick the right one.... All in the... letter."

Colin blinked back tears. "You got it."

"Want you... to go there... Go through... my stuff. Choose something... to remember me by."

Colin wiped his eyes. "Like I could ever forget you."

Ray put the mask back, his own eyes growing moist. Colin held his hand gently, stroking the back of it. Ray glanced at Ed. "You've got... a good man here."

"Don't I know it."

"So tired," Ray murmured. "Maybe I... should sleep." He closed his eyes.

"You sleep if you need to." Colin kept up the gentle stroking, hoping it soothed him.

Suddenly Ray's eyes flew open. "Loved you... " Before Colin could respond, he closed his eyes, his breathing changing. His face relaxed, all the lines smoothing away. It was only the continual low whine of the heart monitor that told Colin he was gone.

Colin sat there, still clasping Ray's hand. "He went so quickly."

Ed rubbed his shoulder. "It's like Julie said. He was ready." He leaned forward. "I'm gonna step outside for a minute, okay?" Colin turned to regard him, and Ed stroked his cheek. "Thought you'd like to say goodbye on yer own." He patted Colin's shoulder and then left the room.

Colin stared at the still form of his first lover, so many memories clouding his head, coming at him thick and fast. He got to his feet and leaned over Ray, cupping his face. Carefully, so, so carefully, he removed the air mask and placed it on the pillow beside Ray's head.

"Goodbye," he whispered, before brushing his lips over Ray's. He straightened and walked away from the bed, toward the door beyond which Ed waited.

"It's a nice little flat," Ed commented, glancing around at the living area. "I can see why Ray loved livin' 'ere."

Colin smiled. "The reason Ray loved this place is down there," he said, pointing toward the window. "His walks along the river bank were important to him." He'd wanted to see it one more time, because in all likelihood, he'd hire someone to pack up all Ray's belongings prior to passing it into the hands of an estate agent.

"Are you gonna choose something like Ray said?"

Colin had been thinking about that. For the life of him, he couldn't think of anything.

"Tell you what," Ed said at last. "Why don't I put the kettle on, while you 'ave a look around?"

"Would you understand if I said it feels weird to be going through his things? That it still feels like he'll walk through that door any minute?"

Ed sighed. "More than you'd think. I remember when me dad passed on. I kept thinkin' it was a joke, that he wasn't really dead, just hidin' in a cupboard somewhere, waitin' to jump out an' scare the shit out of us all."

"Yes," Colin breathed. "Exactly."

"An' it's not like you're rootin' through 'is stuff to find the bleedin' Crown Jewels, right?" Ed cocked his head to one side. "Did you wanna stay here tonight?"

Colin shook his head. "I couldn't. Can't really explain why."

Ed's smile was kind. "No problem. I'll call that 'otel we stayed in last time, see if they've got a room."

"Actually...." Colin gazed at the small flat, his chest tightening. "Can we go? Let's do this tomorrow, before we go to the airport."

Ed nodded. "Let's get out of 'ere. You're right. It's too close to 'im goin.'"

His words mirrored Colin's thoughts precisely. Ray's scent permeated the flat, but beneath it was a faint medicinal odour that brought back recent events.

"We don't 'ave to do this tomorrow, even." Ed leaned against the kitchen work top and regarded Colin keenly. "Let's wait until we hear from Ray's solicitor. We can always come back another day, when everything's less raw than it is right now."

Colin shuddered out a breath. "I know it was my idea to come here, but you're right. I can't do this now."

Ed beckoned him with a finger. "Come 'ere." Colin walked over to him and Ed put his arms around him. "Just stop for a minute. Breathe."

Colin leaned against him, his face buried in Ed's neck.

"That's it. Just take a moment to be still. You 'aven't stopped since you left the office, 'ave ya? Dashin' to the airport, makin' it there with ten minutes to spare, runnin' for the gate... You only stayed still on the bloody plane because you 'ad no choice. Then the taxi..." Ed held him close. "All over now. You got there in time, you said goodbye. An' now you need to let it all go."

Colin inhaled slowly, breathing Ed in. "How do you do this?" he asked softly.

"Do what?"

"Be exactly what I need, exactly when I need it."

Ed chuckled. "Guess that's part 'n' parcel of lovin' someone. You've 'eld me together plenty of times. It's my turn to 'old you. Only, you're not comin' apart, are ya? You're 'angin' on in there, 'cause you're a strong man." He rubbed firmly over Colin's back. "An' you *know* Ray's not in any more pain, right?"

Colin nodded. That was the one thing that eased his heart.

"Then we'll check there's no nasties lurkin' in the fridge, although I think we'd know by now if there were—the place would stink to high heaven. Someone must've cleaned it out before Ray went to the hospice. Maybe Kelly."

"That's possible."

"An' then we'll be on our way." Ed pulled his phone from his pocket and scrolled through.

Colin listened absently as Ed booked them a hotel room. Maybe a quiet dinner with Ed and an early night was just what he needed. Except he didn't think it would be that simple.

He had a feeling it would be a while before the ache in his heart began to fade.

Chapter Twenty-Six

August 19th - the big day

"You've got the rings, right?"

Will gave Angelo a hard stare. "You've asked me three times already. Any more, and I shall walk off in a huff." Then he grinned. "Relax, will you? Everything is perfect."

Angelo groaned. "Oh, God, don't say that. Now you've jinxed it for sure."

Rick landed a quick swat on Angelo's behind. "Only if you keep on saying stuff like that." He was feeling remarkably calm, which was probably a good thing, judging by the state of Angelo's nerves. Elena was just as bad, fretting over numerous things: the flowers, Angelo's cousin Paula who was due to sing, but was experiencing a bit of a cough, whether there were enough chairs...

I seem to be the only sane one around here.

That wasn't quite true. Will was pretty relaxed too. He, Blake and the children had arrived just after Rick, Angelo and Elena. Sophie kept twirling in her new dress, until she did it so much that she got dizzy, and then Blake made her sit on a chair and stay there. Nathan was securely fastened in his pushchair, dozing off now and then.

The chairs were beginning to fill, slowly but surely, even with an hour left until the ceremony. Franco had arrived, dressed in a black suit and tie. He too seemed calm, but every time Rick glimpsed him, he was engaged in conversation with Anthony.

Rick had to smile. Anthony had shown yet again what a godsend he was with Elena. He'd taken her under his wing—and out of their hair while he and Angelo got changed into their suits.

Blake walked toward him, followed by a tall, thin man who carried a briefcase. "Rick, this is Mr. Newton from the General Registrar's office."

Rick extended a hand. "Mr. Newton, the one who makes it all legal."

Mr. Newton smiled and shook hands with him. "I have the licenses. I just need to check them before the ceremony." He glanced around. "I'm guessing that table over there is for me?" Rick nodded. "Perfect. Then if you and Mr. Tarallo could join me in about five minutes, we can go over the paperwork."

Rick glanced around. Angelo was talking to Will, who thankfully was having a calming influence on him. *Thank God*. Rick had enough to deal with.

"Are Ed and Colin here yet?" Blake joined Rick, scanning the assembled guests.

Rick shook his head. "No sign of them yet." He wasn't concerned, however. If there was a problem, one of them would have called.

Blake looked over his shoulder and smiled. "Lizzie and Dave just arrived."

Rick turned, just as a small missile in the shape of Justin collided with him. "Whoa there!"

Justin peered up at him, grinning. "Uncle Rick! You're getting married today."

Rick crouched down. "That's the plan. Don't *you* look smart?"

Justin scowled and pulled at his shirt collar. "Dad made me wear this."

Dave walked up behind him, holding Molly's hand. He rolled his eyes. "I told Justin that you and Angelo wouldn't really appreciate his Batman costume."

Rick bit his lip. "Yeah, but imagine Angelo's face if he had."

"Justin is sulking," Molly told him with an air of superiority.

Rick snorted. "And you, of course, have *never* sulked."

Molly opened her eyes and mouth wide, but before she could speak, Dave leaned closer. "Remember what happens when you tell lies?"

Molly instantly covered her nose with both hands, and Rick guffawed. "I spy with my little eye, someone who's been watching Pinocchio."

Lizzie giggled. "Yesterday, in fact."

He shook his head as Lizzie approached. "Do you want a little help there?"

Lizzie glared at him. "I know, I know, I'm as big as a house, and I still have a few weeks to go."

Rick took her arm and helped her toward a chair that she sank into with a sigh of relief. "This row is for you lot." He peered closely at Lizzie. "Hey, are you okay?" She was a little flushed.

She huffed. "I just didn't have a good night, that's all." Then she smiled. "But you have more pressing things to think about, like letting Angelo make an honest man of you." She winked. Rick feigned indignation, but Lizzie laughed at him. "Yeah, like I buy *that* look anymore."

He kissed her cheek. "Glad you're here." Rick left them to get settled.

"Rick!" Angelo pointed to behind him. "Your family has arrived."

Rick turned and smiled to see his parents waving as they walked towards the loggia. He grinned at the sight of Maggie in a long, pale blue dress. "Wow. Don't *you* scrub up nicely?"

Maggie scowled and his mum arched her eyebrows. "You've got her in a dress. Don't push your luck."

Rick snorted. Maggie was never one for dressing up. He hugged her and whispered in her ear, "You look beautiful, Mags."

She tightened her arms around him. "I've never seen you look so handsome. Dark green really suits you." Then she chuckled. "But oh my. Could Angelo look any more Italian?"

Rick released her and feasted his eyes on Angelo, resplendent in his pale suit. "I think he looks amazing." He returned his gaze to Maggie and winked. "But then I am a little biased."

Maggie stared at him, her eyes shining. "I love the way you look at him, like he's—"

"The best thing that ever happened to me?" Rick finished for her. "Maybe that's because he is."

His dad gave him a brief firm hug. "You look very smart."

"Doesn't he?" Mum's face glowed.

Rick wasn't used to praise. "Come on, your seats are on the front row." He led them to where they would be sitting.

Mum glanced across and waved at Elena. "I must go and say hello."

"Rick!" Angelo was beckoning him.

"Sorry," he apologized to his dad and sister.

Dad snickered. "It's going to be a long, busy day for you." He paused. "Can I give you a word of advice, son?"

Rick stilled. "Sure." He wondered what was coming. Dad wasn't one for man-to-man stuff.

"I know there's going to be a lot happening, but this is a day you'll want to remember. So, don't think about what's coming next, who's doing what—stop every now and then, step back, and take a moment to breathe it all in, take in everything." He smiled. "Your granddad said that to me on my wedding day, and it was good advice. I remember that day like it was yesterday."

Rick's throat tightened, and he hugged his dad fiercely. "Thank you." He gave Angelo an apologetic glance. "And now I'd better see what my husband-to-be wants."

He left them and walked over to Angelo. "What's up?"

Angelo arched his eyebrows. "Only the small matter of the licenses. Mr. Newton, remember?"

Rick chuckled. "Oh, is that all?" He dodged Angelo's hand as it made its way toward his backside. "Well, come on, then. Let's go make sure it's all going to be legal."

He felt like a little kid on Christmas morning.

That's not a bad way to be on your wedding day.

"I'm sorry I made us late," Colin whispered as they walked briskly toward the loggia. Laughter and chatter carried on the warm breeze, along with the strains of violins, weaving a beautiful harmony.

Ed's hand clasped his. "It's okay, we're 'ere now." It had taken the whole journey to the castle for him to calm down. When Colin had announced that he didn't really feel up to attending the wedding, it had taken every ounce of effort on Ed's part not to react. He'd played it cool, all the while knowing that this was exactly what Colin needed—a day with friends who loved him, a day when the past could be recalled, but the emphasis was on the future. Rick's cheerful text, telling them how much he was looking forward to seeing them, had been the deciding factor.

I owe Rick for that. His timing couldn't have been more opportune.

Colin gazed at their surroundings. "Wow. What a perfect spot for a wedding."

"I couldn't agree more." Ed had seen the photos online, but they didn't do it justice, in his opinion. "And thank Gawd the weather played nice for 'em." It was a gloriously sunny day, and the way the stone columns of the loggia caught the light and reflected it was just beautiful.

They stepped into the cool shadows of the arches, and Angelo walked over to them. "We were beginning to think you weren't coming."

"Shouldn't you be standin' at the front, gettin' ready?" Ed asked with a grin after hugging him.

Colin frowned. "Something's going on." Voices were raised in agitation.

Angelo left them and hurried over to where a crowd had gathered on one side of the arranged chairs.

"What's goin' on?"

Blake emerged from the crowd and strode over to them. "There's been a hitch. The wedding may have to wait a little while."

Ed looked past him to where Angelo and Dave were supporting Lizzie, their arms around her. "Oh Gawd," he groaned. "Don't tell me..."

"Her waters broke about three minutes ago. Dave has called for an ambulance." Blake motioned to Will, who rushed over to them. "Tell Dave we'll look after Molly and Justin, okay?"

Will nodded. "Peter's going with them. Anthony has given him the keys to the golf buggy he uses to get around the place." He shook his head. "Talk about timing."

Rick joined them, and they watched as Dave helped his wife into the waiting golf buggy, gripping her hand tightly. Lizzie's face was strained, but when the buggy lurched off, she blew Rick and Angelo a kiss.

A tall man in a dark grey suit approached the grooms. "Gentlemen, if we can get all the guests in their chairs, we can start."

"Thanks, Anthony." Rick tugged at Angelo's arm. "Lizzie will be fine, and Dave will keep us up to date with what's happening."

"You go stand where you're supposed to be," Ed told them. "I'll round up the sheep." He grinned.

Rick pointed to the two last chairs on the second row, both with reserved notices. "Those are for you." His gaze met Ed's. "You'll have a bird's eye view of the whole shindig. And never mind the sheep—Angelo's brothers are acting as ushers. Let them do their jobs."

Ed flicked his head toward the front, where a very handsome man in black was staring at them pointedly. "I think the hottie in black wants to talk to ya. Somethin' about gettin' married today?"

It was Angelo's turn to tug Rick. "Come on. Everyone's here."

Rick smiled and walked side by side with Angelo to the front of the chairs where Will and Maria stood, watching them.

Ed sat with Colin, automatically taking his hand and lacing their fingers. "Weddings, eh?"

Colin gave a half smile. "To be honest, I haven't been to that many weddings, and this is my first gay one. I don't imagine it will be all that different."

Ed snorted. "Knowin' those two? Anything's possible." He leaned against Colin's arm. "You all right, Col?"

When Colin didn't respond immediately, Ed knew all wasn't well.

"It wasn't that I didn't want to see them get married, you know," Colin said quietly. "I was just feeling a little low, and I didn't want to spoil their day." He gazed at Rick and Angelo, standing with Franco, the three men talking in low voices. "But you were right. It feels good to be here." When he smiled again, this time it reached his eyes. "And any day when you get to see two people in love commit to each other, has to be celebrated."

Ed couldn't have agreed more.

From somewhere off to their right, music filtered through the air, and it took Ed a moment to recognize it. He snickered. "Leave it to two gay guys to have Bette Midler singing Wind Beneath My Wings to kick off their wedding."

Then he forgot all about the music as he watched Rick and Angelo face each other, their gazes locked on each other as they held hands.

Ed knew love when he saw it. It was the same love he saw every day in Colin's eyes.

Colin listened in rapt attention as Rick and Angelo made their vows.

"Thank you for literally being my hero," Rick told him. "I will never forget how you rescued me, not just from someone's unwanted attentions, but also from a life that was missing something vital. You."

Colin's chest tightened to hear the love in Rick's voice as he promised to love and cherish Angelo for the rest of their lives together. In front of him, Rick's mum and sister were already sniffing into white handkerchiefs. Beside him, Ed was seemingly lost in the whole experience, his hand wrapped around Colin's.

Colin could understand that reaction. It was a perfect summer's day, and the sound of birdsong filled the air, which also carried the sweet fragrance of flowers. The sunlight reflected off the warm-coloured stone arches, giving everything a soft glow. Rick and Angelo's words were easily audible, their voices rebounding around the space.

Everyone fell silent as they exchanged rings, Will and Maria looking on as Angelo slipped the white gold band onto Rick's finger, before lifting Rick's hand to his lips to kiss it. Low *aws* filled the air when Rick repeated the action.

When Franco placed his hands on their heads and blessed them, Colin caught his breath. It was a fragile moment, beautiful and poignant. Then Franco whispered to them, and Rick and Angelo turned to face the rows of chairs filled with their friends and family.

"Ladies and gentlemen, I have the honour and joy to be the first to introduce to you, Rick and Angelo Tarallo." He regarded the two men before him. "And now the moment you've been waiting for." Franco smiled. "Would the newlyweds like to share a kiss?"

Angelo grinned. "We thought you'd never ask." A heartbeat later Rick was in his arms and they kissed, a lingering embrace while applause broke out, swelling in volume as the kiss showed no signs of stopping.

"Hey, bro, take a breath," one of Angelo's brothers called out, grinning.

At last they broke the kiss, and Rick and Angelo faced their audience, both smiling widely.

"Rick and Angelo are going to sign the register," Franco announced. "But please, stay in your seats, because we're not finished yet."

To Colin's surprise, Franco walked over where Ed and Colin were seated, and bent over to take their hands. "Come with me," he told them.

Colin blinked. "What?"

Ed gave a shrug. "Just go along with it. We'll find out soon enough what else Rick an' Angelo 'ave up their sleeves."

"Okay," Colin agreed, rising from his chair and pulling his hands free to follow Ed and Franco to the front where Rick and Angelo had stood previously. The grooms were standing by the registrar's table, both of them grinning like idiots.

Colin gave Rick a hard stare. "What are you up to?"

Rick opened his eyes wide. "Me? I'm innocent, honest." That had several snorts and chuckles coming from their guests.

Franco took up his previous position. "Today is all about love and making commitments, and sharing that love and commitment with those who matter to you." His gaze flickered to Ed. "Isn't that right, Ed?" Franco was smiling.

When Ed turned to face Colin, taking hold of his hands, the light began to dawn.

No. He hasn't.

Colin took a deep breath and regarded Ed, hardly daring to move. "Are we... getting married?"

Ed chuckled. "What gave it away?"

Logic took over. "But... you need a license."

Ed pointed to where Rick and Angelo stood. "Oh, you mean like the one that man is waving at you right now?"

The registrar was indeed waving a long slim envelope.

Colin blinked again. "But we can't get married. None of your family is here to see it. And let's be honest here. If we got married without telling your mum, she'd have your guts for garters."

Ed grinned. "Col? Look behind you."

He turned, to be greeted by the sight of Ed's mum, his sisters, brother and their spouses, and Ed's nephew and niece. All of them were standing in the back row and waving at him, clearly dressed for a wedding.

When did he sneak them in?

Slowly Colin turned back to Ed. "Did *everyone* know about this apart from me?"

Laughter broke out among their friends. Will and Blake shook their heads, both obviously as surprised as Colin.

"Nah. The only people in on it were Rick, Angelo, Franco an' the registrar." Ed took Colin's hands, his expression growing more serious. "I know this is what you want too."

Colin couldn't deny that. "But... we don't have rings."

Rick walked over to them, holding out a small, black velvet bag. "Then what are these?" He held them out to Blake. "We thought you might like to be best man."

Blake joined them, standing at Ed's side. "I'd be honoured." His voice cracked slightly.

"Thanks, mate." Ed flashed Blake a smile and then returned his attention to Colin. "I know these last few months 'ave been challengin' for ya. But I 'ope you know I've been there for ya." He sighed. "I knew what you were doin'. You've been tryin' to shield me, 'aven't ya? You kept so much of what you were feelin' inside, maybe because you thought you were protectin' me to a certain extent." He locked gazes with Colin. "But you don't 'ave to. I want us to share everything. The good days *an'* the bad days. Because it's you an' me, Col, together. If you're 'urtin', then so am I, but I'll also be the one 'oldin' you until it's passed. You'd do the same for me, right?"

"You know it," Colin whispered, his heart full of love for the wonderful man before him.

Ed turned to Franco. "Then let's do this. No vows written, so we'll 'ave to do it the old fashioned way."

Franco smiled. "I think everyone here just heard your vow, Ed." He addressed the guests. "Ladies and gentlemen, we are here to witness the joining in marriage of these two beautiful men." His eyes shone. "Because men in love are always beautiful."

Colin tightened his grasp on Ed's hands and mouthed, *I love you.*
Ed's slow smile lit up his face. *Love you too.*

Chapter Twenty-Seven

Rick leaned back against Angelo's chest with a contented sigh. "This is heaven."

Angelo couldn't agree more. The bath was easily big enough for two, and the hot, scented water was very soothing. Rick sat between his legs, which caged him while Angelo languidly stroked Rick's chest with a soft flannel. Rick's head lay against his shoulder, now and again turning to give and receive kisses.

Rick reached over to the stool beside the tub, on which sat two champagne flutes. He picked one up and took a sip from it before replacing it and sinking back against Angelo's warm, firm body. "It doesn't feel real, does it?" he murmured. "After all these years, all this planning... we're finally married." Rick chuckled. "Although nothing has changed, right?"

Angelo raised Rick's left hand, where a white gold band shone in the lights above them. "Well, that's new, for one thing." He brought his lips to Rick's ear. "And no more discussions. No more fittings. No more wild suggestions for the reception," he whispered.

Rick laughed. "Yeah, there *is* that. Though you have to admit, those olive trees were gorgeous. All those tiny white lights, twinkling..."

"You weren't too aggravated by my family, were you?" Angelo asked.

"Hmm. Yes, Mr. Tarallo, I have a bone to pick with you." Rick twisted his head to stare at Angelo. "When, exactly, were you going to tell me that all your Sicilian relatives were going to share a certain Italian wedding custom at our reception?" He settled back against Angelo's chest, stroking his thighs in a leisurely manner that made Angelo's skin prickle, and his cock stiffen.

Angelo shifted a little. "I know. I should have said something. I thought you liked it at the wedding in Italy." It was the custom for a guest to tap their glass with a knife and say loudly, "Ba-cio!" repeatedly, until more guests would join in, demanding a kiss from the newlyweds. The thing was, *every* time it happened, the couple had to kiss.

Angelo's family had been very, *very* keen to see him and Rick kiss. Again and again.

"Do you think it was the novelty factor? Seeing two men kiss?" Rick grinned. "Ed and Colin's faces when Elena demanded that they kiss too." He chuckled. "Ed certainly got into the spirit of things, didn't he?"

Angelo laughed. "That might have had something to do with the amount of champagne he'd drunk." Ed had been in a brilliant mood all evening, and Angelo had never seen Colin so relaxed. Even some of Angelo's most liberally minded relatives had appeared amused by the sight of two large men slow dancing in each other's arms, occasionally pausing to kiss. "Ed approached me during the dancing. He wanted to pay for half the reception."

"Aww. That was nice of him. What did you tell him?"

"I told him no. We were getting married anyway. What he'd arranged didn't cost us anymore, except for adding his family." Angelo regarded him. "Are you okay with that? I just felt they'd both been through enough the last few months. I didn't want him dealing with finances today."

"I'm with you, babe."

Angelo hadn't really thought Rick would mind. "Besides, I told him if he was serious about paying, then why not take the money he was going to give us, and donate it to a charity instead?" He smiled. "He liked that idea. He told me he's giving it to the hospice that took care of Ray."

"That's a great idea." Rick sat up and reached behind him. "And speaking of great ideas... "

Angelo let out a soft moan when Rick's fingers caressed his dick, stroking it to full hardness. "What did you have in mind?"

When Rick glanced over his shoulder, grinning as he guided Angelo's stiff cock to his hole, Angelo sighed happily. "How come we've never had sex in a bath before?"

Rick snickered. "Because our flat only has a shower? Now, no more talking. Make love to me, husband." He sank down onto Angelo's shaft with a full body shiver.

Angelo had no problems following instructions. "Yes, Mr. Tarallo. Whatever you say."

"I never realized you were so sneaky," Colin remarked as they strolled from the Pavilion through the rose garden. All the guests had departed, and they were the last to leave.

Ed chuckled. "It's part of me charm, the ability to pull a fast one now an' again. Gotta keep you on yer toes, right?"

Colin squeezed his hand. "I didn't have a clue. How long had you been planning this?"

"Since the first of April."

Colin came to a stop and stared at him. "You managed to keep quiet about this for over *four and a half months*? I'm amazed. You can never keep secrets."

Ed arched his eyebrows. "Well, that just shows you don't know me as well as you think you do." His phone buzzed in his pocket and he pulled it out. He smiled when he opened the text. "Helena Jane Thurston made her appearance at ten twenty-eight, weighin' nine pounds, two ounces. Mother and baby are doin' fine."

"Aw, that's great."

Ed pocketed his phone and retook Colin's hand. They continued walking for a few more minutes before Colin came to another dead stop. "Do you want to tell me where we're going? Because I'm pretty sure the car park is over to the right and we're heading away from it."

Ed chuckled. "Aw. You tellin' me you're not enjoyin' a little night stroll in the moonlight with your new 'usband?"

Colin laughed. "That's one word I didn't anticipate hearing when I woke up this morning." He fixed Ed with a stare. "Well, Oh Sneaky One? Where are you taking me?"

Ed didn't reply, but kept hold of Colin's hand as he led him through the gardens to their destination. He came to a halt in front of an old building, complete with wattle and daub. "Here." He withdrew a key from his pocket and unlocked the wooden door.

Colin followed him inside. "What is this place?"

Ed led the way through the oak-floored hallway to another door, which he opened. "This is our wedding night." He stepped aside and let Colin enter. He'd already seen the room when he booked it, during one of Colin's visits to Edinburgh.

He knew by Colin's soft gasp that he'd seen the seven foot wide bed. "Well? What do you think?"

Colin shook his head, smiling. "This is wonderful." He stepped into Ed's arms and kissed him on the lips. "Thank you. For all of this, the wedding, this gorgeous place... for putting up with me these last months."

Ed snorted. "Putting up with ya? I love ya." He cocked his head. "You sure you're all right? I know that letter from the solicitor this mornin' is what got you down."

Colin gave a sad smile. "It was just another reminder that he's really gone. I know I'll feel bad all over again when we go up to Edinburgh to pack up his things before the sale goes through. And again when we go through all his stuff. I have to trust that the ache will go away, little by little."

"'Ave you given any thought to what you might want to keep of his?"

Colin nodded. "Somewhere in the flat there are photos, because I don't believe for a second that Ray would have got rid of them."

"Photos of you two?"

Colin smiled. "In much happier times, when I was barely out of my teens and head over heels in love."

Ed stilled. "I'd love to see those." Then he groaned. "Fuck. Photos. I 'aven't got any photos of us today."

Colin laughed. "I think that between them, our friends and family will have taken plenty. We'll have enough to remind us of today." He glanced at the huge bed. "I still can't believe you organized all this."

"You didn't really think I was just gonna take us 'ome, tonight of all nights?" Ed chuckled. "Besides, neither of us can drive after all the champagne we drank."

Colin walked slowly over to him and began to unbutton his shirt. "I hope you didn't drink too much, Mr. Fellows. I wouldn't like to be disappointed on my wedding night."

Ed grasped his wrist and slowly brought Colin's hand down to his crotch, where his dick pushed against the fabric. "I don't anticipate any problems," he said with a hopefully wicked smile.

When Colin sank to his knees, Ed sighed happily. "No problems whatsoever."

Epilogue

October

"Can he hear yet?"

Will sighed inwardly. Sophie had been bouncing with excitement ever since they'd arrived in Dr. Michael's office. "Not yet, sweetheart."

Nathan sat on his knee, clutching a brightly coloured ring they'd purchased just for this special occasion.

If all goes well today, that toy will deliver quite a surprise.

"Sophie, come over here." Dr. Michaels beckoned her.

When she gave Will an inquiring glance, he nodded. Sophie walked over to Dr. Michaels who pointed to the laptop on her desk.

"You see this? It's going to play some noises through Nathan's new processors that only he will be able to hear. Isn't that cool?"

"But how will we tell if he can hear them?"

Blake chuckled. "Imagine if you heard noises for the first time. Do you think you'd be surprised?" Sophie nodded. "Then I think all you'll have to do is watch Nathan's face." He glanced at Will. "Time to make an activation day video of our own."

Dr. Michaels smiled. "I always have a camera ready on such days." She stood up. "I'll be back in a minute, and then we'll start." She left the room.

Blake held out his arms for Nathan, and Will handed him over. The last three weeks had been better than he'd anticipated, but the memory of Nathan's surgery day still lingered. Those hours that had crawled by while they sat in the waiting room, trying not to glance at the clock, and definitely not trying to think of their little boy, and drills, and anaesthetic...

When Dr. Michaels and the surgeon had come out to tell them everything had gone well, and they could see Nathan, Will had fought the urge to weep with relief. Alarmingly, the first thought in his head had been the memory of his own father, telling him that boys didn't cry, that men who cried weren't men at all...

God, I am so thankful Nathan will never have to meet him.

Sophie bounced over to Nathan and knelt down in front of him, holding up a book. "Look at the animals, Nathan!" She pointed to the pig and then made the sign for it, pushing up her nostrils. Nathan's gaze alighted on the colourful images of farm animals and he leaned forward, his fingers clutching at the pictures as if he were trying to lift them from the page.

Will ran his fingers gently over the bulge where Nathan's left implant lay beneath the skin, and a shiver of anticipation rippled through him. The wait was over and they were finally ready, after spending an hour going over the logistics. Dr. Michaels had joked that they had to do this first, because the second the processors were activated, they'd probably only recall about ten percent of what she was telling them.

Will had a feeling this was the voice of experience talking. She'd taught them about the batteries, the parts of the processors, the cables and headpieces, and how to maintain them all.

Dr. Michaels and another staff member came back into the office, carrying a small video camera and tripod. The staff member walked to the corner of the room to set up the camera and Dr. Michaels watched Sophie bouncing around and talking.

"Children are such balls of energy at that age, aren't they?" She smiled as she watched Sophie's antics.

Will snickered. "She certainly earns her nickname." When Dr. Michaels gazed at him inquiringly, he smiled. "Cyclone Sophie."

She laughed. "Sophie, why don't you sit on your daddy's knee while we do this?"

Will caught Sophie as she launched herself towards him. Her familiar weight on his lap was a comfort, and he put his arms around her. She tilted her head back and gave him a kiss.

Now he was ready.

"Okay, gentlemen, let's get this little man hooked up, and then we'll see how everything is working." Dr. Michaels grinned at them. "This is the fun part."

She hooked up the processors to the programming interface, then read them out into the software. Nathan kept turning his head while Dr. Michaels attached the processors to the implant via the headpiece magnet. Will could see why the headbands had been recommended to keep everything in place with an active baby.

"Right, the first thing we're going to do is play some sounds and look for a reaction. We want to find a comfortable volume level for him across the frequency spectrum so that his first sound program or map can be set. It's important to remember that only Nathan will them. Since he can't describe the sounds he's hearing to us, this involves a lot of guesswork on my part. Also keep in mind that what we do in the next few minutes, and even the rest of today's appointment, is only a starting point. This is not a flip of the switch process." She turned to the laptop.

Will wasn't looking at her anymore. He was focused on Nathan.

Suddenly Nathan opened his eyes wide, and his mouth fell open into the widest grin they'd ever seen.

Blake caught his breath. "Oh wow. No mistaking that reaction, is there?"

Will couldn't move. He watched, spellbound, aware that every time Dr. Michaels played another sound, Nathan's reaction was everything they could have hoped for and more. After several minutes Dr. Michaels sat back and smiled.

She looked at Sophie. "You did so good being quiet. Are you ready to talk to your little brother?"

Sophie nodded and bounced so hard on Will's lap that he almost dropped her, but he completely agreed with her sentiment.

"Let me remind you... Children have different reactions the first time they hear a voice. Don't worry if he cries. This is huge for Nathan."

Blake nodded. "Okay." He held Nathan tight, bending over to kiss his head.

Will's eyes focused on him for a moment, and he saw in Blake the same excitement, the same elation.

"Here we go." Dr. Michaels said, then gestured that the microphones were activated.

Will leaned forward. "Hey beautiful," he said, his voice quavering slightly.

Nathan just kept playing with his feet, and Will looked across at Dr. Michaels, perplexed. *Is it working?* Sophie shook Nathan's toy in front of him, and the beads rattled loudly. Nathan's eyes widened and he lunged, chubby hands grabbing it.

Sophie burst into an excited peal of laughter. "He heard it!"

Nathan looked at his sister, his eyes still wide, and promptly burst into tears. Will blinked, his throat tight. He had never been happier to hear Nathan cry. Beside him, Blake made a croaking sound, and Will reached for his hand. They took a moment to soothe Nathan with some backrubs. When he quieted down, Will looked at Dr. Michaels.

"Try again," she said softly, picking up the toy that had fallen to the floor and handing it to Blake.

Will found himself holding his breath.

Blake took the toy from her and shook it. This time their little boy let out an explosion of giggles.

"Oh God," Blake said.

Nathan turned his head in the direction of the words, his eyes large and round.

Blake couldn't contain his emotion a moment longer. He bent over until he could see Nathan's face. "Hey, Nathan."

Nathan giggled and patted Blake's mouth. It was more than Blake could stand. Tears rolled down his cheeks, and when he looked across at Will, he was in a similar state.

Sophie slid off Will's knee and knelt down again in front of her brother. "Nathan!" she shouted.

Nathan shuddered as though an electric shock had coursed through him, and then burst into tears.

Will wiped his eyes. "Maybe that was a little too loud," he suggested.

Sophie flushed. "Sorry." She took Nathan's hand in hers. "Nathan? I'm Sophie." Her voice was softer.

Nathan focused on her and smiled, reaching for her face.

Will cupped Nathan's face. "Hey, beautiful boy. We love you."

Nathan stared at him and then laughed, a joyous, natural sound.

Sophie stared at him and then brushed the palms of her hands together twice.

Blake knew sign language when he saw it. "What does that mean, sweetheart?"

Sophie regarded him with wet eyes. "It means happy, Papa."

Blake couldn't think of a more appropriate sign.

The End

***

If you enjoyed this book about friends and found family, then you'll love meeting my Maine Men. Keep scrolling for details of the first book in the series.

Maine Men

Levi, Noah, Aaron, Ben, Dylan, Finn, Seb, and Shaun.

Eight friends who grew up in Wells, Maine.

Different backgrounds, different paths, but one thing remains solid, even eight years after they graduated – their friendship. Holidays, weddings, funerals, birthdays, parties – any chance they get to meet up, they take it. It's an opportunity to share what's going on in their lives, especially their love lives.

Back in high school, they knew four of them were gay or bi, so maybe it was more than coincidence that they gravitated to one another. Along the way, there were revelations and realizations, some more of a surprise than others. And what none of the others knew was that Levi was in love with one of them...

Finn's Fantasy

It's been twenty years since Joel was with a man, and he doesn't want to screw this up. Especially with Finn.

A secret desire

By day, Finn builds houses on the coastline of Maine. Afterhours, Finn dreams of the hot older guy who walks his chocolate lab on Goose Rocks Beach. The man of his dreams ticks all his boxes. Salt and pepper hair. Strong jawline. Blue eyes.

His dream man is perfect fantasy material. As for actually speaking to him?

As if. Their paths won't ever cross, and the guy is probably straight.

A new chapter

Recently divorced Joel is finally living as a gay man, but he's not sure he's ready to jump into a relationship. That doesn't stop him from noticing his new contractor's muscular build, hewn from hard, physical work, or his storm-colored eyes. Or the way he wears his tool belt slung low on his hips. The icing on the cake? There's more to

Finn than good looks. Maybe he's the perfect guy to share long walks on the beach and warm nights in front of a fire.

But it's been twenty years since Joel was with a man. While he's not forgotten how to flirt, he's nervous about making a move.

Especially with Finn.

<u>Get your free copy here!</u>[1]

---

1.   https://books2read.com/FinnsFantasy

CONTACT K.C.

Website: www.kcwellswrites.com[1]

Newsletter: http://eepurl.com/cNKHlT

I'd love to hear from you, so if you want to say hello or have any questions, please contact me and I'll get back to you:

Email: k.c.wells@btinternet.com

---

1. http://www.kcwellswrites.com/

2.   https://www.facebook.com/KCWellsWorld

3.   https://www.goodreads.com/author/show/6576876.K_C_Wells

4.   https://twitter.com/K_C_Wells

5.   https://www.bookbub.com/authors/k-c-wells

6.   http://www.instagram.com/k.c.wells

About the author

K.C. Wells lives on an island off the south coast of the UK, surrounded by natural beauty. She writes about men who love men, and can't even contemplate a life that doesn't include writing.

The rainbow rose tattoo on her back with the words 'Love is Love' and 'Love Wins' is her way of hoisting a flag. She plans to be writing about men in love - be it sweet and slow, hot or kinky - for a long while to come.

Also by K.C. Wells

---

1. https://books2read.com/u/3JR8lB

2. https://books2read.com/SnarlSplashShock

3. https://books2read.com/u/3LwlZD

Bromantically Yours
BFF[5]
<u>Collars & Cuffs</u>
An Unlocked Heart
Trusting Thomas
Someone to Keep Me (K.C. Wells & Parker Williams)
A Dance with Domination
Damian's Discipline (K.C. Wells & Parker Williams)
Make Me Soar
Dom of Ages (K.C. Wells & Parker Williams)
Endings and Beginnings (K.C. Wells & Parker Williams)

<u>Secrets – with Parker Williams</u>
Before You Break
An Unlocked Mind
Threepeat
On the Same Page
<u>Personal</u>
Making it Personal
Personal Changes[6]
More than Personal
Personal Secrets[7]
Strictly Personal
Personal Challenges[8]
Personal – The complete series[9]

---

4.   https://books2read.com/u/bzdA1n

5.   https://books2read.com/u/3JnzKE

6.   https://books2read.com/u/bzBLJj

7.   https://books2read.com/u/m2ExzO

8.   https://books2read.com/u/bPeZVA

9.   https://books2read.com/u/mYx6kG

Confetti, Cake & Confessions (FREE)[10]

<u>Christmas</u>

Connections

Saving Jason

A Christmas Promise

The Law of Miracles

My Christmas Spirit

A Guy for Christmas

Dear Santa[11]

<u>Santa's Secrets[12]</u>

<u>Island Tales</u>

Waiting for a Prince

September's Tide

Submitting to the Darkness

Island Tales Vol 1 (Books #1 & #2)

<u>Lightning Tales</u>

Teach Me

Trust Me

See Me

Love Me

<u>A Material World</u>

Lace

Satin

Silk

Denim

<u>Southern Boys</u>

Truth & Betrayal

Pride & Protection

---

10.   https://www.prolificworks.com/book/33626

11.   https://books2read.com/u/bMw8E8

12.   https://books2read.com/SantasSecrets

Desire & Denial
The Southern Boys Trilogy[13]
Maine Men
Finn's Fantasy[14]
Ben's Boss[15]
Seb's Summer[16]
Dylan's Dilemma[17]
Shaun's Salvation[18]
Aaron's Awakening[19]
Levi's Love[20]
Maine Men – the Complete Series[21]
Salvation
Wrangled[22]
Second Sight
In His Sights[23]
In Plain Sight[24]
CrossBow Protection
Broken Warrior[25]
Standalones

13. https://books2read.com/u/m2l0NG

14. https://books2read.com/FinnsFantasy

15. https://books2read.com/u/md77JW

16. https://books2read.com/u/m2RjJR

17. https://books2read.com/u/bQV6pv

18. https://books2read.com/ShaunsSalvation

19. https://books2read.com/u/mvWWvz

20. https://books2read.com/LevisLove

21. https://books2read.com/u/bMz8J7

22. https://books2read.com/Wrangled

23. https://ooks2read.com/u/4NoWOW

24. https://books2read.com/u/3GGadK

25. https://books2read.com/u/3R5DwB

Kel's Keeper[26]

Here For You

Sexting The Boss

Gay on a Train

Sunshine & Shadows

Double or Nothing

Back from the Edge

Switching it up

Out for You[27] (FREE)

State of Mind[28] (FREE)

No More Waiting[29] (FREE)

Watch and Learn[30]

My Best Friend's Brother[31]

Princely Submission[32]

Bears in the Woods[33]

Holy Hell – with Parker Williams[34]

Teasing Tim[35]

Str8 B8[36]

Anthologies

<u>Fifty Gays of Shade</u>

Winning Will's Heart

---

26.   https://books2read.com/u/b5vjV6

27.   https://www.prolificworks.com/book/62550

28.   https://www.prolificworks.com/book/74720

29.   https://www.prolificworks.com/book/82301

30.   https://books2read.com/u/boEK9Z

31.   https://books2read.com/MyBestFriendsBrother

32.   https://books2read.com/PrincelySubmission

33.   https://books2read.com/u/3LRVLX

34.   https://books2read.com/HolyHell

35.   https://books2read.com/u/bOJRAW

36.   https://books2read.com/u/4X0dj6